SADDLED WITH MURDER

PHILIPPA LEE MORS

FJORDHILL
PRESS

SADDLED WITH MURDER
(An Edwardian Cozy Mystery)

First Edition: December 2024
ISBN (paperback) 979-8-9893179-5-0

Cover design and illustrations by John Mors

Edited by Adie W.

Fjordhill Press LLC
2800 E Enterprise Ave Ste 333
Appleton, WI 54913

https://www.philippamors.com

CONTENTS

To John,
for teaching me to laugh in all our adventures

PROLOGUE

THE CAT CREPT through the dark woods, slinking silently over roots and under brambles. He was far from his cozy basket in the tack room, but he was no stranger to the woods at night. Tasty morsels could be found here—morsels that squeaked beautifully when they were caught—and besides, the warmth and comfort of the tack room always made him feel a little too domesticated. Better to be hunting on a moonlit night like this.

Tonight, he was hunting something larger than usual. He had to trot to keep his prey in sight. Though the actions of humans rarely interested him, it was irresistibly odd that the two young ladies had entered the woods in the middle of the night. They were hurrying along ahead of him, whispering animatedly to each other. The cat wasn't sure why they bothered to whisper—no doubt they thought they were moving quietly enough, but their long skirts found every twig and weed. All the delectable little mice and tender young rabbits must've heard them coming a mile off.

"Are you certain about this?" the slim one said, pausing to retrieve her hat from the branch that had snagged it.

"Quite certain," said the other, who was built like a work-horse but wore a remarkably decorative hat. Artificial grapes crouched together on the hat's broad brim, looking startled to find themselves in the woods at night. "Mrs. Granger—our cook, you know—told me that Mr. Malcolm told her that Mr. Scott saw it with his own eyes. Out there on the moor, plain as day. Though it was night at the time. It only comes out very late at night, after the pubs close."

"After the pubs close? Surely that explains it," the first girl said, puffing a little. The path was growing steeper as they neared the moor.

A few more minutes brought the strange procession to the tree line. The two young ladies halted at the ragged edge of the moor, and the cat crouched in the undergrowth a few paces back. Only his unblinking eyes were visible, dimly reflecting the moonlight.

"Oh," the stout girl said, scanning the empty expanse before her. Though she had uttered only a single syllable, the disappointment in her voice was palpable.

"Cheer up, Olivia," her companion whispered. "It would be very odd if it appeared exactly when we got here. But I still don't understand why you want to see it. Won't it . . . won't it make you feel worse, somehow?"

Olivia turned to face her, eyes large and solemn. "I don't know, Viv. But I can't help but try to see it—to see him. There must be a reason he's still here. Out here, where it happened. Perhaps it's a message to me, like—"

The one called Viv let out a muffled squeak (much like the squeak of a nice, plump mouse, the cat thought bitterly) and grabbed Olivia's arm. Olivia spun back to the moor so swiftly that one of the grapes bounced off her hat and rolled into the long grass at her feet.

The cat gathered himself to pounce on the tantalizing thing, but then he thought better of it. The humans were unusually tense. They were watching something he couldn't see from his hiding place—but he could hear it.

Still distant but growing ever closer, the cadence of hooves broke the stillness of the night. The young ladies froze, mouths agape, as a galloping horse appeared to the west. Edged in stark moonlight, the horse and his rider were a single inky silhouette against the silvery moor.

"I knew it!" Olivia hissed. "It *is* true. There must be some reason he can't leave the land of the living. He's stuck some-where between the terrestrial and the celestial, just as Madame Itovsky says."

Passing a dozen yards from the crouching girls and never slowing or faltering, the horse and rider soon disappeared to the east.

"I could hear the hoofbeats clearly enough," Viv said doubtfully. "It sounded like a real horse. And with those horrible hillocks and all the mist, everything up here looks unearthly. Are you sure that was him?"

"Yes," the other girl breathed, a look of rapture on her pretty face. "That was Father. I know it." The grapes swayed perilously as she whirled to grab her friend's shoulders. "That was Father's ghost—and I think he's telling me what I must do."

"What?"

The cat's face grew increasingly sour as the girls continued to speak. He was far more interested in humans sneaking through woods than in humans discussing plans. After a few minutes, he turned in disgust and stalked back down the path. There weren't any woodland creatures to be had, but there was still a chance he could charm the old groom into bringing him a saucer of cream. Being domesticated had its perks, after all.

A SADDLE FOR A SÉANCE

"Is it beyond all hope?" Lady Chedington asked. The woman was leaning over my shoulder, wafting floral perfume and a sense of despair.

I eyed the jumbled object on the workbench before me. It was a monstrous thing, a military relic of an older age, a veteran of countless rides in dirty weather. In short, it was a very ugly saddle indeed. From the feel of the saddle's underside, years of horse sweat had compressed the wool stuffing into an impassive brick. I shook my head. With Sir Algernon's considerable weight, this saddle must have become an instrument of torture to his horses. Perhaps it was no wonder his prized stallion had bolted with him in such a lethal way. For all their strength, horses were sensitive creatures.

"And the hole, my dear," her ladyship fluttered. "Fletcher said it has developed a mysterious hole!"

Lowering the magnifying loupe on my spectacles, I flipped the saddle over. There it was, a ragged hole in the middle of one of the stuffed panels. It was just over an inch in diameter, with tufts of dirty wool bristling out of the opening. I could see little black specks stuck to the wool inside. Mouse droppings. Lovely.

"It apparently housed a mouse at some point," I said.

"Mouse?!" she shrieked, leaping backward. She was remarkably agile for someone with her elaborate taste in gowns. I hoped her black bombazine mourning dress was stiff enough to keep her upright if she fainted.

"It's not actually in residence at the moment," I assured her. "The little thing chewed through and made a cozy bed in the wool. Probably last winter. Clever mouse."

"You mean to say that there was a rodent living in . . ." She whirled to glare at the aged tabby cat lounging in the corner of the tack room. Always unimpressed by humans, he appeared to be trying to skewer us with his gaze.

"Treacle Tart, you lazy cat!" Lady Chedington said.

The cat stared malevolently at her, his green eyes unblinking. Then a deep, rumbling purr began—a gesture of defiance, no doubt.

"Oh I told Fletcher that cat is too old!" the woman wailed, turning back to me. "He lazes about and can't be bothered to hunt anymore. Mr. Hastings' brilliant mouser had a litter of kittens a few months ago, and I told Fletcher to see about getting one for our stable, and do you know what he said? 'I won't have Treacle Tart'—such a ridiculous name for a cat—'I won't have Treacle Tart being shown up by a youngster now, at the end of his days. Let him be master of his stable till the end.' Absurd man. And now the mice are taking up residence inside the saddles!" She scowled at the cat.

Treacle Tart stood, turned contemptuously, and lay down again, this time facing the wall.

"Well. I shall tell Cook there is to be no more cream sent to the stable for that sluggard," she sniffed, turning back to me.

"Now, tell me the worst. Is it a lost cause? Can you possibly rejuvenate the thing?"

I glanced around the tack room. The place was simply lousy with sleek, elegant saddles on racks of polished wood. Becketts, the Chedington's sprawling estate, had produced fine Thoroughbreds for generations, and although some of the other saddles were old, none compared to the monstrosity before me. With a dozen more pleasant saddles to choose from, why was the woman fixated on this one? Because it was the saddle her husband had died in, or died falling from? A rather macabre thought. Whether she planned to use the saddle or brood over it, I should advise her to let the old thing go, closet it away somewhere and turn her thoughts to brighter things. But, as usual, I found myself wavering between this nobler instinct and the thought of a paycheck.

"It looks like it can still hold stitches," I said, my mercenary side prevailing. "Yes, I should be able to patch it."

"You are a treasure, an absolute treasure!" Lady Chedington declared, clasping my shoulder and nearly swooning with relief. She looked like a faded Gibson girl, with a petulant rosebud mouth and soft, gray-blonde hair piled loosely in the latest fashion. I found myself wondering what it would be like to go gray gracefully—my own dark hair had developed a startling streak of gray at my right temple. But if I had hair as graceful as Lady Chedington's, I'd have to live up to it. And I'd already accepted that I would move through middle age in variations of "molting skunk."

"I can't possibly bring that saddle into the house, smelling as it does," Lady Chedington lamented. "It positively reeks of rodents!"

"Into the house?"

"For the séance, my dear."

I blinked. Her ladyship's way of speaking often put me out to sea. In a fog. Without an oar.

"According to Madame Itovsky," she continued, "if we're ever to communicate with my husband's spirit, we must form a circle of power around his favorite chair."

"I see," I said slowly, sensing a break in the fog.

"We've had no luck with any of the furniture in the house. But Algernon spent more hours in that saddle than he ever spent in any chair. The saddle is the key to reaching his spirit—I'm sure of it!" Her pale blue eyes were large and earnest. "Madame Itovsky says it must be restored to pristine condition. But the smell, my dear, the smell!"

"I'll replace the wool flocking and give the whole thing a vinegar wash. Unless your séance involves sticking your nose between the panels, it shouldn't be too offensive."

"Sticking my . . ." she said, taken aback. "My dear, I can barely stand being in this tack room at all! It positively gives me the shivers, you know, being down here with all of those"—she waved a hand toward the stable aisle—"those hideous creatures." A whinny sounded from somewhere in the stable, and the woman proved her point by shivering dramatically.

"The Becketts horses are lovely," I ventured.

"Lovely, yes," she said, "and positively gluttonous. I just received the latest hay bill, and no one can tell me why the silly animals eat so much. They are kept very comfortable indeed, while their never-ending demands for food and care send me to the poor house."

I was saved from replying when the tack room door creaked open and Fletcher stuck his head in. "Miss Cobb?" he said to me and then blanched when he saw his employer.

"Close the door, Fletcher!" Lady Chedington bellowed. The

elderly man slipped obediently inside and closed the door, much to Treacle Tart's dismay. The cat had been slinking silently toward the door in a bid to escape Lady Chedington's perfume. "That cat is not to leave this tack room, do you understand?" she blazed. "He shall stay put until he remembers his job!"

I gave Fletcher an apologetic smile. There were bits of hay on the old groom's ancient tweed hat and coat. No doubt he had been up since dawn, handling horses and all of the dirty work they involved.

"Very good, my lady," he said smoothly.

Lady Chedington turned a more cheerful countenance on me. "I shall leave you to it, then! Be sure to come up to the Hall before dinner and tell me of your progress." She whisked smartly out the door, leaving the tack room smelling oppressively of roses.

Fletcher grimaced and turned to me. "Apologies, Miss Cobb, but could you come out to the trainin' field? Miss Olivia is off-kilter again."

"Not again, Fletcher, surely?"

"She can't seem to find the center." His mouth twisted, drooping at the corners. "She's hintin' it may be the saddle, but if you ask me, I'd say it's the rider. Either she's leanin' to port, or the whole world is tiltin' starboard when she gets in the saddle."

I would've used less poetic language to describe the silly girl's shortcomings. Miss Olivia Chedington was a very pretty creature, but the sight of her struggling to ride a horse was hardly pleasant.

"Thank you, Fletcher," I said with a sigh, cramming my old black straw hat onto my head. "I'll come take a look, shall I?"

We left the tack room and made our way toward the open

doors at the rear of the stable, passing the gleaming wooden stalls that flanked the wide aisle. Fletcher still had the build of the jockey he had once been, whip-thin and slightly bowlegged as if born to the saddle. I towered over the little man as I towered over most men. As a startled old gentleman on the street had once informed me, "My dear, you are unreasonably tall!"

From my height, I could see that most of the stalls were empty. Most of the horses were out to pasture, but I knew the last stall at the end of the aisle was occupied. I also knew that things were about to become unpleasant if I couldn't get past that stall unnoticed. As we approached, I ducked my head and scurried for the doorway, ignoring Fletcher's surprised look. Unfortunately, at my height, I stand out even when I'm standing still—in short, I scurry like a Clydesdale.

"Ahem." The sound came from the depths of the stall as I passed.

"Blast," I muttered.

Fletcher was watching me in wonder. This was obviously not what he expected from a woman of my age and class—presumed class, that is. I was a bit of an anomaly in Pelgren Vale. I knew I was widely referred to as "that tall, swarthy woman" or "the one sayin' she's a saddler." But as I'd had the money to purchase a cottage in an impressive part of the county, the people of the Vale seemed to be withholding sterner judgement until they could plumb the mystery of my history. And I was dead set they never would.

"A-HEM," came the sound, louder and more insistent this time. I knew that, to Fletcher, it was only the sound of a horse whickering, but I glanced at his face just to be sure.

"Sounds like he's missed you, Miss Cobb," he said. He

spoke with a horseman's typical wryness and no indication he'd heard anything unusual.

I approached the stall with a shrug. "He's quite attached, poor old boy. I should spend a moment with him. I don't suppose you'd mind . . .?"

Though it was probably the first time Fletcher had been asked to excuse himself for a tête-à-tête between woman and horse, he handled it with a curt nod and went out the big stable doors. I turned back toward the stall.

"Yes?" I whispered, looking through the bars. Bertie stared back at me blandly. He was a tall, gray horse of rather hazy bloodlines, but handsome in spite of his prominent Roman nose. His body had faded to white in places, but he still had striking gray dapples over his neck, shoulders, and haunches. The Roman nose usually gave him an air of austerity, but at the moment, the effect was being slightly undercut by a single stem of straw hanging comically from his mouth. There were tight wrinkles above his nostrils—a clear sign of annoyance.

"Poor *old* boy?" the horse said. "My dear Harriet, even if our ages were measured on the same scale, you'd still come out in the lead."

"A figure of speech, Bertie. We're both going gray, so what does it matter? You may call me 'old girl' if you like."

He shook his head and snorted. "Well, *old girl*, you've been wandering around in that contraption again."

I looked at him blankly, then reached up and snatched off the eye loupe spectacles, dropping them into my skirt pocket.

"Thanks for that," I said. Feeling that I owed him something in return, I indicated the straw between his lips. "You've been sampling your bedding?"

He ducked his head and rubbed his muzzle on his foreleg to free the stem. "I finished my hay hours ago. The straw was merely an experiment. We both know it's no substitute for the pasture I was promised." He frowned at me through the bars, ears swiveling back and wrinkles appearing above his eyes.

"I know," I sighed. "I'll talk to Fletcher and get it sorted."

"I was told there would be pasture. Miles of green, you said. Clover and timothy and delicate thistles." He drew up his big, smoky neck and glared down his nose at me from an impressive height. Horses have been looking down their noses at humans since the dawn of time. It's an intimidation tactic, but I know the gag, so it doesn't work on me—well, it hardly works on me.

"I'm sure I didn't mention thistles. I still can't believe you eat those. Just keep quiet, and I'll do my best to get you your own lovely patch of green."

The big horse sighed, blowing air noisily out of his nostrils. "I suppose now you're going out to stretch your legs? Taking a nice little ramble under the open sky? Communing with the glories of nature—"

"I'm heading out to the training field. Miss Olivia is flopping around again, and she's blaming the saddle."

Bertie seemed to perk up, his ears swiveling forward and his liquid eyes brightening. "Enjoy that," he said. "It is an incontrovertible fact that when there's a saddler around, all the incompetent riders discover problems with their tack."

I smiled wanly at him. "If you want to stretch your legs, I could take you along as a replacement mount for her."

His ears swiveled backward in alarm. "Actually, old girl, despite these prison bars, I'm beginning to feel quite at home in this stable." Eyes drifting closed, he dropped one hip, the perfect picture of a slumbering horse.

"Alright. I won't sacrifice you to Miss Olivia. You can graze while we watch her ride."

He snapped brightly awake. "Very well! There is something satisfying about sampling the greenery while watching other horses work."

"But I should warn you. I'm getting that feeling again," I said.

"Which feeling?"

"The feeling that I should march up to Becketts Hall and admit to Lady Chedington that my services are unnecessary. We've been in Pelgren Vale almost six months, yes? And in that time, Lady Chedington has paid me to come and adjust no less than ten saddles for Miss Olivia. The woman's wasting her money. No amount of saddle adjusting will ever make a rider of her daughter, and it feels dishonest not to tell her so."

Bertie rolled an eye at me. "Plucking the low-hanging fruit has never bothered you before."

I glared at the horse. "Perhaps not," I said tartly, "but moving to Pelgren Vale was supposed to be a new start for us. We agreed to go straight, remember? No more bending the truth to line our pockets."

"Failing to mention something is hardly the same as bending the truth," he protested.

"All the same, every time I watch that girl ride—if you can call it riding—I feel dishonest."

"Ah. Then it's a matter of vocabulary," he said. "Don't think of yourself as dishonest. Think of yourself as an expert in the art of omission. It's for a good cause after all. That cottage roof won't re-thatch itself."

Sighing inwardly, I took the leather headcollar from its brass hook on the stall door and buckled it around Bertie's large head. We stepped out into the sunlight, Bertie muttering about the possibility of thistles in the training field, and I wondering again about the dubious honor of being able to talk to a horse.

2

THE GHOST ON THE MOOR

THE WARM SEPTEMBER sun shone cheerfully on the clean brick stable yard, but Bertie's mention of roof thatch left me feeling rather gloomy. Gloomy, dull, and deflated—exactly the state of the thatched roof on my cottage across the valley.

The name "Sunnythatch Cottage" had seemed to me a good omen, but after moving in, I realized the name was simply a sample of the local sense of humor.

"Surely buckets would be a better choice," Bertie had said, watching me from his pasture in the spitting rain.

"Using anything as large as a bucket feels like surrender," I had told him, and I emptied another of the cooking pots I was using to catch leaks from the old roof.

Our meager savings showed very little progress, so I emptied pots with one hand, ferreted away money in the tea tin labeled "New Roof" with the other, and continued to take ridiculous saddlery jobs for the only neighbor who would hire me.

"Alright?" Fletcher asked, approaching to pat Bertie's neck. There was a stiff hitch in the man's stride, not uncommon in his breed. Most weathered old horsemen bore the scars of a lifetime with the spirited and unpredictable animals.

"I think he'll appreciate a little walk," I admitted.

"Or a five-acre pasture," suggested Bertie, nudging my elbow with his heavy muzzle. "If not, feel free to leave my stall door unlatched, and I'll make my own way to that grassy little stretch along the front avenue."

"Talkative old chap, ain't he?" Fletcher ran his eyes over Bertie appraisingly.

An icy tingle ran down my spine. "Talkative?" I said, trying to achieve a normal tone and failing miserably.

"Aye, just like a mare I trained years ago," Fletcher said. "Always whinnyin' and whickerin', she were, always had somethin' to say. One of the best, that mare. Restless, like this one, but one of the best."

I breathed a sigh of relief and shot Bertie a warning look. He gazed placidly back and then gave an exaggerated, toothy yawn. The horse always made light of my concerns that someday, someone other than me would be able to hear him speak.

"They'll most likely put you in a circus," I had told him. "Some sort of freakshow where you'll have to perform like a trained monkey."

"And achieve worldwide fame? Have books written about me? It doesn't sound such a bad life," Bertie had said, winking wickedly.

"What about scientists? They'll want to study you. Conduct experiments on you. They'll be stumbling all over themselves to get samples of your brain." It was this more sobering scenario that finally convinced Bertie to keep his wry comments to a minimum in public places. But, as he pointed out, he couldn't be expected to keep his considerable wit under wraps at all times.

"Bertie might do better with a little grazing," I said to Fletcher. "I'll bring him along now, but could we find him a bit of grass later?"

"'fraid there's no grass in the single paddocks. But there's a little meadow up near the Hall. I s'pose we could turn him out there overnight, if the weather holds. Fence is old, but so long as he don't push on it, it should hold him well enough."

I assured him that Bertie was not a known pusher-of-fences, adding, "But I don't think we'll be here overnight. Just a few hours will do."

The man's wiry brows raised in surprise. "Her ladyship said you'd be stayin' over."

"Did she indeed? She never invited me."

He nodded gloomily. "Very good at assumin' things, she is," he muttered.

Bertie shot me a sympathetic look. "It seems I'll be bedding down more comfortably than you," he said. "As long as Fletcher is handing out favors, why not ask him for a cot in the tack room?"

I glared at the big horse. He knew very well my aversion to grand houses—or rather, to the people one usually finds in grand houses. I'd give my right arm to bed down in the tack room rather than occupy one of Lady Chedington's guest rooms. I still might be able to weasel my way out of it, but if my only client insisted we stay, then stay we must. And if I knew the woman, she would faint dead away at the mention of sleeping on a cot in the tack room.

Fletcher eyed me a tad sternly. "I think she's over-worried 'bout gettin' that saddle sorted. I told her it shouldn't be used, you know. Makes the horses sore, hard as it is. Seems a blessin' the mice got at it."

"But she only wants it for a séance."

That was a mistake. The man snorted loudly, looking nearly as sour as Treacle Tart. "A séance," he growled. "Nonsense, I say. Dabbled in them séances years ago, she did, an' it never brought nothin' but trouble. An' now she's startin' up again." He shook his head grimly.

"I expect she wishes to speak with her husband one last time. People look for comfort in the oddest places."

"An' I expect it's that ghost on the moor that did it," he said.

"Ghost?" Bertie and I said together.

"Oh aye," Fletcher said. "Sir Algernon's ghost. They say you can see him ridin' the moor at night, out there where he were ridin' the day he died." He turned his eyes on the broad pastures beyond the stable yard, a rich, undulating green dotted with grazing horses. The lush valley was bordered by dark woods that rambled lazily up the surrounding hills, growing wilder and more ancient as they sprawled away toward Exmoor.

Following his old eyes to the distant moor, I repressed a shiver. "You've . . . seen his ghost?"

"Me? No. Not with these old eyes—but there's plenty of folks as have."

"Lady Chedington?"

"I don't think she's seen him," he said. "She never said so, in any case, and she ain't one to keep her lips buttoned 'bout somethin' like that. But she couldn't help but hear the rumors down in Pelgren village. Rumors started a year ago, just after my master died."

"It's bad logic to include a horse in those rumors," Bertie mused. "It can't be the ghost of Sir Algernon's stallion. That fellow is in the stable, and as far as I can tell, he displays all the symptoms of being alive."

Fletcher looked amused at Bertie's rumblings and reached

up to scratch his dappled neck. The old horseman's hands were rough and gnarled, with joints like knots in tree bark. "Now, I don't know as I believe them rumors, Miss Cobb," he said, "but I can't help feelin' a little happier because of 'em."

"Yes?"

"Makes me happy, like, if my master is still doin' what he loved to do. Ridin', that's what he loved."

"I've heard so much about his passion for horses. I wish I could have met him." Lady Chedington often deplored her late husband's horse obsession in melancholy tones—the way he could read "the silly beasts" with ease but couldn't come up with "two words to rub together" at social gatherings. Every word of censure she uttered about him had only made me like him more. I had the sense that Sir Algernon would have thoroughly enjoyed sleeping on a cot in the tack room.

"I taught Sir Algernon to ride when he weren't barely old enough to walk," Fletcher said, his rugged face crinkling into a smile. "Never knew a child so taken with horses. One day I found him toddlin' along behind a horse, holdin' the tail for balance, and I decided he'd be better off on top than behind. Taught Miss Olivia too. Sat her on her first pony at the tender age of five."

"How did she ride, as a child?"

"She cried and fell off."

"Ah."

"My master wanted her to ride. But her ladyship, she wouldn't have none of it. Said there weren't no need for the girl to learn to 'bump a horse.' Said she would only get hurt an' she should keep herself indoors and learn to be a lady."

"But Miss Olivia rides now," I pointed out. "I've adjusted no less than three saddles for her in the past month."

"Oh aye, she rides now, if you can call it ridin'," he said, echoing my opinion. "She bought some new ridin' clothes an' she comes out every day with a smile on her face. Can't fault her for tryin', I guess, but the result's always the same. Tipsy as a sot ridin' home from the pub." His eyes flickered to me and his wrinkled cheeks grew warm. "If you'll excuse my sayin' so, Miss Cobb."

"Have no fear, Fletcher. I've seen her ride. And she always looks so uncomfortable—and frightened—that I don't know why she even wants to."

"It's that same ghost," he said darkly. "She took it into her head that her father's spirit won't rest 'nless she keeps the stud farm goin'. An' rides his stallion."

I stared at him, thinking I must have misheard. "The same stallion that caused her father's death?"

"The same. Brioso."

"Brioso?"

"Foreign name," he said with a grimace. "Italian, they tell me. Means lively. Energetic, like."

"A rather unfortunate name for a horse that bolted with his master," Bertie observed, wryly cocking an ear.

"I don't envy you the task, Fletcher," I said. "Teaching Miss Olivia to ride—and on a wild stallion, no less."

"Oh, the Miss is out of my hair now. Lady Chedington found a new riding master. She may be . . . she may be thinkin' of replacin' me."

"Surely not! She couldn't fire you!"

He nodded, his shoulders more stooped and fragile than I had ever seen them. "She could and she may. But she calls it 'retirement.'"

"Horrible idea," Bertie whispered. "This man is one of the few in my acquaintance who knows his way around a curry comb."

"Miss Cobb," Fletcher said, folding his hands before him and straightening up as if preparing for a recitation. "I don't s'pose . . . what I mean to say is, if it weren't too much trouble . . . but perhaps you'd rather not."

I looked at him expectantly.

The watery old eyes met mine. "I don't s'pose you'd put in a good word for me with Lady Chedington? She respects your opinion, she does. Not a day goes by but what she isn't sayin' she needs Miss Cobb to come and sort things out for her. She's come to rely on you."

I stared at him blankly. Respect my opinion? Rely on me? The old groom must be mistaken. "But I'm just the saddler," I faltered. "She's certainly been very kind to me . . ."

I still wasn't sure whether "kind" was the word. Robust and impulsive, Lady Chedington had welcomed my saddlery skills with open arms, literally. On our first meeting, she had given me a fluttery embrace and announced that while everyone else in the neighborhood deplored the idea of a female saddler, *she* thought it a very good thing, and wouldn't I come in for some tea and a chat? That first tea had turned into many more, and I soon realized the reason. Her state of mourning provided Lady Chedington very few opportunities to socialize, and roping the saddler into listening to her long monologues was the best she was bound to get.

Before I could reply to Fletcher, we heard a "Halloo!" and saw a tall young man coming toward us from the direction of the training field.

"Well, if it isn't the poet himself," Bertie said with satisfaction.

3

THE POET AND HIS EYELASHES

BROAD-SHOULDERED and dressed in unassuming tweeds, Mr. Stanley Langford approached us with the light, cheerful air of a man who has no idea how attractive he is.

He was not, in fact, a poet. I had once told Bertie that Langford's chestnut curls and sensitive face reminded me of a portrait of John Keats. Bertie replied that Langford did look the type that would spend entirely too long contemplating a Grecian urn—and had taken to calling him "the poet." But this didn't mean he disliked the man. Bertie was a great admirer of the poet's ability to find the exact spot on a horse's neck that longed to be scratched.

"Miss Cobb! A pleasant surprise on a pleasant day," Langford said, coming to a stop at Bertie's shoulder and giving me a gallant little bow. Bertie had an almost Pavlovian response to the man, leaning toward him and squinting with an expression of anticipated bliss. "And you've brought this handsome fellow along, I see." He reached up a gloved hand to scratch the underside of Bertie's neck. The horse closed his eyes in ecstasy. He was practically purring.

"It's good to see you too, Mr. Langford," I said, and meant it. Although I appreciated seeing Bertie turn to mush around Langford, I had another reason to like the man. Besides Lady Chedington, he was the only neighbor who hadn't looked uncomfortable at the mention of my profession. And, of course, he was also exceptionally easy on the eyes. The chestnut curls were in full force today, tumbling out from beneath his cap in tousled magnificence.

Bertie caught me gazing at Langford and fixed me with a sardonic eye. The big horse enjoyed twitting me about my fascination with Langford's looks, and at forty-five, so few people are suspected of falling in love that I felt a little flattered. But Bertie didn't know the full reason I was interested in Langford. I had designs on the man, certainly, but they weren't the kind of designs that required quoting poetry. My designs were purely mercenary. Langford had a stable of fine hunters, and he appeared to be comfortably situated—in a saddler's eye, the poet was a very attractive mark.

"May I take you across to Miss Olivia?" Langford asked. "She's been—no, Fletcher, we won't impose on you anymore. I can escort Miss Cobb to the training field."

Fletcher wavered a moment, then gave a nod and turned back to the stable. From his tweed cap to his old boots, he appeared diminished, walking slowly as he favored his bad leg.

"Don't you have something to say to the man?" Bertie demanded, pushing me hard with his nose.

Blast the talking horse. "I'll . . . I'll try to talk to Lady Chedington about what we discussed, Fletcher," I called after him. The old groom turned, grinned, and gave me a jaunty little salute.

"Salt of the earth," Langford said as we watched him go, and then he opened the pasture gate to let us through.

We entered the first of many pastures that spread out from the stables in a broad patchwork divided by thick hedges, stone walls, and post-and-rail fences draped with ivy. Bertie made the most of the slack lead I gave him by snatching mouthfuls of grass as we walked, ever on the lookout for young thistles or sweet clover. In truth, this thick turf was one of the reasons the horse had chosen Pelgren Vale, while I had staunchly maintained that the Highlands of Scotland would suit us better.

"Plenty of thistles up there," I had said, "and very few people. Perfect for us, I should think."

"But a horse cannot live on thistles alone," Bertie had replied. "Have you ever tasted heather, Harriet? Tough, bitter stuff. And whatever grass manages to survive up there thinks itself heather. That's the flavor, anyway. Besides, unlike you, I find people intriguing. How am I to study human nature with only sheep for company? No, much better to set our sights on points south-southwest."

And that is how we found ourselves in Pelgren Vale, with plenty of luxurious green to please the big gray horse, and for me, the comforting sense of being ensconced by the hills all the way down to the sea. The only hitch was that we had nearly exhausted our savings buying a cottage in such a desirable district, and it became a necessity to hunt for saddlery clients among our wealthy neighbors.

"Is the saddlery trade thriving these days?" Langford asked.

"Oh, it's . . . marching on," I said. Then, seeing my opportunity, I added, "I would be happy to visit Maplehurst any time, you know. Lady Chedington had me inspect all of her saddles and bridles, and I could, of course, do the same for you."

"Easy, old girl," Bertie murmured from behind us. "Directness is not really the thing in polite society. You must play the fish, not flog the water."

Langford's long lashes widened a fraction at my suggestion, and he stuttered, "Oh— yes. I do hope to have you come to Maplehurst, of course. It's just that my tack room is in the middle of rather extensive renovations—lumber and sawdust everywhere, you know. The tack is being stored in a stall at the moment, and there's so much dust and not enough light—"

"Renovations?" I said brightly, putting him out of his misery. I knew rejection when I heard it, and Bertie was probably right. Over-eagerness was not the thing. Bertie was sometimes more properly human than I was—he honed his sense of human civility, while I stomped along like an unschooled mare of questionable breeding.

"I've had the notion to renovate for a few years," Langford said, "and I'm finally seeing it come to fruition. I think the tack room of a stud farm should be a place for people to gather—a welcoming place where potential clients can enjoy a drink while discussing bloodlines and breedings."

"It sounds very grand," I said.

"Oh, it will be. I plan to have a parquet floor and a wall of windows, and electricity for the whole stable—when the lines stretch that far. But this probably doesn't sound so very grand to you, Miss Cobb. I suppose the stables in Walsall already have electric lights. You came here from Walsall, did you not?"

I only hesitated a moment before replying. "Yes, Walsall."

Bertie shot me an amused look. I hadn't exactly come to Pelgren Vale *directly* from Walsall.

"But I worked in a saddlery factory there," I added, "not in any fine stables with electric lights."

"Walsall, the pinnacle of British saddlery," Langford mused.

"And then you decided to move to our humble little corner of the world last spring?"

"Yes. Six months ago." This was only partially true. I had left the dim, dreary factory in Walsall over a year ago. It was a place where men were quickly promoted while women carried out the tedious work of stitching, earning half the salary of their male counterparts. But when I left the factory, I had headed to Wolverhampton. Money flowed like water at racetracks, I had reasoned, and I didn't see why it shouldn't flow into a saddler's pockets as well.

Lean months had followed, months of bending the truth to make a living, and then—meeting Bertie, and the plan we hatched to change our fortunes. Wolverhampton had been the making of us, Bertie and me, but our dubious activities there made me reluctant to reveal my connection to the place. Walsall was a much safer word, and I kept it ready on my tongue for situations like this.

"Is Miss Olivia riding alone at the moment?" I asked, eager to change the subject.

"Have no fear, Miss Cobb," Langford said, giving me a knowing wink. "The Major is with her."

"The Major?"

"Major Peter Collings. Lady Chedington hired him to assist Miss Olivia with her riding."

"But surely Fletcher could coach the young lady, couldn't he?"

He nodded. "He could and he did . . . until Miss Olivia set her sights on riding Brioso. Sir Algernon's stallion, you know. Then her ladyship decided to call on a professional."

"The stallion," I sighed. "Fletcher said Miss Olivia believes her father's ghost is telling her to do it."

"Her father's ghost?" Langford said, halting in surprise.

I also stopped walking, and Bertie bumped his grass-stained muzzle into my back. A constant and close proximity to this muzzle had taught me to wear only dark colors, so a new grassy smear didn't concern me. Bertie always stuck close when a conversation caught his interest—he was fascinated by human drama.

"The ghost on the moor," I said, smiling. "Surely you've heard about it? Sir Algernon's ghost has been seen riding the moor at night, and Miss Olivia thinks it's a message to her—it's the reason she's so keen to ride Brioso."

His shapely brows rose in disbelief, and he shook his head slowly. "I don't think that's her reason," he said. "But everyone loves a ghost story, I suppose."

We continued walking, and after a moment, Langford said, "It's absurd, of course. The ghost, and Miss Olivia's plans. The stallion is dangerous, as everyone knows, and the girl's riding skills are . . . but of course, you've seen her ride?"

I nodded unhappily. "And I've heard Lady Chedington refer to the stallion as, 'that beast' or 'that mad creature.' "

"She even forbade Fletcher to ride him," he said. "She keeps the horse locked in a box stall around the clock."

"If she's so deathly afraid of him, why on earth would she allow her daughter to ride him?"

"I don't think it's a matter of allowing, Miss Cobb. Miss Olivia is twenty, and her father left the horses to her in his will."

"Indeed?" This answered the question I'd been rolling on my tongue for weeks. Every time Lady Chedington wailed to me about the cost of keeping a stableful of horses, the obvious question jumped to my lips—*Why don't you just sell them? I* always bit my tongue in time, reminding myself that my current salary depended on the woman *keeping* the horses. I wasn't about to plant the idea of selling if she wasn't bright enough to land on the thing herself.

"The girl hasn't ridden Brioso yet," Langford continued. "I advised her to learn how to ride first and leave the stallion for later. But Lady Chedington is worried about her even on the quiet horses."

"That solves one mystery," I said thoughtfully. "Last month, Lady Chedington asked me if I could make some sort of belt that would keep Miss Olivia firmly attached to the saddle. She called it a 'saddle sling.'"

Langford whooped a laugh. "Did you explain to her how dangerous that would be?"

"Yes. I told her that one should never firmly attach oneself to a saddle, as being dragged by a panicked horse is far worse than simply falling off."

"And how did she take it?" he asked, his eyes twinkling with mirth.

"She asked me to come up with some sort of glue which could be applied to the seat to keep the girl 'sticky enough to stay upright' but 'not sticky enough to be dragged.' "

"And?"

"I told her I'd look into it, but that it could take months or even years before it's ready." I gave him a sly smile.

"You're a saint, Miss Cobb."

I laughed. "Hardly. But how is the Major faring with Miss Olivia, in the absence of glue?"

"See for yourself," he said, and opened the gate into the training field.

4

A TALL AND MIGHTY RAMPART

FLETCHER HAD ONCE TOLD me he favored this field for young horses who were still too capricious to be trusted riding out alone.

"With a barrier like that," he had said, indicating the tall hedges that lined the field, "when somethin' startles the horse, you can be sure you won't find yourself t'other end of Exmoor. As close to sure as anythin' gets with horses, that is."

I shivered, imagining Sir Algernon's stallion galloping wildly across the moor. I could almost hear the ghostly hoofbeats. Actually, I did hear hoofbeats.

A large piebald horse was bearing down on us, his ears pricked cheerfully despite the floundering rider on his back. Wearing a stylish black riding habit, patent leather boots, and a look of terror, Miss Olivia Chedington was indeed "off-kilter." She was riding side-saddle, though riding was a rather generous term for what she was doing at the moment—listing dangerously to the left while pulling ineffectually on the reins. Horse and girl swept by us at a leisurely pace. It was obvious the old gelding was a seasoned schoolmaster, used to holding steady no matter what storms broke upon his back.

"Sit up! This is why you must sit up!" came an angry voice. A thin man, presumably the Major, was standing half a dozen yards away, face flushed. His neat gray coat was without a wrinkle, and his knee-high boots gleamed with polish. He would have been the picture of military poise had he not been wildly swinging a thick leather riding crop and quivering with rage.

"If you sit like a sack of potatoes," he thundered at the young woman, "you will fall like a sack of potatoes!"

I frowned. Logical, perhaps, but not exactly helpful instruction. Miss Olivia didn't seem to glean any inspiration from the comment. There was no change in her alarmed expression or her tilted posture. The Major glowered at his pupil, compulsively stroking his delicate mustache and growing redder and redder as girl and horse circled the field.

"She looks terrified," I said to Langford, "and that gelding is as calm and smooth as a carousel horse. Isn't she even more afraid of riding Brioso?"

"She may be afraid of the stallion, but she's more afraid of losing the estate."

I stared at the man, and even Bertie stopped chewing and raised his head. "Are they in danger of losing the estate?" I asked, looking Langford full in his tanned face.

"The horses have always supported Becketts, Miss Cobb. The sales of homebred youngstock, the stud fees from breeding, those profits have always gone back into the estate. The horses support not only themselves but also the running of the Hall, staff salaries, repairs—all the expenses that one is saddled with when one inherits an estate."

I began to reply but was interrupted by the Major, who seemed to be reaching the end of his tether.

"If you do not sit up," he shrieked at his hapless pupil, "we will keep your horse cantering until you do so!" I wondered if he was using the royal "we," since Miss Olivia was flopping and had no control over her horse's gaits. She made a valiant effort to right herself but was either too tired or too frightened to make much of a change.

Not for the first time, I was grateful that women's fashions had changed so dramatically. Gone were the long, flowing skirts that threatened to tangle one between saddle and hooves in the event of a fall. While I had escaped those trends by riding astride—all my skirts were split to allow me to do this without completely thumbing my nose at propriety— Miss Olivia certainly couldn't be expected to behave in such a way. While still modestly *aside*, she was sleek and trim and her riding habit was short enough to reveal a glossy boot in the stirrup. If the girl did fall off, she had a much better chance of getting clear of those hooves than she would have in the fashions of twenty years ago.

"I understand that Becketts relies on the stud farm to stay afloat," I said, turning back to Langford. "But I don't see why Miss Olivia feels she needs to ride the stallion in order to run the stud farm. There are plenty of breeders that do not ride their own horses."

He shrugged. "There is only one stallion at Becketts, Miss Cobb—and he killed his former master. The neighborhood feeling about Brioso is a bit . . . shall we say, restive? I advised Miss Olivia to wait it out, keep Brioso out of the public view for a while. But then Byerley stuck his oar in and gave her the idea of making some sort of grand public display."

"And who is Byerley?"

Langford's eyes flickered with amusement. "You've just made my day, Miss Cobb. That you haven't heard of Lord Byerley is now one of my favorite things about you. He and his family would be quite shocked to know there's a person living in Pelgren Vale who doesn't know the Byerley name. But I'm afraid my enjoyment will be short-lived. The younger Lord Byerley is currently a guest here at Becketts, so you can't help but stumble across him."

"And this Lord Byerley advised Miss Olivia to ride the stallion?" I said indignantly.

"He must've done. She was bursting with the idea after talking to him. She believes that to continue the stud farm successfully, she will need to restore the stallion's reputation very publicly. What better way than by demonstrating he can be handled by a delicate young lady?"

"What better way? Literally *any* other way would be better!"

"Could be entertaining, though," Bertie said from just behind my left ear, making me jump.

"I wouldn't be surprised if Byerley is rather hoping something will go wrong," Langford said darkly. "Then the girl might finally sell Brioso. Byerley's been itching to get his hands on that stallion. He's spent all this week mooning about Brioso's stall, staring at him . . ." He trailed off as if lost in thought. "But I digress," he said, his brow clearing. "Thankfully, Miss Olivia has agreed to ride this old gelding first so that she can get her seat sorted before throwing a leg over the stallion."

I smiled at this typically male expression. Fine ladies did not throw their legs over anything. But I caught his drift.

"And when will she be throwing a leg over the stallion?"

"Ideally, never." He suddenly turned to me, clasping my

free hand in both of his. "Miss Cobb," he said, "say you'll help me convince Miss Olivia not to go forward with this scheme. We must keep her safe." His expression of mournful entreaty made him more poetically beautiful than ever, and I found myself transfixed by his long lashes.

"Of course," I breathed.

Bertie snorted a laugh, and I hastily reclaimed my hand and my common sense.

"That is, I could try to convince her," I said, "but I'm just the saddler."

Miss Olivia thumped past us, miraculously still in the saddle. "Major?" she called, gasping to catch her breath. "If I could just . . . take a . . . a tiny little rest . . ."

The Major smacked his boot hard with the heavy crop and then visibly winced. In his fury, he had turned the crop around until the molded metal handle was at the bottom, and it was with this heavy piece that he had cracked himself soundly on the ankle. He was bony all over, padded only by a modest paunch at the midsection.

"Miss Chedington," he called out in a new, flinty tone, "you will amount to nothing! You stand on the backs of giants. Your father built a castle of horseflesh, and you are but the crumbling rampart of that once-great fortress! It's a shame you were not born male, but you can avoid heaping more shame on your father's good name if you quit your hysterics and . . . SIT . . . UP!"

Already pink with exertion, Miss Olivia's face flushed a dull crimson.

Next to me, Bertie let slip an expletive that would have done credit to any sailor. "You know," he said, "I've never much cared for Miss Olivia. But bringing up her father seems a step too far. Shall I rescue her? I could do a little herding, run out and stop that spotted fellow in his tracks." He nodded toward the piebald gelding.

Before I could decide how to reply without actually speaking, Langford gallantly intervened. "Hello, Major! I've brought Miss Cobb, the saddler. Perhaps she can assist."

The Major turned abruptly and grimaced as if noticing us for the first time. "A moment, if you please," he said. He turned stiffly back to his pupil, but the consciousness of an audience transformed him. He stopped swinging the crop, lifted his chest and his chin, and began to speak with the measured tones of a distinguished parson on Sunday morning.

"As I was saying, you must imagine yourself the rampart of a castle," he said, his voice quavering with refinement. "A tall and mighty rampart, defended in glorious battle. Or perhaps . . . the mast of a tall ship? Or a tree. A tall tree. Not one of the leaning ones," he finished lamely.

Bertie stared at the man, his jaw slack with wonder. I was just as flummoxed as the horse. I had observed many riding masters in my years of saddlery work, but I had never seen or heard anything like the Major. If the man was trying to be unhelpful, he was doing a bang-up job.

And then, something happened. For the briefest of moments, Miss Olivia struggled herself upright, and for a stride or two, she bumped squarely on the saddle. Then she collapsed again, grabbing for the horse's mane.

The piebald, being both bored and rudderless, altered his course and came to us. He stopped neatly in front of Langford, affectionately nosing the young man's chest and leaving a smear of saliva on his tweeds. Langford simply chuckled and started scratching the old horse's spotted neck.

"Whew!" Miss Olivia said. She dropped the reins and reached up to adjust her modish hat over her blonde curls.

She was a pretty girl in a blooming roses sort of way, with round cheeks, dimples, and an attractive pout. Smiling cheerfully down at us, she seemed to have completely recovered from the Major's rudeness.

"Miss Cobb," she said, fanning her pink face with a gloved hand, "I'm so glad you're here! I'm afraid this saddle slips me to the left. Could you possibly take a look at it? Or perhaps I could try a different saddle or . . . a different horse?" Her eyes landed on Bertie, who tensed next to me as if braced for flight.

I had been feeling sorry for the girl, but now I felt a twinge of indignance. Did the silly girl not realize her old gelding had been taking care of her? Riding any other horse, she would have ended up with skid marks and a painfully intimate acquaintance with the ground. I replied in the most sympathetic tone I could muster. "Perhaps a change of saddle is in order. Why don't we go back to the stable—"

"Miss Chedington!" the Major barked, marching up to us with eyes blazing. "Did I tell you to halt?"

"Well, no, Major," the girl said, flashing him one of her most charming smiles, "but the horse came over to say hello—"

Her smile was not having the intended effect. The Major glared stonily at her, his wispy mustache curving downward. "I see. The horse makes the decisions, does he? And when the horse decides to take you into the path of a train or over a cliff to the sea, you will let him?"

The girl giggled. "But there *aren't* any cliffs or trains around here, Major," she said playfully. She picked up the reins and clumsily turned her mount in the direction of the stables, calling over her shoulder, "Don't worry, Major! I'm sure Miss Cobb will find a saddle that suits me by tomorrow."

Langford followed her after a glance at the Major, who

was standing open-mouthed, staring daggers at his pupil's retreating back. It seemed that allowing the pupil to make the decisions fell into the same category as allowing the horse to do so.

The Major turned to me. "Coddled," he declared, in a tone that indicated it was the worst possible epithet he could conjure.

"Perhaps," I said. "But that gelding has the constitution of an elephant. Miss Olivia doesn't seem to be doing any harm."

"My dear Miss Cobb," said the Major, leveling me with his beady eyes. "That young lady is a moron. If you flip to the word 'moron' in the dictionary, her image is sure to be there." He slapped his boot with the crop. "Coddled moron!"

The man was getting my dander up. Yes, the girl was incompetent. Perhaps she was even a moron. But this was certainly a case of the old pot and kettle, and I had my own opinion of whose image belonged on that page of the dictionary. "She did straighten up for a moment," I said coldly.

"Did she?" He paused in his turn toward the gate.

"Yes, didn't you notice? She sat up a little taller. Just for a moment. It was after you said that little thing about the trees." I made sure my tone conveyed exactly what I thought of that little thing about the trees. "She might even become competent with *proper* instruction." I tried to channel Treacle Tart's most disdainful expression and skewered the man with my gaze. At least, I thought I did.

But the thunder cleared from his sallow face, and he looked suddenly gratified. "Ah yes! Proper instruction, quite. I'm glad you've noticed her improvement under my instruction. I have often been told I have a way with words, a unique skill, you know, a kind of innate eloquence. It has often helped me to succeed where others have failed." His voice was reaching Sunday-parson pitch again. "And I thank you for your words of affirmation, Miss Cobb."

With that extraordinary comment, he did a swift about-face on his heel and headed off toward the stable with a new lightness in his step.

"Seems a fine fellow," Bertie said around a generous mouthful of grass. "Not sure I would've encouraged him like that, though."

"Encouraged? But I didn't . . ." I closed my eyes. "Never mind. Any more useful observations?"

"He may benefit from a dose of castor oil."

"Not the Major," I said. "Miss Olivia. Did you notice anything new that might be upsetting her balance?" I had come to rely on Bertie's shrewd eye when evaluating riders and their saddles. Horses really are the best riding masters, and Bertie prided himself on catching the details I missed.

"Other than the Major's mishmash of metaphors? She did seem overly concerned about that hat of hers. Perhaps the hat was slipping to the left, and she was trying to get her body back under it."

"Very helpful, old boy," I said, and I stomped after the Major with Bertie in tow.

5

THE MERITS OF MULES

BERTIE SUDDENLY HALTED, looking back toward the far edge of the field. "What in Epona's name is that?" he said. As a rule, Bertie didn't invoke the name of the horse goddess lightly, and I swiveled to see what had arrested him.

A galloping horse was approaching from outside the back hedge. It was a mousy creature and smallish, and the rider crouching low over its neck was clothed in the most vivid spring-green color I had ever seen. The rider aimed the horse directly for the hedge, and I caught my breath as I realized the fool intended to jump it. Impossible, on such a small horse. Heart thudding, I watched as the little horse rocked back on its haunches and leapt, soaring through the air and clearing the hedge with a foot to spare. I felt the wild urge to applaud, though I didn't act on it, and even Bertie let out a loud snort of relief.

The rider gathered up his mount, patted its neck, and they continued toward us in a light, lilting canter. By this time, I had noticed something odd about the horse, something

Bertie's keen eyes had seen from the start. Its ears were much longer than they should have been.

"It's . . ." I said.

"A mule," confirmed Bertie, his neck arched high for an eagle view. "I believe it's the grocery mule. Lady Chedington's cook drives that chap into Pelgren for supplies. She insists on choosing the ingredients herself, doesn't trust any delivery service. Wise woman." He noticed me staring at him. "What?" he said. "What do you think I do at Becketts while you're grappling with saddles? I watch and listen."

The peculiar duo meandered across the field, but the brightly-clad rider didn't seem to have a destination in mind. He guided the mule in a variety of figures, sometimes trotting and sometimes cantering, doing circles, figure-eights, serpentines and the like. The mule, who was an interesting bluish-brown color, moved as gracefully as some well-bred horses. This was obviously due to the skill of the man on its back. Still and erect, he rode with a quiet mastery that could only be achieved through many focused years in the saddle.

"At least he can bump a horse," I murmured.

"Mule," corrected Bertie. "But well said, old girl." There was an edge of admiration to his voice, and this was praise indeed. Bertie rarely admired anything that wasn't directly related to his own comfort. "Spectacular creatures, mules," he said. "I once saw one jump a stone wall from a standstill. Many of these young gentlemen fussing about with Thoroughbreds would be much better served by a good, solid mule. This fellow seems to have figured that out," he flipped his nose at the pair. "And it's oddly satisfying to know that there's a person on this earth who'd dress up to ride a mule."

I couldn't agree with Bertie there. For all his understated

skill, the rider looked a bit of a dandy. His chartreuse coat was paired with a dazzlingly gold waistcoat and matching gold cap. I could admire each item of clothing separately, but together they gave the impression of being ordered from a Savile Row tailor as "one springtime outfit for a country gentleman."

As they finally neared us, the rider used the lightest touch to bring the mule down to a walk and then eased the animal into a standstill. He was a young man, impossibly fair, and his white-blonde hair and washy skin looked even ghostlier against the colorful attire. He gazed at us with cool nonchalance and no greeting whatsoever.

I stared back at him, and the silence stretched uncomfortably long. The young man's eyes matched the rest of him—very pale like polished silver, and just as cold. As he looked at Bertie, his impervious eyes running over the big horse's body, his face turned thoughtful. Bertie didn't seem to notice the scrutiny. He was busy gazing at the mule with an expression of profound respect. I felt the rider's strange eyes shift to me, and he looked me slowly up and down, his mouth twisting slightly. Was the man trying to intimidate me? From his expensive boots to his thin, colorless lips, everything about him declared the aristocracy. At this realization, I squared my shoulders and firmly met his gaze, feeling my sense of equilibrium returning. I knew his class better than he could ever guess. I hadn't been a saddler forever.

I had grown up around people like this man, though none of them had been so pale. The man I had called Uncle had been a groom on an estate far grander than Becketts, the estate of a viscount rather than a mere baronet. Through what was later deemed a misguided sense of charity, the viscountess had invited me to live in the grand house as a companion to her daughter.

"Such charming black eyes," her ladyship had breathed, though my parentage remained a mystery, and her fine friends never failed to remind her of the dubious influence I was sure to have on her daughter.

They weren't wrong, those satined and bejeweled ladies.

"You're a lucky girl, Harriet, never forget it," my uncle told me.

I knew I was lucky to be educated alongside the viscount's amiable daughter. Better yet, I'd been given my own horse, a plucky cob named Barnum. Yes, I knew I was lucky. But, being a child, I had no memory of being *unlucky*. I didn't know that lucky meant things could be taken away.

My uncle disappeared when I was twelve. "Fly-by-night," some murmured, and the debts he'd had made it likely. But it was easy to ignore my uncle's absence while exploring York-shire's hills and dales on horseback with the viscount's daughter.

A few more years found the young lady chafing at the strictures of her privileged life. As her intrepid companion, I frequently devised entertaining schemes and forbidden adventures for us. When our exploits were inevitably discov-ered, I was the one punished, more often than not with a strap across my backside or my hands. But I simply laughed and came up with better schemes. Even at that age, my feathers were well-oiled.

When my companion and I were found riding our horses bareback one moonlit night, Barnum—my delight and my soulmate—was promptly sold to the chubby son of an earl. "What to do with her" and "send her away," fragments caught while listening behind doors—none of them hurt the way Barnum's loss had shattered me, but I knew it was time to leave. So I crept away from that grand house, armed only with a love of horses and a deep distrust of people like the man currently staring me down.

"Byerley!" The Major's voice cracked through the air, snapping me back from those cobwebbed years. He was striding toward us, a wide grin on his hollow face. "I see you've found yourself a suitable mount!"

The pale young man looked over at him but said nothing.

"No, no, I understand, my lad," the Major continued, waving his crop as if to wave away protestations. "Big Thoroughbreds can be so intimidating. Much better to start with something smaller, more manageable. And when you finally master this mule, perhaps you could try a lady's mount, what?" He collapsed into laughter, swaying in his polished boots.

Byerley's face showed little concern. He looked almost bored as he observed the Major. "Lady Chedington told me I was welcome to ride any horse," he said in a lazy drawl. "I was going to ride Brioso, but she specifically forbade—"

"The stallion!" said the Major, startled from his mirth. "I should think you'd have the sense to stay away from him, considering his history. The horse is dangerous, a known bolter. And he is under my care, as Lady Chedington has entrusted his training to me alone. No, my lad, you must steer well clear of Brioso and leave his training to a professional. He is no mule, you can be certain of that." He laid the thick leather crop across his chest and glared at Byerley imperiously.

Byerley's light eyebrows raised a fraction, seemingly in faint amusement. "About that training, Major. You must be more skilled than I'd imagined. I've never met a horseman who could train a riding horse without ever putting a leg over its back. I've been at Becketts all week, and I have yet to see you take Brioso from his stall." He shrugged. "So I thought I might give him some exercise." He still spoke with breezy indifference, but his gray eyes were two chips of cold stone.

The Major bridled at this, his face reddening and his lips curling under his meager mustache. "The true horseman," he sputtered out finally, "is an artist. He does his work in private. He needs no accolades and he scorns the praise of onlookers." He stuck out his chest, warming to his topic. "He rises early and communes with his horses before the dawn when the world is silent and Nature speaks loudest."

"Emerson?" Byerley asked pleasantly.

"No," snapped the Major. Then, seeming to compose himself, he continued in a more cordial tone. "I'm explaining, my dear lad, that I train horses at dawn when some men are still sleeping off the previous night's cigars and brandy. Those of us with a profession understand the need to rise early and make the most of the day. Fortunately, you will never need to experience such drudgery, ay, my lad?" He chuckled amiably, but his small eyes glittered.

At my side, Bertie seemed fascinated by the conversation, and he stopped chewing for a moment, watching and waiting for the angry response that was sure to come. Byerley was probably on the downhill slope of his twenties—possibly older, though it was hard to tell—and at that age no man likes to be called "my lad." Especially not in the tone the Major was using, and especially not if one happened to be a lord. But Byerley simply gazed at the Major disinterestedly. Then, a slight smile touched the corner of his thin, aristocratic lips.

"For the privilege of seeing a master at work," he said, "I think I can roust myself from bed and stumble down to the stable tomorrow morning, cigars and brandy notwithstanding." He gave the Major a cool smile. "I would dearly love to watch and learn from a horseman such as yourself."

For the first time, the Major was at a loss for words. His lips worked, but the rest of him seemed frozen. Finally, he reached up to smooth his mustache and seemed to shake himself out of his stupor.

"I'm afraid it would be pointless," he said. "I'm sure you'll agree, professional trainers such as myself have a certain intuition, a certain innate ability to communicate with horses. I can no more explain my training process than Michaelangelo could explain his painting process. The horse behaves perfectly for me, thus you would gain nothing by observing me. As they say, perfection makes a poor teacher." He smiled loftily and seemed exceedingly proud of this philosophy.

"That's one explanation for Miss Olivia's lack of progress," Bertie muttered.

Byerley's light eyes flitted to Bertie's face, and my stomach clenched. Had this pale stranger been able to hear the horse's words? There was no shock in the young man's face, just a curiously blank expression, as if he were doing sums in his head.

"Very well," Byerley said, turning back to the Major. "I shan't attempt to learn anything at all from you."

The Major's face relaxed, and his flushed cheeks drooped in relief.

"I shall observe your ride tomorrow morning as I would the Sistine Chapel," Byerley continued pleasantly, "in pure admiration of art." He stared levelly at the Major.

After a long moment of silence, the Major sucked in a breath, drawing himself up. Worry lines appeared between his brows.

"Very well," he announced, louder than necessary. "I shall

ride Brioso at dawn, and I shall expect you to attend." He turned and tromped toward the stable, shoulders slightly deflated.

"Sounds unnecessarily like a duel," Bertie said, whuffling a laugh.

Byerley, who was gathering his reins, hesitated for a moment and looked at Bertie, his fair head cocked. He looked a bit like a dog trying to understand human speech—a very shrewd Alsatian, I decided, heart thumping. Then the pale eyes slid to my face.

"*Miss* Cobb," he said, with odd emphasis, and he nodded haughtily before turning to follow the Major.

Bertie was absorbed in his grazing again, but I felt the tingle of gooseflesh. Byerley had known my name without ever having been introduced—but perhaps Lady Chedington had mentioned me to her guests. More alarming was the young man's sign-off. Byerley had nodded twice—once at me, and once at Bertie.

6

THE ADVANTAGES OF
BEING A ROSSETTI

I LET myself quietly into the Hall through the back entrance nearest the stable. It was not the dim, cramped service entrance one might expect. In Becketts Hall, where generations of Chedingtons had spent their lives breeding and training valuable Thoroughbreds, this route to the stable was nearly as important as the grand foyer. A wide corridor stretched before me with inlaid wood flooring and high sconces in the shape of rearing horses. Horses surrounded me on all sides—the place was absolutely choked with them in ornately framed paintings and photographs. It seemed Sir Algernon had wanted his house as full of horses as his stable.

"Oh, why did my husband throw away his money buying horses!" Lady Chedington had wailed to me months ago. "Why didn't he spend his money on scotch and gaming and women like any rational red-blooded male? At least those expenses would have died with him."

She had reluctantly acquiesced to necessity by reducing the number of household staff, so I didn't expect to meet any servants on my way through the house. Care of the Hall kept the remaining staff too busy to be meeting guests at the back door. Peters, the ancient butler, was usually missing until dinner, at which time he donned his white gloves and his most dignified expression and tottered about with the gravity of a Victorian ghost.

I paused in front of a rather improbable painting of Miss Olivia in a yellow ball gown, riding a leaping horse over a massive stone wall. Even in the painting, she was sliding to the left.

"My dear Miss Cobb!" Lady Chedington said as I entered the drawing room. She was alone in the room and seemed to be arranging some dishes on the sideboard while holding a glass of sherry in one plump hand. Though not tall, her frame was as solidly built as her opinions. She observed my outfit critically. "Those dark colors make you so statuesque. I can't decide whether you look more like a mother superior or the goddess Athena. Something grand and religious."

"And eternally celibate?" I said, glancing doubtfully down at my charcoal gray shirtwaist and skirt.

"Was Athena? I thought she was the one seduced by a swan." She waved a hand. "Never mind. Though if we did follow that train of thought, you'd make a marvelous Queen Elizabeth. Didn't she go about on a gray horse?"

I made a mental note to tell Bertie that there was talk of him resembling a royal charger. That should please the old boy.

"Do help yourself to these delicious dainties," she said, handing me a glass of sherry and indicating the heavily laden sideboard. "After a long drought, I think I've finally found a cook who understands the concept of *hors d'oeuvres*. Like the French, you know."

The spread was impressive. Mountains of fresh, glistening

fruits, cheeses, and various sweet and savory delights. I filled my plate with sliced pears, blackberries, Stilton cheese, tiny toasts with sliced medallions of foie gras, and a delicate scone with a liberal coating of castor sugar.

Lady Chedington led me to a settee that appeared to be upholstered in actual horse hide, hair included. We sat facing a massive mantel above a modest fire, and I gazed up at the large portrait above the mantel. Painted in oils, Sir Algernon was dressed in a scarlet coat and white breeches, and he sat atop a prancing black stallion—ostensibly Brioso.

"Ridiculous, isn't it?" her ladyship said, following my gaze.

"I'm no connoisseur, but I think it's quite good."

"Oh, the likeness is good enough, but that horse! It's not enough that the creature is living in my stable, I also have to endure him in my drawing room. I had hoped he was lost on the moor, you know. After Algernon fell, the beast was missing, running wild for a night. I thought it served him right. Eaten by wolves might've been nice. But he turned up like a bad penny the next morning." She shook her head sadly. "Now," she said, turning to me with clasped hands and hopeful eyes. "What of the saddle? Will you be able to resurrect it by tomorrow? That's the word Madame Itovsky used—resurrect. Her vocabulary is so spiritual."

"Perhaps," I said cautiously, "you'd let me take the saddle back to my cottage and work on it there? I could deliver it tomorrow evening."

"Oh, no, I'm afraid that's quite out of the question. Do you know much about spiritualism, my dear? The spirit's connection to the terrestrial plane is ever so tenuous. The connecting object must stay where the spirit was most present in life. Cart it away, and the spirit vanishes like a snuffed candle!"

I considered myself fairly open-minded—having a talking

horse as companion put me on a rather slippery slope—but from what I'd heard, Madame Itovsky was a spirit medium of the table-rapping variety. Which is to say, not one. I shifted uncomfortably on the settee. The hide must have come from a remarkably well-groomed animal, as it was slippery and kept inching me toward the edge.

"You must spend the night," Lady Chedington said, and there was a note of triumph in her voice. "I think you'll find Becketts Hall to be vastly more comfortable than your tiny little cottage. Not that there's anything lacking in your property," she hastened to add. "It's such a lovely place, such a quiet little wilderness, just like those American paintings with the tiny people and the vast landscapes." She sighed and observed her sparkling sherry glass. "It wouldn't suit me at all," she declared.

I smiled ruefully. The woman had a habit of teetering every compliment on the edge of demurral.

"It will be so nice to have someone my age at dinner!" she continued. "I've been absolutely besieged with young people this week. As you'll soon see. For me, being the oldest and the wisest at the table is not a position in which I flourish. We shall have to band together, you and I."

I arranged my features into what I hoped was an expression of deep regret. "I'm afraid I must decline. The saddle will take hours, and in the midst of such dirty work I will hardly look—or smell—presentable enough for a dining room."

She gave me a sly glance and wagged a finger at me. "I know that dining with a tableful of strangers is not one of your favorite activities. You'd rather eat alone in the stable, would you not?"

I stared at her. I had thought Lady Chedington as silly and shallow as the next wealthy socialite, yet here she was, revealing a startling streak of intuition. Bertie, old scholar of human observation that he was, had once told me, "Spend enough time with a person, Harriet, and that person will jostle your expectations. And we all need a good jostling now and then. It's good for the circulation and the soul."

"No need to explain!" continued Lady Chedington though I hadn't said a thing. She waved her sherry glass at her husband's portrait. "Algernon was the same, you know. That's how I recognized the symptoms in you, my dear. He was forever out of doors, much more comfortable with horses than with people. He would rather eat brown bread and cheese from a basket in the stable than roast pheasant from fine china in the dining room! I suppose you enjoy eating from baskets in stables? Because I'll be sure to send one down for you, and with more than bread and cheese, you can be certain of that."

"Thank you," I said, letting out the breath I had been holding.

"'Tis a shame, though," she said with a pretty pout that reminded me of her daughter. "You could have helped me watch Byerley at dinner."

"Watch him? Is he in the habit of stealing silverware?"

Lady Chedington chortled at this. "No, my dear! I'm sure he's well supplied with silver in every sense of the word, and much finer than ours. But you could have observed him, read him, got to the depths of his soul with those keen eyes of yours."

"To find what?" I did want to get to the depths of Byerley's odd glances at Bertie, but at the moment I was torn between that and the desire to steer clear of him altogether. "I met Lord Byerley today. Well, not formally, but I saw him riding.

He seemed . . ." I hesitated, searching for something innocuous to say.

"Such a noble bearing," she said wistfully. "I was really very keen on Olivia's snagging him."

Somehow, I couldn't imagine the pale, haughty Lord Byerley with lush, giggling Olivia Chedington. "Isn't she having any success?" I asked.

Lady Chedington shrugged. "I was hoping this week would decide it. If proximity to her beauty wasn't enough, I thought her newfound passion for horses would be added inducement. The Byerleys are all mad on horses, you know, have been for generations. The women as well as the men. The men of the family seem to choose wives as much for their horsiness as for anything else. In fact," she said, the fine wrinkles around her eyes crinkling in wicked amusement, "the current elder Lady Byerley looks rather like a horse. There is a point at which a nose goes from aristocratic to positively equine. Olivia would bring a much nicer nose to that family. And she could introduce them to fabrics other than tweeds!" She chuckled heartily.

"But your daughter neither rides nor resembles a horse well enough to be considered 'horsey.' "

"Too true," she sighed. "She can't find her balance, and she's been that way since she was a child. She used to listen to me and stay off the beasts' backs, but since her father died, she's become a bit willful. If I don't allow her to ride, she says she'll sneak down at night and do it anyway, which would be far more dangerous, as you can well imagine! So I hired the Major. Perhaps she will finally be convinced by someone other than me that riding is not in her future."

"In my opinion, Fletcher would be a much better instructor. The Major may be doing more harm than good. He seems extremely unkind, among other things."

"Unkind?" She tittered a laugh. "My dear, kindness is not a native quality among riding masters. I hope he is brutally honest. It is no kindness to Olivia to encourage her when she is so incompetent." She fixed me with her blue eyes, so similar to her daughter's. "Which brings me to you, my dear."

"Me?" I said, startled.

"Did you or did you not praise Olivia's riding today? The Major was full of it. He came to tell me, and quite puffed up he was. He said that she is showing signs of 'elegance in the saddle.' He said that you were quite impressed with his methods and you praised him soundly. Is that so?" She eyed me sternly.

"Of course not!" I protested, blanching at the memory of Miss Olivia's flushed face bobbing desperately above the cantering horse. Elegance in the saddle, indeed. "I only pointed out that Miss Olivia straightened up for a moment."

"Well. Take my advice, my dear, and do not interfere. Do not encourage Olivia if you can help it. She will only get hurt." She gazed into her empty sherry glass as though it were a crystal ball. "What with bicycles and motorcars, there's very little need for young ladies to spend time with those dangerous beasts. The future has wheels not hooves! But if you must praise Olivia, feel free to praise her to Byerley. He could use the encouragement." She appeared momentarily amused, but then her expression fell and she burst out, "But it may not matter, as Olivia is doing her best to make sure the match will never come off!"

"Does she dislike the man so much?" I asked, relieved at the change in topic.

"Oh, I'm sure she likes him well enough, but the silly girl is throwing other beautiful women in his path!" Finding herself in need of fortification, she stood and marched over to the sherry decanter. "Have you met Miss Seyward, our other guest?"

"No, I only came across Lord Byerley and Mr. Langford."

"Miss Seyward is a school friend of Olivia's. I thought my daughter and I understood each other. I thought she would invite someone of the mousy variety—plain and uninteresting and incapable of upsetting plans. But who appears on my doorstep? Miss Seyward, like she's just stepped out of a Rossetti painting."

"Your daughter is as pretty as any painting," I said, feeling that at least this was an area in which I could safely praise the girl.

"But my daughter is a Waterhouse, and Miss Seyward is a Rossetti."

I blinked at her. "Art is not my strong suit."

"A Waterhouse may be beautiful, but a Rossetti is fascinating. A less beautiful face but a face you want to look at much longer. Why do you think Henry VIII went after Anne when there were much prettier women about? Anne was definitely a Rossetti. That's what men sense about Miss Seyward, and that's why my daughter was foolish to invite her."

There was the sound of an old throat being cautiously cleared, and we looked up to see Peters, the snow-haired butler, standing with rickety composure at the door.

"Excuse me, my lady," he said querulously, "but the gentlemen have gone upstairs to change for dinner, and Mrs. Granger has asked to speak with you about the soup."

"Very well, Peters, I shall attend to it in a moment." Lady Chedington turned to me and fervently clasped my hands. "*Do* help me keep an eye on Byerley, Miss Cobb. I'm sure you'll come across him again in your time here. Or you could fabricate a reason to talk to him! Say you will? I need those sharp eyes of yours to tell me whether he prefers Waterhouse or Rossetti." With a conspiratorial wink, she whisked up and followed the ancient butler out of the room.

I stared up at Sir Algernon's portrait. "I'm just the saddler," I informed him. He gazed benevolently down on me, and it seemed there was also a hint of commiseration in his face.

7

THE BENEFITS OF
NOT BEING BATTY

"HE'S ABOUT SETTLED, MISS COBB," Tom said. He nodded toward Bertie, who was grazing in the meadow Fletcher had reluctantly approved for his turnout. "Gave him a bucket of water. Two buckets actually. Easier to carry when you got two." The stable lad grinned at me and stiffened his arms at either side of his slim body, demonstrating how one would go about holding two buckets. Freckled and possessing an impudent snub nose, the boy had yet to put on the muscle that his twenties would bring. He seemed sprightly enough, but Fletcher had informed me he was "a plodder."

"Luckily, there's a place for plodders in this work, Miss Cobb," Fletcher had said, nodding sagely. "Tom can't ride worth a tinker's damn, but give him a pitchfork an' face him toward the stables, like, an' he'll have the place clean in half the time t'would take a more thoughtful lad."

"You work long hours, don't you?" I said to the boy.

"Sunup to sundown, Miss Cobb," he said proudly. "Sometimes longer if I go to Maplehurst."

"You do stables for Mr. Langford too?" When did the poor boy sleep?

"Not exactly. Mr. Langford, he hires me for the special jobs. He knows I can handle a bit o' construction, like. I'm good at buildin' things with wood, see?" He moved his hands smartly as though tapping an invisible nail with a phantom hammer.

"Yes, I understand, building things," I said dryly. Tom obviously thought I had never handled a tool in my life.

"Sometimes buildin' and sometimes tearin' down," he continued cheerfully. "Last year, Mr. Langford, he were in a right pickle. Said he needed to clear out his tack room, clear it all out, saddle racks an' harness pegs an' all, till it were clean and smooth down to the wall studs. He called on me that time, sayin' it were a rush job an' his boys weren't no good at woodworkin'."

"Last year? He's been working on that tack room since last year? But I suppose a parquet floor takes a good deal of time to assemble. Is it very elaborate?"

"I don't know 'bout any floors," the boy said, chewing his lip. "Mr. Langford wanted me for the tear-down, like, but he didn't need me for the buildin' part. Haven't heard another peep, so he must be 'bout done, I'd say."

And there it was. Mr. Langford's excuse of ongoing renovations was just that—an excuse. He probably didn't want to hire me at all.

"Well," I said brusquely, "you're a multi-talented person, Tom. You can do all the work related to horses, and handle a bit of woodworking on the side. All at your age. That's nothing to sniff at."

"Ridin's the best part, Miss Cobb, but I expect you know that yourself with a big, strong horse like yours." He grinned, tipped his cap to me, and faded away toward the stables. A curious choice of words, I thought, though Bertie would appreciate the description.

I turned and made my way through the vine-laden paddock gate into the little meadow. It was a wild, neglected place, overgrown with clover and thistles and starry violets in hidden hollows. Ancient, gnarled trees crept down from the moor above to crowd protectively around the little wilderness. Keats' "faery lands forlorn" had nothing on this place, I thought, and amused myself with the thought of bringing Langford down for a walk.

"This meadow will do very well," Bertie announced as I approached him. He appeared almost white in the dusk, grazing contentedly under a large oak tree.

"Well," I said, "enjoy the grass, but don't be too devastated if Fletcher tries to put you in the stables overnight."

"I respectfully and preemptively decline."

"I believe he's worried about heavy rain."

Bertie drew himself up indignantly, arching his muscular neck and giving me a sideways glare. "Rain? Oh, I ask you. When has a horse ever been hurt by a nice, heavy pelting? It's as good as a massage. Besides," he said, nodding toward the heavy treeline and thick canopy of branches, "I have plenty of natural shelter, should I need it. And if things were to become truly cataclysmic, I'm near enough the Hall that you would hear my cries of distress." We both looked toward the massive brick walls of the Hall, rising cleanly from the carefully tended lawn just beyond our untamed faery land.

There were nearly as many windows on the back of the Hall as the front. The Georgians had dearly loved their windows, and they lent the place a pleasant symmetry, but they also gave a clear view of the meadow. I imagined Byerley gazing down from one of those windows, reading my lips as I talked to Bertie. He seemed the slippery sort that would be good at reading lips. I frowned, turning my back on the Hall.

"Did you notice anything strange about Byerley today?" I asked cautiously.

"His outfit," Bertie said, speaking around a particularly plump thistle head. He crunched the thing with slobbery satisfaction and continued, "I thought the rich prided themselves on simpler clothes. 'I'm backed by a fortune grand enough that I don't need sartorial support' and all that."

"That's not what I meant. Did you get any strange feeling from him?"

"I felt only admiration for how successful he was at winding up the Major. What do you think? Has the Major ever even ridden the stallion? My money's on no."

I sighed. I would have to spell it out, which never went well.

"I think you should be careful around Byerley. He gave you a look. Two looks actually. Right after you spoke."

Bertie stopped browsing and raised his head, looking faintly amused and less faintly annoyed. "Are we treading this worn path again, old girl? You know where it leads—a dead end. And you and I both hate backtracking, so let's not ride down it at all."

"His looks were definitely related to your speech," I said, wishing the universe had saddled me with a less-obstinate talking horse.

"You know as well as I do," Bertie said, lifting his nose higher so that he could look down it more dramatically, "that in the time we've been together, no one but you has ever been able to hear me speak."

"There was the haberdasher in Bristol."

"Nothing doing. He stared at every horse. Probably wondering whether horsehair bonnets would come back in style. Or whether horse skin could pass for beaver in a pinch. He had that hungry look about him."

"Fine," I said. "I'll give you the haberdasher. What about the livery man on Bell Lane?"

"I'm not convinced he didn't have a glass eye," Bertie said thoughtfully, wrinkles appearing above his own dark eyes. "He gave everyone those odd looks. Rather off-putting, as one was never sure exactly where or why he was staring. I saw more than one gentleman check the buttons on his fly after strolling past that livery stable."

"What about the livery man's *son*?" I said triumphantly.

"Hmm," Bertie said, his eyes narrowing. "Now *he* was uncanny. I'd whinge to myself about the lack of carrots, and next thing I knew, he'd bring me a carrot. But I think he was just a good guesser."

"Really."

"You forget, my dear Harriet, that many people read horses without any speech at all. The keener humans deduce plenty from body language and a simple whinny. Your conversations with me have ruined you for the finer elements of unspoken communication between human and horse."

"Now you sound like the Major," I sighed. "Just . . . please be careful around Byerley."

Bertie stepped close and lowered his wide forehead until it touched mine.

"Don't worry about me," he said. "As you know, I am perfectly capable of appearing as unexceptional and simple-minded as the next horse."

I knew that "capable of" and "willing to" were not exactly the same thing but decided not to push the point. "I think we should head home. I can refuse to do the saddle, say the leather is in worse shape than I thought." I squinted at the hazy dusk sky. "We could be home in less than an hour."

Bertie was eyeing another plump thistle. "Why the rush?" he asked, snaking his neck out to retrieve the blossom. "If Byerley can hear me speak, I should think you'd be relieved."

"Relieved?"

"Relieved to know you're not insane."

Early in my acquaintance with Bertie, the thought had occurred to me that I might be cracking. The impossibility of a talking horse had cost me more than a few nights' sleep, as well as a train fare to London to visit a Wimpole Street physician, who had diagnosed me with a mild case of hypochondria. But, as I had lost my resolve on the way and hadn't actually told the physician about Bertie at all, his diagnosis was as vague as my complaint. Bertie finally pointed out that my brain was incapable of dreaming up all the little witticisms that came out of his mouth, and with that thought, I slept a little better at night.

"You should spend some time basking in the knowledge that you're not batty," Bertie said. "But even if you're not in need of such reassurance, you can't just duck out and leave everyone here in the lurch with their problems."

"But none of it concerns me," I spluttered. "I'm just the saddler." The phrase was becoming something of a mantra. I began to wonder if I should write it on a sign and hang it round my neck.

"As I see it," the big horse said, crunching loudly, "you've got yourself a bit entangled. You promised Fletcher you'd help him preserve his job—"

"I did no such thing! I just said I'd try to put in a good word for him."

"—which you have yet to do in earnest. Agreed? Yes. Well. I also remember a promise to a handsome young poet that you will persuade Miss Olivia not to throw her leg over the stallion. But you muddled that one by telling the Major that Miss Olivia is improving. Your little comment may have given him just the right amount of wind under his wings to fan the flames of Miss Olivia's madness. As I see it, by praising the Major, you've managed to jeopardize Fletcher's job while almost ensuring the girl will ride the stallion. And then there's the little matter of deciding whether Byerley prefers Waterhouse or Rossetti—"

"How could you possibly know that?" I exclaimed, eyeing the horse suspiciously. I looked back at the Hall, judging the distance between our meadow and the drawing room window. Bertie was an expert eavesdropper, but the distance was just too far. "You couldn't have heard that all the way over here."

"My hearing is second to none."

I glared at him, unconvinced.

"Very well," he said. "Fletcher may have asked Tom, that redheaded stable lad, to bring me to this paddock. And on the way, I may have spied an exceptionally delightful bit of clover up near the Hall, directly under the drawing room window. Tom is a slim boy, bit of a featherweight really, and he has yet to learn how to dig his heels into the turf and really take hold of a horse. So, what with this and that, Tom and I ended up spending a cozy half hour stuck to that window like a burr to a saddle cloth."

"Charming," I said. "Now I have the reputation of not training my horse to lead properly."

"As I see it," Bertie plowed on, ignoring my comment as he had ignored poor Tom's hold on his rope, "repairing that saddle is the least of your worries. And it's the least you could do after throwing your spanner into the works."

I dragged myself over to a mossy stump and plunked down disconsolately.

"This is why I wanted to settle in the Highlands," I said. "Far less chance of getting mixed up with wealthy people and their problems."

"People are messy, old girl," Bertie said, swishing his tail in the gathering shadows. "That's what makes them so fascinating. And you've done your best to keep us cloistered away at the cottage, but don't you get the slightest bit lonely?"

I gazed at him for a long moment. "I thought this was our plan," I said finally. "Everything in Wolverhampton, it was all for this. Get our own little patch of green and never be at anyone else's beck and call for as long as we live."

"Yes, but when you put down roots, you find other roots, and before you know it, you're entwined. If we stay in Pelgren Vale, we can't help but be a little entwined. I say, let's embrace it. These seem to be decent people and," his eyes slid slyly to mine, "they seem to have decent bank balances. So go ahead, see if you can be of some small use to Lady Chedington, starting with that hideous saddle."

Trust Bertie to appeal to my avaricious tendencies. "She only wants that saddle for a séance, you know," I mumbled. "Some featherbrained plot to contact her husband. So keep in mind, by repairing the saddle, I may only be lining the pockets of some dodgy spiritualist."

"A séance!" Bertie bobbed his head up, high and startled, ears pricked to attention. "But I've always wanted to witness a séance! Oh, this is very satisfactory. A comfortable meadow, plenty of clover and thistles, and a séance in the offing. Very satisfactory indeed."

"We won't be attending the séance," I said, exasperated. "You in particular. Even if we were staying that long, which we're not, I'd like to see you sidle your considerable haunches into that drawing room."

"That would depend upon how much my new friend Tom learns between now and then about controlling a horse," he said thoughtfully.

I made a mental note to give Tom a little lesson on how to lead unruly horses.

8

A SINISTER FLASK

I LEFT Bertie with a promise to bring carrots in the morning, and headed back to Sir Algernon's smelly saddle. With the impending rain, most of the horses had been brought in for the night, and the stable was full of contented munching and the smell of large, warm bodies moving in clean straw.

As soon as I opened the tack room door, Treacle Tart leapt from his basket and streaked toward the opening. I scooted inside and slammed the door. The cat looked up witheringly from between my feet, buffeted by the folds of my skirt, and I began to feel rather guilty about the whole thing. I had come to Becketts to repair Sir Algernon's saddle, not play jailer to a cat.

"So sorry, kitty," I crooned, and Treacle Tart's expression changed. His ears perked hopefully, his eyes grew round and limpid, and he let out a pitiful, squeaking "mreh?" This was apparently the face that got him bowls of cream from the kitchen.

"Not my decision, I'm afraid," I said, crouching down to pet him.

His eyes narrowed. He pulled away contemptuously and stalked back to his basket.

"Alright, back to work it is." I seated myself at the work bench for the second time that day and rummaged in my tool bag. Plenty of waxed linen stitches would need to be ripped before I could drop the panels and remove the old wool, and the mouse hole would be easier to patch when the leather was free and slack.

Poised with my seam ripper, I heard giggling from the stable aisle. The door was suddenly thrown open, and two bright-faced girls piled in.

"Hello, Miss Cobb!" sang Miss Olivia, almost dancing into the room. "We thought—"

"Shut the door!" I barked, diving for Treacle Tart. Just behind Miss Olivia, the second girl seemed to grasp the situation and whirled to yank the door closed. Foiled for a second time, Treacle Tart galloped to the darkest corner of the room and sat beneath rows of hanging bridles, his reflective eyes winking at us from the shadows.

"Oh, Treacle Tart!" Miss Olivia giggled. She turned her rosy face to me and said conspiratorially, "You know, Mother thinks *I* named the cat. Fletcher was too embarrassed to admit that *he* chose the name himself! As if I would name a cat after baked goods. Treacle Tart, indeed! I wanted to name him Sir Percival Puddlethwaite, a much nobler name, don't you think?"

I was saved from answering when the other girl stepped forward to place a covered basket on the bench. "We're sorry to burst in on you like this, Miss Cobb," she said, "but we wanted to make sure you had something to eat."

There was no question that this elegant creature was Lady Chedington's Rossetti. She had none of Miss Olivia's vibrancy, but the sharp dark brows over keen, widely set eyes gave her a look of quiet intelligence. She wore her dark hair in a simple chignon without the elaborate curls that framed her companion's face, but this understated style added to her air of grace and—what was it? Vulnerability? Lady Chedington was right. There was something uniquely appealing about this girl.

"This is my friend, Miss Vivienne Seyward," Miss Olivia said proudly.

"So nice to meet you," I said, and I was surprised when Miss Seyward reached out to shake my hand. Her grip was firm and cool, and she looked me frankly in the eyes.

"I've been so looking forward to meeting you. An independent woman, a businesswoman, and a woman who rides astride." Her eyes shone with emotion. "You are an inspiration to all women, Miss Cobb."

I was surprised by her fervor, oddly touched, and immediately distrustful of the gratification I felt. A pedestal was a precarious place to be. Bertie's wry observations in my ear had taught me that flattery was more wisely laughed at than accepted.

"I really can't take credit for that last one," I protested. "I ride astride because of a back injury. A horse fell with me at a post and rails, and ever since, my back objects to side saddles. I'm afraid my riding style is dictated by necessity, not by any nobler instinct."

"But you're a saddler," Miss Olivia said, apparently feeling she should shore up her friend's argument. "I've never heard of a female saddler before. You're a pioneer," she said dreamily.

I couldn't stop myself from laughing. "Come up to Walsall with me sometime to my old neighborhood. There are hundreds of women working in the big saddlery factories there, the same ones that gave me my start. It's nothing new. Women have been making saddles and bridles for decades."

Two sets of eyes blinked at me solemnly. I was obviously not giving them what they had hoped for.

"However," I ventured, pausing in my climb off the pedestal, "I do work independently now. Doing saddle repairs and adjustments on my own. I guess that's a little unusual for a woman?"

"Just as we said, you're a pioneer!" gushed Miss Olivia, and both girls clapped me on the back and urged me to look inside the basket they had brought.

I lifted the towel to find smoked salmon, cucumber sandwiches, and the loveliest little bacon sandwiches on fresh, floury rolls. Some of the drawing room blackberries had also found their way in, and there was a large flask, probably of tea. Reaching for the tea, I noticed a smaller silver item near the edge of the basket. It seemed incongruous, a fine, elegant thing among the casual bounty.

"What's this?" Miss Olivia said, lifting it out. It was a slim, silver flask, highly polished, and there was some kind of etching visible on the front. "PBL?" she said, squinting at the engraved letters. "I can't make out the rest of it."

Miss Seyward leaned in. "PLB," she declared. "The 'B' in the middle is larger, so that's the surname. The others are meant to come before."

I took the flask from Miss Olivia. The letters were delicately etched, and I reached into my pocket for my spectacles. The girls were delighted when I swiveled down the magnifying loupe, pleased to see this tool of the trade in action. I peered closely at the elaborate engraving.

PBL
On the Victory of His Horse
Praxiteles
at Wolverhampton
12 September 1902

I FELT A CHILL. *Praxiteles. Wolverhampton. 12 September.* It couldn't be a coincidence. My mind flew back to that damp morning a year ago in Wolverhampton, the silent turf track shrouded in pre-dawn mist, the distant sounds of stableboys beginning their morning duties, and a gray horse looming suddenly before me out of the haze. We had been there, Bertie and I, on the 12th of September. It was the day we had taken the reins of our future—the day we had used an unremarkable colt named Praxiteles to change our fortunes.

The two girls were looking at me, surprised by my silence.

"Well, we all know someone with a 'B' surname," I said casually. "What's Lord Byerley's given name?"

"Peregrine Leopold Byerley," Miss Olivia said, delighted. "Oh, how odd! He must have slipped it into the basket when it was sitting in the corridor, before we came down. A little prank, surely. What's in it?"

I unscrewed the cap and took a whiff. "Whiskey." I promptly tipped it back and took a mighty swig of the stuff, much to the girls' amusement. I was in need of a little steadying. *Praxiteles. Wolverhampton. 12 September.*

"It seems a strange prank," Miss Seyward said. "And Byerley's usually so . . . sedate."

"Maybe that's because he's carrying around flasks of whiskey," I said dryly.

"The Major was certainly in his cups tonight," Miss Olivia said in an uncharacteristically dismal tone. "Oh Miss Cobb, you should have been at dinner! The Major was going on and on about how he's cured me of leaning, but of course no one believed him, and everyone was bored to tears. So then he made a grand announcement, though I really think it was just the gin talking. And do you know what he said?"

I shook my head and was surprised to see tears coming into the girl's big, soft eyes.

"He said that we should host an equestrian gala at Becketts." The tears were coming in earnest now. "He said it will be the perfect event to show off his skills as a horse master, and I will ride Brioso and we'll be the . . . the piece of resistance? At the gala."

"Pièce de résistance?" I said.

"Yes, that's it. How did you know? But . . ." she gave a breathless sob, "but I *can't* ride Brioso, Miss Cobb!"

"Isn't that what you wanted?"

"I thought it was, but the truth is, I'm actually not a very brave person. I thought maybe I could be, but it turns out I'm not. I get woozy just looking at Brioso. All I can think is that he'll do the same to me that he did to Father!" Her lip quivered dangerously.

Miss Seyward reached out and clasped her friend's hand, her darkly elegant brows pinched in sympathy. I felt a little pang of envy. How many years had it been since I'd had a true friend of the human variety? Perhaps Bertie was right. Perhaps there was something to be said for tangling one's roots with other roots.

"Father's spirit won't be able to rest until he knows his legacy is safe," Miss Olivia said miserably. "Riding Brioso in the gala seems the surest way . . ."

"What did the others say about the Major's announcement? About going forward with the gala?" I remembered Langford's forest-colored eyes as he pleaded with me to convince the girl against it, but it seemed she wouldn't need convincing after all.

"Mr. Langford was very angry. He said it was a foolhardy plan, that I would get hurt and it would only make Brioso's reputation worse. Mr. Langford is quite handsome when he's riled up."

"And Lord Byerley?"

"Oh, Byerley's never been handsome!" she giggled, and then shivered. "His skin is so pale it's like the belly of a fish."

"I mean," I said, "how did Byerley react to the Major's announcement?"

"Byerley's been in favor of the thing from the beginning. He said every horseman in the county should have the opportunity to see a fine stallion like Brioso. He and Mr. Langford got into quite the row, and Mother whispered to me that it was a good sign to have two young men fighting over me." She rolled her eyes dramatically.

Not knowing what to say, I handed her Byerley's flask. The girl stared at it, then gave me a quavering smile and tipped it up gracefully, following the dainty sip with a few hearty coughs.

"And I don't suppose your mother's in favor of the gala?"

"Oh, she's not in favor of me continuing the stud farm at all. She says it's disgraceful for a young lady of my class to run any business. Though I can't see why she should think that way. After all, *she* worked when she was my age. She was a performer."

"A performer?" I said, startled. My mind ran through the

possibilities. Music hall? Burlesque? Somehow I couldn't imagine Lady Chedington in costume, stomping the boards and singing satirical songs. Proper theatre, then? It was possible. Her Gibson-girl looks would've been an asset to any production.

"Oh. I oughtn't to have mentioned that," Miss Olivia said. "Mother doesn't want anyone to know. You'll forget I said it, won't you, Miss Cobb?"

"Will you come back to the Hall with us?" Miss Seyward asked, stepping in to rescue her friend. "Lady Chedington asked us to show you to your room. And Olivia and I would love to hear stories about your time in Walsall. You could bring your dinner along, and we could make a little party of it."

"Please, will you tell us about working in the saddlery factories?" added Miss Olivia. "It must've been horrible!" She shivered theatrically, looking bright and interested. The tempests of youth passed quickly, it seemed.

I looked down at Sir Algernon's untouched saddle. It gazed blandly back at me as though its present distress was nothing compared to all the hardships it had faced in the past.

"How are you at wrangling cats?" I asked the young women.

With plenty of crooning and wheedling flattery, Miss Olivia was able to get hold of Treacle Tart long enough to allow me and Miss Seyward to slip out the door. I found myself giggling, actually giggling, as I hadn't done in years, and I didn't think it was all due to Byerley's whiskey. There was something nice about these young creatures and their unhampered desire to hear about my former life.

What a tale I could weave for them, if I chose. I could tell them the true story of a world they would never know, of all the little pockets of despair and the ugly, grasping necessities of survival. They would be quite shocked to know that I had—but of course, I wouldn't tell them any of that. I didn't fancy walking those bleak steps again. As Bertie had said, neither he nor I was fond of backtracking.

9

GETTING THE WHIP
HAND OF THE MAJOR

WE TURNED LEFT toward Brioso's stall and ran smack into the Major. He was standing in the aisle, gazing gloomily at the stallion through the bars. There was a small silver cup in his hand, and when he saw us he downed its contents in a single noisy gulp. Rocking back on his polished heels, he flashed Miss Seyward a magnanimous smile.

"Miss Seyward!" he said. "How glad I am to see you. Come here, come here, you must see this magnificent beast. He is in my care. Did you know? His training is entrusted to me. One needs special skills to tackle a horse like this, what?" By the look of his glassy eyes, he was indeed "in his cups." He swayed gently like a tree in the breeze. A tall tree. One of the leaning ones.

As he leered at Miss Seyward, I noticed him fumbling with his thick leather riding whip. Did the silly man carry it everywhere? Then, he did something so odd that at first I thought it was merely drunken floundering—or a lewd gesture. Flipping the narrow silver cup upside down, he pushed the open end onto the handle of the whip and started turning it like a screw. It fit sleekly, and just a few short turns attached the cup firmly to the handle. What I had taken earlier that day for a decorative metal handle was actually a stirrup cup, meant to hold whatever liquid courage the hunting crowd passed around on horseback. The base of the cup was a fox's head. Tiny red stones winked aggressively from the fox's eyes and the heavy molded snout bared its teeth in a silent snarl.

"—a grand creature, as I'm sure you'll agree," the Major was saying. "Look at those haunches!"

Miss Seyward reluctantly joined the Major in front of the stall and gazed uncertainly at the stallion while trying to keep a little distance between herself and the blustery man. He didn't seem to give a fig about my presence, leaning his spidery frame ever closer to the girl and reaching above her to place a hand on the stall bars.

Repugnant man.

"Haunches?" I said brightly. "Let me see." I marched forward and rudely jostled myself between them, looking into the stall.

The Major stumbled backward, huffed, and bore into me with his bleary eyes. "As I was saying, Miss Seyward," he said, craning his neck to see her, "those are not run of the mill haunches, oh no, my girl. And his neck. Such a neck! Such a shoulder!"

In the stall, Brioso was placidly munching his hay, flickering an ear toward us now and then. Despite the Major's effusions, he looked like a very ordinary horse. His color was striking, certainly—he was as black as Lady Chedington's bombazine, with no white markings anywhere on him. I had expected to be impressed by the stallion, but what I actually felt was . . . disappointment. He was a little too steep in the shoulder and short in the hip, and his neck appeared flat and unmuscled. Of course, Lady Chedington had demanded he be kept in a stall, and the months of inactivity had probably diminished his muscling. I should have felt sorry for the horse, but he didn't seem particularly bothered by his imprisonment. With his reputation as a proud, mercurial creature, I would've expected to find him relentlessly pacing his stall, but at the moment, he looked as calm as Miss Olivia's piebald gelding.

My mind flew back to Langford's words. *"Byerley's been itching to get his hands on that stallion."* This was the stallion Byerley was mooning over? How could someone who rode so well have such a myopic eye for horseflesh? I frowned, deciding that either I was missing something, or Byerley was.

Miss Olivia had managed to sneak out of the tack room without releasing the prisoner, and she joined us at the stall, eyeing the stallion warily.

"Observe his color!" the Major intoned. "The purest jet black you will ever find. You probably didn't know, Miss Seyward, but black horses are extremely rare. He is one in a million, this horse."

"But Mr. Langford has dozens of black horses," Miss Olivia said.

"What?" The Major looked startled.

"Well, maybe not dozens, but I think he has at least five or six."

"I'm sure you're mistaken," the Major said, glowering at her. "Black is very rare. No doubt his horses are dark bay, and you've mistaken them for black. A very common misjudgment."

"But I haven't made a mistake," she persisted. "Mr. Langford talks about his black horses all the time. He's trying to breed a whole herd of them. He has a black stallion too."

The Major's eyes narrowed. "I heard Mr. Langford's stallion died last year."

"Oh! That's right. I forgot about that. I try my best to forget sad things, don't you? But surely he has more stallions. Mother says he collects horses like they're going out of style. But she's convinced that horses *are* going out of style, so I don't know if she means that Mr. Langford is being wise or foolish. What do you think?"

The Major blinked and swayed. His inebriated brain was no match for Miss Olivia. "Well," he said, "if you can't remember which horses are alive and which are dead, we certainly can't trust your judgement on the color of their coats." Snorting, he sidled around to Miss Seyward again, leaning his sunken face uncomfortably close.

"Do you ride, Miss Seyward?" he asked, breathing into her face. I could smell the gin from where I stood. "I could teach you, you know. I've been told I have a way with words, a way with horses, and," he winked at her, "a way with women."

She lifted her chin to meet his smirking gaze. "No, thank you, Major."

"But . . . you would excel, I assure you! With a figure like yours," his roving eyes took in her figure, "you would be a natural. A slim lily, not like that overblown hothouse flower." He waved his whip vaguely at Miss Olivia.

"Alright!" I exclaimed, making all four of them jump, including Brioso. To say I was feeling riled would be an understatement. If the Major wanted a tall and mighty rampart, I could be that. I was nearly a head taller than the man. I drew myself up to my full height and looked down my nose at him, channeling Bertie's most disdainful posture.

"I believe the lady said no, Major," I said. "And I believe you should get some rest before your demonstration tomorrow morning. Brioso will be full of himself, and you'll need your full strength to handle him."

The Major blanched and backed away from the stall a few steps. "Do you think so?" he said. He certainly didn't have the air of a man who had ever ridden the horse before. It seemed Bertie was right.

"Haven't you noticed, Major?" I continued. "It's well known that Brioso is exceptionally spirited at dawn. Think of the energy he'll have after spending months in a stall. I don't envy you, Major. You're likely to have your hands quite full tomorrow morning, and it will take all of your skill to control him." Planting that wicked little seed, I nodded to the young ladies and we swept out of the stable, leaving the Major standing uncertainly in the aisle.

"Is Brioso really so hard to handle at dawn?" asked Miss Olivia. We tromped across the damp grass toward the Hall, which glowed before us like an otherworldly fortress against the deepening dark.

"I have no idea," I replied. "But, from the look of the Major's face, he won't be having very sweet dreams tonight."

Both girls grinned.

I O

A DUEL AT DAWN

THE SODDEN EARTH squelched beneath my boots the next morning as I crossed the lawn in pre-dawn darkness. It had rained heavily, and around eleven o'clock last night Mrs. Granger, the cook, had knocked lightly on my bedroom door.

"Sorry to disturb you, ma'am," she had said, her heavy cheeks taut with concern. "Mr. Fletcher, he went out to bring your horse into the stable, but the horse wouldn't stand to be caught! He went spinnin' an' runnin' like some gray devil, and Mr. Fletcher couldn't lay a finger on him, so he left him out in the storm, and Mr. Fletcher, he hopes you don't mind, ma'am."

I was sorry Fletcher had made the effort, but not surprised. The wiry old groom had firm ideas about what was proper for horses at Becketts, and leaving one out in a downpour must have irked him. After a jolly time with the two young ladies—polishing off Byerley's fine whiskey and regaling them with my most lighthearted saddlery anecdotes —I had left my window open a crack so that I could hear Bertie if he called. As expected, I had heard nothing but rain.

I let myself into the meadow through the rickety gate. The

78

air smelled of damp soil and unshed raindrops, and the bottom of my skirt grew heavy and wet as it brushed against the ragged weeds. I could just make out Bertie's ghostly form against the dark treeline. He must have heard the gate, and I wondered why he hadn't come to greet me. Then I smelled it. Tobacco smoke. I squinted, and for a brief moment I could see the orange glow of a cigarette tip a few feet away from the horse.

As I approached, Bertie flickered an ear in my direction but remained facing forward, head drooping and one hind leg resting in a cocked position. The person standing near him turned, but I had already recognized the man's pale hair under his cap.

"Lord Byerley," I said cheerfully. "If I had known you were taking care of my horse this morning, I would've stayed in bed a bit longer."

"Does he need much care, then?" Byerley asked. "He seems to me rather self-sufficient. Clever horse." He grinned like a bleached Cheshire cat against the backdrop of shadowy trees.

I glanced sharply at Bertie. His big ears lolled lazily to either side, and his lower lip hung stupidly slack. His eyes were hooded, heavy lids drooping with sleepy indifference. It was the most simpleminded expression Bertie could muster, a safety tactic he employed whenever he felt he was being suspected of more intelligence than the average horse. He'd honed the expression for years, and he was immensely proud of it, referring to it as "The Vacant Donkey." Seeing the expression now caused my stomach to tighten. It was as much a warning to me as a blind for Bertie.

"I'm not sure about clever," I said. "A bit stubborn. Like most older horses."

"Yes, I've noticed that about him. Stubborn." Byerley

sounded distant, bored. Then, in the same careless tone, he said, "I'd like to buy your horse, Miss Cobb."

"What? No!"

He gave me a lazy smile. "The stables at Ashwold Abbey, my family estate, are designed with every attention to the comfort of horses. Five thousand acres of lush pasture, plenty of space to enjoy a quiet retirement." He looked back at Bertie. "Think it over," he said, directly to the horse.

The smarmy bounder. "What five thousand acres of lush pasture sounds like," I said, feeling nettled, "is one very ill horse. I'm not sure what would kill Bertie quicker, the laminitis or the debilitating obesity." Byerley started to reply, but I interrupted him. "Aren't you in danger of missing your appointment with the Major? Pistols at dawn, or something like that?"

Byerley smiled faintly and flicked his cigarette into the wet grass. "Miss Cobb, Bertie," he said, giving us the double-nod again.

I watched until the darkness swallowed him, and when I heard the rusty protest of the old gate, I turned to Bertie.

"Am I going mad," I whispered, "or did a lord just try to poach my horse?"

"*Your* horse?" Bertie arched his long neck upward in a stretch before shaking his body like a wet dog. "Good lord, holding that ridiculous expression for more than five minutes is harder than it looks."

"Yes, yes, you're your *own* horse, but he doesn't know that. Or does he? What was he doing in here before I—blast," I said, reaching into my pocket for a carrot and feeling the cold metal of Byerley's flask. "I forgot something. Be back in a moment." I shoved the carrot at Bertie and headed after the lord.

Thunder rolled in the distance, and heavy clouds hung close in the graying sky. The stable windows glowed with faint light, and I could see Byerley approaching the front entrance. With my long strides, I caught up with him just as he reached the massive oak doors.

"Byerley," I said, and as he turned, I tossed him the flask. Surprised, he caught it between his arm and his body.

"Careful," he said. "This flask means a lot to me. Did it help?"

"Help what?" I said, my heart thudding. Rain pattered on the stable roof as the clouds began to release again.

"Jog your memory," he said. "Wolverhampton. September 12th. My colt Praxiteles ran that day. Odds were ten to one on that colt, but he pulled it off, much to everyone's surprise. Except yours." He grinned maliciously at me and then pulled the stable doors open.

A gust of wind hit us. At the far end of the long brick aisle, the rear stable doors were wide open. Silhouetted against the dim sky, a tall black horse stood in the rear stable yard. *Brioso*. Byerley and I moved down the aisle, and as we approached, I could see something on the ground at Brioso's hooves.

Byerley flung out an arm as if to stop me from rushing forward. "Don't spook him," he said, low and even.

"I wasn't going to," I said, and then, "he's caught in the stirrup. He must've been dragged." On the wet bricks at the stallion's left side, a man lay serenely on his back, arms straightened neatly at his sides. He would've been a picture of peaceful repose had his leg not been pulled up awkwardly in the air, caught in the left stirrup of the stallion's saddle.

Brioso stood motionless, his reins dangling and his long body leaning slightly against the pull of the stirrup. He showed no signs of panic—no rolling eyes or restless hooves

—just a wary calm. Big drops of rain began to pelt down, and the stallion's ears flickered toward us as we closed in, but he remained still. Speaking in a low, reassuring murmur, Byerley took hold of his reins.

I stepped forward and looked down to see the Major's face. His eyes gazed sightlessly up into the slate sky, his face slick and pale except for a small red scrape on the left side of his forehead. He seemed remarkably undamaged for having been dragged by a horse. I crouched down next to the man, reaching to feel for a pulse.

Keeping my fingers on his clammy skin, waiting for the flutter of a heartbeat that I knew would never come, I tried to avoid his blank eyes by concentrating instead on the the little mark above his temple. There was no blood, and what I had taken for a scrape was actually a squarish blemish, like an angry red stamp on the sallow skin. I leaned closer. It was a strangely symmetrical indentation made of three sunken parallel lines, the top one curved like a cap. The stack of three lines gave the impression of a crude square not much bigger than a fingernail. What kind of object in the pasture had left that oddly specific mark? The corner of a stone, perhaps, buried for years until it found the man's head as he was dragged?

"Miss Cobb!"

I rocked back and released the Major's silent neck.

"No pulse?" Byerley said. He was stroking Brioso's neck, soothing the horse.

I shook my head.

Thunder growled, nearer this time. We couldn't trust Brioso to keep calm in a rising storm, and he would drag the body farther if he broke away from us. The Major needed to be freed as quickly as possible. I reached for his boot, which was jammed through the stirrup iron to the ankle. Raindrops spattered the polished black leather, and my hands slipped as I tried to push the heel back through. Even in death, the Major was impeccably groomed. I paused in my struggle, staring down at the body. Impeccably groomed. No mud, no grass, not even a streak of dirt marred his tawny waistcoat and gray jacket. Only a few shreds of straw clung to him like gruesome confetti.

"What are you waiting for?" hissed Byerley.

"He's clean," I said stupidly, staring down.

"Miss Cobb!" Byerley's voice lashed out like the end of a whip. "Either get his leg free, or come hold the horse and I will do it."

With some effort, I dragged my eyes away from the Major and met Byerley's rigid gaze. In the dimness, he was a creature of black and white, stone-faced with harsh hollows under his aristocratic cheekbones. Even in the presence of death, he managed to look condescending.

I grabbed the boot with renewed determination. It wouldn't come. Shoved home through the narrow iron, the heel angle was all wrong to slide back out. I reached up to where the stirrup leather attached to the saddle bar, thinking I could remove the whole stirrup. The thick leather wouldn't slide.

"The girth," Byerley said.

I cursed and grabbed for the saddle flap. Unbuckling the girth would release the whole saddle and free the Major that way. As a saddler, I knew the equipment literally inside and out, but when it came to detaching a corpse I was coming up all thumbs. I slid my hand under the flap to reach the girth buckles, but the weight of the Major's leg on the stirrup pressed the flap down and I struggled to get my hands around the straps. Byerley, still holding Brioso's reins with one hand, reached his other hand around to the other side.

Then, it happened. Thunder cracked directly overhead, and at the same time, a sudden flurry of brown and white streaked across the stable yard, yowling loudly and racing directly through Brioso's legs.

Brioso had valiantly handled both the corpse and the breaking storm, but he was no match for Treacle Tart. The horse flung his head in the air and reared, jerking harshly on the reins in Byerley's hand. Something in the bridle gave way, and as Byerley moved toward the horse, the stallion pulled back and the whole bridle ripped off, landing at the lord's feet in a jumble of leather. Brioso wheeled and tore away through the open gate into the first pasture, and the Major's body—still caught in the stirrup—was jerked forward, dragging alongside the stallion's frantic hooves.

In a moment, Brioso was transformed from a domesticated horse into a panicked beast, reduced to the one powerful instinct that had kept his prehistoric ancestors safe—flee the predator. As soon as it started to slide, the Major's body became a dark pursuer, doggedly matching the horse's speed and sending him bucking and kicking in a primitive race for survival. Byerley cursed loudly and we both stood in the pelting rain, watching helplessly.

The body bounced and rolled like a rag doll but the stirrup held fast. I found myself wondering with strange detachment if it was one of the stirrups I had reinforced in a previous visit. If so, what a testament to my stitching. I choked back a giddy laugh that caught like a sob. *Pull yourself together, old girl.* As Bertie would say. *Bertie.*

I raised my fingers to my mouth and let out a piercing whistle, three times.

"I doubt a whistle will stop him," Byerley said bitterly, watching the stallion recede into the distance.

"Not him," I said.

There were a few long moments of silence, and then from behind us came the clatter of hooves sliding on bricks. Bertie was barreling down the stable aisle, pale and fearsome, ears flattened and muscles surging. Seeing me, he shifted his weight back on his haunches and made as if to stop.

I flung a pointed finger toward the pasture. "Brioso," I said.

Bertie rocketed off his coiled gray haunches and leapt forward again, tearing out into the open green.

Byerley turned and stared hard at me. His white hair was plastered to his forehead, and rivulets of rain ran down his face.

"He understands speech," he said. It was not a question.

"Of course not. He understands whistles and hand gestures."

Byerley looked as though he was going to argue, but I turned and moved a few steps away, watching the horses.

With Bertie's heavier build and additional years, he might not have been able to catch the Thoroughbred in a fair race. As it was, Brioso's gruesome baggage was a significant handicap, and soon Bertie and the stallion were racing neck and neck with Bertie on the right side and the Major still dragging on the left. Bertie surged ahead by a nose and used that nose along with his shoulder to push Brioso into a broad leftward arc. Fractionally slowing his strides while blocking any movement to the right, Bertie was setting a calmer pace and gradually herding the stallion into a circle. Brioso tried to break away just once, and Bertie pinned his ears and bared his teeth, fiercely nipping at the stallion's neck to remind him who was in charge. Soon the two horses had slowed to a controlled trot, then a walk, and then they finally halted twenty paces from us, both heaving and dripping with rain and sweat.

"You ask me to believe your horse did that all on his own," Byerley said, suddenly appearing at my side. There was a head collar and lead rope in his hand, which he must have retrieved from the stable.

I whirled on him. "*You* were the one being clever about Wolverhampton. If you know Bertie was there, you must also know he was a track pony. For years. It was his job to lead nervous young Thoroughbreds to the gate and to catch them when they bolted or lost their riders. Bertie was simply doing what he was trained to do."

"Of course," Byerley said absently, and he moved toward the horses in rain that had slowed to spittle.

11

THE USEFULNESS
OF HAVING THUMBS

I HAD no headcollar for Bertie. Though Byerley was already onto us like a strike-hound at a hunt, I didn't want to push it further by flaunting the fact that Bertie didn't actually need a headcollar. Brioso's bridle lay in a sodden tangle a few feet away, and I hurriedly scooped up the jumbled thing and set out across the field.

As I strode up, I was relieved to see that the Major had ended face-down. Seeing those empty eyes once before break-fast was enough. Brioso was tense and watchful, his neck high and the muscles quivering across his shoulders and chest, but he allowed Byerley to buckle the headcollar around his head. The stallion's wary ears were fixed on Bertie rather than the corpse, which was no wonder, as Bertie bared his teeth at any movement from the dark horse.

Giving Bertie a wary glance, Byerley reached between the two horses and fumbled for the girth buckles. "Don't bite me by mistake," he muttered, and Bertie's ears relaxed a fraction.

I lifted the saddle flap on Brioso's other side and found the Major's leg to be more compliant than before, though I didn't want to think about why, and I was easily able to release the girth. Byerley freed his side, and the girth dropped to the wet earth with a cheerful jangle of metal buckles. The saddle immediately gave way to the pull of the Major's weight and slipped off, landing directly on the corpse with a dull thud. With Bertie's smoldering eyes trained on him, Brioso only slightly shied at the sound.

"That could've been handled better," I said, wishing I had thought to catch the saddle. As disagreeable as the man had been in life, it seemed rather indecent to pummel him with saddles in death.

"Don't worry. He didn't feel it." Byerley gazed stonily down at what used to be the Major, then reached up to pat Brioso's dripping neck and started toward the stable with the exhausted animal. "Stay with the body," he flung over his shoulder.

I watched them go, man and horse walking on sanguine green under a lifting sky, for all the world as if they had just finished a day's hunting. Byerley had traded the previous day's chartreuse coat for an equally startling purple number—it would have been more fitting in a ballroom than in a field. Freed of his dogged pursuer, Brioso playfully nosed Byerley's pockets as if expecting a reward. The lord obliged, feeding him some morsel and placing a quieting hand on his neck as they walked. I turned to Bertie and found him watching the pair with mild disgust.

"Didn't know our lord had food on him," he said, nostrils pinched in disapproval. "What does one have to do to get a bit of sugar around here? Oh yes, go absolutely batty and drag a man to his death. It seems I've been going about it the wrong way all these years."

The big horse was drooping slightly, water dripping down

his forelock and off the end of his rain-darkened muzzle. His flanks were steaming in the chilly air, but his breathing was normal. He was a wonder, this loyal, gracefully graying brute next to me. Perhaps the same quirk of nature that rendered him able to speak had also blessed him with unusual hardiness.

"Thank you," I said to him.

"Don't mention it," he said, bowing his Roman nose imperiously. "Actually, I wouldn't mind if you mentioned it now and then. Focusing on the part where I caught a Thoroughbred half my age. In muddy footing. It might be nice to keep that memory alive for a few years at least."

"I'll make a note. And just out of curiosity, did you jump or plow through?"

Bertie looked offended. "Jump, of course."

"Well done." It was much easier when Bertie jumped out of a paddock rather than resorting to more destructive methods of escape, which he only employed if a fence was far too high to be jumped. I may not have been entirely truthful when I told Fletcher that Bertie wasn't known to push fences, and I didn't relish the prospect of repairing a shattered fence. Or, worse yet, having Fletcher do so.

"It seems Byerley made a rather snap judgement," Bertie said, eyeing the body. "About his being dead, I mean. I can smell death within a few moments of its happening—and yes, in case you were curious, by that reckoning he is indeed dead—but don't you humans need to check a pulse or hold a mirror to the nose?"

"He was dead when we found him, Bertie. Lying in the stable yard with his foot in the stirrup. I checked his pulse."

"He was already dragged?" Bertie looked incredulous, his square chin hanging slack. "Impossible. I heard no hoofbeats until just before your whistle, and while my coat may be fading with age, my hearing is certainly not."

"You were with Byerley," I pointed out. "Perhaps the Vacant Donkey was taking all your concentration."

"Even so, if I missed the sound of galloping hooves in a silent valley, I appear to be slipping."

"I don't think he was dragged at all. Until later, that is. He was clean when we found him, perfectly clean, except for a few pieces of straw. *Straw*, Bertie, not grass and not dirt. And he was on his back, neat and straight, with his leg twisted across his body to the stirrup. If he'd been dragged, he would have looked like this." I indicated the crumpled form before us.

Bertie lifted his neck high and fixed me with a considering eye. "If he wasn't dragged, how did he die? Apoplexy?"

"If he'd been in the saddle when it happened," I said, "his fall would've spooked Brioso into bolting, wouldn't it? And I'm not sure he could've fallen from that height into the perfect position we found him in."

"Perhaps he put his foot in the stirrup and had an apoplectic fit before he could swing up?"

"It would have taken some clever maneuvering to push his boot all the way through the stirrup while standing on the ground. It's easy to slip a foot through from up on top, but it's harder to do from the ground. Not impossible, though."

"You said he was clean, but did he have any marks on him?" Bertie said. "Could he have been injured, then struggled his way over to the stirrup before fainting dead away, literally?"

I paused, remembering the Major's milky, lifeless face. There was the little red blemish, vivid on the clammy skin. "He had an odd mark on his head," I said. "Squarish. Very near his left temple. I saw it while checking his pulse. No blood, just a mark with three lines, like a stamp on the skin. I only got a quick glimpse of it."

"Well?" Bertie said, glancing quickly around and then back to me.

"Well, what?"

"It seems the universe has arranged for us to have a bit of a private conference with the Major here."

I eyed the corpse warily. "I'm not sure we're supposed to touch him before the doctor or police or someone qualified takes a look."

"That ship has sailed, my dear Harriet," Bertie said. "It left port about twenty minutes ago. If you wanted to preserve evidence, you shouldn't have let him take that muddy little jaunt round the field and then dropped a saddle on him. I can't see how taking a peek now would make things any worse than they already are."

"To what end, though?" I said.

"To satiate our curiosity."

"I'm not that curious."

"You're also not that good at poker. It's obvious you've got a case of the old bated breath. I have enough curiosity for the both of us, but I'm lacking the necessary thumbs, so if you could just lend me a hand—"

He lowered his big nose and pushed gently under the Major's side. I crouched down next to the body, taking hold of a shoulder and rolling it toward me while Bertie assisted with his nose. As the body finished its revolution, I let out the breath I had been holding. The eyes were no longer staring. The mud had softened and coated the face in a comforting camouflage. It was no longer the Major, just a clay figure not yet completed by the artist.

With this thought, my stomach stopped flipping and

curiosity began to nibble around the edges of my mind. I reached into my pocket for my spectacles, flipped down the eye loupe and leaned close, searching for what I had seen back in the stable yard. The exposed skin around the temple was now muddy and battered, and I could barely make out the faint, purply-red patch among the other scrapes. Gone was the clear stack of lines that had given the impression of a bizarre stamp. The indentation had been muddled and obscured by subsequent injuries.

Bertie suddenly flickered an ear and raised his head. "It seems we have company."

I heard a shout and saw Fletcher hurrying toward us, hobbling in his rubber boots. I rocked back on my heels and stood, feeling suddenly chilled as my wet skirt draped around me. I flipped the broken bridle around Bertie's neck, pretending to hold him steady.

Fletcher's lined face was set and gray in the dawn light, and he was covered in hay chaff as though he'd rolled in the stuff. When he took in the Major's body, there was neither shock nor pity on his face, just mild disgust. After a lifetime working with animals prone to panic and injury, Fletcher seemed to be meeting this new crisis with the equanimity of an undertaker.

"Lord Byerley said he's dead," he growled, looking down at the still form.

"Yes."

"You saw it? Saw him dragged?"

"No. He wasn't dragged. I mean, he wasn't dragged to death. He was dead before he was dragged. I saw him dragged, not killed."

Fletcher stared at me uncomprehendingly.

"At times like these," Bertie said, "it's a shame I can't do the talking."

I tried again. "He was dead when we arrived, but he was *clean*, Fletcher. His foot was stuck through the stirrup, and Brioso was standing quietly in the stable yard, and the Major was perfectly clean with no mud or grass on him. Lying as neat and straight as if he'd been . . ."

Bertie pushed me hard with his nose, nearly making me stumble.

"Well, as if he'd been sleeping there," I finished lamely. I had been about to say something else, but Bertie's eyes contained a warning.

Fletcher cursed softly and shook his head. "That does it for the stallion, then."

I looked at him sharply. "You don't mean . . . surely not, Fletcher?"

"I know some who'd put him down. This makes twice, remember. Sir Algernon and now the Major."

"But it wasn't Brioso's fault," I protested. "The Major was dead before he bolted, and he wouldn't even have bolted if the cat hadn't spooked him."

"The cat?" The old man looked more dejected at this than when he'd laid eyes on the corpse. "Don't mention that to Lady Chedington, if you can help it. She's never been over-keen on that cat. Nor on Brioso, neither. Last time, when Sir Algernon fell, she said the stallion were a danger to society an' he should be destroyed. Terrified of him, she were. When we found my master's body, Brioso weren't nowhere to be seen. He had run off, like. Her ladyship said, 'Don't look for him, Fletcher. Leave him out on the moor to starve.' She even sent word 'round to all the neighbors that the horse had gone mad an' they should shoot on sight if they saw him."

Bertie pinned his ears and snorted in disgust.

"But surely no one took a shot at him?" I said.

"No, no, 'course not, Miss Cobb. They knew it were just her grief talkin'."

"And she didn't have him destroyed after all. Did you talk her out of it?"

"That's the funny thing, Miss Cobb," Fletcher said, a faint twinkle in his old eyes. "Now, I don't put much faith in society, like, social graces an' what's proper an' what's not. But Lady Chedington, she can't do a thing without announcin' it to all her neighbors, an' most of them neighbors value horses more'n she does. They talked sense into her. Told her, these things happen with horses an' he ain't dangerous, just spirited. So she dropped the idea of puttin' him down. She cares plenty 'bout her social standin', she does, and she wouldn't go against the crowd."

"And now Brioso belongs to Miss Olivia," I said. "Sir Algernon left the horses to her in his will."

"That's 'bout the size of it."

"What do you think she'll do with him?"

"Hard to say," he grunted. "But now it's two deaths, people might not be so quick to overlook it. One can be explained away, like. But two . . . when a thing happens twice, that's when you find out just how superstitious people are. An' Sergeant Harrison, he ain't much of a horseman himself. Things could get bad for Brioso when the police show up, that's certain."

Bertie had done all the hard work that morning, but I suddenly felt weary and waterlogged. I looked down at my sopping skirt and hunched my shoulders against the fresh breeze. *Not much like a tall and mighty rampart now, old girl.* I was supposed to be resurrecting a saddle for a séance, not standing over a corpse.

"Miss Cobb, you don't look well," Fletcher said, his old brow wrinkling even more than usual. "Why don't you head up to the Hall and get some tea? I can stay with the . . . the body."

The Hall wasn't attractive to me at the moment—Byerley was probably up there right now, imparting his dire news— but from where I stood, the stables looked comfortingly familiar and utterly oblivious to what had occurred at dawn. Filled with the sensible smell of horses and a bit of ammonia to clear one's head. That was the place to be in a crisis.

"Thank you, Fletcher," I said, "but I think I'll take Bertie back and see about his legs."

12

A BROKEN BIT

"I WOULDN'T BE SURPRISED if that soft fellow comes up lame. But I think you'll agree that I possess the coolest, tightest legs in all of Becketts," Bertie said.

He wasn't wrong. His solid legs showed no signs of the mad gallop in the mud—except for the mud, which I had wiped clean before giving his legs a rub-down. We were in the large stall at the end of the stable aisle, Bertie was nose-deep in a generous portion of hay, and I was desperately trying to come up with a reason not to go up to the Hall. Presumably, Lady Chedington now knew she had a corpse on her hands and that the corpse had been found with the same horse that killed her husband. And I didn't want to show my face till the first violent palpitations were over.

"Well, old girl," Bertie said from the depths of his hay, "you've rubbed my legs to within an inch of their lives. You've brushed me and rugged me and fluffed my bed, and unless you plan to read me a story, I think it's time for you to go and face the music."

This reference to reading stories was only half sarcastic—

the big horse loved to be read to. He had developed a knack for predicting the endings of stories, frequently ruining the stories for me when he guessed right. We had worked our way through Austen, Collins, Dickens, and Stevenson, and were currently tackling the works of the recently-knighted Sir Arthur Conan Doyle. I felt a little pang of homesickness as I thought of comfortable evenings in our home pasture, a good book in the gloaming and not a corpse in sight.

"The young women are there to comfort Lady Chedington," I said, fidgeting. "If she needs a broader shoulder to lean on, she has the two men. I think Mr. Langford can more than make up for what Byerley lacks in empathy. I'm just the saddler."

"Do you trust Byerley to give a true account of what happened this morning?"

"What do you mean?"

"If we believe that little mark on the Major's head is a sign of foul play, we shouldn't be overeager to trust anyone."

I considered this. "Mr. Langford said Byerley is obsessed with the stallion. In which case Byerley will doubtless make it very clear that the horse was not to blame for the death. Especially if it means saving Brioso's life."

"But if the poet is right and Byerley is obsessed, our lord may be just as eager to blame everything on the horse in order to to spur Miss Olivia to sell him. Or, if we're acknowledging other suspicions, to cover up a crime."

Blast the big horse and his convoluted mind.

"Let's see what the doctor says," I decided. "For all we know, Brioso could have swung his head into the Major and cracked the man's skull."

"We horses do have very solid heads," Bertie mused.

"Some are more hard-headed than others," I muttered.

"But did that little mark look like a head-butt to you?"

"No," I admitted. "But I have no experience examining corpses, thumped in the head or otherwise."

I went to the corner of the stall to retrieve Brioso's bridle, which I had unceremoniously dropped there before treating Bertie to the best grooming of his life. As I lifted the thing, I noticed that the jointed metal bit was broken. It was an oddly shaped bit, but I'd often found unusual bits in the Becketts tack room. The two curiously curved sides, which should have been joined at the center, were swinging freely on their leather straps. This answered the question of what had given way when Brioso had panicked.

"Odd, that," Bertie said, bobbing his nose toward the bridle. "One doesn't often see broken bits." He frowned. "It might've been nice if you'd mentioned that detail while we were hashing out theories on how the Major died."

"It broke after the Major was already dead," I said, "when Brioso panicked and Byerley was holding his reins."

"It must have been very worn. Seems you let that slip when you inspected all the bridles last month."

"I was very thorough." I looked down at the thing. "If the joint had been thin enough to break, I would've caught it. That's one of the spots I check." A thought crept into my mind. "But thank you for pointing it out, old boy. I think I'll take it to the tack room where I can examine it in better light." I darted for the stall door.

"A bit rich, isn't it, to resume your work while there's a corpse in the field?" Bertie glared through the bars as I closed the stall door behind me. "I think you should go up to the Hall and get the lie of the land, then report back to me. After that, you can examine every bit in the place if you'd like."

"This bit is related to the accident," I protested. "Indirectly, maybe, but it has to do with Brioso. No one would blame me for taking a few moments to give it a once-over."

Bertie snorted and went back to his hay.

On my way to the tack room I paused at Brioso's stall, peering in at the plain animal and wondering whether Fletcher was right. Did the morning's events spell a death sentence for the stallion? Would he end up in the Becketts drawing room as upholstery on another settee? Or would he be bought for a song and live out the rest of his days in luxury under Byerley's inexplicably admiring eye? Brioso seemed unbothered by these questions, chewing his hay with an unfettered air. It seemed Byerley had fed him and wiped him down. The pale young man was odd and off-putting, but he was no slouch when it came to horse care.

In the tack room, I pushed Sir Algernon's saddle to the end of the work bench to clear a space. It collapsed to one side, giving me a reproachful grimace.

"I'll get to you eventually," I told it. I donned my spectacles and unbuckled the bridle straps to free the bit.

The two brass segments were tarnished a dull brownish-gold, not new but not as old as some of the other bits hanging on crowded pegs behind me. Some people favored brass for its purported warmth and softness in a horse's mouth, but according to Bertie, that was bunk. "It's the hands at the other end of the reins that make a bit soft or hard," he said. "A steel bit in light hands beats a brass bit in heavy hands any day."

The circular center joint on one of the halves was still intact, but on the other half, the interlocking joint that should've held the two pieces together was ripped and ragged. The edges of the metal were so thin that it wouldn't have taken much pressure to break through.

I considered the metal, frowning. How could one side of

the joint have worn dangerously thin while the other side was solid as the day it was forged? I had seen jointed bits worn to breaking point before, but both sides were equally thin in those cases. I leaned in, making the most of my magnifying loupe. The inside of the broken joint was not tarnished like the rest of the bit, and the metal was not worn smooth by use. It gleamed yellow, like new brass, and there were scratches and notches along the torn edges. I stared. These marks were not caused by the slow erosion of time, nor were they the result of tearing metal. These gouges were deliberate. Man made. Made by something sharp and abrasive.

I snatched my tool bag to me. Inside, the larger tools were still in their proper places, but a single glance told me that the smaller, more delicate instruments had been jumbled about. I fished through the pockets until my fingers found what they were looking for. A thin triangle file. It tapered to a point at one end, and the thicker end transitioned abruptly to a flat steel projection made to slide into a wooden handle. I only used it for the most detailed tasks, so I hadn't attached any handle, which would have made it hard to get the right angle in tight spaces. Without a handle, the fat side of the file ended in sharp points, and I always wore gloves when I used it.

Even at arm's length, I could see that the metal was oddly discolored. I hesitantly brought the thing closer. My breath caught. There were rusty-red smears around the thick end of the file. My eyes shifted to the surface of the old table, and I leaned close, peering through my eye loupe. A fine scurf of metal filings coated the rough wood.

I leapt up and fled to Bertie's stall, still holding the broken bit in one hand and the stained file in the other.

"It was deliberate," I gasped from outside the stall. "Look." I held the edge of the file to the tiny gouges at the broken end of the bit.

Bertie bowed close, giving a sidelong glance through the bars. He snorted sharply. "Do I smell blood?" There were wrinkles above his large, liquid eyes, but the eyes themselves were alight with interest.

"That's what I was going to ask you," I said grimly. "If you say it's blood, it's blood." Horses were no scent-hounds, but, being prey animals, they were especially sensitive to scents that had spelled danger to their wild ancestors. Like blood. "Whoever used the file didn't think to wear gloves. It's sharp in places, and they would've needed a lot of pressure to file through that brass. And they didn't even think to wash the file or clean off the tabletop. The place was lousy with filings."

"Not a very experienced prankster, then," Bertie said.

"Prankster? Don't you mean 'criminal'?"

"You said the bit broke after the Major was already dead. So, it really didn't contribute to his death at all. Thus, it remains a prank."

"But the intent!" I said. "It was too vicious to be a prank. With Brioso's history, the person must have known that if the bit broke while the Major was riding, Brioso would've bolted and the Major would've been injured, or worse. It seems to me there was clear criminal intent."

"Harriet, you said the person didn't think to wear gloves when using a sharp file, then didn't even clean the file or the table. What does that point to, old girl?"

"Someone in a hurry. Or someone very stupid."

"I don't doubt they were both," he said. "But, more importantly, it points to no attempt to cover their tracks. Criminal intent means a criminal mind, and a criminal mind would've at least thought to wash off the blood and brush off the table.

Or take the file with them in a pinch. Thus I deduce that the person was a prankster rather than a criminal. Those two are not mutually exclusive, however. There's nothing to say that the person who planned this little premeditated prank couldn't later have been swayed by the winds of passion to thump the Major in the head. But when the person handled that file, they were not yet a criminal."

He should've been a barrister. "So, we need to look for a wounded hand," I said. "Byerley was lurking about in the wee hours, gracing you with his presence before dawn. Did you notice anything odd about his hands, any wound or bandage? I can't remember. It must've been him. He loathed the Major."

"Everyone loathed the Major," Bertie said, and then suddenly swiveled, ears at attention.

I turned to see Byerley standing just a few paces away, his washy face made washier by the purple coat. How long had he been standing there? And how had he sidled up the aisle without even Bertie noticing? I glanced suspiciously at the man's feet, somehow expecting to see sneaky purple slippers but finding instead very ordinary leather boots.

Byerley was gazing just as suspiciously at me, and I realized I was still holding the broken bit in one hand and the stained file in the other.

Blast.

"Lady Chedington is asking for you," Byerley said, staring at the two objects. He didn't exactly look shocked, but I wasn't sure the insipid fellow was capable of looking shocked. I fought the urge to stuff the bit and file into my pockets, or fling them through the bars into Bertie's stall.

"Very well," I said with as much nonchalance as I could muster. "I need to stop by the tack room first." I turned and walked away with stately, measured steps, trying to channel Lady Chedington's suggestion of a mother superior.

Closing the tack room door behind me, I paused, panting. It probably wasn't wise to carry evidence around in my damp pockets. But I also couldn't just dump the things on the table-top. What if our prankster-criminal, growing wiser after a few hours, returned to dispose of evidence? If Byerley was our man, he wouldn't return with me to the Hall. He would stay down here to raid the tack room. And even if he wasn't our man, he would no doubt stay to pester Bertie and possibly make his way into the tack room anyway. I frowned, looking around for a place to stash the things.

In the corner of the room was a narrow cupboard, behind rows of cluttered bits hanging on dusty wooden pegs. I crossed the room and tugged it open to reveal a variety of bottles and jars. Liniments and medicinal draughts, no doubt. A large leatherbound ledger lay on the top shelf. I set the bit segments and file carefully on the ledger, closed the cabinet, and exited the tack room.

Byerley was standing in front of Bertie's stall with his arms folded and a look of sardonic amusement on his face. A glance through the bars revealed that Bertie had not gone to the trouble of the Vacant Donkey this time, but had simply turned his ample haunches toward the man. An unmistakably cheeky gesture.

"Will you escort me to the Hall?" I asked Byerley, figuring it was worth trying to extricate him from Bertie. "I'm feeling a little faint. As though I might faint, that is. I may need a steadying arm. Ladies' nerves, you know."

Byerley grinned wolfishly at me. "I suspect your nerves are every bit as tough as Bertie's, Miss Cobb. And at your height, I'm not sure I'd be much of a prop. But if you really think you'll need help reaching the Hall, I can wheel you up in that." He indicated the wheelbarrow used to muck out the stalls.

"Your arm will do," I said coldly, and then it registered. The hand he had waved lazily toward the wheelbarrow was wrapped in a fine, ivory-colored cloth. I took a shaky breath and then threaded my arm through his and pulled him with me into the sunlight.

13

PAYING DEBTS

THE MORNING WAS MARCHING ON, turning the wet grass to diamonds and the walls of Becketts Hall a rich reddish gold. It all seemed rather impudent, like a perky grin at a funeral. Byerley and I were out of sync, walking with the uncomfortable rhythm of a dancing couple when both are trying to lead, but I refused to release his arm. I had planned merely to keep the slippery fellow away from Bertie as long as possible, but now I had a new objective—find out what was beneath the silk handkerchief tied around his hand like a hasty bandage.

"You've been busy this morning," Byerley said.

I didn't like his tone. "What does that mean?" I said crossly.

"You were up mysteriously early and then, upon discovering a corpse, you were mysteriously slow to detach said corpse from a horse known to bolt. Then, you absconded to the stable with that horse's bridle and were seen using a file on a mysteriously broken bit. It's all rather mysterious."

My heart thudded. I had been so busy suspecting Byerley that I hadn't considered how my own actions might appear.

"I wasn't using the file," I said finally. "And I could say the same about you. About failing to detach the Major, that is. You could've unbuckled that girth sooner." It was a little unfair, since I hadn't thought of the girth any sooner than he had, but I was feeling ungenerous. "That boot was jammed solid, the leather was wet, and my hands weren't strong enough."

"From the lack of circulation in my arm, I'd say you're stronger than the average man."

I relaxed my vice grip on his arm. "How is Lady Chedington?" I asked, deciding that drawing room etiquette was called for. When someone is banging on about something unpleasant, a lady should introduce a mutually acceptable topic as soon as possible. Especially if that lady needs to decide in short order how to rip a bandage off a lord's hand.

"Surprisingly well," he said, "or rather, alarmingly well."

"Indeed?"

"After the first shock, followed by a tipple of sherry, her ladyship became preoccupied with something else."

"Really," I said, and then, as he made no effort to continue, I pulled him to a halt and turned to face him. We were nearly to the Hall, and I needed more time to get to the bottom of that bandage, literally. "Enlighten me."

"Did you tell her, Miss Cobb, that she needs to repair a saddle in order to conduct a séance?" Those impossibly-silver eyes were cold and disconcerting.

"What? She's going on about that? Now?"

"It seems her ladyship has been *led* to believe that this séance scheme is of vital importance. So important, in fact, that the corpse in her field pales in comparison. When I told her the Major is dead, she gaped at me, downed a bit of sherry and said, 'Then there's not a moment to lose!' Then she started babbling about you and a saddle and a séance. So I'd like to know what you're playing at, Miss Cobb."

"What I'm . . . Lord Byerley, am I to understand you think I'm responsible for this séance nonsense?"

"I've known her ladyship a long time," he said, with more than a bit of an upper-hand air. "When I was a child, a spirit medium came to Pelgren Vale. Madame Tournier, she called herself. She was a very clever woman, using neighborhood gossip to produce her readings, which caused no end of strife for the people here. It was she that told Lady Chedington her husband would be killed by a black stallion—everyone knew that Sir Algernon was rather taken with black horses, so there was nothing very mystical in that prediction. The police finally took notice of Madame Tournier, whose true name was Mrs. Turner, and ran her out of Pelgren Vale as a charlatan, but the mischief had already been done. Many of the people here were never able to shake the influence of her predictions —including Lady Chedington. When Brioso was born, she was terrified of the colt, much to Sir Algernon's dismay."

"And what does this have to do with me?" I said.

He gazed at me stonily. "Lady Chedington is easily influenced. She never mentioned séances or spirit mediums again —till you came into the neighborhood."

"I have nothing to do with . . ." I started vehemently, then stopped. And laughed. It was too much—the virtuous thunder on his brow and the bizarre accusation on his lips. And it was too predictable. Of course, the strange, tall, black-eyed woman that infiltrated the neighborhood and lived in a solitary cottage and carried odd tools about on horseback and wore peculiar spectacles (yes, they were still perched on my nose)—she was certainly the one spreading witchcraft.

I laughed in his startled face, and at that moment, an idea came to me.

"Lord Byerley," I said, holding out my hands, "give me your hands."

He looked surprised, then guarded. "Why?"

"If you give me your hands, I will tell you something true about yourself. Have you never heard of palmistry? We spiritualists can read a whole life in the lines of a palm."

He hesitated for a moment, and then smiled faintly. "Very well. If you'll also tell me something true about your horse."

"No." My response was flat, instinctual.

"Still no trespassers?" he said, his bleached eyebrows lifting. "Fine. Something true about you, then."

He gave me his hands, palms up. His skin was as cool and colorless as the rest of him but surprisingly calloused for a member of the peerage.

"I'm afraid we'll need to—" I indicated the silk handkerchief. He nodded his haughty assent but made no move to remove the thing, so I carefully untied it myself.

There, across the center of his right palm, was a small red gash. It was not deep, but the center was torn enough to have left the blood I found on the file. There were pink rub marks at either end of the wound, and the whole thing looked painful but hardly serious.

I raised my eyes to Byerley's tight, wary face. The Hall loomed behind him, and Lady Chedington appeared in the drawing room window, looking small and peaked. "How did you get this?" I demanded. Direct, yes, but there was no time for dilly-dallying.

"I thought you could divine that," he said pleasantly. "And you may be suffering from amnesia. A horse pulled violently away from me this morning, and forgive me if I'm wrong, but

I thought you were there. The rein ripped my hand." He smiled angelically at me.

It was possible. Probable, even. Brioso had jerked away with some force, and I had seen similar outcomes when people neglected to wear gloves while handling horses.

"Well? Shall I continue reading my own palms?"

"Here's your reading," I said. "Something true about yourself, yes? Here it is. You don't know much about desperation."

The white brow wrinkled in confusion.

"It's not your fault," I continued. "Your life hasn't given you the opportunity to learn about desperation. Perhaps Lady Chedington didn't dabble in séances before I arrived in Pelgren Vale, but the baronet passed away just before I arrived. This interest in séances is likely the desperate fixation of a desperate woman."

The gray eyes were like two stones from the ocean floor. "You're wrong, Miss Cobb," he said. "I know my fair share about desperation. And I know that a time of desperation is the easiest time to take advantage of someone."

Do you indeed? I thought. I knew where his comment was aimed, but my mind fled back to the plain black stallion in the stable and the corpse in the field. In this desperate situation, it would be very easy for Byerley to acquire the stallion.

Byerley reached into his pocket and pulled something out. Then, to my astonishment, he placed it into my hand.

I stared suspiciously down to see a lump of sugar and a gold sovereign. "What is this?"

"Price of a palm reading. And something for Bertie."

It was more likely the price of one hundred palm readings, but it didn't matter. I didn't want even a farthing from the man. And although Bertie might be less quick to turn up his nose at the sugar, I was loathe to provide any bridge between him and Byerley.

"The first reading is free of charge," I said, holding the things out to him.

He backed away. "I always pay my debts, Miss Cobb." There was iron in his voice and in his eyes, and he fixed me with a long look that seemed to mean more to him than it did to me. Then he turned and walked to the back door of the Hall, opening it and standing aside for me to enter. I shivered as I approached him. Had there been something sinister in that last comment, or had my imagination supplied it? Had he repaid a grim debt to the Major before visiting Bertie that morning? This ghostly young man, with his unyielding face, seemed exactly the type that would let resentment fester until it burst like an ugly boil.

His arm came down just before I stepped over the threshold, blocking my way but not touching me. I looked into the pale eyes, silently cursing my hammering heart. It was absurdly silly for a woman of my stature to feel like a cornered rabbit, but in that half-second I ran through all the woodland creatures, and rabbity was exactly how I felt.

"Have you forgotten our agreement?" Byerley said. He seemed to be enjoying my discomfort.

"What agreement?" I managed, in my least-rabbity tone.

"I let you read my palm. Now you're supposed to tell me something true about yourself."

"Ah," I said, willing the strength back into my voice. "Here it is. Listen closely. Are you paying attention? Good. I've never been to a séance in my life, nor do I know anything at all about palmistry."

I reached forward and grabbed the fine purple cloth of his sleeve—whipping his arm up and out of my way—and as I swept through the doorway, I flipped the gold coin and sugar lump at him. He caught the things clumsily, grinning in spite of himself. I was halfway down the horse-laden corridor before it occurred to me that his startled, unguarded grin was a vast improvement on the Cheshire ones he preferred to throw around. Perhaps he practiced those the way Bertie practiced the Vacant Donkey. A defense mechanism, no doubt.

I desperately wanted to flee back to Bertie and tell him all about Byerley's sinister pride in paying debts—leaving out the bit about the sugar, of course—but I owed my own debt to the forlorn woman waiting for me on the other side of the drawing room door.

14

THE SPECKLED BITS

"OH, MISS COBB!" Lady Chedington said, crossing the room to clasp my hands with crushing fervor. "What luck you were here! This morning! To help Lord Byerley. Such an auspicious occurrence! Your being here, that is. What of the saddle? I trust you're nearly finished?" Her tone was much too bright, but I was relieved to see dark smudges under her eyes and worry lines on her brow. The woman appeared manic, but she certainly knew the gravity of what had taken place that morning.

"Lady Chedington," I said, leading her to the horsehair settee and sitting with her on the horrible thing, "have you sent for the doctor? The police?"

"Yes, yes, there's trouble at Mr. Foster's place," she said, waving a hand.

She seemed to consider this a sufficient answer, but I raised my eyebrows pointedly at her until she continued.

"The Hastings' splendid mouser had a litter of kittens—do you recall?—and everyone in the neighborhood wants one, of course. Mr. Hastings is wild about those kittens, absolutely agog says Mrs. Hastings, and he couldn't choose which one to keep for himself, so he declared he will keep them all. Mrs. Hastings declared that he will not, that she can barely stir without stepping on kittens, so she gave one to Mr. Foster. On the sly, that is."

"Lady Chedington, I don't see how—"

She sighed deeply. "When Mr. Hastings uncovered the scheme, he marched over to the Foster's and demanded the kitten, but Mr. Foster declined. So Mr. Hastings locked himself and the kitten in Mr. Foster's tack room and refuses to come out. He's been in there since yesterday."

I stared at the woman. Perhaps she had lost her senses after all. A glance at Byerley revealed nothing helpful. He was leaning against the door frame looking irritatingly unconcerned, and I felt a sudden desire to someday see the man's feathers well and truly ruffled.

"And—?" I ventured, turning back to the lady.

"And so," she said, fidgeting with the lace handkerchief in her lap, "Doctor Reed and Sergeant Harrison are there at Mr. Foster's, sorting things out. Luckily, the Fosters have a telephone, so when Dr. Reed's secretary told me where he was, I was able to ring Mrs. Foster and hear the whole story straight from the horse's mouth." She grimaced as though tasting something bitter. "Horse's mouth! Horses! I shall have to alter the way I speak as I never want to hear those creatures mentioned again!" She buried her face in the lace handkerchief.

Two thoughts sprang into my head. One, that the people of Pelgren Vale had a penchant for locking cats in tack rooms. And two, that it was oddly comforting to live in a place where a dispute over kittens took precedence over a dead body.

"But they will come?" I asked. "The doctor and the sergeant?"

"Yes, they will come, though I don't know why Sergeant Harrison need be involved. Surely it's just a case for Doctor Reed?"

"I believe they need to rule out foul play," I said, my eyes flitting to Byerley's face. He had a blank, preoccupied look, and he stared back at me impassively.

"A foul deed by a foul beast!" choked Lady Chedington. "I should think that's plain enough. No doubt the sergeant will demand the horse be destroyed for the safety of the neighborhood. My husband thought that creature would be the savior of Becketts, but the beast turned out to be its downfall! Unless . . ." She reached out to grab my hand and said in a voice of husky urgency, "The séance is now of utmost importance."

If her burdened brain needed to focus on the séance, so be it. And it could be a two-birds-one-stone opportunity—keep the woman occupied until the doctor and police arrived, and show Byerley that I was not some sort of sinister spiritualist puppet master.

Placing my work-worn hand over her soft one, I said, "Lady Chedington, you need to explain to me why this séance is so important." I spoke loudly enough for Byerley to hear, but when I glanced at the doorway, the man was gone. *Blast.* "I'm sure it would be a great comfort for you to speak to your husband—"

"Oh, pish posh, my dear," she said, waving the handkerchief in the air. "I've never been very sentimental, you know." She frowned up at her husband's portrait above the mantel. "But it would be a great comfort to finally get an answer about Algernon's bits."

"His . . .?"

"His bits, my dear! My husband had an unhealthy obsession with his bits."

I felt laughter bubbling up at Lady Chedington's choice of words. It was a shame horses weren't allowed in drawing rooms. Bertie, being less fond of earthy humor than I was, would have been able to silence me with a glare. But by imagining his expression of refined disapproval, I was able to keep a straight face.

"Bits," I said, coughing a little. The Becketts tack room was packed to the gills with bits, but no more than any other tack room belonging to an estate of the same equestrian éclat.

Lady Chedington rose from the settee and went to a writing desk in the corner, rifling through a pile of papers. "Algernon had a hobby. Well, it became more like a religion, as he tried to convert every horseman in sight. He designed bits for horses."

My mind flew to Brioso's bit, the odd shape of the mouthpiece, and all the other oddly-shaped bits hanging in the tack room.

"He was convinced that the types of bits already manufactured were not good enough for his horses," she continued. "Not effective, too heavy, the wrong shape, too light, at first he was content to simply whinge about it. Then he got it into his silly head that he was a scientist, some sort of pioneer in the field of horse bits. He made sketches of his ideas and had Mr. Malcolm down at the forge produce his prototypes."

The woman crossed to me and dropped a sheaf of papers on my lap. On the fine, cream paper I saw painstakingly detailed sketches of horse bits in various shapes, from absurd to conventional. Accompanying the sketches in a strong, slanting hand were notes outlining the possible effects of each mouthpiece.

Lady Chedington made her way to the sherry decanter and proceeded to fill a sparkling glass while continuing her story. "After testing them on his own horses, Algernon hawked his bits to all his friends like some sort of deranged street vendor. It never went anywhere, of course. No one else in the neighborhood wanted to try the strange bits he produced. But Algernon didn't care. He carried on making bits that no one wanted, very pleased with himself indeed." She stopped pacing and glared up at the portrait.

"And you need to contact your husband about those bits?" I asked, trying to follow the woman down her winding road.

She waved a hand. "Oh, I don't care about *those* bits. They're probably cluttering up the tack room and annoying Fletcher. He never had any use for them, and neither do I. No, the bits I'm looking for are quite different. Can you believe— and this may shock you, my dear—Algernon wanted to commemorate his two favorite designs, those he was most proud of, so he melted down his mother's jewelry and had two bits cast *of gold*!" She gripped the back of the settee, swaying over me.

"Pure gold?" I said, dropping an exact sketch of Brioso's bit into my lap.

"Yes. Old Lady Chedington wasn't one for tin and paste."

"But surely not actual bits? Gold is far too soft to put in a horse's mouth . . ." My mind spun as I struggled to picture the golden tone of Brioso's broken bit. Could it . . .? But no, that was impossible. If the stallion's bit had been pure gold, it would have been badly warped and covered in teeth marks. And although life hadn't afforded me many opportunities to handle pure gold, I trusted I could still tell the difference between gold and brass.

"Oh, yes, my dear, they are full-size. Or rather larger.

Great, ugly, whopping things, as if made for some legendary horse from Greek mythology. What's more, they're crusted in jewels, absolutely crusted!"

I breathed a sigh of relief. Brioso's bit was definitely not crusted in jewels.

"My mother-in-law herself was always crusted in jewels. Crusty old—well," she said, reining it in. "It wasn't enough for my husband to make bits of his mother's gold, he also had to stick the family jewels onto them till they looked like they had the pox! Those speckled bits were worth more than the horses and this Hall combined."

"Were?" I said, noting her tone of desolation.

"Were," she agreed. "Olivia and I haven't seen those bits since a month before Algernon's passing. He used to keep them on his desk in the library. It tickled him to use them like some sort of bizarre paperweights. But then one day he spirited them away somewhere, and never said a peep to anyone."

"The baronet had no private safe, no favorite cupboard?"

"No. We have looked, my dear! At first I wasn't worried, as I was sure the location would be written in his will, but when the will was read, there was no mention of the golden bits at all! The last paragraph read, 'To my dear wife Cressida and my darling daughter Olivia, I leave my greatest legacy and a potential fortune in the form of a family business. I desire them to produce and market horse bits, based on my prototypes, under the Chedington name.'" She sat heavily on the settee and observed the portrait with an expression of thorough disgust.

"I take it you don't intend to start such a business," I ventured.

"Oh, it's all nonsense, my dear! It's just Algernon's parting shot." She lifted her sherry glass to the portrait in a sullen salute. "He resented me for my lack of faith in his bits. But when I speak to him in the séance, he must tell us where to find those golden bits. I shall appeal to his paternal compassion, reminding him that Olivia should have her grandmother's jewels no matter what ridiculous shape they are currently in." She sighed deeply and turned to me. "It seems Olivia will need those jewels. She hasn't been making any headway with Byerley at all. And now that the beast has struck again," ostensibly referring to Brioso, "the stud farm is doomed. No one will breed to a murderous monster nor buy his offspring. There is no doubt about it—we shall have to destroy the creature or we shall be ostracized, simply ostracized. And we'll be penniless unless we find those bits!"

In the past, I'd had both ostracism and penury lapping at my toes like a bleak, recurring tide, and I didn't think Lady Chedington and her daughter were in any real danger of drowning. Still, there was something pathetic about the landed gentry— saddled with an ancestral estate but without the cash to maintain it. And without the cash to regularly pay a saddler.

"Let's wait to hear what the doctor has to say," I soothed. "It's possible it wasn't Brioso's fault at all. Did Lord Byerley tell you the Major was dead when we arrived, before he was dragged?"

Her round eyes were brimful as she took in my face. "Yes, but he was with the beast! With his foot in the stirrup, no less! We shall never be able to convince anyone that the stallion is innocent, with a body count of two."

I heard voices from the corridor and turned to see Miss Olivia, Mr. Langford, and Miss Seyward coming through the door. All three were dressed and combed and didn't appear to have come down in any haste. The expressions on their faces showed early morning brightness, nothing more. Langford and Miss Seyward gave me warm smiles, but Miss Olivia came across and swept me into an enthusiastic embrace.

"Thank you for your stories last night, Miss Cobb," she whispered, sparkling at me from beneath her golden curls. "You inspired me to take action. I did something very brave last night, and I shall tell you all about it when we have a moment alone together." She winked, then headed cheerfully to the silver coffee service on the sideboard.

I stared after her. What did the girl mean? What 'brave' thing had she done? Could she—but no, that was ridiculous. Or was it? I gazed at the girl as she browsed the breakfast dishes, noticing how strong and sturdy she was. Daily riding, however ineptly accomplished, would give her the strong muscles and familiarity with horses necessary to—I mentally shook myself like a dog coming out of water. Ridiculous.

"Rather early for breakfast, isn't it, Mother?" Miss Olivia said. "Lord Byerley said you wished to see us. Oh!" she clapped her hands in delight, hovering over a platter of pastries. "Cook made whortleberry tarts! Sarah is such a dear, berry picking in all sorts of weather just to be sure Cook has what she needs. Just think, this tiny tart could include whortleberries from all over Exmoor! We should each have one and then try to guess where the berries came from." She laughed very prettily at her own wit.

"I suppose there's no point in keeping it from you," Lady Chedington said, rising with a curious mixture of reluctance, resolve, and regality, like an aging monarch set to deliver a dreadful proclamation. "The Major . . . is dead."

For a moment, there was complete silence, and then the sound of a whortleberry tart falling onto the sideboard and rolling to the floor. Miss Olivia stood frozen, shaken, her empty hand in the air. Langford looked confused, as though he was sure he'd heard wrong, and he opened his fine mouth to speak. Then, a strangled gasp came from another direction. I turned to see Miss Seyward, her face porcelain-white, crumpling senselessly into the arms of Lord Byerley, who had just stepped into the room behind her.

Lady Chedington observed the unconscious girl in the arms of the young lord and said dejectedly, "Score one for Rossetti."

15

PLAYING WATSON

"I SHALL BE ETERNALLY grateful to Miss Seyward for fainting like she did," I said to Bertie. I was hunkered down in the corner of Bertie's stall, wrapping up my whispered account of the morning's events. "There is something calming about taking care of an invalid in a crisis. It diverts the attention, gives everyone something to do."

"It apparently didn't give our lord enough to do," Bertie said, the gray skin above his eyes wrinkling in a frown. "He sauntered through here not fifteen minutes ago. Presumably going out to join Fletcher and the corpse."

"Byerley's always lingering near doors and disappearing when no one is looking," I said. "It seems he can barely stand being in a house at all."

"Sounds familiar," snorted the big horse, shooting me an appraising look, which I ignored.

"Byerley's unbothered by anything," I said. "I'm surprised he even caught Miss Seyward when she fell."

"He does seem the type that would lend a fainting lady nothing more than an ironic eyebrow."

"It must've been a reflex. He unloaded her onto the settee as soon as possible. We were all around her, and Mr. Langford was exceptionally quick-witted, loosening her collar and calling for water and salts—"

"Ah," Bertie said, "so the poet isn't flighty in an emergency?"

"He is remarkably level-headed for someone with eyelashes like his."

"And the lady rallied?"

"She did. With some cool cloths applied to her face, and a sniff of Lady Chedington's vinaigrette, and some gentle murmurings from Mr. Langford to bring her out of her stupor."

Bertie cocked his head. "The poet seems unusually attentive. Perhaps Miss Seyward is his muse?"

"He was simply being a gentleman," I sniffed. "It's lucky for Miss Seyward that she came round when she did. I had half a mind to rip open her shirtwaist and loosen her corset. But she came right in the end, no disrobing necessary. Miss Olivia immediately tried to force her to eat a pastry, and Lady Chedington offered her a massive tumbler of sherry, and when Langford pointed out that she might not be able to handle all that, Miss Olivia said, 'A small sip of something stronger!' and proceeded to call for Byerley and his whiskey. That is when we noticed he was gone. Langford said it was a bit unmanly for Byerley to scurry out on a lady in distress, and I happen to agree with him."

"You did a neat bit of scurrying yourself," Bertie said. "Did you even pause to observe how everyone was handling the news of the Major's death?"

"I observed," I said, a little offended.

"Care to enlighten me?"

"We need to take a step back. As soon as she entered the room, Miss Olivia came directly to me and whispered that she did something 'very brave' last night. She said my saddlery stories from Walsall 'inspired' her to do it."

The horse gaped at me. "What kind of stories did you tell her? You didn't do away with anyone in Walsall, did you?"

"Don't be ridiculous."

"What 'very brave' thing did she do, then?"

"She didn't elaborate. But she looked very cheerful and pleased with herself, not at all like she'd just killed a man."

"Unless she's a psychopath," he said. "I've always thought there was something sinister about her frequent giggling. How did she react when she learned that the Major is no more?"

"She seemed very shocked, but she didn't go white, she went pink."

"Guilty pink?"

"I have a feeling her complexion is the type that goes pink in every situation," I said.

"Fair enough. And the poet?"

"Mr. Langford seemed confused, then surprised, and then just grim and practical while dealing with Miss Seyward."

"And Miss Seyward?" the horse said. "Other than turning white and fainting?"

"Isn't that suspicious, though? Her face . . . it was horrible. I didn't know if she would scream or faint. But isn't the fainting a bit of a tell?"

"You spent too much time on the back streets of Walsall, Harriet. Women there didn't faint, they couldn't afford to. You need to readjust your expectations to our new life and class.

This is Pelgren Vale, where fine ladies faint and police mess about with kittens."

"And lords get away with murder?" I suggested.

"That remains to be seen," he said. "He could very well be telling the truth about how he injured his hand. And remember, a cut on the hand doesn't rule anyone in or out. It just shows who hated the Major enough to try to knock him down a peg. By the by, there is one more suspect that wasn't in that room, and he had just as much reason as anyone else to knock the Major off his high horse."

"Fletcher? But he wasn't even here. He goes back to his cottage every night, doesn't he?" The old groom's cottage, a humbler version of my own, was across the narrow north pasture from the stables. It was close enough that he could be quickly roused if there was trouble at night, but far enough that he could maintain a bit of privacy when desired.

"From the look and smell of him this morning, I think he slept in the hay barn," Bertie said.

I considered this, remembering Fletcher's disheveled, chaff-covered appearance in the field. "He was rather piqued about a certain gray horse weathering a storm in the meadow," I said. "After he paid you that visit last night to invite you back to your stall—"

"Which I declined."

"—he must've decided bedding down in the hay was a cozier prospect than hoofing it back to his cottage in the rain. There now, don't you feel a tad guilty about that?"

"I would," Bertie said, "if I didn't know that Fletcher habitually sleeps in the hay."

"What?"

"Remember, I hear things," he said. "And I see things. Since Fletcher's gotten a bit long in the tooth, he's been taking little naps now and then in the hay barn. With that oddly-named cat. He keeps a cozy horse rug stowed in there for that purpose. I also heard Tom tell Sarah, the housemaid, that Fletcher frequently spends whole nights in the hay. So, I'm afraid Fletcher remains on our list of suspects. Did you notice any cuts on his hands?"

"No," I admitted uncomfortably. "I've been distracted."

"And you've been certain that Byerley's your man." Bertie flipped his nose airily. "Don't let your dislike for the lord cloud your judgement. A rookie mistake, that."

"How is it that I'm a rookie and you are not? As far as I know, you and I possess exactly the same experience solving crimes. Having read *The Moonstone* and *The Woman in White* three times each is hardly a solid qualification, old boy."

Bertie's thick lashes dropped low, and a slight smile played at the corner of his gray lips. He looked about as sly as it is possible for a horse to look. "I had a life before you, Harriet. We've shared a few stories, you and I, but there are plenty left to tell. When the time is right. Suffice it to say, you've spent your life avoiding people, while I've spent mine serving and observing them. And until horses are allowed in houses, you'll need to be my eyes and ears in the human sphere."

"As you wish, Inspector," I said. "I'll do the observing, you do the deducing. Starting with Byerley's remark about paying debts."

"We need to backtrack farther than that. If you recall, our lord paid me a little visit this morning before dawn."

With all that had happened, I had almost forgotten the strange interlude in the dark meadow. "Spill," I said.

"He was there only a few minutes before you showed up. But Harriet," he said, eyeing me carefully, "Byerley was trying to shock me into a response, so he told me something he knew would be of interest to me. He owned a colt that ran at Wolverhampton. A colt that won against stiff odds. Named Praxiteles."

"I know," I sighed.

"You know?" The big horse arched his muscular neck and glared down his long nose. "That would have been an observation worth sharing. Perhaps I was wrong about your poker skills. What else have you got up your sleeve?"

I waved this away. "Was he speaking to you or at you? Did you let on that you understood him?"

Bertie blew an exasperated snort. "Do you have so little faith in the Vacant Donkey? Yes, he was speaking *to* me, without a doubt. No, I did not let on that I was anything more than an average, aging, slow-witted horse. I was very convincing. I even drooled a little."

I relaxed against the rough wood of the stall wall, relieved. Tom had arrived, and I could hear the comforting scrape and scatter of his hefting pitchfork.

"His colt ran on the 12th of September," I said. "It's definitely our Praxiteles. Byerley has the date engraved on a flask."

"Ah! You've been picking pockets? Very satisfactory."

It was my turn to glare. Bertie frequently overestimated what I had learned on the streets of Walsall. He liked to imagine me as some sort of canny, street-wise maverick, when in reality I had been a very ordinary factory worker.

"I didn't pick his pocket," I said. "He wanted me to see the flask, so he slipped it into my meal basket last night. But it doesn't matter. We don't have to see Byerley's heavy-handed hints if we don't want to. He's just trying to wind us up because he thinks I'm trying to take advantage of Lady Chedington, and he thinks you're a talking horse."

"Which I am," Bertie said, with a wink. "But I'm in no real

danger, as he can't share his suspicions about me without sounding insane. He could, however, do real damage to your reputation by spreading rumors about certain . . . unconventional behaviors at the track in Wolverhampton."

We shared a long look. "Then we'll have to make sure he doesn't," I said.

Bertie cocked his large head and swiveled his ears, very still for a moment.

"Don't tell me Byerley's sneaking up the aisle again," I hissed, pressing my forehead against the polished bars and craning my neck to see both ways.

"No, but I think the cavalry has arrived." He paused, listening intently. "One horseless and one horsed, I should imagine."

The sound of an engine was still relatively rare in Pelgren Vale, but I could hear the rugged, chugging vibrations of a motorcar gradually approaching.

"Remember," Bertie said, "observation first, deduction later. You're the Watson, the eyes and ears of our little outfit."

"And the muscle? Watson tends to be the muscle. Yet I seem to be lacking the requisite revolver."

"Slow your gallop, old girl. You're going to harness a different strength. I know you'd rather wait and see what the doctor chap has to say, but you'll need to speak up about that head wound."

"Won't the doctor find it on his own? I was only joking about the revolver, by the way. I'm not planning on taking any active part in this business. The woodwork is a nice, cozy place to be, and I plan to stay there. I'd rather not insert myself into things at all."

Bertie snorted. "And I'd rather not spend the next twenty years wondering which of our neighbors is a murderer. The doctor may suppose that the injury happened during the dragging, but you must tell him it happened earlier, which should interest the police as well. You and I are quite capable of solving the mystery of the broken bit, so feel free to keep that close to your vest, but in the matter of murder, it may be informative to observe the police at work."

"Really, Bertie, this doesn't concern us," I said, frowning. "We'll let the doctor decide how the man died."

Wrinkles appeared around his nostrils. "As usual, you're swinging your putter when the green is miles away. Try the long game, Harriet. If they hang this death on the stallion, his reputation—and possibly his life—will be finished. Even if the police don't recommend destroying the fellow, Lady Chedington will convince her daughter to sell the horses. Becketts will crumble, and you will lose your only consistent client. And when you're sitting in your cottage on a winter's eve, boiling your coffee beans twice because you can't afford fresh ones, gazing out at my grave because you couldn't afford oats . . . you'll think back to the day you could've saved your job, your coffee, and your handsome horse simply by mentioning a little bruise on a man's head."

I eyed him skeptically. "You're forgetting the other way we might save Becketts and ensure a steady supply of coffee and oats."

"Don't keep me in suspense."

"We could find Lady Chedington's golden bits for her."

"Ah!" he chuckled. "Good show, but it won't do."

"Won't it?"

"From what we know of Lady Chedington, that money would be spent on afternoon teas. On garden parties and galas—and not of the equine persuasion. Perhaps she'll even buy a motorcar or a fleet of bicycles, but she'll never give Miss

Olivia money to support the horses. No, I'm afraid your best chance of staying employed is to keep the stallion in the clear, which means a mention of murder. Remember, Watson, stay close, try to hear everything they say, and speak up when the time is right."

16

ONE HORSELESS AND ONE HORSED

THE MOTORCAR ROLLED SLOWLY around the circular carriageway, passing the Hall and coming to a shuddering halt in front of the open stable doors. Tom paused in his chores to gape at the thing.

"Don't those beat horses, then," he breathed, drinking in the sight of the newfangled machine. "They go where you tell 'em, stop where you tell 'em, and no cleanin' up after 'em." He waved his pitchfork at me, grinned, and went back to his cleaning.

I supposed it was a lovely motorcar, as the things went. All deep glossy blue with brass fittings, it was larger than most of the motorcars I had seen, with two rows of high open seats rather than one. I had very little use for the internal combustion engine but, as with all new technology, Bertie was fascinated by it.

"Imagine a world, Harriet," he had said, "in which the drearier work of hauling and dragging and transporting is all done by engines rather than horses."

"I'd like to hear you debate this with other horses, if other horses could talk," I had said. "Most horses wouldn't be very grateful to become obsolete. For horses that outlive their usefulness, the knacker is a more likely end than a retirement pasture."

"And saddlers? How will they fare in the age of the motorcar?"

"Fine, just fine," I had said. "We will stitch leather seats. Motoring gloves and caps. And," with an evil smile, "the demand for strong horse harnesses will increase, since horses are forever being called on to rescue those silly machines when they get stuck in the mud! Trust me, Bertie. It will be hundreds of years before motorcars replace horses completely."

In the glistening contraption before me sat a burly man, his barrel chest straining the buttons of his police uniform. He noticed me watching and gave me a nod, then ostentatiously jiggled and fussed with a few levers. Behind the motorcar, coming up the drive at a smart trot, was Bertie's "horsed" visitor. The solemn black buggy looked old and worn, but the bay mare in the traces seemed cheerful and light-footed. She tossed her fine head gracefully, and I could hear the jingle of tiny bells as the driver brought her to a dancing halt.

"Whoa, Beauty!" he called to the horse, and I smiled to myself. The number of horses named "Beauty" had significantly increased in England since the publication of a certain famous book over two decades ago.

The big man in the motorcar climbed heavily down, straightening his sergeant's uniform and his bristly red mustache. "Well, Doctor?" he called to the buggy driver. "I arrived first again, you'll notice. Never took her out of first gear, yet she still beat your beast."

The other man, a spare specimen dressed in a neat black

suit, paused in his climb down from the buggy. "Was it a race, then?" he said, blinking owlishly behind his round spectacles. He stepped carefully to the ground, and I could see white hair beneath his black bowler hat. He appeared to be nearly as old as Fletcher, though he moved with the same lightness his horse displayed.

"Was it a . . ." it was the sergeant's turn to blink. "Yes, Doctor! Didn't we agree, in front of Foster's stable, that I would keep my motorcar in first gear and you would keep your horse in trot and we would see who arrived the fastest?"

The doctor considered this, then shook his head. "I remember it very differently," he said. "I remember you positing a theory with which I concurred."

"But . . . it was a wager! You shook my hand!"

"I did wonder why you wanted to shake hands," the older man said. "You said, 'Even in first gear, I think my Wolseley can beat your horse, what do you say, Doctor, care to shake on it?' And I said, 'Of course,' and I shook your hand. Because I agreed with you. It is highly logical that your engine can beat my Beauty. After all, it has six horses, and Beauty has only herself." He affectionately patted the bay mare's shiny neck.

The sergeant opened his mouth to protest but then seemed to think better of it. "Seven and a half," he mumbled.

"What was that?" the doctor asked. He was in the process of strapping a canvas nosebag around his horse's muzzle, an action I had only seen before from the most conscientious London cabbies.

"I said, seven and a half," the sergeant said gruffly. "This Wolseley has seven and a half horsepower, not six."

"Ah," the doctor said cheerfully, "you see? Then it is even more logical." He stepped back from his horse and watched her munching the feed in the nosebag, a faint smile playing on his lips. "A spot of feed keeps the digestion flowing," he announced, to no one in particular.

As if on cue, the little mare lifted her tail and deposited a large, fragrant pile onto the white gravel.

The doctor observed this with immense satisfaction. "Good, good," he murmured, taking a small notebook and pencil out of his pocket and making a note.

The sergeant grunted. "If you're quite finished recording your horse's bodily functions—"

"Quite," the doctor said, snapping his notebook shut.

"Oh, Dr. Reed! Sergeant Harrison!" Lady Chedington was coming down the gravel drive from the direction of the Hall, supported by Mr. Langford's sturdy arm. Although the lady wore an expression of dogged determination in the face of doom, she swayed slightly in spite of her escort.

"I never thought the day would come that I should see you again under these circumstances," she said to the newcomers. "You must think Becketts full of murderers! Two victims in less than six months! But I assure you, there is only one murderer."

Dr. Reed moved forward to take her ladyship's hand, but Sergeant Harrison paused and straightened. His bushy red eyebrows lowered over eyes that were suddenly very keen.

"Murderer?" he said. "Two victims? I was told there was a simple horse accident, one man involved."

"I believe her ladyship is referring to the late baronet's accident," Langford said. His sensitive brow was pinched, but he stood stalwart and steady, a fixed point of poise in a world gone akimbo.

"Accident, nothing!" exclaimed Lady Chedington. "It's that same wretched stallion. The beast has murdered again!"

"Ah, well," Sergeant Harrison said, relaxing. It seemed

murderers of the equine variety troubled him less than the usual type.

"And what of Mr. Hastings?" her ladyship said, suddenly changing tack. "Were you able to rescue the kitten?"

"The kitten was never in danger," Dr. Reed said, patting her hand reassuringly. "It was not an obsession of the violent variety. Classic fixation disorder, I should think. Though I will be meeting with Mr. Hastings very frequently in the next few weeks to clarify my diagnosis. Just think! I may be in a position to publish the first study ever done on the phenomenon of feline fixation."

Lady Chedington looked vague.

"Chap's in love with his kitten, that's what the good doctor is trying to say," the sergeant said. "Never seen a fellow so obsessed with an animal." His eyes landed on the doctor, who was gazing past Lady Chedington to smile blithely at his bay mare. "Almost never," the sergeant grunted. "Lady Chedington, perhaps you could start by telling us the name of the unfortunate man? An employee, you said? Not old Fletcher, is it?"

"Heavens no! He was not permitted to handle the beast. No, Sergeant, it is . . . Major Peter Collings!" She collapsed against Langford, who handed her his own handkerchief and gallantly stuffed her undoubtedly damp one into his pocket.

"Collins?" The sergeant's brows furrowed.

"Collings," Lady Chedington corrected from the depths of Langford's sleeve. "Surely you've heard of Major Peter Collings? The famous horse master from York?"

"Can't say as I have. Don't really hobnob with the horse crowd, myself. Famous, you say?"

I wondered if the man knew that the word "famous" was always suspect on Lady Chedington's lips. The woman had a charming habit of exaggerating the rank and skills of the people around her to reflect the value she assigned to them.

"He won the jumping at Olympia," she declared.

It was my turn to frown. If the man I knew as the Major had won anything at the most prestigious horse show in London, I would eat my own hoof, as Bertie liked to say.

"I remember a Collings doing very well at Olympia," the doctor said, tearing his attention away from his mare. "He surprised everyone by winning the jumping on a draft horse, of all things, the only horse that could carry his weight. That was back in 1888, the first year Olympia was held, which is why I remember. It is always regrettable when horsemen run to flesh, as it puts undue stress on the horse's spine. Collings was much too broad and heavy to be jumping, yet he cleared those jumps by dint of spur and whip. Very regrettable display."

Langford caught my frown and raised one fine eyebrow. It was indeed an eyebrow-raising question—could fifteen years turn a broad, heavy man into the cadaverously thin Major? It was possible, perhaps, but unlikely.

Lady Chedington hesitated for a moment, apparently considering the same question.

"He has slimmed marvelously since then," she decided. "No doubt in dedication to his craft. He is—he was very dedicated. It seemed such a boon, such a stroke of luck when he showed up on my doorstep! I needed the stallion trained and my daughter coached, and he appeared as if providence itself had sent him!"

Sergeant Harrison and Dr. Reed exchanged a look, but neither said what I was also thinking. A famous horseman from York just happened to show up on her doorstep? The twist on the sergeant's face revealed he didn't like the smell of it.

"You didn't invite him, then?" the sergeant said. "He didn't come here on the reference of some acquaintance?"

"No, oh no. That is what made it so positively auspicious! Kismet, I say. The Major said that many horse masters in York have a high opinion of the Becketts bloodlines. He said when he heard about my husband's passing, he wanted to offer his help. A gesture of respect for my husband's memory, no doubt." The lady noticed the narrow glances being exchanged, and a bit of indignant color came into her cheeks. "I'm not so unguarded as you seem to think, however. In all diligence, I did ask my solicitor to verify that Major Peter Collings competed at Olympia. He found that it was exactly as you said, Doctor. 1888 was the year."

"Well. We'll circle back to that later," the sergeant said, but he had the look of a hound on a scent.

"Perhaps you could show us to the body?" added the doctor, in the same bright tone one would use to say, "Perhaps you could show us to the rose garden?"

"Mr. Langford will do those honors," Lady Chedington said. "Seeing one corpse in six months is enough for me. I refuse to set foot in that"—she waved a hand at the stable —"that house of horrors! I never want to see a horse again. The stallion must be destroyed, Sergeant. He's far too dangerous to keep, and I can't possibly sell him in good conscience. You must tell Olivia what's to be done, as she'll never listen to me."

"Well," the sergeant grunted, "we'll come to that when we come to it."

"I need to talk with you later, Sergeant, about the possibility of acquiring a motorcar like yours," she said.

The sergeant smiled expansively. This was obviously one of his favorite subjects. "Good, very good! I'll take you motoring, shall I? I think you'll find the small quirks of the motorcar are nothing to the quirks of horses."

I wondered how Lady Chedington would feel about the quirks of motorcars when she was kneeling in the road, struggling to change the rubber tube that fit inside the tires. Stray horseshoe nails were forever puncturing the things, and I often saw motorists in this position, surrounded by pleasantly jeering spectators.

The three men turned toward the stable and then paused, arrested at the sight of me. I shifted uncomfortably. I usually tried to avoid standing places that emphasized my height, and it was probably a little startling to be confronted by a towering, darkly-clad woman in the doorway of the stable.

"Oh! This is Miss Cobb," Lady Chedington said. "Have you never met? Miss Cobb, Sergeant Harrison, Dr. Reed," she waved a vague hand to indicate introductions. "Miss Cobb is a very skilled saddler. Of the highest order—from Walsall, if you believe it, the very zenith of saddlery! She bought old Mrs. Haigh's cottage across the valley. A very convenient proximity. And it was she that found the Major this morning, with Lord Byerley. They caught the monster that was dragging him."

The doctor, who had looked instantly interested at the mention of saddlery, doffed his bowler hat charmingly. "Hello, Miss Cobb. I may wish to speak with you later about Beauty's saddle. It appears to be rubbing along her withers—"

"A pleasure, I'm sure," the sergeant interrupted loudly, nodding curtly at me.

I moved aside as the three men came forward, and Sergeant Harrison paused as he passed me, his keen eyes appraising. "Becketts is a popular place these days," he said. "Famous horsemen and famous saddlers showing up out of the blue to offer their services to a grieving widow. Remarkable."

"I'm hardly famous—" I protested, but the sergeant had already turned away, following Langford into the stable.

17

A BOUQUET OF JUNIPER

I WAS SURPRISED to see Byerley and Fletcher standing at the far end of the aisle, flanking a flat handcart parked in front of Bertie's stall. Made for carrying hay and other farm materials, the cart now held a long, lumpy form shrouded in a woolen horse rug. Brioso's saddle lay in a forlorn heap in the corner of the cart, looking as though it felt a little ashamed of itself.

Sergeant Harrison's throat rumbled ominously as our little group came to a stop around the cart. "Lord Byerley. Fletcher. You felt the need to move the body, I see."

Fletcher seemed a little crestfallen at this, but Byerley lounged lazily against the cart with the dispassionate ease of a large, pale cat.

"We thought it best not to let him bake in the sun," he said.

I glanced at Bertie, who was watching intently through the bars of his stall, and I wondered at Byerley's choice of this exact spot. Perhaps he hoped a front-row seat to the proceedings would cause Bertie to give himself away.

With clinical efficiency, Dr. Reed rolled back the rug, releasing faint odors of earth and torn grass. The mud was nearly dry on the battered form, and Byerley and Fletcher had left the saddle attached with the stirrup iron still firmly around the ankle.

"Hmph," Sergeant Harrison said, breaking the silence. "Well. Seems straightforward enough. Not the first time I've seen a dragging. Silly, panicky creatures, horses."

Bertie's eyes narrowed and his ears swiveled back a fraction. Byerley observed this with faint amusement and lifted a mocking eyebrow at me.

"I'd like to conclude this as soon as possible," the sergeant continued. "Lady Chedington is already in a state, so I'd like to get this corpse out of her hair. I assume, Doctor, that this is not the fat Major Peter Collings you saw at Olympia in 1888?"

"That's impossible to say conclusively, of course," the doctor said, using his stethoscope to listen for a heartbeat. "But it is unlikely. That man was very large, very broad. A body does become diminished and sunken when life is extinguished, but the height of the frame, the width of the shoulders—"

"I'll put you down for a 'no'," the sergeant said.

"A 'probably not' would suit me better," the doctor replied.

"And none of the rest of you had ever met the man before, or know anything about him?" Shaking heads all around. "Then there's the rather pressing matter of determining who this chap is and why he showed up on her ladyship's doorstep under a false identity. He was obviously dragged, so I'll just need the bare bones." He grimaced at the unfortunate choice of words. "The scenario, as it were." He turned to Byerley. "What time did it happen?"

"First light," Byerley said. "Just before dawn."

"Damned queer time to be riding."

"Yes."

The sergeant waited for more, but Byerley wasn't as generous with his words as he was with his gold sovereigns. "You saw him fall?" the burly man finally prompted.

"No. He fell before we arrived."

That's something, I thought, relieved that Byerley wasn't changing the story, though the word *fell* felt a bit misleading. The young man didn't trouble himself to add any more details, and I was about to speak when I noticed everyone staring at Dr. Reed.

The doctor was leaning down, his lips hovering as close to the corpse's muddy lips as it was possible to be without actually kissing. At the same time, he reached out a hand and pressed down on the still chest. We watched in thick silence. No doubt we all shared the same shivers of revulsion, with the possible exception of Byerley, who looked a bit bored.

"Doctor?" the sergeant said, his ruddy mustache twitching in disgust.

The doctor straightened up. "Juniper," he declared, readjusting his spectacles. "A bouquet of juniper." He looked around in satisfaction, his smile only faltering when he noticed our blank expressions. "Gin," he stated, as though it was obvious. "The man consumed a large quantity of gin shortly before his demise. The smell is still strong within him."

"Ah." Sergeant Harrison seemed pleased. "The most common cause of horse accidents."

"Indeed?" The doctor blinked behind his spectacles. "Gin? Fascinating. When was the study done? I wonder what properties cause gin to be more dangerous to the equestrian than other alcohols—"

"Not gin, Doctor," growled the sergeant. "Riding while drunk."

"Oh. Oh yes, of course." The doctor looked distinctly disappointed.

"It seems rather cut-and-dried, then," Sergeant Harrison said. "A drunken man rides a spirited stallion in the dark. He falls or passes out, his foot gets stuck in the stirrup, and the horse drags and tramples him. We'll just need a cause of death, Doctor. Is there any way to tell which blow actually killed the man?"

"He was already dead when we arrived," I cut in.

The sergeant's eyes flitted to me. "If the horse was already on the run when you arrived, you have no way of telling whether he was dead or just insensible." The big man's dislike had been palpable ever since Lady Chedington sang my praises in her overblown way.

"He was dead before he was dragged," I said firmly.

The sergeant and Langford stared at me, one in disapproval and one in confusion, but Dr. Reed looked instantly interested.

"How do you mean, Miss Cobb?" he asked.

I described the scene we'd encountered—the still horse, the Major lying in that oddly serene position with perfectly clean clothes, my checking his pulse and finding nothing.

"You checked his pulse too, Lord Byerley?" the sergeant interrupted.

"No. I was holding the horse."

The sergeant's flat gaze fell on me. "A pulse is sometimes hard to feel, Miss Cobb. Even for those who know about such things." His tone made it clear that, in his estimation, I did not belong in the category of those who knew about such things. Turning back to Byerley, he said, "Can you confirm the state of his clothes when you arrived? No mud, no grass?"

"His clothes looked clean from where I was standing. But I

never got close." Byerley's light eyes were inscrutable, and he didn't seem interested in offering anything that wasn't directly asked for. I would have to take up the slack in the reins.

"There was a bit of straw on his clothes," I said. "Just straw, no grass."

The sergeant eyed me again, eyebrows hunched like a rusty sunset on his stormy brow. "If the horse was calm and Lord Byerley was holding it, how is it that the man was then dragged?"

"The stallion spooked," I said simply. Fletcher had wanted the cat left out of it, and I could be as reticent as Byerley with the details that didn't matter.

"The bridle did break," Byerley interjected, "lest anyone get the wrong idea about my ability to hold a horse. The stable cat ran out, spooked the horse, and the bridle broke."

Fletcher looked very glum at the mention of Treacle Tart.

"Cat." The sergeant spat out the word as though it pained him as much as the word *horse* pained Lady Chedington. "Everything comes down to cats today." He glared at me and Byerley as though the cat belonged to us. "How long was the man dragged before you caught the stallion?"

Byerley spoke first. "Bertie went after him almost immediately—"

"Bertie?"

"Miss Cobb's horse," Byerley said, pointing at the stall. Sergeant Harrison turned and stared at the big gray horse, who appeared to be dozing.

"Bertie? Named after the king? A bit disrespectful, that," he growled. "You were also riding before dawn, Miss Cobb?" It sounded like an accusation.

"I wasn't riding," I said, and stopped, sensing thin ice. I had no wish to reveal the extent of Bertie's independence that morning.

"So, this horse, *Bertie*, bolted with the stallion? Saw him running and decided to join in? No wonder the man looks abused. Trampled by two horses."

Bertie maintained his sleepy aspect, but tight wrinkles of disdain appeared around his nostrils.

"Bertie caught the stallion," Byerley said, stalking over to the stall. "Brought him to a stop in less than five minutes. An admirable display by a very intelligent horse."

At the word "intelligent," Bertie's nose relaxed and he swiveled an approving ear toward the young man, who offered him a lump of sugar. The horse took the morsel, looking only mildly sheepish when he caught my eye. The big turncoat.

"In my experience," the sergeant said, "horses do not catch other horses. Their riders do. And bolting horses always cause other horses to bolt. Have you ever been hunting? Once one horse starts running, all the others join in, and then it's a bloody free for all." He shivered as though remembering a particularly harrowing experience on the hunt field.

"This horse is different," Byerley said, flinging me a wicked smile.

So, the lord had found his tongue and was all too ready to use it, if just to curry favor with Bertie. As for me, I was happy to let Sergeant Harrison believe that Bertie had trampled every person at Becketts if it meant we could drop the matter, but Byerley seemed ready to elaborate if I did not.

"Bertie was a track pony before he joined me—before I bought him," I corrected. I didn't like the reference to buying and owning any more than Bertie did, but sometimes conventional language was necessary. "He was trained to stop bolting horses on the track." I hoped my tone of cold finality would put the discussion to rest, though anyone who had ever visited a track knew that track ponies did not do such things on their own.

From the look on the sergeant's face, his credulity had been stretched past breaking point. "It's more likely the two horses simply tired in less than five minutes," he muttered. "So! A drunken man passes out while mounting. He is the victim of strong drink and bad timing. He ends up insensible, on the ground, with his foot caught in the stirrup, and then a wayward cat jumps out and all hell breaks loose. Miss Cobb's horse joins the fray, and the man is dragged and trampled into the condition we see before us."

"A drunken man would've still possessed a pulse before being dragged," Dr. Reed reminded him.

"We're not certain that he didn't," the sergeant said.

"I'm quite certain," I said. I was watching the doctor's nimble fingers as they probed the Major's skull through gritty, greasy hair. "There was a mark on his head before he was dragged. It looked like it could have been a wound."

All the men stared at me in astonishment, with the exception of Dr. Reed, who had reached the corpse's left temple and was palpating the area with intense interest.

"Did you see the mark?" the sergeant barked to Byerley.

"No," he said, "but I didn't get close."

Dr. Reed straightened up. "Perhaps you could point to the mark you saw, Miss Cobb?" The excitement in his eyes was magnified by the thick lenses, and it was obvious that he had found what he was looking for.

I swatted my eye loupe into place and leaned in. The three lines had faded from existence, but the squarish blemish was still visible. I pointed to the spot.

"Exactly," the doctor said triumphantly. "The man has a skull fracture in the exact location Miss Cobb has indicated. There has been significant crushing of bone—would you care to feel, Sergeant?"

The sergeant looked a bit squeamish. "I'll take your word for it. Kicked in the head, then? While mounting?"

"Unlikely," the doctor said, hunching down to corpse-level again. "What Miss Cobb saw is a small contusion of unique shape. The man received a very concentrated blow with a narrow object in the shape of . . . a square. The mark is still visible on the skin, and the fracture beneath confirms it."

There was silence for a moment as we all weighed the implication.

"Square, you say? Like a mallet?" Since coming to Becketts, the sergeant had displayed mild suspicion and irritation, but until this moment, I had never seen him look like a police officer. His muscles tensed, his burly shoulders squared, and his mustache bristled like the rising hackles of a hound.

"No, no," the doctor said, "nothing so large. It is, in fact, quite small—see?"

The sergeant leaned down to examine the spot, and Langford came forward as well, peering closely with grim interest. Byerley remained aloof, leaning comfortably against Bertie's stall as if he owned both the horse and the stable.

"The damage was probably magnified by the negligible size of the object," continued the doctor. "All the force was concentrated on a very small area in a very fragile region of the skull. It could even have been something as unlucky as falling against an unyielding projection while drunk."

"Would he have been knocked out straight away?"

"It's hard to say. There may have been a period of lucidity

before he succumbed, or he may have lost consciousness immediately."

The sergeant looked deflated. "Then it's a search," he said bleakly. "I suppose there's nothing else to be done. I will ring Constable Ellis—we'll need to comb the place for a square object that could have made that mark. Head of a bolt? Is there any bolt sticking out of the stable walls or fences, Fletcher?"

Dr. Reed's face brightened. "You know, my Beauty used to struggle on the roads. Dry clay is better than mud, yes, but that hard-packed clay doesn't provide much traction. Beauty used to slip now and then, even when the roads were dry—"

"Doctor." The sergeant scowled at the smaller man. "As much as I enjoy discussing your horse's many shortcomings, now is not the time."

"The point is," replied the doctor, "I finally had Beauty's shoes fitted with studs."

"Studs." The sergeant looked blank for a moment, and then the significance of the word seemed to break over him. "Studs!" he crowed. "Could a square stud in a horseshoe have done the job?"

"I would need to see the stud, of course, but that is the appropriate size."

"If the stallion kicked the man . . ."

"Yes, from just the right angle and just the right distance, so that the stud in the shoe carried all the force but the rest of the hoof made very little contact . . . it is just possible it could have caused the injury we see before us."

"I could kiss your Beauty," breathed the sergeant, unguarded in his relief that a full property-combing would not be necessary.

Dr. Reed took the little notebook and pencil out of his

pocket and began writing. "I feel the need to record that little comment," he said, "for posterity."

I caught Bertie's eye. The horse was staring very hard at me from behind Byerley's shoulder, and I knew what he was thinking. A horseshoe stud might be the perfect size and shape to make that mark, but no stud I had ever seen would have left those three little lines.

18

THE ADVISABILITY
OF STUDS IN SHOES

"FLETCHER!" bellowed the sergeant, though the old groom was only a corpse-width away from him. "We'll need a stud from the stallion's hind shoes."

Fletcher looked bleak. "Brioso doesn't wear studs," he said.

"Yes, he does," countered Langford, and we all looked at the poet. "I believe the farrier may have fitted him with studs on Monday."

Byerley straightened up as though interested in the discussion for the first time.

"But . . . Mr. Langford," Fletcher said with some confusion, "Sir Algernon's horses never wear studs. He didn't like the things, thought the horses would twist a leg in pasture. Said if hooves were meant to grip like that, the good Lord himself would've made 'em knobbly. Said if a smooth sole were good enough for the Almighty, it were good enough for him."

"Sir Algernon is dead," Langford said, but his gentle tone stole any sharpness from the words. "Did you specifically tell Malcolm not to add studs on Monday? He's a great believer in studs. The man has added studs to my horses' shoes on more than one occasion without even consulting me." He smiled kindly at the old groom. "It's a profitable habit, no doubt. Likely to add a few shillings to the job and the owner is none the wiser."

"Beggin' your pardon, sir," Fletcher said, "but Mr. Malcolm always resets shoes exactly as he finds 'em. Never adds nothin' extra just to pad his prices. Honest as the day is long, is Mr. Malcolm." Fletcher spoke placidly, as all rough old horsemen did when they inevitably contradicted their betters, but Langford's innocent jest about Malcolm had awoken a tiny flame of indignance.

"Perhaps the Major requested the stallion be fitted with studs," Langford said. "After all, he took over Brioso's care when he arrived, did he not?"

Fletcher looked bleak at this mention of his diminished position. "That's so," he muttered.

"Well, seems to me we have only to look at the stallion's hooves," Sergeant Harrison said. "You weren't permitted to handle the stallion before, Fletcher, but I doubt Lady Chedington would mind if you brought him out to us, just this once?"

"No need for that," Langford said, "I'll bring him out. Fletcher needs to stay safe and healthy now that he's back in charge of Becketts." For once, I found myself less than impressed with Langford's gallant streak. There was a fine line between kindness and condescension, and although I couldn't decide which this was, Fletcher's face made no bones about it.

Despite Langford's insinuation that the horse was unsafe, Brioso meekly followed him out of the stall, shuffling along like an aging Labrador retriever. The frenzied gallop seemed to have stolen any last bit of spark the plain horse possessed.

He came to a clumsy stop in the aisle before us, only sparing one leery glance at Bertie.

"Care to do the honors, Sergeant?" Langford asked.

The sergeant moved back a fraction of a step. "I don't intend to get anywhere near this devil's hind hooves."

Byerley pushed himself off Bertie's stall and strode forward. "I'll do it," he said, giving the sergeant a withering look. "Fletcher? Would you mind getting the pliers?"

Fletcher nodded smartly and headed off to the tack room.

Byerley had no trouble lifting each of Brioso's hind hooves to reveal that the stallion was indeed wearing square studs. With the aid of the pliers, he loosened one stud and then used his long, pale fingers to unscrew it from the metal shoe. I found myself rather wickedly hoping that the wound on Byerley's hand would make things uncomfortable for him. He hadn't replaced his bandage, and Brioso was enjoying this new human prop by resting as much weight as possible on him. But the young lord's nimble fingers didn't falter, and there was only a hint of color in his face when he straightened up.

Sergeant Harrison took the small, threaded stud from Byerley, contemplated it for a moment, and then handed it to Dr. Reed.

"Yes," confirmed the doctor, holding the thing to the corpse's left temple and crouching low for a parallel view, "it appears to be a match." The sergeant satisfied himself with a brief look and then straightened up, dusting off his hands as though he had done all the work.

"So," he said, looking around at us, "the stallion kicked the Major in the head, either while he was mounting or earlier, in which case the man still managed to stick his foot in the stirrup before passing out. Lord Byerley and Miss Cobb arrived, and the rest played out as they described." His eyes landed on Brioso, who was nearly asleep, lower lip drooping like Bertie's Vacant Donkey. "I shall have a talk with Lady Chedington about what's to be done with this animal. Bolting with the baronet was one thing, but kicking a man in the head—"

"He weren't never known to kick, sir," Fletcher said, coming quickly forward, "even when he were young and my master first started him. He always had a little spirit, like any young horse, but never a bad bone in his body. An' after my master died, he seemed to feel it. He was quieter then, after it happened. Apologetic, like. An' he's been that way ever since. Calm, almost lazy. It changed him somehow, my master's death. I can't see him ever kickin' a man, not meaning to, anyhow. Before that, maybe, if he were startled, he had just that bit of spirit, but since then, with him feelin' sorry 'bout it, I just can't see it happenin'.'"

Sergeant Harrison's eyebrows should have been a warning to Fletcher, sinking lower and lower during his little speech, but perhaps the old groom didn't care. Brioso's life was on the line, after all.

"Am I to believe, Fletcher," the sergeant said, his whiskers twitching, "that you think the horse capable of remorse? That you believe this stallion feels sorry for what he has done and plans to change his ways—like some thundering great reformed criminal in horse clothing?"

"Yes, sir," Fletcher said, twisting his cap in his hands. "I just don't think he should be put down for somethin' he must've done by mistake. An' the Major weren't no horseman at all. Mr. Langford an' Lord Byerley can tell you that. An' Miss Cobb."

"It's true," Byerley said. "But I believe Miss Cobb spoke

highly of him yesterday. That is what the man told us at dinner. Perhaps she saw something we did not?" He turned his sardonic eyes on me.

The bleached bounder was trying to rile me, and it was working. "I did see something you did not," I said. "I saw a silly man shouting abuse at a girl who was trying her best. I told the Major that Miss Olivia was improving, just to . . . to get him off her back. I wasn't bestowing a knighthood or anything like that, though he seemed to take it that way."

"I think we can all agree that the Major did not live up to his reputation," Langford soothed. "And if he was an imposter, as you seem to suspect, Sergeant, he may have known very little about handling horses. So I agree with Fletcher. The stallion shouldn't be held responsible for something that, at best, was just an accident, and at worst, was caused by cruel, drunken mishandling of a horse."

"Here, here!" Dr. Reed agreed, no doubt hearkening back to the book that had given his horse her name. *Black Beauty* had brought the abuse of horses into the forefront of the British consciousness, and I thought I remembered at least one account of drunken mishandling in the book.

Sergeant Harrison remained dubious—he had apparently not read the book. "That will be a discussion for another day. One death could be overlooked, but two . . . Well. I'll send Mr. Wilson up to collect the body, and I won't disturb Lady Chedington any further today. I'll ring her after I've confirmed the man's identity. You gentlemen can explain to her how the thing happened?" He looked past me and Fletcher to the poet and the lord, who nodded their assent. "Good. I'll leave it in your capable hands, then."

The big man straightened his uniform smartly, took the little stud from the doctor, and turned to leave. Brioso was innocuously dozing, but the sergeant pressed up against the side of the aisle as he skirted the stallion, trying to stay as far as possible from those murderous hooves.

The sound of another hoof rang out sharply. I knew it was a heavy hoof at the end of a pale leg, flung against the inside wall of Bertie's stall. The big gray horse glared at me, and although I couldn't read the old boy's mind, I could translate his expression well enough. *Rampart time, old girl.*

19

SUSPICIONS

"Sergeant Harrison!" I called, hurrying after him. "A word, if you please."

The man turned and fixed me with a wary look. "Yes, Miss Cobb?"

"Could you join me in the tack room for a moment?" I asked.

He narrowed his eyes, hesitated, and then strode into the room with me at his heels. "Make it quick, Miss Cobb. I have an investigation to begin. Assumed identity. Unless you have some idea of the man's true identity?" He cocked his head. "Perhaps he was a friend of yours? You both drifted into the neighborhood very recently, did you not?"

"I don't know the man," I said. "I am a *resident* of Pelgren Vale, Sergeant, in a cottage I purchased free and clear. I've been living here six months, and the Major just arrived this week. I met him only yesterday, and I only knew him as the Major."

"Then what is it, Miss Cobb?"

"May I see that stud for a moment?"

The sergeant's eyes narrowed, but he handed me the thing. It felt cool in my palm, its surface dull and flat—no lines. I grasped the threaded end and pressed the square end firmly into the skin on the back of my hand.

"Miss Cobb!" he exclaimed, grabbing and wrenching the stud away from me. "Are you trying to injure—what are you playing at?"

"There was more than a square on the Major's head before he was dragged," I said, trying to force as much tranquility and elegance into my voice as possible. The man was more likely to listen to a proper lady than the dodgy saddler he believed me to be. "The mark was like a stamp on the skin. Three parallel lines, the top one curved, all red and sunken. They faded after he was dragged, but they were there. And, look." I held out my hand to him as though presenting it to be kissed.

He looked at the mark on my skin. "No parallel lines," he grunted. "Just a square."

"Just a square," I agreed.

The man was now looking keenly at my face as though seeing me for the first time, and I felt a fragile stirring of hope. He looked as though he might believe me. Byerley—or whomever—would not get away with murder, the stallion's reputation would not be beyond redemption, Lady Chedington would not need to give up the stud farm, and my saddlery skills would not be rendered redundant.

"You wear very interesting spectacles, Miss Cobb," he said, and hope withered as I realized he had been observing my spectacles, not my face.

"Yes." I swatted the eye loupe up and out of the way. As Bertie so often reminded me, I had a bad habit of going around with the thing flipped down in front of my eye. It was a habit formed in the Walsall factory, where long hours in low light had rendered the loupe a necessary part of me.

"They're quite unusual," he continued. "Powerful, no doubt. Able to make up for a serious deficiency of sight. Tell me, Miss Cobb, were you using that—" waving his finger at the folded loupe, "that contraption when you saw those three little lines?"

"No," I said. "I use the loupe for my work. Close stitching and such. But I could see the lines quite clearly without it."

"It was raining, was it not?" He spoke as though he was humoring a child. "Easy to see all sorts of lines and squiggles with raindrops running into your eyes."

"The three lines were there," I said doggedly. "I saw them clearly, I assure you."

"And? What do those three lines mean to us? You think the man hit a different object altogether? Do you expect to search the entire estate for a rock or tree or bolt with three little lines? Ridiculous. It would be beating a dead horse."

I took a deep breath. "I don't think the Major hit anything. I think he was hit. By someone. With some object that left those lines stamped on his skin. It may have happened in Brioso's stall, which would explain the straw I saw on him. Then he was arranged in the impossibly neat position we found him, his foot forced through the stirrup to give the impression of an accident. I don't know why the stallion didn't move before we arrived, but as Fletcher said, the horse has been calm and lazy since Sir Algernon's death—"

"Oh, come, Miss Cobb!" the sergeant thundered, his face rapidly reaching the same shade as his hair. "I don't know where you come from, but this is Pelgren Vale! I can personally vouch for the respectability of every person on this estate, with the clear exception of *you*! And the dead man himself, of course. You think the man was murdered?" His snapping eyes took in my clothes, from my unconventional split skirt to my plain black straw hat. "Where do you come from?" he said. "It must have been quite the place, as you've developed the habit of seeing murders around every corner." He took out a little notebook and pencil very similar to the doctor's, and looked at me expectantly. "Well? I'll need the full address of your former residence. After the stunt pulled by that man out there, I think it behooves me to pay closer attention to every person popping up in our neighborhood."

Blast Bertie and his investigative ardor, promoting me to the rank of Watson just to amuse himself. The situation was unfolding exactly as I'd feared. Leaving the woodwork to stand in the spotlight was well and good for those without a past, but Bertie should have known it would turn the screws on me.

"Walsall," I said, feeling a sense of defeat, and I gave the address.

"You were living there up till the time you came to Pelgren Vale? Six months ago?" he asked, scribbling with extreme deliberation.

"Yes," I said, but the man noticed my slight hesitation. As Bertie had said, I was rubbish at poker.

"I shall check this, Miss Cobb, and get a full account of your activities in Walsall," he said, tapping the pencil on the notebook page. "Sensationalism might be the thing in Walsall —all the cities and newspapers seem to offer nothing but sensationalism these days—but the Vale is full of good, quiet, respectable folk. And we don't take kindly to rabble-rousers. Especially those without evidence."

"I have evidence," I blurted. "Evidence that someone disliked the Major well enough to try to harm him." Bertie would not be pleased, as he had wanted to keep the broken-bit investigation to himself, but my dander was up and I was rapidly running out of anything to lose.

"The evidence of your own questionable eyes? Or something more solid?"

"Lord Byerley wasn't exactly accurate when he said the stallion's bridle broke. It was the bit that broke."

"Really, Miss Cobb—"

"Someone used one of my files on that bit. Filed the center joint until it was weak enough to break at the slightest pressure. Even if the Major had succeeded in mounting Brioso, the bit would've broken during his ride and he would've fallen. I can show you the file marks on the bit—and there's blood on the file. I think the person cut his hand while doing the job."

The mention of blood gave the big man pause, no doubt awakening that hound-like instinct present in every officer of the law. "Blood, you say?"

"Yes. I can show you." I crossed over to the corner cabinet. Perhaps, if he became interested in new evidence of foul play, he would forget all about nosing around my background.

The old hinges creaked in protest as I opened the cabinet and reached for the top of the ledger. My fingers found only the smooth leather cover. I stared and wrenched open the second door for more light, but it was quite clear that the file and the bit pieces were gone. Diving in to the elbow produced nothing but dusty fingertips. The bit and file had been removed.

I turned back to Sergeant Harrison, my hands empty but my mind full—full of Byerley's shifty nature, his catlike slinking and quick retreat from the drawing room that morning.

"Well?" the sergeant said, one heavy eyebrow aggressively cocked.

"They're not there," I said weakly. "I put the broken bit and the bloody file in that cabinet—"

"Ferreting away evidence, eh? A bad move, Miss Cobb. Moving evidence around. Makes one look amateurish at best, quite guilty at worst."

"Then why would I be telling you about it? Just a moment." I crossed to my tool bag, which was now resting on the floor at the foot of the long table. Someone had moved the bag, and the bridle—I raised my eyes to Brioso's rack and saw his bridle hanging neatly there with a different, intact bit buckled into the straps. An old set of broken reins lay carefully folded over the bridle. Cursing under my breath, I heaved the tool bag onto the table and glanced inside. The file was there, stuffed into one of the inside pockets, but as I gingerly lifted it out, I already knew what I would see. No blood marred its silver surface. In the cheerful sunlight slanting down from the high windows, the file gleamed with a cleanliness it hadn't known for years.

The sergeant took it from me, gave it a cursory glance, then snorted.

"Someone must have washed it," I said, but I knew how ridiculous that sounded.

"Perhaps so, perhaps so. Or perhaps you've imagined again that you saw something no one else saw, for the second time in one day! Really, Miss Cobb. I appreciate that a woman of your," glancing again at my clothes, "your questionable means would wish to render yourself indispensable to a wealthy widow. And prove the usefulness of your skills with bits and bridles and saddles. Solving a crime with those skills would certainly impress your new neighbors, what? But let me give you a word of advice." He leaned toward me with a menacing light in his beady eyes. "Leave the crime solving, and the crime spotting, to the professionals! Sensationalism won't sell in Pelgren Vale. And neither will your saddlery skills if you persist in creating these dangerous fantasies. Desist, Miss Cobb. Leave well enough alone. I shall have my eye on you."

He marched to the door, and then paused and turned back. "A bit of friendly advice, since I've encountered women with wild imaginations before, and I'd like to save us both a bit of time. You'll probably find a thousand items on this estate capable of making three little lines, and a hundred of them might look like weapons. But listen carefully. I don't want to hear about them. I'm a busy man, and I would need more evidence than the suspicions of a dodgy interloper from Walsall!" With one last reproachful glare, he huffed out of the room.

2 O

INJUSTICES AND WHAT
TO DO ABOUT THEM

"Not the brightest thing you've ever done, old girl," Bertie said, giving the kind of crooked, exaggerated yawn that only a horse can give. "I thought we agreed to keep the 'bit bit' to ourselves."

The stable was bathed in the soft gold and lengthening shadows of evening, and a delicate breeze whispered through Bertie's stall, no doubt teasing him with tales of dewy grass and drowsy thistles. The old boy had been shut up all day. After learning about Bertie's early morning escape, Fletcher had been very reluctant to turn him out again.

"Keep him in a stall till evenin', Miss Cobb," he had said. "Best not chance him gettin' loose again for a few hours at least. Not sure her ladyship could handle the sound of runnin' hooves, the state she's in."

The airy stable was a welcome change to the close atmosphere of the tack room, where I had spent the afternoon stitching away under Treacle Tart's resentful glare. Once the Major's body had been carted away, Lady Chedington made it abundantly clear that tomorrow's séance would go forward as planned, which meant that finishing the saddle was "vital, my dear! Absolutely vital!" I didn't mind. The calming texture of old leather under my fingertips was just the balm I needed after my bruising interview with Sergeant Harrison. As far as I was concerned, the sooner I finished the hideous thing, the sooner Bertie and I could head for home. But I was keeping this last thought to myself, as I was fairly certain the big horse didn't share my eagerness to part ways with Becketts.

"You were the one convinced we should declare murder from the mountaintops," I said to him. "How was I to know Byerley had managed to wash the file and rearrange the bridle? And it was Byerley, you know."

"Yes, the languid lord was the only person to saunter through here before the stable lad showed up. Byerley has a remarkably soft step. I wonder if lords are taught to be furtive in childhood?"

We heard a light whinny and a snort from somewhere farther down the aisle. As all but two horses had been turned out for the day, there was no question which horse had made the sound.

"Not that I have an abundance of love for that silly stallion," Bertie said, "but it does seem rather harsh to keep the chap locked up around the clock. At least I possess the reasoning skills to understand why I'm stuck in a cell, and the brains to keep myself occupied. But Brioso's probably spent months puzzling over why the grass is always greener on the other side of the fence. And that one can never be solved, just like the tree falling in the forest—"

"Unlike you," I interrupted, "he seems to enjoy a stall. He was happily dozing when I walked past. I've never met a stallion so lazy. And Lady Chedington said she won't stand for him to be turned out as he could 'escape and murder all the neighbors.'"

"Miss Olivia hasn't decided what to do with the poor fellow, then?"

I shrugged, and the big horse glowered down his nose at me.

"Harriet, have you even been up to the Hall today? You're supposed to be nosing out clues. I'm imprisoned and obviously can't, but I should have thought you'd at least try to work your way into the thick of things."

"I had to finish the saddle," I said indignantly. "And yes, I went up to the Hall. Once. To get a dish of cream for Treacle Tart. He was locked in the tack room with me all afternoon, and he has a very expressive face. He seems to consider the whole business my fault."

"Ah. And how did he take the olive branch?"

"He sniffed the cream like a sommelier sniffing wine and then dove in without giving me another look. But I left the tack room feeling slightly less reviled."

"Congratulations. And kitchens are splendid places to pick up gossip. I don't suppose you heard anything while you were begging cream off the cook?"

I considered for a moment. I had no wish to encourage Bertie's investigation, but the poor boy had been locked up all day and I probably owed him something. "Mrs. Granger told me that Miss Olivia has been moping about all day. Very prettily moping. Mrs. Granger said 'the young gentleman is pushin' her to sell him the stallion'—I think we can safely assume she meant Byerley—'the other one is pushin' her to keep him, an' says he'll help her make a go of the business'— that has Langford's gallantry all over it—and 'her ladyship is pushin' her to destroy the horse.' No great surprise there."

Bertie snorted in disgust. "And the sergeant? Any news on which way the wind of the law is blowing?"

I shook my head. "Sergeant Harrison isn't likely to send me any telegrams," I said.

Wrinkles appeared above Bertie's eyes. "Having no great love for horses himself, he may come around to Lady Chedington's point of view and advise Brioso be destroyed. Little Miss Olivia might hold out for a short time, but I doubt she has enough iron in her spine to refuse a direct order from the law, if the law decides Brioso is a danger to society. Best keep your ear to the ground on that one."

I squared my shoulders, stiffening my spine and my resolution. "Come nightfall, I don't intend my ear to be anywhere near Becketts. I shall be in my own bed tonight, and the only thing in my ear will be the sound of crickets. And the sound of you, munching grass in your pasture." I threw in that last bit rather hopefully, thinking that a mention of his home pasture might soften him up. It did not.

"We can't leave," he said, his ears flattening.

"There's nothing more for us here, Bertie. We have nothing more to contribute. I told the sergeant what I knew, and you know where that led. Byerley plans to keep poking at me until I deflate like a punctured balloon, and poking at you until you finally tell him off. And no matter how many expletives you use, he'll be very pleased to hear you speak. Continuing our little investigation will only raise eyebrows—and questions. I'm just the saddler. As I see it, the only real responsibility I've ever had to Becketts was to restore a saddle for a séance. The saddle is finished, so we're free to leave."

Bertie looked at me thoughtfully. "Why did you become a saddler?"

"What?"

"Your career choice. Why become a saddler? Surely there were easier pursuits."

I eyed him suspiciously. The horse was obviously leading me down some path of his own, and I was loathe to follow him until I could see the footing. "Leatherwork was the only thing I was ever good at," I said. "My Victorian childhood was full of needlework and horses. When I found I had to support myself, saddlery work combined those skills quite nicely."

"But you told me something else about your Victorian childhood," he said. "You told me that you once read an article about the cruelty of tight bearing-reins on carriage horses. The habit of fastening carriage horses' heads unnaturally high in the name of fashion. You said you went down to your bene-factor's stable and removed all the bearing reins from all the harnesses. Buried them in the back field, I think you said. To be sure they would never be used again."

I looked at him mutely. I still remembered the feel of the shovel, the feel of satisfaction as I looked at the damp earth where the straps were buried, and the feel of the Viscount's cane when my unladylike behavior was discovered.

"Do you think everyone who read that article did the same?" Bertie said. "Not likely. You told me that story as a silly little anecdote of your childhood, but I found it rather telling. Even at an early age, you were the type of person to notice injustice to horses."

"The Viscount's horses were always blamed for things that weren't their fault," I said. "Anyone could have seen that. They sometimes stumbled while pulling the carriage, couldn't get their balance because their necks were cinched up so high. Sometimes they went down because of it, and all they got was the sharp side of the lash. Yes, I suppose that little sense of injustice probably went into my desire to be a saddler."

Bertie's eyes grew bright. "And when I first met you in Wolverhampton, dressed as you were, I knew at once that you were that rare thing, a person who not only noticed injustice but would also do something about it."

I straightened up and went to the bars of the stall, craning my neck to look both ways down the aisle. Empty. I settled back against the stall wall. If anyone was sidling around the stable, this was not a discussion I wished them to hear. "In Wolverhampton," I whispered, "dressing as a man—living as a man—I didn't do it out of any crusading interest. It was purely mercenary. I learned in the Walsall factories that men were promoted and women were not—"

"A grave injustice, that."

"Yes. But my decision to go to Wolverhampton and live as a man, it wasn't a social statement, it was all about money. Where there is horse racing, there is money, and I followed the money to Wolverhampton, where a female saddler would have been laughed off the track. I did what I had to do to earn a living. It was all about padding my pocketbook, nothing more noble."

"And then you put that pocketbook on the line to rescue a certain handsome gray horse from a life of servitude." The corners of his heavy muzzle lifted with satisfaction. "Saving another horse from injustice."

I smiled faintly at him. I could have said, *But you weren't just another horse. You were a friend by that time, and I didn't want to part with you. It was as much about me as it was about you.* Instead, I said, "Well, the next time I need a little pick-me-up, I'll ask you to tell me the story of what a selfless creature I was in Wolverhampton. Don't forget, Bertie, I also profited quite nicely from our little gamble."

He gave a long snort, which could have been a sigh. "What

we have before us now, Harriet, is the ultimate injustice against a horse. Brioso may be destroyed for a crime he didn't commit. Such a precedent in Pelgren Vale—our new home, in case you forgot—makes me a bit jittery. So jittery, in fact, that I might not be comfortable staying in the Vale."

I stared at him in dismay. "But . . . we can't move again!"

"Then it's time for you to reach deep within yourself and find the little girl that ripped all the bearing-reins off the Viscount's harnesses. It's up to us to solve this thing, and probably save that silly stallion's life." His eyes became suddenly sly. "Unless you don't think you're a match for Byerley."

I pushed myself off the wall where I had been lounging. "I can handle Byerley," I said, with a little more confidence than I felt.

The big horse didn't waste a second. He knew capitulation when he heard it. "I've been considering that," he said, "and I think it may be time for me to have a chat with that self-satisfied lord."

"But that's exactly what he wants!"

"Exactly. And considering the transactional nature of the titled classes, I believe he may be ripe for a bit of quid pro quo. A hostage exchange, if you will."

"Tell me," I said, and he did.

COW-EYED POETS

"LET IT COME ABOUT ORGANICALLY," Bertie said, after divulging his idea. "Don't track him down. Wait until chance brings you together, and be sure to secure all of your hostages before bringing him to me. I'm sure you can find him slinking about later tonight. But at the present moment, you need to go in for your evening feeding."

"What?"

"You shall attend dinner in the Hall. To keep an eye on everyone, see how they're handling the death. It's bound to be uncomfortable—"

"You think so?" I said icily.

"—and uncomfortable situations are the most telling. People give away the most when they are uncomfortable. All you have to do is find another wounded hand, and viola! The mystery of the broken bit is solved. There's your warm-up."

"Warm-up?"

"Warm-up to solving the actual murder. Remember, the person who filed that bit isn't necessarily the person who thumped the man in the head."

"Byerley is still my favorite on both counts, though you seemed quite cozy with him today."

"No use antagonizing our antagonist," Bertie said, arching his dappled neck. "Especially when there's sugar in the offing. And besides, his lordly face looked as shocked as the rest when you said your piece about the head wound."

"By that measuring stick, none of them did it," I said. "And why would he have washed the file and fiddled with the bridle if he wasn't trying to cover something up?"

"Perhaps he was covering for someone else. What about your acolytes? The young women? I don't suppose you tracked down Miss Olivia to find out what 'very brave thing' she did last night?"

"No," I said. "I'll corner her tonight. And the cook said Miss Seyward was shut up in her room all day, recovering from her faint."

"She's a dark horse, that one," Bertie said thoughtfully. "But we must consider motive. You told me the Major was a bit of a lech toward her—"

"More than a bit."

"And probably had been all week. The young lady had reason to resent him, and time for that resentment to build. Then there's Miss Olivia. She'd been under his fiery gaze all week, trying and failing to 'bump' a horse. He was exceptionally rude, and as every horse knows, when a spoiled filly gets jostled, someone is going to pay."

"I don't think so," I said. "At least, I don't think Miss Olivia could keep quiet about anything big. She says whatever comes into her pretty head. Who else have you got?"

"There's the poet. He didn't want Miss Olivia to ride in that gala, and it seems the Major was rather keyed up that she should. After your little bit of encouragement, that is."

I glared at him. "That's hardly a reason to kill a man."

"Unless the poet is in love with the girl. Who knows what passions lurk in the heaving breast of a poet? His concern for her safety could have pushed his gallantry over the edge. Does he go cow-eyed when he sees her? That would be something to watch for at dinner."

I sighed. "Cow-eyed poet. Check. Anything else I should be watching for, while I struggle to remember which fork to use?"

"Lady Chedington didn't want her to ride the stallion either."

"Oh come, Bertie. Can you see that fluttery lady handling a corpse, and Brioso—a horse that terrifies her? Or any horse? And besides, she hired the Major, so she could just as easily have fired him."

"Well, there's only one other suspect, and he won't be joining you for dinner."

"Fletcher?"

"Fletcher. He is in charge of Becketts again." He looked hard at me through the gathering shadows. "There's motive enough to butter your bread." His big head swung suddenly toward the stable aisle, ears pricked.

There was a giggle from somewhere down the aisle, a very pretty giggle, unmistakably Miss Olivia's. Then came a voice, deep and melodious, the kind of voice that could handle a line of Keats without sounding at all sarcastic.

"I shall need an answer soon," Langford said.

I stepped carefully toward the bars and looked down the aisle, but the angle blocked my view. I could just see the lavender edge of Miss Olivia's skirt as she stood somewhere near the tack room, and I couldn't see Langford at all.

"Things will be much simpler," he continued. "Just say the

word, and I'll lift these responsibilities from you. You'll never even have to look at a horse again if you don't want to."

"I don't know," Miss Olivia said. "I mean, I think I'd like to look at a horse again. They're not bad to look at. A bit painful to ride, but not bad to look at."

Langford spoke again, and there was a hint of exasperation in his voice. "Of course, you may look at them all day if you wish. I was just trying to say that you won't have to make any decisions about the horses because I will handle all that."

"Alright," she said uncertainly.

"Alright?" he said. "Does that mean what I think it means?"

"I mean, it doesn't mean yes," she said, giggling again, but it sounded a rather nervous giggle. "I need to think it over a while longer. You won't be angry?"

"Not at all." The warmth had returned to his voice.

"See you at dinner, then," she said. The skirt whirled and moved out of view as her light steps receded.

I looked at Bertie and whispered, "Offering to help her with the horse business, just as Mrs. Granger said."

"Or something more momentous." His long gray ears were thoughtful. "It's a shame we couldn't get a look at his face. I wonder if there was a bovine expression."

I shook my head. "He didn't sound cow-eyed."

Footsteps came down the aisle toward us, and I scurried behind Bertie. If Langford noticed me in Bertie's stall, he would know I had been eavesdropping. I didn't even have a brush or a pitchfork to explain my presence in the stall.

Bertie lifted his front hoof, the one nearest me. "You're checking my shoe," he informed me, and I grabbed the hoof and leaned over it in an attitude of intense scrutiny. At first I thought the footsteps had passed the stall, but then I heard them falter and stop.

"Why, Miss Cobb!"

I straightened up, releasing Bertie's hoof. "Mr. Langford! You startled me. I thought everyone was up at the Hall. Lady Chedington's fondness for drinks before dinner, and all that."

His finely-lashed eyes narrowed imperceptibly, but his sensitive poet's lips relaxed into a smile. "I should have known you'd be down here tending to your horse. You're a remarkably attentive horsewoman. No problems with that hoof, I hope?"

"No. I thought he had loosened a shoe in that mad gallop this morning, but everything's tip-top."

"You have a fine horse," he said, gazing through the bars and running his eyes over Bertie's topline. The horse arched his big neck proudly, as he always did when he was the subject of admiration. "I wish I could have seen him catch Brioso this morning. I suppose Byerley remarked on the chase? Was he surprised that your horse could so easily catch the stallion?"

"Surprised?"

"Surprised that your older horse could match Brioso's speed," he said, and Bertie deflated a little at the word *older*. "He has a very high opinion of Brioso's speed and stamina, Byerley does. I thought perhaps he mentioned something after seeing the stallion run."

"He didn't mention anything," I said. "But Brioso had a significant handicap."

"Ah. Quite. A bit of dead weight." We were silent for an awkward moment and then Langford said, "Keep an eye on Byerley, Miss Cobb. He's quite used to acquiring whatever he sets his sights on—whatever horse he deems worthy of his stables at Ashwold Abbey. With the endless resources of his inheritance, he rarely fails to get what he wants. He's been obsessed with Brioso for a while now, but I noticed him looking at your horse overlong today. Take care, Miss Cobb. He may wish to steal your mount out from under you."

I smiled. "I think I can handle Byerley."

His forest-glade eyes crinkled with warmth. "You know, I rather think you can. And what of the séance? Are you prepared to handle the whims and vagaries of the spirit world?"

"I hadn't planned on staying for it."

"I believe Lady Chedington is counting on your presence."

I stared. "I never agreed to it. Actually, she never even invited me—"

"So you never had the chance to refuse," he said, grinning. "Her ladyship has a way of roping people into things without actually extending an invitation, because people have a way of turning down her invitations. She's found it's much more effective to just say, 'Ah, but I was sure you would attend!'"

"But . . . I'm just the saddler," I spluttered.

"You're much more than that, Miss Cobb," he said. He spoke solemnly, but his eyes twinkled. "You're number seven."

I blinked at him.

"It seems there's something wrong with the number six, did you know that?" he continued. "If you don't attend the séance tomorrow, there will be six people including Madame Itovsky. Apparently six is a very unlucky number, but seven is a different story altogether. Lady Chedington declared that you will be there to make a seventh and 'stand in the gap between us and the devil,' I believe she said."

Had we been alone, Bertie would've been wickedly grinning at me, but as it was, he contented himself by muttering, "I always said your black hat makes you look like a vicar."

I sighed and cocked an eyebrow at Langford. "So it's the

old, 'Thank you for fixing the saddle, and now could you stick around to ward off the devil' gag?"

He smiled apologetically but his eyes were still dancing. A poet with a sense of humor was a rare creature indeed. "And you probably thought life in Pelgren Vale would be boring," he said. "Consider yourself forewarned. Shall I see you at dinner?"

"I don't suppose it matters that I haven't been formally invited," I said.

He grinned. "I think we can safely assume that a place has already been set for you." With a nod, he made as if to continue down the aisle, then stopped and turned back.

"Have you seen Fletcher? I need to ask him a question about this." He lifted his hand, which had been obscured by the front of the stall, revealing a heavy riding whip. The handle end was bare except for narrow piece of threaded metal. It was the Major's whip. Bertie snorted, moving swiftly up beside me to stare through the bars. "I'm looking for the handle attachment," Langford continued. "It's a stirrup cup, shaped like a fox's head, and it screws onto the whip—here." He pointed to the threaded end. "I don't suppose you've seen it laying around anywhere?"

"No," I said, feeling a little breathless, and then I added somewhat idiotically, "That's the Major's whip."

"Oh, the Major was carrying it around, but I believe it actually belonged to Sir Algernon. Lady Chedington wasn't pleased to see the Major with it but decided to let sleeping dogs lie. The stable lad found the whip in Brioso's stall this morning while he was mucking out. It was buried in the straw, but I have yet to find the stirrup cup attachment."

"Why is he looking for it?" Bertie murmured.

"Why are you looking for it?" I said.

"Lady Chedington has been asking for it," Langford said. "She's been on the rampage, gathering up anything of value—anything with gold, silver, or jewels—saying that she will need to pawn it all to keep Becketts afloat. An exaggeration, I'm sure, but if it makes her feel better . . . The cup is only pewter, but she said it has tiny rubies for eyes, which could bring a good price. You're sure you haven't—Ah!" He looked down the aisle. "Just the man I wanted to see. Fletcher!"

The old groom came into view and limped his way over. His bad leg seemed to be causing him more pain than before, after a long day tending to the horses.

"Mr. Langford, Miss Cobb," he said, nodding respectfully.

"Have you found that stirrup cup, Fletcher?" Langford said, waving the end of the whip. "Lady Chedington is very keen on having it. I think it would put her mind at ease to add it to her stash of assets. Did you happen across it? It may have been in Brioso's stall, somewhere in the straw."

Fletcher looked sourly at the waving end of the whip. "No, Mr. Langford," he said. "Haven't seen hide nor hair of it."

"You'll bring it to me, if you find it?"

Fletcher nodded slowly, his dull expression never changing.

"Good man," Langford said. "And I'll see you at dinner, Miss Cobb." He bowed with a gallant flourish and strode off in the direction of the Hall.

The old groom snorted as he watched him go, then turned to me and nodded toward Bertie. "Got a few more things to finish up, Miss Cobb, but I can turn him out in the meadow. You best not be late for dinner, an' all that."

"Thank you, Fletcher," I said, "though I'd rather stay in the stable with you."

His worn face creased into a smile and he moved off down the aisle, whistling softly to himself.

I whirled to Bertie. "We need to find that stirrup cup," I hissed.

"Yes, but Harriet—"

"The whip was in Brioso's stall, so the cup is probably in there too. Buried in the straw—maybe Tom missed it. I can do some digging before I go up to dinner, though I may reek of manure after, but that will serve Lady Chedington right for wanting a saddler at dinner—"

"Slow down, old girl, I—"

"That fox's head, swung at the end of such a heavy whip, hitting that man's skull in just the right place . . . I'll need to see the thing to know for sure, but I'll bet that fox's snout is just the shape to leave three little lines—"

"Harriet!" Bertie's eyes were blazing with impatience, his nostrils flared. "I'm trying to tell you that I already know who has the stirrup cup."

I stared at him. "You do?"

"You're not going to be pleased."

"Who."

Bertie snorted. "Fletcher walked through here this afternoon, right past my cell, whistling a little tune and tossing something from hand to hand. I didn't know it was meant to attach to a whip, but I thought it an odd thing for him to be carrying around. It was a metal stirrup cup with a fox's head."

A FORMAL DINNER

"HAVE YOU A BROTHER, MISS COBB?" Byerley said, gazing down the table at me.

I paused with my spoon in the air, then carefully lowered it back into my bowl of lobster bisque. That single spoonful had already cost me a bit of consternation—I had very little appetite, as the circulation in my stomach was being far outpaced by the circulation in my brain. In short, I was thinking furiously. Fletcher had the stirrup cup, and he didn't want anyone to know he had it. At least, he didn't want Langford to know.

"Don't confront Fletcher now," Bertie had said in the stable. "You'll need to be at dinner with the rest, as expected. Plenty of time to drill into him later, when there's no chance of being interrupted by the others coming to fetch you for dinner."

"Lying about that cup doesn't necessarily mean he was the one to use it," I'd replied. I was becoming something of a last-ditcher in my desire for Fletcher to be innocent. "Perhaps he saw something or knows something and wants to keep the evidence safe until he can give it to the police."

"Perhaps," Bertie said. "Or perhaps it's not the murder weapon after all and he's just a common thief, stealing those little rubies for himself. Anything's possible. Go up to dinner and look for a wounded hand so we can put that first mystery to bed. Watch and listen for other clues. The sergeant fellow told you he would need more proof than an object capable of making three little lines."

I was considering these things in the dark-paneled dining room of Becketts Hall, my eyes floating absently around the table, but looking directly at Byerley had been a mistake. He had caught my eye and commenced his attack.

"You must have a brother in Wolverhampton," he continued. "I remember a man at the track who bore a startling resemblance to yourself."

"Oh, really, Byerley!" tittered Lady Chedington, swatting a hand in the air. "No lady wants to hear such things! A man that resembles Miss Cobb, indeed!" She wagged a finger at him, a gesture of almost maternal disapprobation. "You always were one for speaking nonsense at table. Give us some of your other nonsense, dear boy, but leave out the men resembling women, or women resembling men." Lady Chedington had been using this familial tone toward Byerley all evening, and I couldn't decide whether it was that she wanted him as her son-in-law, or that she had already consumed an impressive amount of sherry.

"The likeness really is uncanny," drawled Byerley, ignoring his hostess and fixing his pale eyes on me. "The same dark eyebrows, the same nose, even the same chin. You have a brother in Wolverhampton, Miss Cobb. I'm certain of it."

I gazed coolly back at him across the table. If the young

lord was going to behave like a circling hawk, I was certainly not going to turn rabbity again. I knew him better now, knew his proclivity to poke and prod and pull the wings off flies, metaphorically speaking. I also knew that his desire to be in Bertie's pocket provided me some sort of protection.

"Sorry to disappoint," I said, "but I have no brother, in Wolverhampton or elsewhere." To emphasize the finality of my statement, I took a bite of soup and blithely chewed a rather tough morsel of lobster, keeping my eyes fixed on his the whole time. Bertie would've been proud.

Byerley smiled faintly. "I suppose you—"

"Speaking of racing," Langford interrupted, proving that chivalry was not entirely dead, "any news on who's to ride Rock Sand in the St. Leger?"

Byerley hesitated, considering me for another moment before deciding to give up the hunt. "Danny Maher, I should think," he said, turning to Langford. "Seems they're onto a good thing with that pair. Why would they change it up with the Triple Crown in sight?"

"Oh, come! Are the walls of your Ashwold Abbey so thick? You must be the only man in England that doesn't know the story. Maher had a bad spill last week. A young horse panicked and went through the rails. Put his shoulder out, Maher did, and they're trying to judge whether he'll be sound enough to ride in the St. Leger."

"If they were so keen on him riding the last leg of the Crown," Byerley said, slowly turning the stem of his wine glass, "they should have stopped him riding any other horses in the interim."

"Easy to say, but I'm sure Maher doesn't have the means to just stop riding," Langford said. "He's a self-made man. He doesn't have unlimited family resources."

Those last words sounded a bit caustic, and I curiously observed the two men as the discussion devolved into a heated and nonsensical debate. I had the pleasure of seeing two spots of high color come into Byerley's cheeks, and storm clouds settle on Langford's placid brow. There was obviously no love lost between the two.

Lady Chedington ate her soup with an air of resignation, probably regretting the odd seating arrangement. In a thinly-veiled ploy to separate Byerley from Miss Seyward's Rossetti allure, she'd put the men on one side of the table and the women on the other. Byerley and Miss Olivia were seated at Lady Chedington's right and left, then Langford and I, and then, to my left and pointedly without a partner, Miss Seyward. Flanked by the two girls, I'd thought it would be easy to snatch a glance at their palms, but in the normal use of table utensils, one's palms are rarely exposed.

I observed Miss Seyward between bites of soup. From the look of her, spending the day in bed hadn't helped the girl at all. She was nearly as pale as Byerley, dark eyebrows punctuating her face like ink on parchment. Gazing into the empty shadows across the table, she limply spooned her soup, paying no attention to the bickering men.

"Miss Seyward," I whispered, "are you quite alright?"

She turned her eyes to me, those lovely green eyes that had been so full of laughter the night before—now grayish and dull. "Fine," she said absently. "I'm just fine. Tired, that's all."

"Miss Cobb," Lady Chedington called down the table. "You haven't touched your Chablis. Perhaps you would prefer something sweeter? A nice Sauternes, no doubt. Peters!" she bellowed for the ancient butler. "Where is that silly man?"

At my right, Miss Olivia was unusually subdued, and I wondered about the difficulty of eating soup while maintaining such an attractive pout. The girl finished with glum determination and then settled back, watching the two men across the table.

"My money will be on Rock Sand, regardless of who rides him," Langford was saying.

"His odds are too short to please me," Byerley said, picking at the bread roll on his plate. "Rising Glass will bring a better return."

"By that logic, you should just put your money on Flotsam and be done with it." Langford's expression was cordial again, but his words were clipped. "That would be nicely in line with your preference for misfits. Speaking of which, were you or were you not riding a mule yesterday?"

"And you always prefer to bet on a sure thing," retorted Byerley, "but how has that turned out for you?" His silver eyes searched Langford's face. "Or perhaps you prefer the race to be rigged from the start," he said slowly.

"Why are there so many marine names in the race?" interrupted Miss Olivia. The two gentlemen looked at her, startled out of their tête-à-tête. "Flotsam, Rock Sand, Rising Glass," the girl continued, "they all remind me of the ocean. And if I were to choose, I would choose Rising Glass, because glass is the most beautiful form of sand."

There was silence for a moment and then Langford nodded. "I agree," he said, raising his glass. "To the most beautiful form of sand," he declared.

"Here, here," Byerley said, joining in with a sardonic smile, and the ominous cloud that had been hanging over the two men dissipated as the rest of us joined in the silly toast.

Lady Chedington smiled alternately at Byerley and her daughter as though the young lord's raised glass was a marriage proposal. Then her blissful blue eyes fell on the empty soup bowls, and she turned in her chair, craning her neck for the delinquent butler.

"Peters? We're ready for the—oh, bother!" She heaved herself up and marched toward the corridor, grabbing a silver handbell from the sideboard as she passed. In a moment, the air was filled with a cheerful row as Lady Chedington stuck her arm out the doorway and swung the bell with ragged determination.

"Father always said our home was not big enough to warrant electric bells," sighed Miss Olivia. "Much to Mother's annoyance. The old bell-pulls were removed during renovations a few years ago, so she's had to rely on that din ever since!"

Lady Chedington floated back to the table, rubbing her ear.

"There," she said. "Peters probably went for a lie down, but that was loud enough to rouse the dead." She gazed at her wine glass contemplatively. "Unless he actually *is* dead, of course. Bound to happen one of these days."

"May I ask you something about your horse, Miss Cobb?" Byerley said, giving me an angelic smile.

"No."

My stark response brought looks of surprise all around, but Lady Chedington swooped in with one of her exuberant laughs. "No! Quite right, my dear. No. Couldn't have said it better myself. Those animals were not to be mentioned in my presence ever again, yet the young gentlemen have been talking of nothing else! I find my mind flitting away to that monster in my stable. No horses, Byerley, if you please. You must tell us of motorcars instead, as I am dead set on acquiring one!"

"He's not a monster," Miss Olivia said.

"What was that, Olivia?" said her mother. "I believe that bell has made me half-deaf. Speak up, my dear."

"I said, Brioso is not a monster!" the girl said, this time at impressive volume.

In the moment of silence that followed there was a squeaking from the corridor, and Peters tottered gravely into the room. He was followed by Sarah, Lady Chedington's girl-of-all-work, pushing a wooden cart on wheels that were desperately in need of oiling.

"Nonsense, Olivia." Lady Chedington glared at her daughter. "You've always been afraid of him, even before he killed your father. When Algernon was first training the beast, you told me he pinned his ears at you—bared his teeth, stomped his hooves, and I don't know what else. But it sent you into palpitations, I remember that quite clearly."

Sarah was smartly removing the soup plates while also watching in trepidation as Peters delivered the main course, plate by quavering plate. I didn't blame her for being worried. The butler's gloved hands trembled with age, and the plates were piled high with heavy slices of meat.

"That was before I got to know him," Miss Olivia said, and her chin rose with a hint of defiance. "He's really quite a nice horse."

"Got to know... of what are you talking? You mean to say you used to be terrified of that beast, but today, after he's killed a second man, you think he's a nice horse? Really, Olivia. You know nothing about it. And nothing about horses."

Peters reached around my shoulder and wobbled a plate of lamb in front of my nose. The plate made achingly slow progress toward the table, and I let out a sigh of relief when it found terra firma instead of my lap.

"That's right," the girl said, her face blooming into angry pink. "I know nothing about horses. But who's fault is that? When I was afraid to ride all those years ago, you and Father were both convinced that I would never be any good with horses. You told me so. And I believed you! So I never really tried. But then Miss Cobb told us her stories, and I decided to—"

"Miss Cobb?" Lady Chedington said.

"Miss Cobb?" I said.

"Yes." Miss Olivia turned to me with a bright smile. "You told us so many interesting stories last night, about horses and saddles and bridles and bits, all the work you've done and all the horses you've known, it was so fascinating! Like a whole new country, a country that I've been living on the edge of but never entered. So I decided to enter it last night. After we left your room . . . I rode Brioso."

23

RESCUING A DAMSEL IN DISTRESS

"RODE THE STALLION!" exclaimed Lady Chedington, her face frozen in horror.

Peters was evidently tiring, and I heard him sigh deeply as he extended the last plate around Miss Seyward's shoulder. It hung in midair for a moment, and then it began to dip and topple. If she had been a fraction slower, Miss Seyward would have been wearing roast lamb and mint sauce, but her left hand shot out reflexively to grab the edge of the plate. She flinched, almost dropping the plate, but then her lips pressed into a firm white line and she lowered the plate to the table. As she released it, I caught a glimpse of dull red across the milky skin of her palm. The girl dropped her hand quickly into the folds of her skirt, but then she raised her eyes to mine, shame flooding her face. She knew that I had seen.

"I didn't actually ride him, ride him," Miss Olivia was saying. "But it was kind of riding, I guess. Viv came down to the stable with me, but I sent her to the tack room because I knew it was something I had to do alone. Just me and Brioso, you see?"

"Miss Cobb," whispered Miss Seyward, glancing fearfully around the table. The others were arrested by Miss Olivia's story, but Miss Seyward leaned close, her breath a delicate flutter against my face. "You know how I got that scratch on my hand, don't you." It wasn't a question, just a statement of dull certainty.

"Yes," I whispered back.

On my other side, Miss Olivia seemed to be relishing her story. "I was so afraid, entering his stall," she said, her voice dripping with dramatic tension. "He looked so tall, so power-ful, and I kept thinking of what he did to Father, and I could barely open the stall door, my hands were shaking so much."

Miss Seyward's whisper came again. "I didn't mean him to die, Miss Cobb, you must believe me." Her Rossetti eyes were fever-bright and tortured, and her words came tumbling out, soft and desperate. "It was just a silly trick. I thought the bit would break and he would have a little fall, but I didn't think he would be killed." Tears welled up, her face relaxing in the relief of her confession. In a moment, the floodgates would burst and everyone at the table would know her secret.

"Hush," I hissed, trying to channel Bertie's sternest expres-sion. "We'll discuss this later." The girl shut her mouth and the waterworks receded.

At the head of the table, Lady Chedington was gaping at her daughter. "You could have been killed, Olivia!"

"That's just it, Mother. I saw Brioso's eyes, and they were kind. Calm. Nothing like the hard, proud looks he used to give me. He just seemed . . . softer, somehow. And I went in. And he let me pet him and scratch his neck and walk all around him, and he just stood there. And I wasn't afraid anymore, because I could see he would never hurt me. So I found a bucket and turned it over, and I stepped up on it and flung myself over his back and wriggled and wriggled until I could get my leg over him. And then I was sitting on him, and he was fine and I was fine and the whole world was fine."

"Oohhh," Lady Chedington moaned, covering her face with her hands. "Bareback and astride! Olivia, this is hardly a story to share at dinner!"

"That's why I don't think he's a monster." Miss Olivia's eyes swept earnestly around the table. "He isn't. He's a sweet horse, a real gentleman, and the Major must have done something horribly wrong because Brioso wouldn't hurt a fly. And I don't think he should be punished for something he could never have meant to do."

Lady Chedington looked rather wrung-out. She took a mighty swig of her wine. "You were just lucky, my dear," she spluttered, reaching over to pat her daughter's hand. "You must let older, wiser heads decide what's to be done with that stallion. Perhaps he was only half-awake when you visited him. Or he was biding his time. Horses are devious creatures, and your little stunt does nothing to change the fact that the horse has killed two men. I believe Sergeant Harrison will recommend destroying him, for the safety of the neigh-borhood."

There was the loud scraping of a heavy chair sliding back, and suddenly Miss Seyward was on her feet. Her face was the color of slate, but she stood steadily enough, her delicate chin jutting out as though in defiance of some invisible foe. If ever there had been a tall and mighty rampart in human form, it was this woman.

"I have a confession to make," she announced. "It was my fault the Major died."

The air in the room seemed to disappear in a collective

gasp. I stared up at the girl, feeling suddenly lightheaded. What was the little fool doing?

"I went to the stable with Olivia last night, like she said, and she asked me to wait in the tack room so that she could be alone with Brioso. All the saddle and bridle racks are labeled, and I noticed that Brioso's bridle looked a little dusty." She paused, running a tongue across her dry lips.

I tried to corral my racing thoughts. The girl obviously thought that the broken bit was responsible for the Major's death. Was it possible that no one had told her—that she hadn't heard the results of the investigation? She had been in bed all day . . .

"I was just going to try cleaning and oiling the leather, because Miss Cobb's stories inspired me to take more interest in the finer points of horse tack, but then I . . . I did something that I'm so ashamed of. I didn't think it would cause any serious harm, but I—"

"You let Treacle Tart out of the tack room!" I said, jumping to my feet and nearly upsetting the table.

The girl blinked at me in surprise, a single tear running down one porcelain cheek. It would've make an excellent painting, if only an artist could've captured it. "Miss Cobb," she said, "don't try to protect me. I'm guilty, and I should pay for my actions."

"Yes, yes, I know you feel guilty about setting the cat free," I said, taking hold of her shoulder and pressing her down. She resisted for only a moment, then her knees gave way and she wilted into her chair. "You were frightened to admit it to her ladyship, were you not?" I babbled. "You knew she wanted that cat to stay in the tack room. But what's done is done, and I'm sure Lady Chedington will agree that there's no use crying over spilt milk, is there? Or spilt cream, in this case." I gave a giddy laugh and then, noticing that no one else was laughing, I hurried on. "Because it involves a cat. And he likes cream, you see? No harm done, really."

Everyone was staring up at me in wonder and confusion, and there was a curl to Byerley's thin lips, but I couldn't tell whether it was of scorn or amusement. From the look in his pale eyes, it seemed to be both.

"But I don't understand," Lady Chedington said, blinking down the table at us. "What does this have to do with the Major's death?"

"Miss Seyward has been in bed all day," I said. "No doubt she heard that the cat spooked the stallion. But she didn't hear the actual results of the investigation." I turned away from the others and stared hard at Miss Seyward, lifting my eyebrows for emphasis. "She didn't hear that the Major never even rode the stallion," I said, directly to her. "She didn't hear that he was dead *before* the cat spooked the horse and *before* the bit broke. He was hit in the head earlier. None of those other little things caused his mur—caused his death." I thumped back down into my chair, grabbed my wine glass and took a sustaining gulp, hoping that no one had noticed I'd almost said "murder."

"Oh, poor Viv!" Miss Olivia said, reaching across my plate of lamb to clasp Miss Seyward's hand. "You thought you were responsible? How horrible!"

"Yes, yes, it's quite regrettable," Lady Chedington said, frowning at Miss Seyward. She was probably regretting the attention the girl was getting. Miss Seyward's Rossetti face had been lovely in tragedy, but relief now transformed her into a creature of otherworldly beauty, eyes glistening and skin softly glowing. "You shouldn't have let that cat out, my dear," her ladyship continued, "but, as Miss Cobb said, there's no real harm done. Perhaps the cat will even venture out onto the road, which is used by more and more motorcars every day, and then who knows what luck we may have!"

24

THE DIFFICULTY OF
MAKING A HAY WISP

"Miss Cobb," Miss Seyward said, floating to my side as I moved down the great, echoing corridor. "I want to explain. I—"

"Not here," I said sharply, glancing behind us. After an awkward finish to dinner, Lady Chedington had sent the young gentlemen to the study, where they could "make use of Algernon's cigars and brandy, which I'm sure are already quite stale." Neither man seemed eager to spend another moment in each other's company, but as the woman immediately began lecturing Miss Olivia, the two men chose the lesser of two evils and stalked off toward the study.

"I need to check on my horse, Miss Seyward, and you shall come with me," I said, and we made our way through the maze of horse paintings and stepped out into the night. The full moon hung above us, broad and benevolent, transforming the meek little lawn into a grand, silvery carpet.

"Oh!" Miss Seyward's breath caught when we reached the meadow gate, and I turned to see her gazing across at Bertie. "He's beautiful," she breathed, and she was right.

Framed by a filagree of black and silver weeds, the big gray horse was glowing. His ever-lightening coat, such a worry to him as it faded with the years, seemed to reflect the moonlight.

"He doesn't look like a normal horse, somehow," the girl said. "He looks as though he should have wings. Oh, that sounds silly."

"Not silly at all," I said, and we approached him through the tall grass and weeds. I had often thought the same, watching Bertie from the window of my cottage. There was a beyondness about him on moonlit nights—a hint of something other, a gleam in his coat that had none of the earthiness of other horses. He liked to joke that I was older than he—and of course I was, as it was ridiculous to think a horse could live to forty-five—but he had never actually told me his age. Looking at him now, I wouldn't have been surprised to learn that his life stretched all the way back to ancient Greece. Standing still and proud, Bertie could've been carved out of marble by Praxiteles himself.

"I don't know what made me do it, Miss Cobb," Miss Seyward said. She reached up a tentative hand to stroke Bertie's neck, and the old boy rolled an inquiring eye at me.

"Yes, you do," I said.

She hesitated, then nodded. "Yes, I suppose I do. It's just . . . well, Miss Cobb, I didn't grow up on a grand estate like this. My parents were very poor, so they sent me to live as companion to my great-uncle. It was a man's house, with my uncle's male acquaintances and business clients coming and going. Some of those men bothered me. They thought they could take advantage because I was poor and my uncle was inattentive. I've been told I'm pretty . . ."

"An understatement," Bertie said.

"You're beautiful," I said.

"But my looks have brought me nothing but strife, Miss Cobb," she said. "In those days, I'd have traded my looks in a heartbeat for a shred of autonomy. It was better when I went away to school. When I left my uncle's house, I told myself I'd never let a man make me feel small again. And I thought those days were behind me. Then the Major . . . well, the Major brought the old days back, and he made me feel small with his leering and grinning and suggestions."

"Repugnant man," Bertie agreed, "but is she trying to say she killed him or she just fiddled with that bit?"

"Does that soft little whinnying sound mean he likes me?" Miss Seyward said, eyeing Bertie uncertainly.

"I think he does," I said, "and I don't blame you for that little prank with the bit. It was only natural, after the way the Major behaved toward you."

"It wasn't just about me, though!" she said. "I wouldn't want you to think I did it all for revenge. I mean, I am a rather selfish creature. At least . . . at least, I hold tight to lovely things when I find them. When I went away to school and met Olivia, she was so lovely and kind to me, she didn't care at all that I didn't come from money. She stopped the other girls bullying me, just gave them one of her proud looks and a few clever words and stopped them in their tracks."

"Clever words?" Bertie said. "Miss Olivia has been holding out on us."

"She made me feel like I could be someone—we have dreams together, you know. We plan to start a business together someday. We don't know what it will be, but we're on the lookout for it. Then we shall be independent, I from my uncle and she from her mother. And so . . . I was worried about Olivia, Miss Cobb. For all her practice, she isn't much of a rider—"

Bertie whuffled a laugh.

"—and I was sure that if she rode Brioso, I mean truly rode him, she would get thrown or trampled or something worse. And I couldn't bear the thought of losing my one true friend. But I knew if the Major took a little tumble off Brioso, Olivia would see how dangerous the horse is. And when my eyes fell on that bridle, I suddenly remembered the story you told us last night, and that's what gave me the idea to use the file on that bit."

"The story I told you?" I said, frowning.

"Yes, when you were with us last night, you told us those funny stories about your career. Your story gave me the idea."

Blast Byerley's good whiskey. I must have let my mouth run away with me.

"You said you warned a jockey that the joint in his bit was wearing too thin," she said, "but he was a proud fellow and said he hadn't time to switch bridles. And then the bit broke during the race, and he didn't fall off, but the horse ran round and round and took ages to catch, and when it was finally caught the jockey slithered off like a wet noodle and said, 'Cobb! Where's Cobb? That saddler's bad luck, an' no mistake!'"

I closed my eyes and sighed. "Yes, now I remember telling you that story."

Bertie nudged me. "Well done, old girl! The story that launched a thousand ships. Now think back. Did you tell anyone a story about thumping someone with the business end of a stirrup cup? That might give us a clue as to who our murderer is."

I glared at him, then turned back to Miss Seyward. "What's

done is done, and I don't think we need to reveal any of this to anyone else. The bit didn't cause injury to the Major, but telling your story might cause injury to you—embarrassment and misunderstanding, or worse."

"Oh, thank you Miss Cobb!" she breathed, eyes shining in the moonlight. "I know I don't deserve—"

"Hallooooo!" came a voice, light and cheerful, followed by a giggle. We turned to see Miss Olivia traipsing through the rough undergrowth. "The two of you abandoned me to Mother's remonstrances! Have no fear, I don't hold it against you. I escaped as quickly as I could. I knew I'd find you down here, as Miss Cobb is always escaping to her horse, and I can't say I blame her. When I was with Brioso last night, I hadn't a thought for anything else in the world! Being with a horse seems a remarkably good way to empty one's mind. I feel in need of a little mind-emptying myself at the moment. And look what I brought!"

The girl came to a breathless halt, dropping an object into the grass before us. It was the old wooden grooming box from the tack room, full of brushes, combs, and other grooming tackle.

"I thought you could teach us the proper way to groom a horse," she said to me. "And look!" She lifted a lumpy, ragged thing out of the box and held it proudly aloft for our appraisal. "I made it myself," she said.

"It's lovely," Miss Seyward said uncertainly.

"What is it?" I said, looking skeptically at the bristly mass. It looked like a double-handful of hay wadded up into an untidy ball.

Bertie was a little quicker on the uptake. "Good heavens," he said, staring at the thing in horrified fascination. "Don't let her touch me with that, Harriet."

"It's a hay wisp," Miss Olivia said. "I followed the instructions in *The Illustrated Manual of Horse Care for Young Ladies*. That book said it should be used on the muscles 'with a pounding, sweeping motion, to stimulate the circulation and bring a shine to the coat.' It didn't turn out exactly like the illustration, and the book said it's better used by men since young ladies lack the strength, but that just made me mad. I'm strong and I'm game to try it. Your horse is quite calm, is he not, Miss Cobb?"

She stepped toward Bertie, brandishing the hay wisp like a weapon, and the horse receded like a wave from the shore.

"I'll take that," I said, reaching over to pluck the shaggy thing from her hand. "I applaud your initiative, and it's not bad for your first go, but these are hard to make from an illustration. Better ask Fletcher to teach you."

"I'll do that, Miss Cobb," she replied, and the two girls rummaged in the brush box for more conventional grooming tools.

Fletcher . . . I looked over at Bertie and found him watching me.

"You'll need to track him down tonight," he said, as though reading my thoughts.

I nodded.

Seeing the young ladies armed with sensible, non-threatening brushes, Bertie came forward to accept their ministrations. I showed them how to use firm, quick strokes, working gradually from the neck along the body to the haunches, and at last the horse declared they were, "becoming quite skilled. Especially Miss Olivia, she really puts her heart and soul into it."

"Do you think Mr. Langford knows how to make a hay

wisp?" Miss Olivia asked, swiping masterfully at Bertie's haunches.

"I'd assume so," I said. "I think young boys are taught the skill when they're taught to ride."

"And girls are only taught to sit atop a horse and look marketable," she sighed. "Well. I hope Mr. Langford knows how to do it. He proposed to me, you know, and I don't think I'd like to marry a man who can't make a decent hay wisp."

25

A MEDDLING SADDLER

"Proposed?" I said.

"Marry?" Miss Seyward said.

"I knew it!" Bertie said.

Miss Olivia's eyes faltered, and she went back to her brushing with renewed vigor. "Yes," she said. "He proposed to me this afternoon."

"But . . . you didn't say yes, did you?" Miss Seyward asked. She seemed wilted and diminished, as she had been in the dining room.

"No, I didn't say yes. But I didn't say no, either. Oh, I know, this changes everything! Our plans to be independent—independent together, that is, with our own business. But, you know," she said, frowning, "I haven't been able to come up with any business ideas anyway. I thought I could gather bunches of ideas into the nest of my mind and sit on them until one of them hatched—"

Bertie emitted something between a cough and a laugh.

"—but I've hatched nothing!" she continued in maudlin tones. "My mind-nest is barren. I know I won't ever be really clever, but as I see it, the death of that silly man has made everything quite simple. Brioso was Father's joy, and as a faithful daughter, shouldn't I protect that? If they tell me to destroy Brioso, Mother and the police and the neighbors, well, I'm just not sure they'll take no for an answer. 'No' from a girl like me doesn't carry much weight."

"She's going to marry the poet to save Brioso," Bertie said, eyeing Miss Olivia with something like admiration.

"And you think 'no' will carry more weight coming from you and Mr. Langford?" I said.

"Yes."

"Can't you just ask him to stand up for Brioso?" Miss Seyward said. "Or did he refuse to do so unless you marry him?" The girl was no longer wilting. She looked distinctly rampart-y, tall and indignant.

"No, no," Miss Olivia sighed. "Nothing like that. He's always been kind, especially since Father died. He would stand up for Brioso, of course, but it wouldn't mean much just coming from a friend of the family. I would still bear all the responsibility for Brioso. A silly girl who doesn't know a thing about horses with a supposedly dangerous stallion on her hands. But if I married Mr. Langford, he would own everything, and everyone would rest a little easier knowing a man was in charge."

"A marriage would mean much more—and last much longer—than the act of saving a horse," I said.

"That's why I can't make up my mind, Miss Cobb," the girl said miserably.

"I think the usual method is to decide whether or not you love the man," I said.

"Oh, yes, I love him. Just like I love Byerley."

Miss Seyward and I blinked at her.

"You're in love with both of them?" Miss Seyward ventured.

"No, not *in* love," the other replied with a nervous giggle. "I love them like brothers. I've know them since I was a child, you know. They were the sons Father never had. They spent so much time here at Becketts, learning from Father about horses and bloodlines. Father knew I would never be any good with horses—and of course, I was a girl, much to my detriment—so he poured all his knowledge into those two instead."

"They don't appear to like each other at all," I said, remembering the tension I had witnessed at dinner.

"Oh, they've always had some kind of rivalry, a silly sort of competitiveness. And it's never really gone away. Fletcher always favored Byerley, but Mr. Langford and Father were always the closest. So . . . it's like he already has Father's approval. Oh, Miss Cobb, how do you make the big decisions of life?"

"There is another option, you know," I said thoughtfully, "if you really do want to start a business."

"Careful, Harriet," Bertie murmured. "Your stories seem to spur these ladies to action, and neither seems particularly well-equipped to run away to Walsall."

"Your father's bits," I said to the girl.

"But we don't know where those bits are!" she replied. "Mother and I have looked everywhere for them."

"Not the golden bits. Your father's bit *designs*. He wanted you to carry on with those designs, making and selling his bits under the Chedington name."

"He did?" she breathed.

So Lady Chedington hadn't even told her daughter about

it. "It was in his will," I said. "He referred to it as 'my greatest legacy and a potential fortune.'"

"Mother said I didn't need to bother my head with reading that will," she said. "I don't think she wanted me to know about that at all! Oh, Miss Cobb, if Viv and I could manage to make money, we could find a way to protect Brioso . . . with money comes influence, you know. Mother is always telling me that. Thank you, Miss Cobb! I knew you would know what to do." The two young ladies beamed at me.

I raised my hands and took a step back. "I'm just the saddler. It wasn't my idea, it was your father's."

"I find I'm in need of some water," Bertie said. "Now that you've nixed an engagement and launched a business, perhaps you could wander up to the stable with those buckets and manage to run into an elderly groom with a secret."

I left the young ladies working industriously on Bertie's mane and headed over to the fence line. There were two buckets there, both full. I dumped one in the grass and struck off for the stable, empty bucket in hand.

The brick aisle was already swept clean for the night and the place was very still and silent, with most of the horses out grazing in the mild night air. Seemingly unbothered by his imprisonment, Brioso barely cracked an eye as I walked past. I marveled again at his calm temperament. The stallion was snoozing happily in an empty stable, while most horses would've been pacing their stalls and screaming for their companions. As herd animals, horses are rarely pleased to be left alone. Sir Algernon's death aside, Brioso certainly didn't live up to the reputation he had earned in his youth.

A rhythmic squeaking came through the open doors from the rear stable yard. There was a figure standing at the outdoor pump, moving the old pump handle up and down like an automaton. Once the water spilled out in earnest, the man reached his hands under the current and began scrubbing vigorously. With the splashing of the water, he didn't notice my approach until I was nearly on top of him.

"Oh, Miss Cobb!" he exclaimed, straightening up and taking a step back. In his right hand, shimmering wet in the moonlight, was the stirrup cup.

"A little late to be doing the washing up, isn't it, Fletcher?" I said.

The old groom followed my eyes down to his hand. "Just washin' this," he said, holding it up. The pointed fox ears and snarling snout looked sharper and more sinister than I remembered them. I had expected embarrassment and unease from Fletcher, or a furtive attempt to slip the cup into his pocket, but the man seemed almost proud as he displayed the thing.

"Why are you washing it?" I asked suspiciously. There couldn't have been any blood. If that squarish snout had left the mark on the Major's head—and it looked the right shape —it hadn't even broken the skin.

"Found it in Brioso's stall," he said, "an' Dr. Reed would be happy to know that the stallion's digestion is movin' along as it should be." He chuckled. "There were proof of that on this cup. But her ladyship, she wouldn't like that, to be sure. She ain't so interested in the natural functions of horses, like. So I thought I'd give it a good scrub."

"You're planning to give it to Lady Chedington?"

"Of course," he said, looking a little startled. "She's been askin' for it, just like Mr. Langford said. She said the cup belonged to Sir Algernon, but the rubies belonged to her mother, an' she's right keen to have those back. An' anythin' else of value we can find in the stable, if it comes to that. Plans to pawn it all, far as I can tell."

"It's just . . . when Mr. Langford asked you about it, you said you hadn't seen it."

"Oh, aye, Mr. Langford," he said dryly. "He wanted to give the thing to Lady Chedington himself. Very helpful, he is."

"Isn't he?"

"Lately. But he weren't so keen nor so helpful before my master died."

"I thought Mr. Langford and Sir Algernon were good friends?"

"Aye, they were," he admitted. "But they had their differences, now an' then. An' they weren't over-reasonable 'bout those differences, sometimes. Mr. Langford's been helpful since my master died, always hangin' about an' tryin' to give advice. Makes me think he feels a bit guilty 'bout some of those rows with my master. Well. I just didn't want Mr. Langford to take it. I thought, might be nice to remind her ladyship that ol' Fletcher can still be useful, so I wanted to be the one to give her that cup, Miss Cobb."

"The cup and whip were found separately?"

"Tom found the whip first, muckin' out Brioso's stall. I dug around in the straw a bit later an' found the cup. It still smelled of gin—an' horse dung, 'course. If the Major were drinkin' in there before his ride, he could've got kicked, I guess." His lips twisted as though he still resisted the possibility. "Some horses get real nervous 'round drunkards, smellin' the drink and sensin' the strange behavior, so it could have set him off." He frowned and shook his head. "But I don't think so. You've seen Brioso enough to know, Miss Cobb. Do you think that stallion," he waved a hand toward the stable, "would kick a man in a stall?"

I shook my head. "No, I don't. He seems calm as a kitten."

"Aye," he said. "He weren't so calm before, but I stand by what I said. My master's death changed him. An' Tom and I will be standin' in front of his stall with pitchforks if that sergeant comes to put him down."

"I'll join you," I said. "And Bertie too. He can be very intimidating when he wants to be. But Fletcher, you didn't see or hear anything in the stable this morning? Anyone coming or going? Anyone who could've harmed the Major and arranged things to make it look like a horse accident?"

He didn't look as surprised as I expected, but he shook his head resolutely. "No, Miss Cobb. I were sleepin' in the hay last night, you might know, but nothin' woke me. I don't see nor hear half as well as I used to, though." He grimaced a little. "Don't mention that to her ladyship, if you can help it."

"I'm sorry, Fletcher. Sorry that having Bertie out in the meadow caused you so much worry that you stayed and slept in the hay barn."

"Oh, it weren't exactly that," he said slowly. "I sleep in the hay now and then. Like to keep an eye on the horses, make sure no harm comes to them. 'specially the stallion."

"Do you expect Brioso to be harmed?" I said, surprised.

"Oh. No. Not exactly." His eyes shifted away from mine. Was the man embarrassed? Perhaps he didn't want it known that his gruff exterior housed such tender solicitude for his charges.

"Could I have a look at that cup, Fletcher? Over there, in the light."

"Actually, Miss Cobb, I'm wonderin' if you could hold onto the cup for me tonight. Too late to take it up to Lady Chedington now, an' I'd rather not keep it myself. Don't look right, you know, employees holdin' onto valuables overlong."

I agreed, and he handed the cup to me. Bertie would be very pleased with this development. The only thing better than knowing who had the cup was having the thing ourselves.

"It's bent," he grunted. "Brioso must've knocked it about. I wanted to straighten it out a bit before givin' it to Lady Chedington. Rubies are still there, at least." He reached a gnarled hand up to touch his cap and gave me a weary smile. "'Night, Miss Cobb. And thank you." He moved off into the darkness, but not in the direction of his cottage. He was heading for the hay barn again.

I hurried down the stable aisle toward the tack room, where I knew I could find better light. Shoving my spectacles onto my nose as I went, I stared into the fox's menacing face. The rubies were indeed still there, little red chips winking balefully at me from the depths of the pewter eyes. The fox's snout canted slightly to the right. Brioso would've crushed the soft pewter had he stepped directly on it—something else must have caused the damage. A heavy blow, no doubt. I stared hard at the end of the snout. The top of the nose was curved, and below, lifting away from the teeth in a vicious snarl, the lips formed two straight ridges. Three lines, the top one curved.

I lifted the latch on the tack room door, swept breathlessly inside, and found Byerley seated at the heavy oak table.

26

A HOSTAGE EXCHANGE

"Miss Cobb!" he said expansively. There was a large ledger open on the table before him, papers scattered everywhere, and he was leaning back in his chair with his booted feet resting casually on the tabletop. Lord of the manor, indeed. All that was missing was a pair of wolfhounds gnawing bones on the floor. Then I saw Treacle Tart curled in his lap, and the feudal image faltered. *This* was the person the cat chose to be chummy with?

Byerley's pale eyes shifted to the stirrup cup in my hand. "What have you there?"

Blast.

"Sir Algernon's stirrup cup," I said, a tad defiantly.

"Come to hide it away in the cupboard?" He flashed a wicked grin. "Don't let me stop you."

"I won't be making that mistake again," I said. "Now that I know there are unscrupulous characters wandering about." My eyes landed on the contents of the table, and my breath caught as I saw a few of Sir Algernon's oddly-shaped bits scattered amongst the papers. Had the slippery lord found the golden bits? But no, all of them appeared to be steel and none of them contained jewels, as far as I could tell. "Fiddling with the baronet's bits?" I demanded, and immediately regretted my choice of words when Byerley laughed aloud.

"His designs are actually quite good," he drawled. "You should let Bertie get his mouth on them sometime and tell us what he thinks."

I scowled at him. *Us*, indeed. "Speaking of bits, why did you feel the need to cover up that broken bit and file? Surely you knew I could easily spot who did it."

"You were barking up the wrong tree," he said. "You and Bertie were discussing the thing rather freely this morning—not a wise choice, you know, when you want to keep your horse's abilities a secret, and when there are unscrupulous characters about. When Miss Seyward fainted and I was obliged to drag her across the drawing room, I saw the wounded hand you were looking for. And I thought it would be a shame for that young lady to be mixed up in a police investigation."

"Perhaps you were worried that any police scrutiny of wounded hands would also include you." I stepped forward, looking down at the papers on the table. The document closest to the young man showed two illustrations of a horse, left and right perspectives, along with a branching chart of names written in fine script. "Studying Brioso's pedigree, are you? Making plans for his future at Ashwold Abbey? Tell me, Lord Byerley, what were you doing this morning before you paid Bertie that little visit?"

"You're barking up the wrong tree again," he said, and he brought his feet and the chair down with a thump. Treacle Tart leapt to the floor and shot me a withering look. He'd been onto a good thing until I'd interrupted their little tableau. "I don't want Brioso, Miss Cobb. And I might ask you the same thing about this morning. Why were you up before dawn? Surely Bertie doesn't need such constant attention."

"I was curious to see the Major ride Brioso. And of course, I checked on my horse first."

"Ah!" He grinned blithely at me. "Exactly my morning schedule as well. Except I'll admit to wanting a chat with Bertie. As you see, I'm an open book. You, on the other hand, seem to have plenty to conceal. And now I find you wandering about under cover of darkness with an object last seen with the murder victim—"

"You agree he was murdered?" I said quickly.

"Of course. A corpse doesn't fall into that perfect position without a little help. He looked like he was already laid out for his coffin. And, let me guess," he slid the chair back, rose, and came around the table toward me, those odd silver eyes never leaving my face, "The fox muzzle on that stirrup cup could make a dent the size of a horseshoe stud." He unfurled a graceful hand—not the injured one—and stood before me, hand outstretched, patiently waiting.

I tallied my options. I was taller and broader than the young man, and I stood between him and the door. He wouldn't be able to flee with the thing, and I thought I'd have the advantage in a physical contest. This was what my life in Pelgren Vale had come to, I thought. Contemplating how to take down a lord, literally. I handed him the cup.

Byerley gazed keenly at the end of the fox's snout, and then, using the same logic I'd used earlier that day, he pressed the thing firmly against the back of his hand. I swatted my magnifying loupe into position and leaned in, forgetting my distrust of the man in my eagerness to see what I knew would be there. On his translucently pale skin were three lines, still pink from the force he'd used, one curved from the shape of the nose, the others straight. To the naked eye, all of them together would give the impression of—

"A square," Byerley said.

"I'd like that cup back," I said, and held out my hand, less elegantly than he had.

He smiled and placed the cup in my hand before stalking back to his seat. "As I see it," he said, "there are a few reasons you might want that cup. Perhaps you simply want to sell it and make away with the cash—nothing sinister, just an ordinary case of sticky fingers. Perhaps you really do believe someone murdered the Major, and you plan to give it to the police. Or perhaps, and I think this the most likely, you killed the Major yourself and you plan to destroy the thing or 'lose' it permanently."

It was pleasant to look down my nose at him, but he seemed to gain some sort of power when he was seated and I was not, and I wasn't keen on the lord-and-vassal dynamic. Pulling out a stool—where had the man found a chair with a back?—I seated myself across from him.

"I didn't kill the Major, Byerley." We were becoming cozy enough to drop the "Lord," I thought.

"Then why won't you say who did?"

"Because I don't know who did!"

"I find that very unlikely."

"Why?" I said, glaring at him. "Why are you so certain I know something about it? Does being a lord mean you're allowed to turn your suppositions into facts?"

"The incontrovertible fact is, there was a witness to the Major's death—and you're the only person in this world that can get an answer from him. If you haven't already done so, it's probably because you murdered the man yourself and don't need answers. But if you did already question him, I can only assume your silence means you're protecting the murderer."

I frowned. "Do you mean Bertie? You think Bertie witnessed the murder? But he was in the meadow—"

"Not Bertie," he said. "Brioso. The stallion witnessed the murder."

I stared at him for a long moment. "You think I'm able to hear Brioso speak? Because you believe I'm able to hear Bertie speak?"

"Oh, come off it, Miss Cobb!" he said, then slumped back in his chair and began to laugh. "I heard you and Bertie speaking together this morning. Discussing the bit and the file. Let's just agree that you and I can both hear Bertie speak."

"If you can hear horses speak," I said sweetly, "why don't *you* ask Brioso who the murderer is?"

"Because I don't think Brioso can speak to humans."

"Then how could I have questioned him?"

"You couldn't." He laced his long white fingers together on the table before him. "Miss Cobb. You possess a unique gift, one that most horsemen would sell their souls for. You have a talking horse at your disposal." He leaned forward, a bright gleam coming into his eyes. "Why don't you ask Bertie to question Brioso? Surely Bertie can communicate with him, horse to horse, and get a full account of the murder."

"I'm sure Sergeant Harrison would be thrilled to receive that eyewitness account. And why don't you ask Bertie about it yourself?"

"I don't think he'll talk to me without permission from his owner."

I kept a straight face, but inside I was crowing. The pasty

lord had just handed me the means to start my hostage exchange.

"He prefers the term 'keeper,'" I said, dangling the carrot.

Byerley's eyes narrowed and he smiled. He had the look of a cat that had just been given cream, believing I had stumbled into that little admission about Bertie. We sat there, eyeing each other in silence, and I let the silence go on until he opened his mouth to speak—then I pounced.

"If I give Bertie permission to speak to you," I said, feigning reluctance, "will you agree to stop your public hints about my time in Wolverhampton?"

"Meaning I can still twit you about it in private?" he said, but his smile looked a little less wolfish than before.

I refused to be bated. "Will you agree not to tell anyone what you know about my . . . unconventional choices there?"

"Do you mean race-rigging or disguising yourself as a man?"

"Both. Although I feel quite safe on the first count, as no one would believe you anyway—and you yourself made a pretty penny on that win." I smiled thinly at him.

"Tell me, Miss Cobb, did you wear a different disguise at each track you visited? Sometimes the fine lady and sometimes the humble saddler, changing it up so you wouldn't get caught race-fixing?"

"There was nothing nefarious about my choice to wear men's clothes. It was the only way I could make a decent living. But I'm not sure that explanation would cut any ice in Pelgren Vale, if the fact were to come out. No one would hire a woman who had lived as a man at a racetrack. Bertie and I would be forced to leave the Vale."

He considered me for a moment. "Fine," he said. "I agree. We all have secrets, Miss Cobb, and I have no real wish to divulge yours. And I'm eager that Bertie should stay in Pelgren Vale."

"Do you agree that I'm just a saddler, and I'm not trying to fleece Lady Chedington?"

"Oh, that," he said, waving a lazy hand. "I do probably owe you an apology on that one. When I shared my concerns about you with Olivia—none of your secrets, mind you, just my concerns that you were swindling her mother—she was very robust in her defense of you. She told me all about the golden bits, and she also informed me that her mother was holding séance parties last year when I was in Wolverhampton—long before you came to the Vale. It was some sort of attempt to become a more popular hostess, an excuse to hold more parties at Becketts." He grinned at me. "So it seems you may be just a saddler after all. A saddler with a talking horse."

"Then we're agreed? On all counts?" I said.

"Yes."

I held out my hand, and he looked at it.

"Gentlemen's agreement," he mused. "How appropriate."

We shook.

27

RELEASING CATS IN
MIXED COMPANY

BERTIE SAW US COMING. By the time we reached him, he'd assumed his Vacant Donkey disguise, chin hanging and ears lolling. The young ladies were gone but they had outdone themselves. I restrained a laugh when I saw that their zeal had extended so far as to braid chicory flowers into the horse's mane and tail. The result was quite festive, made sillier by Bertie's dull expression.

Byerley eyed the horse skeptically. "What happened to him?"

"Miss Olivia and Miss Seyward," I said. "They've discovered the joys of grooming."

"Ah."

Bertie's lips tightened a little. It seemed the Donkey was displeased.

"Well?" I said, arching an eyebrow at the young lord. "You have questions?"

He stepped forward and folded his hands before him like a schoolboy about to recite a lesson. I found myself enjoying this new Byerley. He wasn't so sure of himself after all.

"Bertie," he said, "Miss Cobb and I have reached an agreement, and she gives her permission for you to speak to me."

Bertie rolled a quizzical eye at me. "Hostages?" he asked.

"Exchanged," I said.

"Satisfactory," he said, and shook himself violently, freeing most of the flowers from his mane. "Those young ladies seemed to think I would be joining a parade—or a circus." Nostrils wrinkling, he turned on Byerley and demanded, "Do you approve of trussing up horses with flowers and weeds?"

The lord looked startled. "No," he said, adding, "at Ashwold Abbey, the horses are never subjected to such things."

Bully for them, I thought, glaring at Byerley. He obviously wasn't going to give up trying to coax Bertie to his estate.

"Now," Bertie said, "you have questions for me. I may have answers. But your agreement with Harriet does not afford carte blanche with me. Some things I may choose not to answer, but your word to Harriet is still binding, as she has upheld her end of the bargain by giving us permission to speak." His large, dark eyes were dancing as he said this. He didn't need my permission any more than he needed a tail full of flowers.

"I understand," Byerley said. "And first, I'd like to know what you've learned from Brioso. Did he tell you who murdered the Major?"

"No," Bertie said.

"Then come to the stable with me now and ask him about it."

Bertie let out a great, whuffling sigh. "I can't talk to other horses," he said. "I don't know how it is that Harriet—and you, apparently—can hear and understand me, but I can't hold verbal conversations with horses any more than you can. I can only communicate with other horses the way normal horses do, through instinct and body language. I can't access anything intellectual in their brains if there's nothing intellectual already there."

"If that's the case," Byerley said, his face hardening, "how did you convince my Praxiteles to win that race?"

"Convince is probably the wrong word," Bertie said, his ears flickering thoughtfully. "*Goad* would be more appropriate. And I don't intend to explain that one to you. Not yet. Let's just say I used the same technique you seem so fond of—intimidation."

Byerley thought about this for a long moment. "How many races did you . . . interfere with?"

"One."

"One?" Byerley looked surprised. "Why only one?"

"Because it took a lot of planning and preparation, and I'm actually a rather lazy creature. Because it was not a very clever plan, so simple that someone would have caught on had we repeated it. And because one race was all that was needed to buy my freedom."

"But . . ." Byerley said, "with your abilities—a horse being able to observe other horses and predict winners—surely you and Miss Cobb could have planted yourselves at the track and made a fortune. Just playing the odds and winning."

Bertie arched his neck and looked down his Roman nose at the man. "Harriet and I have a little creed. It may sound strange to you, a person born into considerable wealth, but Harriet and I know a thing or two about want. For us, true wealth is not about acquiring vast sums of money. True wealth is being able to thumb our noses at doing anything we don't want to do. We have enough for that, therefore we consider ourselves sufficiently wealthy."

This seemed a new concept to Byerley, who murmured, "I

see," though his frown said otherwise. Then, as if mentally shaking himself, he said, "As to the more immediate matter, why is Miss Cobb in possession of Sir Algernon's stirrup cup?"

"Why were you pouring over Brioso's papers if you don't want him?" I countered.

"The stirrup cup?" Bertie said, looking inquiringly at me.

"Yes."

"How did you manage it?"

"Are we releasing cats in front of the lord?" I asked him.

He nodded his heavy head austerely.

I drew the stirrup cup out of my skirt pocket and held it up for the horse to see. "Fletcher found it in Brioso's stall. He gave it to me for safe-keeping tonight as he doesn't want to be accused of taking valuables home—a wise choice, it seems, with all the accusations of thievery floating around." I shot Byerley a look. "He's feeling the urge to curry favor, so he means to return it to Lady Chedington himself."

"Do you believe him?" Byerley cut in.

"Yes," I said, "but I have no evidence that he didn't do the thing. Just my impression of a truthful old man with a limp so bad it would make dragging a corpse near impossible."

"Lord Byerley," Bertie said, turning his squinted appraisal from the stirrup cup, "it's your turn to answer Harriet's question. Why were you pouring over Brioso's papers if you have no interest in the horse?"

The young lord's face turned guarded, cool marble under the moonlight. "I didn't say I had no interest in him," he said. "I said I didn't want him."

"Why not?" Bertie said. "Wouldn't his Becketts bloodlines be an asset to your Ashwold stables?"

"Perhaps. But I'm more interested in uniqueness." He

began to speak with a new earnestness, words tumbling over each other. "As you say, I was born into wealth, and when you have the wealth that my family does, and you're able to buy the best of everything, it all gets rather . . ."

"Crowded?" I suggested.

"Dull," he said. "Deeply, depressingly dull. Where's the challenge when you've scooped up the best horses in the country? Where's the tension, the skill, the art of it all? I've found more satisfaction in training unknown youngsters from dodgy bloodlines, and finding moderate success, than I ever have in sweeping the boards with a ready-made champion. Horses with faults and foibles, those that no one gives a fig about, the lost causes and dead-enders . . . those are a trainer's true test."

"You're addicted to the underdog," Bertie observed. "That explains Praxiteles."

I remembered Langford's words to Byerley at dinner. *That would be nicely in line with your preference for misfits.* And the lord's odd choice yesterday, riding the grocery mule when he had all the fine Becketts Thoroughbreds at his disposal. He just might be telling the truth.

"But your fixation on Brioso," I said. "Why the interest in his pedigree? Mr. Langford said you've been 'mooning over' the stallion all week. And you advised Miss Olivia to hold that equestrian gala when the mourning period is finished, to ride Brioso in front of a crowd—even though you knew how disastrous that would be. She could have been badly hurt."

"Both of you can read horses," Byerley said. "Do you think that stallion would've hurt her?"

"He seems a remarkably lazy creature," Bertie said, "but his reputation is well-known. It was before we arrived in the

Vale, but we've heard he was exceptionally spirited and difficult when Sir Algernon was training him."

"Some of those rumors came from Lady Chedington, you know," Byerley said. "She was always convinced the horse would hurt Sir Algernon."

"Which he did," I pointed out.

"Any young horse could've done the same," Byerley said angrily. "Bolting is not the same as purposely killing a man." He took a deep breath and seemed to compose himself. "When I arrived here last Sunday and found Brioso such a . . . a changed creature, I told Olivia I'd help her ride him. She said she and Miss Seyward were looking for a way to earn their own living. I said, 'the horses are yours, why not continue your father's legacy and carry on with the stud farm?' She was showing an interest in horses for the first time in her life, and her father would have been proud. I believed she could learn to ride, eventually." He lifted his chin with a hint of the old haughty manner. "I still believe it, and I still mean to help her. If she's able to keep Brioso."

Addicted to the underdog, indeed. I smiled.

"In other words, you'll help her make a go of the business," Bertie said with emphasis and then stared hard at me. My smile faltered as I heard the familiar words. What had the cook said when I went to the kitchen for Treacle Tart's cream? *The young gentleman is pushin' her to sell him the stallion. The other one is pushin' her to keep him, an' says he'll help her make a go of the business.*

"You don't want Brioso," I said slowly. "Mr. Langford does."

"Yes." Byerley's white jaw tightened. "He's always wanted him. He's been trying to get him from Sir Algernon since the stallion was a yearling."

"Why?" I spluttered. "Nothing about that stallion strikes me as exceptional."

"You should have looked closer at those pedigrees, Miss Cobb. Brioso is Horizon's last foal."

"Horizon?" The name meant nothing to me.

Bertie stepped in. "Horizon was the ultimate underdog," he explained, his tone uncharacteristically reverent. "Diminutive in appearance, under sixteen hands tall, onlookers jested that he couldn't even see over the fences, let alone jump them. Yet he won the Grand National in 1871 and again in 1874. Sheer spirit."

I eyed the gray horse. Someday I would get answers about his past life, find out how he could rattle off racing statistics like a bookie.

"Sir Algernon wanted to tap into that spirit," Byerley said. "He believed his mare Obsidian was the perfect complement to Horizon, that the cross would produce something exceptional. But the stud fees were very high, and Sir Algernon . . ." his lips twisted slightly, "well, he was never any good with money. With the cost of running Becketts, his constant spending on the horses . . . he often found himself running dry."

That explained Sir Algernon's stirrup cup, I thought—pewter, not silver, and adorned only with jewels he'd swiped from his wife.

"I was away with my runners at the time, but Langford was also keen to have a foal from that cross, and he offered to front the cash for the stud fees for two breedings. The first foal would go to Langford and the second would go to Sir Algernon, but both would carry the Becketts brand on their shoulders in acknowledgement of Obsidian's lineage. The baronet happily agreed and two foals were produced, a year apart, both colts and both pure black like their mother. The younger was named Brioso, and the elder was named Dolce."

"Dolce. Langford's stallion that died," I said.

"I never saw Dolce," Byerley said. "I was away too often, and Langford and I had grown apart. But I heard that he was unhappy with Dolce. Both colts were said to be unremarkable, but where Sir Algernon's experience and skill allowed him shape Brioso into a promising young competitor, Langford struggled to make anything of Dolce."

"Bloodlines will only take you so far," observed Bertie. "As the saying goes, you can't ride a pedigree. The skill of the trainer and the horse's own idiosyncrasies play a strong part."

"Exactly," Byerley said.

"And Dolce died last summer before Langford had any success with him. Rotten luck," I said, feeling a pang of pity for the poet.

"Perhaps it was just rotten luck," Byerley said, "but I think otherwise. Did you see that ledger in the tack room, Miss Cobb?"

I nodded.

"Sir Algernon was an indifferent bookkeeper," he continued. "He rarely updated accounts in that ledger, using its pages as some sort of personal journal instead. And tonight, when I was reading through his scribblings from last year, I found this." He reached inside his fine coat and withdrew a folded paper. "Even in the moonlight, it's too dark to read, but I'll tell you what it says and you can examine it later. Sir Algernon wrote that he didn't believe Dolce's death to be mere chance."

"What?" Bertie said, nostrils flaring in surprise.

"You see, he and Langford had another agreement. Horses being the fragile creatures that they are—no offense, Bertie—"

"None taken," Bertie said. "As a species, we have our constitutional weaknesses, more prone to illness and injury than dogs or cats."

"Just so," Byerley said. "And because Langford paid both stud fees, Sir Algernon signed an agreement that if Langford's foal died, ownership of the other foal would revert to Langford."

I felt prickles on the back of my neck. I thought I could see where this little path was leading, and I didn't like it one bit.

Byerley held up the paper, sharp and angular in the moonlight like the edge of a blade. "Sir Algernon wrote that when Dolce died last year at the age of six, Langford immediately produced their written agreement and demanded to be given Brioso. Sir Algernon refused and pointed out that the original document said 'foal,' and Dolce was already a full-grown horse when he died. The lawyers agreed with the baronet, and the matter was dropped. But Sir Algernon had another reason for refusing Langford. He writes here that he suspected Dolce's death to be unnatural, that Langford somehow caused the death in order to get his hands on Brioso."

"Did Sir Algernon have evidence?" Bertie asked. His ears were flattened, and there was dark fire in his eyes.

"None that he writes here," Byerley said. "He mentions 'suspicious behavior' on Langford's part around the time of Dolce's death, nothing more. But there were pages missing from that ledger. A whole later section had been torn out. I think this page had only been overlooked because it was between pages of actual farm accounts."

We all stared at each other in silence.

"Langford didn't want Olivia to ride Brioso," Byerley said, "because she might have found she was able to, and then she would have carried on her father's business and would never have considered selling the stallion. So I believe Langford hired a man come to Becketts and present himself to Lady Chedington under the guise of a famous trainer."

"The Major," I breathed.

"Yes. Langford's instructions to 'The Major' were clear—make certain everyone, including Olivia herself, believed she would never be any good with horses. Discourage her completely, snuff any desire to ride."

"But the Major started to enjoy his fictional life," Bertie mused. His equine eyes were keen and bright. He loved predicting the end of a story, after all. "He started believing that he could have an easy career at Becketts, especially after receiving a little praise—"

"It wasn't praise," I growled.

"—and so," Byerley said, taking the reins once more, "he double-crossed Langford and encouraged Olivia rather than discouraging her. Langford saw Brioso slipping away from him again. And that is why he killed the Major this morning."

28

THE SÉANCE

THE DAWN MISTS were creeping away, leaving shimmering jewels of dew on each blade of grass. I wondered if Lady Chedington would find that "auspicious"—a meadow full of jewels to remind her of those she intended to find by harnessing the spirit world. I smiled as I struggled through the gate with Sir Algernon's saddle slung over my arm. There was a new development that I knew would please Bertie, and I was looking forward to springing it on him. But the horse's gray ears swiveled backward when I approached, and he gave the saddle a dubious look.

"Out of the question," he said. "I know I've helped you in your saddlery work before, but I refuse to play mannequin to that hideous piece of hide. Try it on the grocery mule if you must, but leave my back unsullied."

"What did I tell you before, Bertie?" I said, lowering the thing onto a fallen log. "It's a saddle for a séance. The only surface this saddle will grace is a table." I straightened up and looked back toward the Hall. "Ah. You see? The table cometh."

Tom and Langford were slowly crossing the trimmed

lawn, carrying the round drawing room table between them. Behind them in a solemn procession came Byerley, Miss Olivia, Miss Seyward, Sarah, Mrs. Granger, and Fletcher, each carrying a wooden chair. Lady Chedington, chairless, brought up the end of the bizarre parade, speaking animatedly to a slim woman draped head to foot in black gauze.

Bertie gaped. "I believe I owe you a debt of gratitude, Harriet," he said. "You knew I wanted to witness a séance—how did you manage to convince Lady Chedington to bring the whole thing to me?"

I spoke low and kept my back turned on the approaching group. "I'd love to take credit," I said, "but she came up with it all on her own, as a way to lure Sir Algernon back from the afterlife. She's decided his spirit won't manifest in the drawing room, as 'he could never be bothered to come to that room in life, so he certainly won't make the effort in death.' She said he loved the outdoors and he loved this little wilderness, so this is where it must be held."

"And Byerley?" he said, cocking an eye at me. "Lords must rise remarkably early, as he did stop by to ask me whether I was ready to divulge our race-rigging methods. I declined, and told him to find an opportunity to search Langford's room. Did he?"

"Not yet," I said. "But Byerley told Lady Chedington that he'll go back for the final chair. Knowing our slippery lord as we do, I think it's safe to say he'll also slither his way to Langford's room. But if those missing ledger pages are so important, I doubt Langford left them in his room. He might have them on him now, or perhaps he already burned them."

"It's worth the search," Bertie said. "Other than Byerley's suppositions, we have no evidence Langford has done anything wrong. If the poet did remove those pages, there must have been something incriminating in them."

"But could anything Sir Algernon wrote last year prove what happened yesterday?"

"Prove, no. But there may be clues from which we can assemble a clearer motive. And I believe our lord is harboring additional suspicions. He didn't let all his cats out of the bag last night, and after careful consideration, I think I can deduce the dimensions of the remaining cat."

I eyed him narrowly. "Care to throw a lowly dog a bone?"

"Later," he said, looking smug. "I may be wrong, and I don't want to cloud your judgement with unnecessary suspicions."

Or tax my tiny brain with ideas too hefty, I thought, feeling a bit sore that he was playing a lone hand.

Lady Chedington's high, quavering voice split the air. "What is *that*?!" she called. I turned to see her halted at the gate with her darkly-clad companion. The others were making their way toward me, but Lady Chedington stood frozen. "Oh no, no indeed," she continued, pointing an indignant finger at Bertie. "I won't have one of those . . . those *devils* loose among us as we sit at our spirit table. Being seated, we shall be defenseless against his teeth and hooves. I shouldn't wonder if he killed us all when our backs were turned!"

"Lady Chedington," I called, "Bertie is a very old horse—" Bertie glowered at me "—and quite safe, I assure you. Besides, you said Sir Algernon preferred the company of horses to the company of people. Wouldn't his spirit be more likely to join us with an equine presence nearby?"

This logic seemed to arrest the lady. The woman in black spoke a few soft words to her, and they both proceeded through the gate, Lady Chedington still looking less than pleased.

"Madame Itovsky agrees with you," she said tartly. "But if that creature approaches me, I shall expect the young men to ward him off."

Langford nodded and then turned his dancing eyes toward me, and I forced myself to smile back. Just like the old days, I thought, a saddler and a poet joined in mutual appreciation of absurdity. Except that now I suspected the poet of murdering a man—and possibly his own horse. I sighed inwardly. I should have known a poet with a sense of humor was a thing too good to be true.

Byerley, dressed unremarkably for once in a coat of solemn navy, deposited his chair and retreated.

"Now, where to put the table . . ." Lady Chedington said, looking around in bewilderment. This was probably the farthest she had ventured into nature in a long while. I looked past the floral decorations on her broad-brimmed hat to see Byerley striding back toward the Hall.

"You may wish to create some extra time for our intrepid lord," Bertie muttered.

"I think we should walk around and try to find the place that feels the most spiritual," I announced to the others.

Langford gave me a sharp look, but Miss Olivia chimed in immediately, "Oh, that's just what I was going to say!" We all moved off, leaving Sarah, Mrs. Granger, and Tom standing awkwardly with the jumbled furniture. Fletcher had wisely slunk back to the stable.

After a good tromp and a few silly disagreements, most of which were manufactured by me, it finally occurred to Langford to ask where Byerley was. We all looked around, and I was relieved to see the fair-haired lord slipping back through the gate, the final chair cradled in his arms. Lady Chedington directed everyone to carry the furniture to the south end of the meadow, to an "exceptionally spiritual" place under the old oak tree. I scooped up the saddle and trailed along. Following at a respectful distance, Bertie browsed like the old grazing horse he was supposed to be, ignoring Lady Chedington's dark looks. I caught Byerley's eye—once—and raised an eyebrow at him, and he answered with an almost imperceptible shake of the head.

When the servants had departed, we seated ourselves around the table. The old cavalry saddle made a very lopsided centerpiece, and it suddenly occurred to me that there was no tablecloth. I looked keenly at Madame Itovsky. She wore an elaborate headpiece sprouting black feathers, which fluttered disconsolately in the breeze. It was impossible to make out her features behind the dark gauze veil. How was the woman going to perform her table-rapping tricks out here in the daylight, without any tablecloth to conceal her movements? It was surprising she'd agreed to the meadow at all. Surely the usual gags like table levitation or ectoplasm were more easily accomplished in a darkened room.

When all eyes were on her, the shrouded lady spoke. "Vee are gathered today to vitness the manifestation of Sir Algernon Chedington." Her tone was impressively funereal, deep and rhythmic, but the accent was patently fake. I wondered who had first discovered that you could have yourself a career in spiritualism just by throwing a few v's into the mix.

"Are zere any unbelievers here today?" she continued, proving that z's were also handy. It was hard to tell where she was looking, but the spidery headpiece turned slowly around the table, confronting each of us in turn. Across the table from me, Byerley's smooth face had turned sardonic again, but Miss Olivia's blue eyes were as round as Treacle Tart's saucer. No one spoke. A dozen paces past Miss Olivia's modish hat, Bertie had laid off grazing and was observing the proceedings with interest.

"Good," Madame Itovsky said. "Any hint of unbelief vill hamper our efforts. Vee must verk together to call him—vee must join hands now, combine our energies, and focus on zee saddle before us. But I varn you. Zee spirit vill not stay long. Vee have not zee power to keep him vith us."

I took Langford's hand on my right, Miss Seyward's on my left, and fell to observing the old saddle. The stitching was a job well done, I decided, eyeing the waxed linen stitches with which I had closed the freshly-stuffed panels.

"Sir Algernon!" Madame Itovsky burst out in a voice deep enough to have come up from her toes. "Vee ask you, husband, fazzer, friend, return to us!"

A light breeze played through her black feathers, and silence reigned. One minute passed. Two. I shifted in my chair, feeling a little disappointed. I had hoped for some clumsy table-rapping at the very least, but it seemed all we were going to get was a theatrical voice with a bad accent. Then, the humming started. It was so low and steady that at first I thought it was just the wind in my ear. As it grew, an achingly slow crescendo, I forgot to focus on the saddle and stared at Madame Itovsky. I was impressed in spite of myself. When was she taking a breath? There was no break in the deep hum. It flowed on and on, a tuneless rush from under the black veil. Then the woman's head snapped back, her body stiffened, and she spoke in a newly delicate voice with no hint of the contrived accent.

"The horseman comes, aloft, alight, through pastures of the spirit night, his brow so clear, his heart so still, his empty saddle now to fill."

Well. It was no Keats, I decided, relaxing back against my chair. Langford probably could have come up with something better.

Madame Itovsky's chin dropped suddenly, decisively, and she said in a newly monotone voice, "I am here."

"Algernon?" Lady Chedington asked tentatively.

The black shroud nodded once.

"Oh, Algernon!" There was a gush of emotion in Lady Chedington's voice, but she blinked away the tears and dove into the business at hand. "There's no time to beat around the bush, my dear," she said. "Look across—do you see your daughter there?"

Miss Olivia wasn't pleased to be singled out. Her pretty face paled, and she looked like she was caught between morbid fascination and a strong desire to flee the meadow altogether. Miss Seyward visibly squeezed her hand, gazing at her friend in concern.

"Your daughter," continued Lady Chedington, "deserves to have a future. Which she will not have unless you tell us the location of those golden bits. You left us near penniless, with nothing but those four-legged fiends."

"A black horse," said the voice.

Lady Chedington glowered. "Yes, yes, that horrible beast. He's the one that killed you. But you probably know that. I don't like to say I told you so, my dear, but I warned you about him, did I not? Now, the bits—"

"There was a struggle."

"Yes, a struggle," her ladyship said. "We know, my dear. That creature was too strong for you."

"Two horses. Two men." The voice was slow and even.

"Two men?" Lady Chedington blinked. "Two men took the bits? Highwaymen, perhaps?"

"There was a struggle."

"A struggle over the bits?" Lady Chedington said hopefully.

"A sound, like the crack of a whip!" the voice hissed.

"Oh," her ladyship said, frowning.

"One man fell into darkness, never to rise again."

I looked across the table at Byerley. He no longer looked amused. His jaw was tight and his brow sharply furrowed. Behind him, Bertie loomed like a gray statue, head high and nostrils flared.

"Who are you?" Lady Chedington asked the veil suspiciously. "Now, look here. I demand to speak to my husband, Sir Algernon Chedington."

"A struggle. The crack of a whip. One man fell."

"No! No more of that nonsense," Lady Chedington blazed.

"Let him speak!" Byerley exclaimed. Rare color had come into his cheeks.

Lady Chedington turned her fury on him. "Silence!" Swiveling back to the spirit medium she said, "You will tell me where to find those golden bits, or I will end this séance here and now!"

This seemed to give the veiled figure pause. There was a shudder and a sudden intake of breath and then, "The bits." The voice was different now, soothing, almost cloying.

Lady Chedington beamed. "Yes. The bits. Oh, thank you my dear. Now, tell us where to find them."

"Oak. Strong oak. Like branches."

"An oak tree?" suggested Lady Chedington, peering upward at the strong branches above us. "The bits are near an oak tree? Is it this one? How auspicious!"

"Buried among many more of their kind." The voice had a sing-song quality, lilting, taunting.

"Buried among many oak trees?" Lady Chedington

blinked. "We have oak trees along the avenue. But, my dear, there are so many! Which one—could you point it out? The beginning of the avenue or the end of the avenue?"

"Buried at the root!" The voice cracked through the air like a whip against flesh. "At the root you shall find them!"

The black figure shuddered violently and slumped forward, shoulders rolling and head drooping. Then, just as the feathered headpiece began to slide, Madame Itovsky straightened up, pushed the veil and feathers back into position, and settled back mildly in her chair.

"Vat did you see and hear?" she queried. "Did Sir Algernon appear?"

"Oh, yes, Madame," bubbled Lady Chedington. "Now, you must tell me more about the oak trees—"

"Zee spirit is gone," Madame Itovsky stated flatly. "I cannot tell you vat zee spirit said nor zee meaning behind it. You must discover zat for yourself. It is your own spirit journey." She rose, stiff and stately, and stalked off toward the meadow gate.

Lady Chedington popped up and hurried along with her. "But my own spirit says I need more information . . ."

I released the hands on either side of me, feeling dazed. Then I realized I was making a movement with my right hand —wiping my palm on my skirt. I glanced sharply at Langford, but he was already rising from his chair and turning away. It was unlike the poet to walk away without a word, but that wasn't what was biting me. His hand in mine had become distinctly sweaty.

EXCAVATIONS

"Leave the furniture!" Lady Chedington bellowed. She was in a foul mood, as it was clear she would get nothing more from Madame Itovsky, who was floating out the gate like a dissipating spirit. "Where's Fletcher? I need that stable lad to bring shovels to the avenue. We shall dig up every oak tree if need be. Though I don't know why Algernon would have buried those bits. Buried at the root, indeed! Ridiculous. Unless he was worried about robbers or highwaymen. Fletcher! Where is that silly man? Come, everyone, to the avenue! Byerley, Mr. Langford, you've handled shovels before, have you not? Olivia! Miss Seyward! Here's your chance to prove you're as good as the men, as you always seem so eager to do." She struck off purposefully and then, noticing the weeds which snagged her voluminous skirts, "I shall need an excavation outfit. Sarah! My old riding habit!"

Miss Seyward, Miss Olivia, and Langford followed her reluctantly, and when the meadow contained only a lord, a saddler, and a big gray horse, Bertie looked at us and said, "Well?"

"Two men," Byerley said. "A struggle. The crack of a whip." His gray eyes were hard as flint.

"One man fell into darkness, never to rise again," I said.

"Yes," Bertie said. "And how is it that she could so accurately describe the Major's murder?"

"She got her wires crossed," I said. "Instead of Sir Algernon, she channeled the Major."

"Oh, come, Miss Cobb," Byerley scoffed. "You're not saying you actually believed that little show? I thought you disavowed all things supernatural."

"That's just it," I said. "I expected a show. A little table-rapping at the very least. But there was something about the simplicity of it that . . . well, it gave me pause."

Byerley snorted, a reaction he had no doubt learned from Bertie.

But the big horse was slower to mock. "Harriet is not wrong to consider the angle," he said. "There are plenty of unexplained phenomena in this world—in fact, you have one before you now."

We stared at him.

"A talking horse," he said dryly, fixing us with a penetrating equine eye.

"Oh," I said.

"Quite," Byerley said.

Bertie sighed and continued. "Accepting, as I necessarily do, that not everything in this world can be explained by science, I do not discount all spirit mediums. And a lack of showmanship is sometimes a sign of the genuine article. But if Madame Itovsky knows something about the murder, I don't think she learned it from the spirit world. Something in that séance convinced me that our sable lady is firmly planted in the land of the living."

"The v's and z's?" I suggested.

"They were appalling, but no. Think back. She abandoned the murder and switched to the bits as soon as her paycheck was threatened."

We absorbed this for a moment.

"What do we know of Madame Itovsky?" I said. "Is she a neighbor?" I turned to Byerley. "You've lived in Pelgren Vale since you were a child. Do you know where Madame Itovsky lives, or how she's connected to Becketts?"

"I've never heard of her before," he said. "And I assume we're agreed that Madame Itovsky is not her real name."

"Go after her," Bertie said suddenly. "Byerley—go after her now. Try to get more information." His dark eyes turned sly. "Rumor has it there's a gold sovereign weighing heavily on your mind—and your pocket. If you're so desperate to get rid of it, why not see if our veiled lady is impressed by the glimmer of gold?"

Byerley flashed a grin and trotted away toward the Hall.

Swinging his big head to me, Bertie said, "Fletcher wishes to give that stirrup cup to Lady Chedington this morning, does he not?"

"He was chomping at the bit about it when I saw him in the stable. He's concerned that the longer we wait, the more likely it is he'll be accused of stealing the thing."

"Go with him now and present it to Lady Chedington. She'll be up at the Hall, sorting out her 'excavation outfit.' You must convince her not to pawn the cup, and after hearing Madame Itovsky's pronouncements, she may be ripe to accept that the thing was used to murder the Major. And Sergeant Harrison may be more tractable if we have Lady Chedington on our side."

"She's a real feather in our cap," I muttered, feeling unconvinced.

The big horse grew thoughtful. "Don't mention that Byerley shares your suspicions. If her ladyship demurs or grows angry with you, it may be wise to leave the lord space to pursue her from another angle."

Nodding reluctantly, I gathered the saddle from the tabletop and sallied forth, the stirrup cup bouncing in my pocket with every step.

I found red-headed Tom standing in the stable aisle holding Treacle Tart. From the cat's bitter expression, it seemed another escape attempt had been foiled.

"Almost got away again," Tom said, stroking the indignant animal.

"It's really too bad, keeping him locked in the tack room," I said, looking sadly at the cat. He glared back, unimpressed with my pity.

"Better'n a horse, I say," Tom said cheerfully. "Sir Algernon's father, he kept a horse in the tack room when he were short on box stalls. That's the rumor, at any rate." He opened the tack room door and dropped Treacle Tart inside, and I followed quickly, closing the door behind me.

Fletcher was in the tack room, hastily stowing something behind the old saddle racks in the corner. His tense expression gave way to relief when he saw me, and I had the feeling he'd been expecting Lady Chedington to burst in on him.

"No digging for you today, Fletcher?" I said, crossing the room to place the saddle on one of the racks.

"Shovels ran out," he said blithely.

I grinned at him. "How unfortunate." I didn't mention that I had just spied the shovel he'd hidden behind the racks. Reaching into my pocket, I withdrew the pewter cup, its ruby eyes glittering in the light from the high windows. "Would you like to take the cup to Lady Chedington before she's knee-deep in a mud pit?"

"I would," he said, taking the cup from me. "'bout time I had somethin' good to bring her ladyship."

I felt a slight stirring of conscience. Lady Chedington might not consider the thing "good" when I broke the news to her that it was a murder weapon.

Staring into the fox's crooked face for a moment, Fletcher reflected, "Can't help but feel like I failed my master. It were my fault that day, you know, that he were ridin' alone. I usually rode with him, Brioso bein' such a handful back then, but I had a spill from a young filly the week before an' broke this leg," he slapped his right thigh. "Sir Algernon rode out alone on Brioso. His lady begged him not to, asked him to take someone along for safety, like, but he said if he couldn't ride his own horse on land he knew like the back of his hand, he didn't deserve to be called a horseman."

"No one could've predicted what happened, Fletcher," I said. "You know as well as I do that even the best horses are unpredictable. You didn't fail him."

"But I did fail Brioso. When I came back after bein' laid up in my cottage, I found he'd been locked in his stall for weeks. He'd lost all his musclin', an' all his spirit too, seemed like. He were a changed creature an' no mistake. Meek an' mild like you see him today. He's so quiet now, I wonder if he could even work up enough steam to breed a mare." A sudden flush came over his rough old cheeks. "Beggin' your pardon, Miss Cobb. Shouldn't have spoken so in front of a lady."

"Rest easy, Fletcher," I sighed. "This lady understands the natural functions of horses." I crossed to him and took his arm. "Care to escort a lady to the Hall?"

The Hall was all but deserted. Peters was probably having one of his lie-downs, and Sarah was helping her mistress with the excavation outfit, so we waited at the bottom of the stairway in the grand foyer. When Lady Chedington finally swept down the stairs, she looked surprisingly earthy and capable in a smart riding habit of brown tweed. The warm tone suited her, and I told her so.

"Plaid in mourning is not exactly the thing, you know," she said, "but it's the only thing I have that won't mind a bit of dirt. And I've already broken that silly social moratorium by holding the séance, though no one need know about that—you won't mention it to anyone of consequence, will you? Perhaps I shall end my mourning period early. More and more people do, you know. Queen Victoria is gone, and we can't all be expected to spend years in black crepe." She turned to my companion. "Fletcher!" She never failed to bark his name. "Have you unearthed more shovels for the . . . the unearthing?"

"No, my lady," he said. "But I found this." He held the stirrup cup out to her.

"Ah!" she said, eyes lighting up. "Fletcher, you wonderful man!" She grabbed the cup from him and examined it closely.

"It's bent from bein' in the stall, but the rubies are still there."

"The jewels are all that matters! They should fetch a good price." She stuffed the cup roughly into her pocket and made for the front door. "Well done, Fletcher," she called over her shoulder. "Bring more shovels to the avenue when you find them!"

Fletcher gave her retreating back a sour look, but there was a new squareness to his old shoulders as he left through the rear corridor.

"Lady Chedington," I called, "I need to speak with you."

"Can't it wait?" She paused with her hand on the door.

"I'm afraid not. It's about that stirrup cup. You can't pawn it."

"Why not?"

"First, do you know Madame Itovsky's real name? Her address?"

She blinked at me. "I've always called her Madame Itovsky. Madame Irena Itovsky. And she's never given me her details—I leave messages for her at the post office, and she always gets them. One assumes keeping things private is part of her mystique."

"Well, do you remember what she said before she mentioned the bits?"

The woman looked at me blankly.

"She said, 'The crack of a whip,' and 'One man fell into darkness, never to rise again.' "

"Oh, that," she said, waving a hand impatiently. "You never know what nonsense you're going to get with Madame Itovsky. Half the time she finds the wrong spirit. It was obvious when she got hold of Algernon because he told us where to find the bits."

"That's just it. I think she got the wrong spirit at first. I think it was the Major speaking, and he was telling us how he died." I took a deep breath. "I believe there was a struggle, and he was struck—with that stirrup cup attached to the whip. I believe he was murdered by a human, not a horse."

She gaped. "What? But . . . he was kicked by that beast! The doctor and the sergeant said so."

"I saw something," I said. "There was a mark, like a stamp on the Major's skin, that could only have come from the snout on that fox."

"Did anyone else see this . . . this snout stamp?" she said, frowning.

"No," I admitted. "It had faded by the time the others examined him. But I'm sure of it. I know what I saw. And the Major's body looked like it had been arranged, and—"

"Did you tell Sergeant Harrison all of this?" she demanded.

"Yes," I said, "but we didn't have the stirrup cup then, so he didn't . . . he wasn't inclined to agree without evidence."

She smiled sadly, came to me and clasped my hands in her plump ones. "My dear," she said, "I know you love horses. I did once too, if you can believe it, but then experience made me wiser." Her eyes changed as she said this, growing hard and cold as the tiles beneath our feet. "I know you don't want to believe the beasts capable of murder, and you'd do anything— imagine anything—rather than admit a horse is evil."

I felt my hackles rising. It was the same word Sergeant Harrison had used—imagine. I bit back an acerbic reply and took a deep breath. "I'm only thinking of you," I said mildly. "If you allow Brioso to be destroyed and then a murder is discovered, what will your neighbor's say when it's revealed that you punished an innocent animal?"

"My dear Miss Cobb," she said, giving a chuckle, "my neighbors know he is not innocent. Only this morning, Lady Carter rang to give her condolences. She said it was just a sad bit of luck that the beast spent his murderous instincts on the Major before he could harm Olivia. She is an influential woman, and the neighborhood will be firmly behind me, I assure you." She swept a loose strand of hair back beneath her hat and patted the rest of the blonde waves into place, the very picture of propriety. "You intend to pursue this stirrup-cup nonsense, with or without me?" The words were clipped but not angry.

"Yes, but I would prefer to do it with you. All I ask is that you ring Sergeant Harrison and tell him about the snout on that cup."

She searched my face for a long moment, and I was surprised to see her expression softening. "Very well," she said. "But I can't say I believe it, and I don't want the police here again disturbing my guests over such a slim suspicion."

Considering her guests were being asked to do hard manual labor at the moment, I thought they'd probably welcome the disturbance, but I decided not to mention it.

"So," she said, drawing herself up with grave determination, "you and I shall ride to Pelgren now and give the cup to Sergeant Harrison."

RIDING WITH A LADY

I BLINKED. That was unexpectedly easy. "I'll ask Fletcher to bring the carriage," I said, turning to retreat before she could change her mind.

"I said *ride*, my dear," she said.

"Ride? But—" I waved a vague hand at the woman who couldn't bear to set foot in her own stable. "Surely you'd be more comfortable in a carriage?"

She looked slightly offended. "The fact that I can't stand the creatures doesn't mean I can't manage to sit atop one of them. The carriage will take too long. We'll get to Pelgren much more quickly through the path in the woods. I have an excavation to attend to, and the sooner we get this silly business out of the way, the better. Besides," she said, looking regretfully down at her brown tweed, "in my carriage on the road, someone might see me out of mourning clothes, and it's best not to break with tradition in such a public way. No one would expect to see me on horseback, and as the police station is at the edge of the village, we can slip in and slip out and no one's the wiser."

"Then I'll have Fletcher saddle . . . do you have a—" I gulped, "a favorite horse?"

She grimaced. "I suppose that spotted beast will do. The one Olivia hasn't yet managed to fall from. If she can stay atop the thing, I don't see why I shouldn't be able to. And don't tell Fletcher—or anyone else—the purpose of our ride. Until something is proven, I don't want anyone else discombobulated by this flimsy tale. I need everyone's minds firmly focused on finding those bits!"

I found Fletcher industriously polishing the brass fittings on the stall doors. It seemed unnecessary, since the brass was already gleaming, but it made a nice alternative to digging up the oaks in the avenue. When I told him what we needed, he goggled at me as if I had sprouted another head.

"Saddle a horse for . . . Ride? Lady Chedington, ride? Beggin' your pardon, Miss Cobb, but surely she said to bring the carriage, not saddle a horse."

"She asked for the piebald gelding," I said grimly. "He is the quietest horse here, isn't he?"

"Oh, aye," he said, still staring at me in wonder. "He's quiet enough. But why . . . "

"We have urgent business in Pelgren, and Lady Chedington says the path in the woods is the quickest way."

Fletcher laid the polishing can and cloth carefully on the brick floor, straightened up, and extended his rough hand to me.

"What's this?" I said in surprise.

"I just want to shake the hand of the only person who's got her ladyship to ride a horse in . . . well, in donkey's years."

I grinned and grasped his hand, saying, "I can't take credit, Fletcher. I wanted her to use the telephone."

"I'll bring the gelding down to you, then," he called, as I

went to retrieve Bertie's tack. "Closest gate to that path is the back of that meadow."

It felt remarkably good to be taking action, striding through the meadow with Bertie's saddle over my arm. Bertie could perform mental gymnastics in an attitude of meditation, resting a hind leg and lowering his gray lashes, but I needed something physical to keep my brain running at full steam. The longer I sat still and chewed on a thing, the more convoluted it became, but a brisk walk or a spirited ride was sure to sort things out. Not that I thought my ride with Lady Chedington would be spirited. But after the inactivity of the last few days, it would feel good to be in the saddle again.

I was gratified to see surprise on Bertie's face for the second time that day. "Ride?" he said, ears frozen in puzzlement. "The sedentary lady means to ride? Well done, Harriet. You must have convinced her beyond a flicker of a doubt if she's so eager for the law to have that cup."

"She's not convinced," I said, snugging up the girth around Bertie's barrel. "She just doesn't want to see Sergeant Harrison's whiskers around here again. They might distract the others from the treasure hunt."

Bertie slipped his head deftly into the bridle as I offered it, taking the mild snaffle bit into his mouth. "Byerley paid me a visit before heading out to the dig," he said.

"And?"

"He begged me again to tell him how we got Praxiteles to win that race. I declined. More pertinently, he said Madame Itovsky remained buttoned up tighter than a corset, gold sovereign notwithstanding."

I frowned. "Lady Chedington said something about her 'mystique.' It seems inscrutability is part of the woman's charm."

"Byerley had the impression she was afraid of him."

"Afraid?"

"He said it was hard to tell behind that dark veil, but she physically recoiled when he reached into his pocket. An odd reaction, to be sure."

His gray ears flickered to the gate, and I turned to see Fletcher leading the piebald gelding, followed at a cautious distance by Lady Chedington. She had donned a more practical hat with veil attached, probably in an attempt to avoid being recognized by any curious passersby. I was impressed by the set of her chin and the determination in her stride. For a woman terrified of horses, she was exhibiting admirable pluck.

I swung astride Bertie, thankful again for the split skirt that made the action possible. Lady Chedington waited in mounting position at the piebald's left side, but curiously, Fletcher remained at the horse's head and made no move to assist her.

"Well?" she finally demanded, glaring at the old groom.

His eyebrows shot up, and he scurried around to help her. "Apologies, my lady," he said, bending low to offer his hands to her lifted boot. Rather than using her opposite leg to push off, the lady put all her weight on the unfortunate man and scrambled upward like she was climbing a ladder—and had no acquaintance with ladders. Once seated, she hooked her right leg awkwardly around the branching head of the pommel, arranged her tweed skirt, and then appeared completely at a loss when Fletcher handed her the reins.

"Remind me," she said. "Do the straps go through the bottom of my hands or the top?"

Fletcher blinked at her. "The bottom, my lady. Above the

last finger." As she still appeared mystified, he reached up and arranged the incomprehensible things for her.

"We should've brought a rope to tether her to us," I muttered.

"Excellent hindsight," Bertie said, moving off toward the back of the meadow, "but we shall have to trust to fate and that spotted fellow's good training."

The old gate at the treeline was well concealed in ivy and nettles, but Fletcher struggled it wide enough to release us into the wild. "Just follow along behind Miss Cobb, my lady," he said, and then he touched his hat in a grim salute and hurried away before his mistress could manage to fall off.

I had expected some sort of lane, but the path that wound through the woods was little more than a deer trail at first. We picked our way carefully along under a dense canopy of foliage, Bertie in front and the piebald following at his tail. When the path began to take us sharply upward, I worried about Lady Chedington on the incline, but as the minutes passed without the lady dropping her reins or losing her stir-rup, I started to relax. This was just the kind of path Bertie and I enjoyed, though we usually sped along at a quicker clip, ducking branches and bounding nimbly over roots and logs. For the sake of our companion, Bertie kept his strides short and measured, but the spring in his step showed he shared my thoughts.

"We should return and explore this path at a better speed someday," he mused, "without the unnecessary baggage."

The "baggage" had been silent thus far, but she soon grew comfortable enough to realize that she could talk and ride at the same time. "Now, my dear," she said, "if you believe a murder took place, you must have some idea of who did it?"

I hesitated. "That's what I'm hoping the police will uncover."

"Perhaps a gang of highwaymen came to Becketts under cover of darkness, meaning to pillage the place! A dreadful thought—Oh, take the path to the left, my dear. That right hand path will lead us all the way to Exmoor, or to Mr. Langford's Maplehurst if you turn off sooner." We followed the lower path horizontally across the slope.

"What do you think of Mr. Langford?" I asked, glancing behind to make sure she was still in the center of her saddle.

"Think of him?" she said. "I can't complain about his behavior to us since Algernon died. He's been remarkably helpful. But he's as hopeless with money as my husband was, and he shares the same obsession with horses. A bad combination, to be sure. He's forever running short. Short of cash, that is, not of horses, and the first is the result of the second!"

"But his Maplehurst is in the midst of extensive—and expensive—renovations, is it not?"

"Oh, that!" she scoffed. "Those renovations are being nicely covered by the insurance money from his stallion. The death of that stallion was the best thing to happen to Mr. Langford in years! That stallion was— no, take the right-hand path, the other leads to the forge—that stallion was useless. You may think me indelicate to say it, but the silly beast had no idea what to do with mares. As a breeding stallion, he was a complete flop."

I smiled at her apt choice of words. It was the second time that day that I'd heard doubts about a stallion's ability to procreate. Maybe there was something in the Pelgren Vale water.

"Mr. Langford and Miss Olivia seem quite close," I said.

"Do you think so?" she said sharply. "They have been

thrown together lately, rather too often for my liking. Luckily, my daughter grew up with his handsome face, so she's as blind as a sibling to his silly eyelashes. But I never considered the effect of her lashes on *him*! He certainly never took notice of her in the past, but when Algernon died, he started spending more and more time with us, giving his assistance and advice . . . yes, perhaps Olivia's beauty has smitten him."

"Or he's smitten with the stallion she inherited," Bertie said.

"I shall have to put a stop to whatever is brewing on that front, to be sure," she said. "By the way, I don't suppose you were able to discover whether Byerley prefers Waterhouse or Rossetti?"

Bertie gave a muffled laugh, and I admitted my ignorance.

The forest floor climbed away to our right while flattening out to our left, and the little path broadened into something like a lane. I decided we could probably ride two abreast, which would save me looking over my shoulder every few minutes to check on my charge.

"Lady Chedington," I said, "it's finally widening out. Do you think you could manage to move up next to me?"

I always wondered if what happened next would've happened at exactly that spot, with or without my suggestion. I heard a harsh equine grunt from behind, and the piebald suddenly shot past me in a streak of black and white.

"He's off!" Bertie said, springing after the pair before I had time to gather my wits.

Lady Chedington gave a piercing shriek, and her mount rocketed into the forest to our left. Bertie was at his heels almost immediately, but the panicked gelding showed no signs of slowing.

"Stop, you monster, stop! Whoa!" howled his hapless rider,

but her flopping and bumping only sent the horse into new heights of frenzy and he thundered on, narrowly avoiding the trees in his path.

Cursing under my breath, I leaned low over Bertie's neck and gave him free rein, my legs clinging grimly to his surging body. As I ducked to avoid being brained by a low branch, I realized that the forest was too dense for Bertie to play the same card he'd used with Brioso. There would be no gradual herding in this rugged place.

"Help!" the lady cried. "For god's sake, help me!"

"I'll get alongside her," Bertie gasped, "you grab the reins she's flinging about."

We moved up, Bertie leaping a fallen tree and then barely missing one in his path, and soon the galloping horses were neck and neck. Lady Chedington was indeed flinging her reins about. Arms waving wildly in the air, she bent over backward, almost lying on her mount's haunches. Seeing Bertie's gray body next to her, she rallied enough strength to hoist herself up, but she overcorrected and landed halfway up the piebald's neck.

"Oooohhhhh!" she wailed. I reached across to steady her but almost lost my seat when Bertie broke away to veer around a tree. When we closed with her again, she was hanging off her mount's side, clinging to his neck in a desperate embrace. I leaned in and reached for the flapping reins, and at the same time, the woman grabbed for Bertie's neck with all the fervor of a drowning swimmer. Bertie stumbled at the additional weight and she screamed and clawed wildly at his head, yanking his bridle over his ears in her struggle.

I snugged up my reins to keep the falling bridle from tangling in Bertie's legs. Losing her grip on that last lifeline,

Lady Chedington finally lost the battle. Gaping in horror, she paddled with her arms and somehow managed to push off Bertie's neck, only to ricochet backward and roll off the piebald's opposite side.

Suddenly, I found myself launched up Bertie's neck as he slammed to a halt. He rocked back on his haunches and reared, lifting his front hooves and spinning sideways, and I was only saved from a fall by grabbing handfuls of his gray mane. His rising neck hit me squarely in the chest. I gasped for air as his hooves found the ground, and then I saw what had caused his violent reaction. Immediately before us the ground ended, falling away into a deep gorge that cut across the hillside in a ragged line.

31

POETS AND THEIR REPUTATIONS

THE GORGE WAS DECEPTIVELY NARROW, and the surrounding trees—which grew benignly up to the edge on either side—gave the impression of an unbroken forest floor. Approaching at speed, most horses wouldn't notice the cruel drop-off until it was too late. I tore my eyes away from the jagged rocks some twenty feet below—a fall which would certainly have broken Bertie's legs and my skull—and scanned the forest for Lady Chedington.

Luckily, the old piebald had eased up and changed course the moment his rider fell, swerving off to the right and moving parallel to the gorge. He had then managed to step on his own trailing reins, the pressure of which had activated years of training and brought him to an obedient halt. He stood heaving and sweating a dozen paces away, still arrested by the feel of his own hoof on the reins.

Bertie backed away from the broken edge and I dismounted. "Lady Chedington!" I called, and was immensely relieved to see the woman stomping toward me, battered hat in her hand and fury on her face.

"What caused that beast to do such a thing?" she thundered, the twigs in her frowsy hair giving her the look of an enraged scarecrow. "Fletcher assured me he was safe. I shall give that man a piece of my mind when I see him next. Safe, indeed! I could have been killed!"

"We both could have," I said, indicating the gorge.

She approached and peered over the edge, her face growing cold. "No one told me there was a chasm in this forest," she snapped.

"How far is Pelgren from here?" I asked. "It must be only another mile or so. If I take your reins, do you think you could manage the ride?"

"I am certainly not going to mount that creature again, with chasms and crevasses at every turn! I was far too optimistic about this little endeavor, but now I've been reminded that optimism has no place with horses. No. I shall not continue. It was a silly errand in the first place. You may go on alone, but I shall go back."

"On foot?" I said, startled.

"Of course on foot," she said. "We're barely off the Becketts land. I may not be much of a rider, my dear, but I can certainly handle a walk of that distance. I shall give you the stirrup cup, and you may ride down and explain it all to Sergeant Harrison yourself. It is your story after all. But I don't know why anyone need bother so much over the death of that silly man. A traveling poet, indeed!"

"Poet?" Bertie and I said together.

"Yes, my dear," she said, "a traveling poet, that's what the Major was! Sergeant Harrison telephoned this morning to give me the news. It seems the man was not a horse master at all. He was in the village pub every night this week performing drunken poetry readings!"

"I don't suppose he did any Keats?" I asked weakly.

"What?"

"Never mind," I said. "How did the sergeant discover that the drunken poet and the Major were the same person?"

"Oh, the drink went straight to the Major's head one night at the pub, and he began crowing about how he had changed professions. He told everyone he was having immense success in the field of equine education. Equine education! Poets are such disreputable people. Vagrants, all of them. I shouldn't be surprised if he was traveling with a whole troupe of them, and the others came to Becketts that night to murder one of their own! One does hear that there is no honor among thieves. I suppose poets are the same. Quoting Tennyson while thumping each other in the head! It's a sordid thought, positively sordid!"

"Well," I said, trying to claw my way back to the surface. "If you give me the stirrup cup, I'll take it along to the sergeant, and he can track down any violent poet-gangs in the area."

She reached into her skirt pockets and a look of concern flickered across her face. "There may be a problem," she said, pulling out the linings of both pockets to reveal they were empty. "It must have fallen out sometime during that mad gallop!"

I looked back the way we had come, observing the distressingly thick undergrowth. It was a wonder we had made it through as far as we had, and finding the stirrup cup in all that brush would be nearly impossible.

"Do you remember where you fell?" I said bleakly.

Twenty minutes of searching resulted in nothing more than an increasingly foul mood in my human companion. "It's hopeless!" she declared. "I won't waste any more time here. The loss of those rubies cuts me to the quick, but there is far more to be gained by finding the golden bits at Becketts." She placed a gloved hand on my arm. "Come back with me, my dear. With your strong arms and your intuition, perhaps you'll be the one to dig them up!" Taking my silence as acquiescence, she plucked a few twigs from her hair, crammed her misshapen hat over the rest, and went to retrieve the piebald.

I looked helplessly at Bertie. His large eyes were nearly closed and he was resting a hind leg. Anyone else would've assumed the gray horse was sleeping, but I knew better. My spirits rose a little. He was working on something in that equine brain of his. Feeling my expectant gaze, he opened his eyes, yawned impressively, and then twisted his head upward to grab a mouthful of some low-hanging leaves.

Well. I couldn't expect him to be brilliant all of the time.

Then, the horse did something very odd. Loudly crunching the leaves, he stretched a hind leg forward and stepped on the heel of his left front hoof. He then jerked the front hoof sharply upward, pulling it quickly out from under the hind one.

"Loose shoe," he informed me blandly.

I stared at him. He waved the offending hoof in the air, and I heard a dull clinking as the metal shoe shifted on its loose nails. From the look of it, by stepping on the heel of his own shoe, he had not only loosened it but had also managed to bend it. It was a neat trick, but I couldn't fathom why he'd done it.

As if reading my thoughts, he said, "I certainly won't get far on this shoe. We shall have to call on that farrier fellow, Mr. Malcolm. Luckily, Lady Chedington already pointed out the path to the forge, did she not?"

Eyeing him suspiciously, I racked my brain for any ulterior motive he might have for visiting the farrier. When was the last time I had heard Mr. Malcolm's name uttered? "I suppose," I said, "you would also like to question him about the rumor that he's in the habit of adding square studs to horses' shoes willy-nilly?"

"Exactly," Bertie said, looking pleased. "Rumors being such insidious things, we might as well try to clear that up."

"But if we believe the Major was murdered with that stirrup cup at the end of a whip, why does it matter that Brioso has studs in his shoes?"

"It may not matter at all. Or it may matter a great deal."

I waited for more, but he just stood there looking smug. "Fine," I whispered. "Keep your cats, then."

Lady Chedington came up, pink-faced and sweating, dragging a very reluctant piebald gelding behind her. "Lazy creature!" she panted. "And very contrary indeed. If you tell him 'whoa,' he runs away with you, and if you want him to move, he can't be bothered. Ridiculous!" She held the reins out to me. "I suppose you'll have better luck towing him along behind your creature."

"Lady Chedington," I said, "My creature has a loose shoe. I'll accompany you back to the fork in the lane, where you said there was a path to the forge, but then I'm afraid you'll need to carry on alone."

Despite her protestations that we could simply send word to Mr. Malcolm from Becketts—protestations that I suspected were rooted in her desire to avoid leading the piebald home herself—we soon parted ways. With thunder on her brow, Lady Chedington dragged her "spotted beast" in the direction of Becketts, and Bertie and I walked down the lower path, eventually breaking from the treeline behind a cluster of stone buildings. The rhythmic double-clang of a hammer on metal confirmed that we had found the forge.

32

A LOOSE-LIPPED LEPRECHAUN

"Why, Miss Cobb!" Mr. Malcolm said in surprise as we entered his cobblestone yard. He stood in a low, open-fronted stone building, shaping a large shoe in front of the coal-fired forge. A massive Percheron stood tied nearby, kindly provided with an ample portion of hay—a tribute to proper digestion that would have pleased Dr. Reed, had he been there to see it.

Away from his forge, no one would suspect Malcolm's profession. He was small and slight, possessing a curiously ageless face, and his twinkling black eyes and spritely ways gave the impression of a latter-day leprechaun.

"People are forever expectin' a farrier to have height like yours, Miss Cobb," he had once told me, "but how would that help, I ask you? My work is crouchin' low with a hoof between my knees, an' I reckon 'twould be that much harder if I were farther from the ground."

After smartly removing Bertie's loose shoe, the man declared cheerfully, "Won't even cost you the price of a new shoe." Everything Malcolm did was cheerful and snappy, like the sparks he wrought from the metal on his anvil. "Nothin' wrong with this shoe save a little wobble, an' that's easily mended."

As he took the shoe to the forge, I said, "I've heard the Chedington horses never wear studs. Is that so?"

"Aye, that's so," he said. "Sir Algernon were always against it. Seems a young mare of his blew out a tendon in pasture, years ago, an' he always said she never would've done it if her hoof'd slid instead of stuck, like. I told him, there's plenty of horses as wear studs and survive, but he were dead set against it an' there weren't no changin' his mind."

"But the Chedington's stallion Brioso is wearing studs. I suppose someone requested them in your last visit?"

The little man looked curiously at me, the orange light of the flames reflected in his dark eyes. "Ah, quite the mystery, that one," he said. "No, no one requested 'em, but I reset shoes exactly as I find 'em, see? An' that stallion's been wearin' studs since last October, 'cause last October I lifted his hoof and found studs already there."

"That was after Sir Algernon's death? And you hadn't put studs on him before that?"

He looked surprised. "Sure, it were after the accident. Sad state of affairs, that. Lady Chedington had that stallion locked in a stall for weeks by the time I saw him. Seemed a bit cruel, but there it is. A sorry sight, he were. Lost all his pride, seemed like. An' the studs I saw on his shoes that day, well, they hadn't been set by me, that's certain."

"Then how did they get there?"

"Oh, I got the feelin' Sir Algernon had been messin' 'bout with those shoes before he died. Makes sense, you know."

"Does it?" I said, confused.

"You know where they found his body."

"Out on the moor."

"Well, there you go, then."

I blinked at him. "I don't quite . . ."

The farrier waved his tongs like an instructor's pointer, explaining, "If he meant to go gallopin' around Exmoor, well, he probably got to worryin' 'bout slippin' an' he added them studs himself, just for a trial, like."

"I see. He knew how to add studs to shoes?"

"He knew plenty 'bout shoes and shoein', did Sir Algernon. Not hot shoein', 'course, but he could do a bit of cold shoein'. He were always tryin' to get away from the missus," he said, grinning broadly.

I couldn't see what that had to do with shoeing, but I smiled helpfully back. "Indeed?"

"Indeed!" he said with feeling. "I always thought that were why he spent so many hours down here with me, learnin' more than most gentlemen ever know 'bout hooves and shoes. But Mr. Langford did too, an' he's not even married."

"Mr. Langford?" I said. Bertie's ears pricked sharply.

"Oh aye, Mr. Langford," Malcolm said, taking the glowing shoe to the anvil. The wide leather aprons he wore over his legs flapped like wings—a winged leprechaun, I thought irrelevantly. "Last year, he came to me to learn, and real keen he were." The little man raised his voice over the clanging of his hammer against the shoe. "No harm in the gentlemen playin' around, like. Makes 'em feel like real horsemen. Sir Algernon just played around, but Mr. Langford, he's been doin' his own hoof trimmin' and shoein' for a while now."

"Why would he do his own shoeing?" I tried to picture the well-coiffed poet shoeing a horse, and failed.

Malcolm approached Bertie, lifted his front hoof, and placed the shoe against the sole. He checked the fit with an appraising eye and then grunted, taking the shoe back to the anvil. "Well, these gentry, they don't have no profession. Don't have no way to make more money, once the money's gone."

He seemed to think this sufficient explanation, but after a moment of silence, I said, "Yes?"

"I reckon Mr. Langford found himself in just that kind of pickle, so he started cuttin' corners, like. Shoein' his own horses an' such."

"But Mr. Langford does have a profession," I pointed out. "He has a horse breeding business."

The little man brayed a laugh. "You know horses, Miss Cobb. Horses ain't no way to make a livin'—unless you're gettin' paid to put shoes on 'em, that is." He flashed me a grin, white teeth in a smoke-darkened face. "Breedin' and raisin' horses, well, it ain't for the faint of heart. Too many things can go wrong with horseflesh, and what can go wrong usually does, that's the rule with horses. Havin' a breedin' farm, well, that's just a fancy way of sayin' you like to gamble. An' Mr. Langford, most of his gambles never paid off."

"Such as?"

"Such as that deal he made with Sir Algernon, payin' all that money just to get them colts by that famous stallion. He got the short end of that stick, Mr. Langford did. His colt Dolce were a disappointment, an' it probably chapped his hide to see Sir Algernon end up with a fine colt like Brioso."

"But the colts were very similar in appearance?" Bertie said quickly. Malcolm looked amused at Bertie's whickering, and I relayed the question.

"Oh, like twins they were, when they were standin' still. But if you saw 'em move, you knew which were which. Dolce, he had a funny way of goin'. Flipped his front hoof, he did, an' no amount of trainin' could take it out of him. Brioso, now, he were a real nice mover, an' with Sir Algernon's good trainin', well, he were set to make somethin' brilliant out of that stallion. Mr. Langford and Dolce, there weren't no brilliance 'bout neither one of them."

"And then Dolce died last year," I said. "Do you know how he died?"

Malcolm's laughing leprechaun eyes sobered for the first time. "Mr. Langford had more'n a bit of bad luck last year. Like I said, he's a great one for cuttin' corners, is Mr. Langford, an' he bought some cheap hay at auction. Real musty stuff, turns out, an' two of his favorite stallions got real sick. The more valuable one died—Dolce. How's that for luck? But maybe it weren't such bad luck after all. Some big city insurance man came down, an' turns out, Mr. Langford had enough insurance on Dolce to dig himself right out of that tight spot he were in." His lips twisted wryly. "For a while, that is."

"What do you mean, for a while?"

The farrier took the shoe back to Bertie and said, "How long do you reckon it takes to renovate a tack room, Miss Cobb?"

"I wouldn't know," I said, surprised.

"Mr. Langford's been renovatin' his for a year."

"Perhaps he's in the midst of something very grand?"

"P'rhaps. Or p'rhaps not," he said, crinkling his black eyes at me. He was certainly enjoying his roundabout tale. Drawing it out of him was beginning to feel like hoisting an anchor from the depths of the sea.

"Yes?" I said. "Have you seen his tack room, then?"

"I ain't been to Maplehurst in a long while. Mr. Langford, he still buys horseshoes from me, comes right here to the forge to pick 'em up. I used to deliver to Maplehurst, but he said them renovations of his are makin' a right muddle of things. Said it's best to steer clear till everythin's sorted. But I don't know 'bout that."

"What don't you know?"

"Well," he said, his small hammer tap-tapping horseshoe nails expertly into Bertie's hoof, "the last time I delivered shoes to Maplehurst, last year, Mr. Langford were actin' real queer, like. Wouldn't let me carry the shoes into the tack room. Made me set 'em out in the stable aisle. An' couldn't wait to get me out of that stable an' on my way. Made me think maybe there were somethin' in that tack room he didn't want me to see." He looked up from his work on Bertie's hoof and gave me an exaggerated wink. "Now, what do you think that could be, Miss Cobb?"

My heartbeat quickened, and I remembered young Tom's words as he held Treacle Tart outside the Becketts tack room. *"Better'n a horse, I say. Sir Algernon's father, he kept a horse in the tack room when he were short on box stalls."*

"A horse," I breathed. It was too low for the farrier to hear, but Bertie's clever ears caught the word and he swung his head my way.

"Nothin', that's what!" Malcolm said, slapping his leg and laughing at his own wit. "There ain't nothin' in that tack room, an' nothin's what he don't want no one to see!"

I frowned, trying to untangle his words. "Why wouldn't he want no one—anyone to see nothing?"

"It weren't me that said it, you understand, but I don't think Mr. Langford's renovatin' that tack room at all."

"No?"

"No."

"Why not?"

"Mr. Langford, he's always been a bit short of the ready."

Tilting his pointed chin, he gave me a knowing look and rubbed his thumb and forefinger together. "Lackin' the needful, if you know what I mean."

"You think he ran out of money?"

"Aye, I think the money ran out an' he's too ashamed to admit it. I reckon that tack room of his looks the same as it did a year ago, an' he don't want nobody to know it." He set down Bertie's hoof and looked at it critically, then turned to me. "He's a proud man is Mr. Langford, an' he were right proud of his grand plans. Told everyone 'bout them renovations. Told everyone to steer clear till it were done, that's how he brought it up in conversation, like. 'Best not come to Maplehurst while things are underway,' he'd say, 'We'll have a grand reveal when it's done.' But I reckon, what with all his debts an' this an' that, he ran clean out of money before he ever touched that tack room. An' now he can't bring himself to say it'll never be finished. Tragic. Like one of them Greek tragedies." From the satisfied look on the farrier's face, he seemed to be rather enjoying Langford's tragedy.

I glanced at Bertie. The horse's gray lashes were lowered and there were wrinkles above his nostrils. It was an expression of rumination that had nothing to do with digestion.

As I paid Malcolm, Bertie shook himself awake and murmured, "Ask him about the ghost on the moor."

"Talkative, ain't he?" Malcolm said, giving Bertie's neck a firm pat.

"I've heard rumors that Sir Algernon's ghost has been seen riding on the moor at night," I said. "Have you ever seen it?"

He snorted. "'Course not," he said, waving a hand. "I don't go in much for that spiritualism stuff, not like Mrs. Jones down the lane. She's the one for ghost stories, she is. Or there's plenty of folks down at the pub willin' to talk, if you wet their whistle first. Might cost you, but I've never known a secret to survive more'n a few pints of ale, so if you're willin' to buy a few rounds, you'll hear your fill. An' you'll find yourself right popular too. That's what I call a win-win."

As usual, Bertie sifted quickly through the words to pick out the salient morsel. Nudging my arm, the horse muttered, "Who is 'Mrs. Jones down the lane'?"

"Ah!" Malcolm said, grinning at my question. "Mrs. Jones." He placed a stubby finger alongside his nose and said in a mock whisper, "Mrs. *Irene* Jones." He looked at me expectantly, but when I only stared blankly back, he ventured, "Wears a veil, though she's not a bride? Likes colors of the darker persuasion?"

Bertie began to laugh, slow and soft, and I said, "Do you mean that Mrs. Irene Jones is Madame Irena Itovsky? The spirit medium?"

The man beamed, immensely pleased that I had guessed his riddle. "There you are, though it weren't me that said it! Likes to keep things secret, does Mrs. Jones. Good for business to keep the gentry guessin', she says. None of them fine ladies wants to find out their spirit medium is a person named Jones. They like them foreign names."

"And by 'down the lane,' you mean she lives near here?"

33

DEDUCING THE DIMENSIONS
OF THE REMAINING CAT

BERTIE and I were soon riding down the broad dirt road that ran past the front of the forge. Branches arched high above our heads, filtering the warm afternoon sun and sending extra dapples of light and shadow dancing across Bertie's coat.

"Are leprechauns the creatures that speak in riddles," I said, "or am I thinking of a different fairytale character?"

"What?" Bertie said, his ears tilting. "Oh, I see. Very apt. Something of a West Country Rumpelstiltskin, I should think."

"Did you know how informative he would be?" I peered down at the horse's arched gray neck, wishing I could see his face. His lofty steps betrayed that he was certainly pleased about something.

"I had hopes," he said. "One good rule of hoof is, never tell a farrier your secrets. They tend to be gossipier than a Kensington carriage horse."

"Which I assume means gossipy."

"Oh, very."

"In that case, I wish you were a bit more like a Kensington

carriage horse. Are you planning to spill your cats before we reach Madame Itovsky's?"

He turned his Roman nose and squinted up at me. "When our diminutive friend was waxing mysterious about Langford's tack room, why did you say 'a horse'?"

"It was something Tom said earlier today, when I said it was a shame about Treacle Tart being locked in the tack room. He said, 'Better'n a horse,' and went on to say that Sir Algernon's father was rumored to have put a horse in the tack room when he was short on space."

Bertie snorted. "It's details like that that aid an investigation," he said. "In the role of Watson, you should consider communicating your clues."

"You could do with a dose of that yourself."

"But I suppose it wasn't a vital detail," he continued. "The stable lad had already mentioned something intriguing about Langford's tack room. Do you remember what he said on our first night at Becketts?"

I tried to visualize Tom's slim, freckled face that night as he stood next to the fence of Bertie's meadow. His young chest had swelled with pride as he told me about his work at Maplehurst—woodworking, he'd said. He was good at woodworking. And building. And tearing down. *"Mr. Langford, he were in a right pickle. Said he needed to clear out his tack room, clear it all out, saddle racks an' harness pegs an' all, till it were clean and smooth down to the wall studs. He called on me that time, sayin' it were a rush job . . ."*

"Langford *is* keeping a horse in there!" I exclaimed.

"And the furtive behavior the farrier described? Langford is not *keeping* a horse in his tack room, he's *hiding* a horse in his tack room. Why would he begin hiding a horse around the same time he received a rather sizeable insurance windfall?" Bertie was practically prancing under me in his impatience.

"Dolce didn't die," I breathed.

"Well done, Harriet," he said. "The poet faked his stallion's death last year. But I don't think he is quite the criminal mastermind Byerley seems to believe. I think the winds of fate sent Langford an opportunity, which he was intelligent enough to see and unscrupulous enough to seize. That bout of bad hay did leave him with an equine corpse—but it wasn't Dolce's. Langford was struggling financially, and Dolce's insurance money must've been tantalizing. He also believed that the little clause in his contract with Sir Algernon would make Brioso his if Dolce died. He had two very good reasons to claim it was Dolce that died."

"But surely the insurance agent would've checked the corpse against Dolce's papers?"

"What do we know about the frequency of black horses at Maplehurst?" Bertie said.

"That Langford collects them like they're going out of style," I said.

"Indeed. Dolce was plain, no white markings, and his only identifying mark—the Becketts brand—is carried by many of Langford's herd. When a horse is alive and standing, especially when moving, he's easy to identify if you know what to look for. But one dead horse with a brand on his shoulder looks very much like another. And if that dead horse was plain and dark enough to pass for black . . . well, it wouldn't take much to fool a city agent coming down from London."

"But Langford can't fool his neighbors . . ."

"Not the horsiest among them. Not if they see the surviving stallion move."

"So he keeps Dolce out of sight in that tack room." My

stomach turned at the thought of a horse closed in darkness, unable to graze or move freely under the open sky. "He's as bad as Lady Chedington, keeping a horse locked up around the clock!"

"Ah, but I don't think we can lay such cruelty at the poet's feet," Bertie said. "Consider the ghostly rumors. The timing fits."

The light dawned. "Langford is exercising Dolce on the moor at night?"

"When it is too dark for anyone to identify the horse," Bertie agreed, nodding.

I considered for a moment. "Committing insurance fraud doesn't make Langford a murderer, any more than our little antics in Wolverhampton make us murderers. He's been hiding his own horse in his own tack room. How does that help us prove he murdered the Major?"

Bertie raised his muscular neck and tilted his head to look up at me. "Haven't you guessed?" he said. "Langford doesn't have Dolce in his tack room. He has Brioso."

It was fortunate that Bertie never let me ride with tight reins, as I probably would have jabbed him in the mouth in my surprise. As it was, the loose reins did no damage, but he felt me startle in the saddle and he chuckled.

"Think back, Harriet," he said. "Brioso ran loose for a night after Sir Algernon fell and died. He 'turned up like a bad penny' at Becketts the next morning, standing patiently at the stable door. I believe Langford caught Brioso that night—perhaps even intending to return him in the morning—but then, upon hearing of Sir Algernon's death, Langford saw his chance and took it. He put Sir Algernon's saddle on Dolce and delivered him instead, under cover of darkness."

"But wouldn't Fletcher have recognized—oh," I said, realization dawning.

"Yes, 'oh.'" Bertie said. "Eloquently put. Fletcher was laid up in his cottage with a broken leg. The well-meaning but less-intuitive stable lad saw only a plain black stallion—who did bear a very close resemblance to Brioso—wearing Sir Algernon's saddle. He put him in Brioso's stall and, on Lady Chedington's orders, kept him locked in that stall for weeks. When Fletcher returned—"

"He thought Brioso had lost all his muscling," I said, "and all his spirit. He thought he seemed diminished, like a different horse, but he thought it was all due to being shut in a stall for so long."

"Or some sort of equine penitence for bolting with Sir Algernon," Bertie said. "Fletcher was plumbing the depths of absurdity in his attempt to reconcile the stallion's change in personality. But as for noticing any physical differences, Fletcher knows he can't trust his old eyes anymore. His vision is fading—he even mentioned it to you."

"But the stallion at Becketts isn't hidden away in a tack room," I protested. "He's there for anyone to see. Someone, perhaps one of those horsey neighbors you mentioned, could have noticed the difference even though he's kept in a stall. Langford was taking a massive gamble."

"Not as massive as you might think. Formal mourning is one of the more tiresome traditions you humans have, but it certainly came to Langford's aid in this case. Lady Chedington has been in mourning for the past year, much to her chagrin, and the neighbors have properly kept their distance. Her ladyship is so desperate to socialize that she's been reduced to relying on a saddler for company."

"Thank you very much," I said.

"Langford thought of nearly everything—except for those studs," Bertie said. "Brioso never wore studs, but Dolce did, and Langford simply forgot to remove them before swapping the horses."

"Is that your only evidence? All of this is built on those little studs? And the fact that everyone has been banging on about the stallion's change in behavior?"

"Until we talked to the leprechaun, yes. But he mentioned something else, something which jogged my memory, if I might indulge in a little pun. When the horse you knew as Brioso was dragging the Major, did you notice anything odd about his movement?"

"The horse or the corpse?" I said. "I was more interested in the corpse."

"And I was more interested in the horse. When I was next to that stallion, bringing him down from his gallop, I noticed he had an interesting way of flinging his left front hoof. He paddled it as he moved. A quirk that Dolce was known to have."

"And then Langford asked me if Byerley said anything about the stallion's movement after seeing him run!" I exclaimed. "He must've been worried Byerley suspected—does Byerley suspect the stallions were swapped?"

"I think he does," Bertie said. "I believe that's the cat Byerley refused to let out of his bag last night."

"And then Byerley suggested the gala," I said. "He told Olivia to invite all her horsiest neighbors, to do a grand demonstration with the stallion. He *knew* some of the neighbors would realize that the stallion was Dolce, not Brioso."

"So did Langford," he said, nodding his big head. "It would've been a very public revelation of his fraud. Thus, he needed to bring a decisive end to any discussion of galas and prove that the stallion was too dangerous for Miss Olivia to handle. It was a clever idea to hire the Major to discourage the girl. But when the Major proved duplicitous, Langford killed him and framed the stallion for the murder. That is our working theory."

We rounded a bend in the quiet road, coming out from under the leafy avenue and moving into sunlight. Ahead on the left was a trim stone cottage, tendrils of blue smoke threading out of its chimney.

"There's one problem with all of this," I said. "What did Langford hope to gain by stealing Brioso? Yes, he has him, but he can't do a thing with him!"

Bertie gave a slow chuckle, so deep and earthy that I could feel it down to the toes of my boots. "Correct. Brioso is most valuable as a breeding stallion. People pay for bloodlines, but if Langford can't reveal that the stallion on his property is Brioso, he can't possibly profit from him."

I snorted. "Unless his obsession drove him batty and he only wants to gaze at Brioso and write poems about him . . . it was a very silly thing to do. He must have nothing but saddle flocking between his ears!"

Bertie cocked his ears thoughtfully. "Perhaps when one is as obsessed as he was with Brioso, one ceases to think clearly. When the object of one's obsession wanders up, reins dragging, free for the grabbing . . . well, I suppose one grabs first and considers later. And now that Langford has had time to consider, he knows that he needs to be seen buying Brioso fair and square—or marrying into ownership of him—if he wants to do anything more than gaze at him in that tack room. That's why he's so desperate to buy Dolce back from Becketts, or marry Miss Olivia."

"Because everyone believes Dolce is Brioso," I said, and

then I began to laugh. "You know, the ghost on the moor is one of the reasons Miss Olivia has been so reluctant to sell the stallion. Langford must find that infuriating."

"The poet certainly shot himself in the foot with that one," Bertie agreed.

The two black horses cantered merrily around my mind, round and round like deranged carousel horses, until I began to feel a bit woozy. *Two horses . . .* I straightened up sharply in the saddle. "Madame Itovsky said 'two horses' when she was talking about the murder. Do you think Langford was worried about Byerley's suspicions and decided to try swapping the horses back? And the Major stumbled drunkenly across the swap?"

"Now you're thinking like a detective," Bertie said, a rare note of approval in his voice. "But if Brioso is as spirited as he is reputed to be, I doubt Langford would have been able to get him to Maplehurst in the midst of a midnight storm. However," he halted in front of the stone cottage, "that is another detail Madame Itovsky should be able to clear up. I still believe she must have seen the murder, or spoken to someone who did."

34

DEAD GIVEAWAYS

THE COTTAGE WAS nothing I would have chosen for the grim and stately Madame Itovsky. With its cheerfully squat appearance, soft blue shutters, and window boxes overflowing with a rampage of yellow petunias, it looked like something Miss Olivia would have fancied. I dismounted and approached the blue door, noting gauzy white curtains fluttering out of the open windows.

"She must be home," I said, but when my knocking produced no result, Bertie crossed the verge and followed me back along the vine-laden side of the cottage.

We rounded the rear corner to see a slim woman in shirtwaist and skirt, pinning black garments to a clothesline. It would have been a very ordinary slice of country life if the clothesline had not been supported by two towering statues, each with the body of a man and the head of a jackal. The line was fastened at either end to the statues' outstretched hands, and the jackal heads glared stonily at each other over the woman's head as she bent to her basket. It was a wonder she could sleep at night with those ghastly figures just outside her back door, but they were probably useful in keeping the neighbors away.

"Anubis, the Egyptian god of the dead," Bertie observed. "If she's trying to keep her two identities separate, someone should inform her that those statues are a bit of a tip-off."

"They're a dead giveaway," I agreed, and the big horse snorted a laugh.

At the sound of Bertie's snort, the woman whirled, holding a length of black cloth in front of her like a weapon. Waves of soft brown hair framed a face which, from its faint smile lines, would have been kind and clever had it not been pinched with worry. She observed us for a moment, then slowly lowered her hand. As she did so, I saw the glint of something peeking out from under the cloth.

"She has a knife!" I whispered.

"Byerley was right," Bertie murmured. "She is afraid of something."

"What are you doing here?" the woman demanded.

"Madame Itovsky," I said, taking a few steps forward, "I'm Harriet Cobb, Lady Chedington's saddler. Do you remember me? I was at the séance this morning, and I need to ask you a few questions."

The woman's face turned wary. "I don't know what you're talking about. My name is Jones. Irene Jones."

I raised my eyebrows and looked pointedly at the unearthly statues that flanked her, then at the unmistakable black gown and veils hanging on the clothesline. Following my gaze, her expression wavered for a moment before collapsing into a sheepish smile.

"Oh, bother," she said, leaning to place the cloth and knife back into her basket. "Lady Chedington sent you, did she? I didn't think she knew where I lived." A hint of worry returned to her face. "But if she knows, I suppose everyone knows."

"No, Lady Chedington doesn't know," I assured her. "The bl— someone else told me."

Something flickered in the woman's eyes. "Not Lord Byerley?"

"No, not him."

She visibly relaxed. "Well, I can't tell Lady Chedington anything more about those golden bits. The spirits have spoken, and as they don't like to speak too frequently, she'll need to wait till the next séance. If she doesn't find the bits in the meantime, that is. Would you please tell her what I've said? Her ladyship is a very persistent correspondent when she doesn't get the information she wants. The postal clerk grows tired of holding all those messages for me."

"I'm not here to ask about the golden bits," I said. "I have questions about the other things you said today."

Her face became as stony as the statues on either side of her. "I didn't say anything," she said. "It was Sir Algernon's spirit that spoke, and I can neither repeat nor explain what a spirit says. You must look deep within yourself to find the truth in his words. Deciphering the spirit's message is a valuable journey for your own spirit."

"My spirit says that you were at Becketts two nights ago."

She gaped at me. "What?"

"Perhaps you were walking on Becketts land sometime that night, near enough to see the stable yard."

"My dear woman," she said, "are you attempting to frame me for murder?"

"So you know there was a murder committed?" I said.

"Everyone knows that military man was killed by the

Becketts horse. And now you're trying to place me at the scene. Did Lord Byerley put you up to this?"

"Why Byerley?" Bertie said, and I repeated the question.

"No reason," she said, and she gazed suspiciously at Bertie for a moment. When her eyes finally shifted to me, the anger in them had been replaced by curiosity. "You might be interested to know," she said slowly, "the druids of old could communicate with animals."

Before I could gather my wits—and a suitably evasive response—Bertie's ears flickered toward the cottage and I heard a cheerful voice saying, "I'm sorry I'm so late, Ma. Her grand highness needed to change. She took a bit of a tumble from a horse—I didn't even know she rode horses!—and I had to help . . ." The speaker came merrily around the corner of the house, a basket in one hand and a half-eaten apple in the other. The words faded from her lips when she saw us. Familiar tight brown curls were visible under her jaunty straw boater hat.

"Miss Cobb!" she said.

"Hello, Sarah," I said, feeling a slow smile spreading across my face. Things were beginning to make sense. "Madame Itovsky is your mother?"

"Sarah has nothing to do with any of this!" the older woman burst out, moving swiftly to stand between us and the girl. For a brief moment, she glanced back at the clothes basket, apparently regretting that she was now farther away from her knife.

"It's all right, Ma," Sarah said. "Miss Cobb is a friend."

"She was at Becketts with—with all of them," her mother replied.

"She's newer to the neighborhood than we are," Sarah said, setting down her basket. "I don't think she knows any of them particularly well." She stepped around her mother and came to Bertie, offering him the apple in her hand. "There's a fine fellow, now," she crooned, as Bertie politely accepted the treat and crunched it with slobbery relish.

"Sarah," I said, "I think you may be able to clear a few things up for us—for me. I think you may have seen something two nights ago at Becketts, and I think you know that the Major was not killed by that stallion."

She stared. "No," she said, shaking her head slowly. "I didn't see anything—you think something else happened to that man?" If it wasn't the truth, it was beautifully done. Her warm brown eyes were wide and guileless, and I felt my resolve faltering.

"In the séance this morning," I said, "your mother described certain details about the Major's death, details that seem to fit with other evidence—to spell murder. How could she have known those details unless she saw it happen, or you did?"

Sarah absorbed this for a long moment. Finally she said, "I could point out that my mother is a spirit medium, and a good one, which is true, but . . . I like you, Miss Cobb. And I trust you."

"But . . . you don't even know me," I blurted.

The girl flushed faintly and smiled, looking very much like her mother, her face creasing prettily in all the same places. "No, I don't know you, but I know more about you than you think. I'm not usually given to listening at doors, but two nights ago, I heard such lovely laughter coming from your room—Miss Olivia was laughing and sounded so happy, happier than she's been in a long while! What with her father's death and her mother's ways, she's had a rough time of it, as you can imagine. When I heard her laughing, I mean really laughing, I couldn't help but listen at your door. And I heard those stories you told, about your time in Walsall and your saddlery work, and I just . . . well, I guess I got to like you."

"Oh," I said, not knowing what else to say.

"I shall need to hear these stories," Bertie murmured. "I'm envisioning a new career for you as an inspirational speaker to young ladies. And prime minister after that, when women get the vote."

"You said you trust me," I said to the girl. "Will you tell me what you saw two nights ago?"

She shook her head. "Nothing, Miss Cobb. I was telling the truth. I don't know anything about the Major's death or murder."

"But your mother said, "Two men. Two horses. There was a struggle. The crack of a whip. One man fell into darkness, never to rise again.'"

Sarah looked across at her mother, whose face was rigid with concern. A thought seemed to pass between them, and the girl turned back to me, her eyes solemn. "She wasn't describing the Major's murder. She was describing what happened to Sir Algernon."

35

A WITNESS

"Wʜᴀᴛ?" Bertie and I spoke together, and Madame Itovsky's clever eyes flitted to the horse again, but I was past caring.

"Tell me," I said to Sarah.

Absently stroking Bertie's neck, the girl began to speak. "Ma and I haven't lived here long, you know. We came to Pelgren Vale last August, from Hampshire, at the invitation of Lady Carter. She knew of Ma's work through a friend in Hampshire—for a spirit medium, you know, it's almost impossible to work in a new place without some sort of introduction, as the police are always suspecting fraud. Anyway, we fell in love with the Vale and decided to stay. Ma's bookings were coming on strong, and I was lucky enough to find work at Becketts. Lady Chedington hired me as a lady's maid to Miss Olivia . . . it was a good position." She paused, her work-worn fingertips playing with Bertie's mane. "Miss Olivia loves those whortleberry tarts, you know, the ones we had yesterday," she said.

That seemed irrelevant, but I said, "Yes?"

"Mrs. Granger never has time to go searching for whortleberries. But I like nature. I like getting up at dawn and wandering through the woods to find berries. They grow best at the edge of the woods, up where the trees meet the moorland."

I nodded slowly, beginning to see how the berries fit into things.

"So," she sighed, "last September, I was berry picking, trying to find the last of the whortleberries. I always went very early, just as the sun was coming up, and I often saw Sir Algernon riding his black stallion. They were such a sight. Beautiful. And a little frightening."

"Frightening?" I said.

"That stallion always played up. I don't know much about horses, Miss Cobb, but it always seemed Sir Algernon had his hands full when he rode that one."

"I see. Go on."

"He was venturing farther and farther from the estate in his daily rides. It worried me a little, and I know it worried Lady Chedington, since Fletcher wasn't around and Sir Algernon was always riding alone. She was certain he would have a bad fall. Well, on that morning in September, someone rode out to join Sir Algernon. At first I was relieved, thinking he'd found someone to accompany him, but then . . ."

"But then?"

"It seemed they were arguing. At first, they were just talking, kind of circling each other on horseback. I was too far away to hear anything, of course. Then I started to hear snatches of raised voices, but it was one of those windy, late-summer days, so I couldn't really catch anything. It went on for awhile, and then the other man raised his hand. Sir Algernon shouted and reached for the hand, and they struggled for a moment on horseback before breaking apart. Then the other man held his arm out again toward Sir Algernon, and I heard a pop and a crack, like the crack of a giant whip splitting the air. That's when I knew the other man had fired a gun."

"A gun!?"

She nodded solemnly. "Sir Algernon didn't appear to be hit, but his black stallion panicked at the sound of the gunshot, rearing and spinning and bolting madly away across the moor. The other rider stayed still for a moment, looking in my direction. I had cried out when it happened, you see. I was shaking with fright, but I was well-hidden in the trees and bracken. And the rider finally turned and galloped away." She took a deep, quavering breath, leaning a little into Bertie's comforting bulk.

"And you didn't tell anyone about this?" I said gently.

She turned her eyes on me, tears welling, and I saw the months of anguish reflected in them. "No," she whispered. "At first, I was too frightened. And then I thought maybe I hadn't seen what I thought I'd seen. Perhaps there was nothing in that rider's hand. Perhaps he had just been pointing his finger, and it was a distant gunshot that spooked the horse. People are always hunting on Exmoor."

"But what about when Sir Algernon didn't return from his ride?"

"Everyone started searching the moor right away. They didn't need me to tell them that's where he'd been riding. I didn't find out he died till that evening, and then I felt so ashamed. I thought I should have gone after him when the stallion bolted."

"You wouldn't have gotten far on foot," I said, offering slim consolation. "You can't blame yourself for that."

"But I had waited all day without saying a thing. I knew I

would certainly lose my position if I spoke up after staying mum for so long. I'd only been at Becketts a short time. We were so new to Pelgren Vale, we were still trying to keep Ma's work private until she could build a solid reputation. A scandal involving her daughter, before anyone really knew us, it would've put an end to her career. Please understand, Miss Cobb," she said, reaching out a shaky hand to grasp my arm. "If a bullet wound had been found, I would have come forward and told what I saw." Her arm dropped limply to her side. "But he didn't die by gunshot. He died falling from his stallion."

"Because of a gunshot," I pointed out, and she dropped her eyes, cheeks flaming.

"What did the horse and rider look like? Could she identify them?" Bertie said. I asked the question, and Madame Itovsky strode over to put a protective arm around her daughter's shoulders.

"She's answered your questions," she said. "She doesn't know anything else."

"But why now?" Bertie persisted. "Why come out with it now, unveiling those details during the séance? Surely there must be a reason."

Madame Itovsky looked hard at the horse. "I can't make out your words," she said slowly, "but I sense you're able to communicate." She looked at me. "Care to translate?"

Under her calm eyes and matter-of-fact certainty, I felt my old denials and deflections begin to crumble. My shoulders felt curiously light as I shrugged and said, "Why now? Why suddenly bring up those details in the séance after all these months?"

"I was worried about—" Sarah said.

"You don't need to say anything more," her mother cut in.

"No, I want to," the girl said, a hint of desperation in her voice. She was like Miss Seyward in that moment, seeking redemption through revelation. "I was worried about Lady Chedington and Miss Olivia's safety. You see, until this week, I had no idea who the other rider was. He was riding a brown horse that day, and there are brown horses everywhere. I don't know enough about horses to tell one brown horse from another. The man was too far away for me to see his face or anything else about him ... except for his coat."

"His coat?" I said, surprised.

"He was wearing a bright coat. Very bright. In that early sunlight, it almost glowed. It was such a vivid yellow-green ..."

My heart dropped. I looked at Bertie. His nostrils flared, and there was a hard light in his eyes.

"It was a color I had never seen on any man, before or since," Sarah continued, "until this week." Her solemn brown eyes found my face. "Two days ago, I saw that coat again, and Lord Byerley was wearing it."

36

REVELATIONS

BERTIE'S CANTERING hooves thrummed out a quick, three-beat rhythm, as impatient and insistent as the words going round my mind. *He did it—he did it—he did it . . .*

"I don't blame them for refusing to speak to the police about it," Bertie said, not winded in the slightest by the exercise. The woods were growing cool and dim around us, late afternoon shadows weaving a grim latticework across our path. "Sarah did not actually witness a murder," the horse continued. "Her account is merely circumstantial. The Byerley family is one of the richest and most influential in the county, as Madame Itovsky pointed out. Byerley could make life very uncomfortable for them."

"I just don't understand Byerley's motive in all of this," I said, ducking a cluster of low-hanging leaves. "There must have been some bad blood between him and Sir Algernon, which I suppose we should ask Fletcher about. And the Major—we're assuming Byerley killed the Major, yes?—what was his motive there?"

"Have you considered that he and Langford might be in this together? They did grow up together, 'like brothers,' Miss O said."

"If that's the case, why would Byerley have—steady on, old boy. Can you at least try to avoid the lowest branches now and then?—why would Byerley have spilled so much to us about Langford? He was definitely pointing the blame, which doesn't smack of a brotherly alliance."

"Perhaps Byerley desired Brioso after all, regardless of his assertions to the contrary. Our fastidious lord is quite taken with uniqueness, which is why he usually buys misfit horses, but Brioso is unique in another way, being Horizon's last colt."

"I suppose," I said.

Bertie cocked an ear in my direction. "I should think you'd be pleased to discover Byerley's guilt. After all, you identified him from the beginning as an unsavory character."

I spent a moment in begrudging self-reflection. "I guess I was starting to like him," I said.

Bertie snorted and his ears flicked forward again. "So was I, old girl. It seems you and I need to spend more time in the company of humans and the study of human nature. It appears we are both rubbish."

The gate to Bertie's meadow had been left open, sagging on its old hinges in grim reproof. Either Lady Chedington had anticipated my return, or she hadn't received the strict drumming that most children did with their first pony—*if you open a gate, close it behind you*. Since I was familiar with the parallel rule, *always leave a gate as you found it*, I rode through without stopping. The séance table and chairs stood forlornly under the big oak, abandoned among the weeds as damp evening air worked its way into the fine varnish. I shivered as we rode past. In the eerie stillness, it was all too easy to imagine wandering spirits making use of those empty seats.

We opened the stable doors to find the place full of life. It was surprisingly bright and warm with the glow of gaslight, the smell of horses in clean straw, and the sound of girlish chatter. Standing halfway down the aisle on either side of a dark horse, Miss Olivia and Miss Seyward appeared to be practicing their newfound grooming skills.

"Oh, Miss Cobb!" called Miss Olivia, pink-faced and smiling. "Come and meet Obsidian. She's the matriarch of Becketts, you know."

Judging by the smears of dirt on their grubby skirts, the young ladies had evidently put their hearts into the afternoon's excavations. Their heads were bare, one dark and one light, both charmingly tousled from their exertions. Obsidian, on the other hand, stood poised and polished, groomed to within an inch of her life and looking vaguely bemused at all the attention.

"She's an old dear," Miss Olivia said, waving her brush at the mare. "Fletcher said she could use some grooming. We were *so* tired after digging in the avenue all day—we found nothing but scads of roots, you know—and we needed some way to unwind. There is something very calming about grooming a horse, isn't there? Oh! I suppose Bertie will need brushing after that saddle comes off?"

Miss Seyward gave me a wan smile, looking very much as though she would prefer a bath and a cup of tea to grooming another horse.

Before I could reply, I felt Bertie grow suddenly rigid next to me. "Where is Dolce?" he said.

I looked past the black mare to the stall on the other side

of the aisle, finding only darkness behind the polished bars. "Where is Dol—Brioso?" I said.

Miss Olivia's dimples disappeared. "Oh, Byerley left with him about an hour ago."

I stared at her. "Byerley."

"Yes."

"You sold Brioso," I said, thinking *he got what he wanted after all, that sly, despicable—*

"Yes," she said, fidgeting with the brush in her hand.

"Where's Fletcher?" Surely the old groom would be able to shed light on Byerley's history, produce something to explain why the lord had taken a shot at Sir Algernon last year.

"He went home. That's one good turn I've done. At his age, Fletcher shouldn't be sleeping in the hay every night, but he's been doing that ever since Father died, just to keep an eye on Brioso. Can you imagine? He said now that Brioso's gone, he can go back to his cottage and sleep in his own bed. He seemed relieved."

I nodded mutely and glanced at Bertie. The big horse's gray lashes were nearly closed. At least the gears were turning in that head of his. Finding Miss Olivia's face again, I tried to decide how much to divulge of the afternoon's revelations.

"Oh, don't look at me like that, Miss Cobb," she said, misinterpreting my gaze. "I know I said I was going to keep Brioso, but I decided it was just too hard on Mother. After all, he was a constant reminder of Father's death, and I knew her sorrow would never heal with Brioso here. So I sold him. It's a bit of a shame, though," she mused, running her brush along Obsidian's swayed back. "I did like Brioso, and I've never really liked any horse before! But today of all days, I felt I needed to be selfless and kind to Mother. She's been in a very bad mood all day. She disappeared while we were digging in the avenue, which is strange, because she usually likes to be in the thick of things, shouting orders like a drill sergeant. When she finally joined us again, she was in an even worse mood!"

"Perhaps that's because she fell from a horse," I said, looking at Bertie for signs of life. He was supposed to be the detective in all of this, using his considerable brain to decide our next move. His languid expression hadn't changed, but the skin on his shoulder quivered for a moment as if shaking off a fly.

"Mother *rode?*" squeaked Miss Olivia, her blue eyes round in disbelief.

"Yes," I said. "That's why she disappeared during the dig. She and I were riding to Pelgren to—to talk to Sergeant Harrison, and her horse spooked and she fell."

To my surprise, Miss Olivia began to laugh. "Oh, I can't believe it! You must be a very good influence on Mother, getting her to ride again after all these years. Well? Did she do her trick?"

"Her trick?"

"Yes, her mounting trick."

"I—I'm not sure I understand . . ."

"I saw her do it when I was a child, when she still rode now and then. She approaches the horse with a few quick steps and then swings herself up into the saddle without even touching the stirrup! It's very impressive. Fletcher remembers her doing it, I'm sure."

I stared at the girl in amazement. "Your mother, Lady Chedington, has a . . . mounting trick?" I suddenly remembered Fletcher standing at the piebald's head, making no move to assist his mistress into the saddle until she demanded it.

"Oh, yes!" she said, eyes dancing. "Not only that, but—oh."

Her mouth snapped shut and her expression fell. "I shouldn't have mentioned that. It's not quite the thing, you know. A lady leaping into the saddle and astride too . . . no offense, Miss Cobb, but she wouldn't want word of that to get around. She hasn't done that since I was a child, after all. You won't mention it to anyone, will you?"

Miss Seyward mildly pointed out that Obsidian was beginning to fidget and perhaps it was time to go up for baths and dinner. Miss Olivia reluctantly agreed, and her friend led the broodmare away, the horse seeming no less relieved than the girl. With a last longing look at Bertie's dusty coat, Miss Olivia hoisted the grooming box and made for the tack room.

"Well?" I said, turning to Bertie.

He opened an eye. "Very odd," he said.

"I'm not talking about Lady Chedington's secret trick. What are we going to do about Byerley?"

"Who are you talking to?" came Miss Olivia's voice from behind me.

"My horse," I said quickly, reaching up to pat Bertie's neck. "It's silly, I know, but it can be useful, like talking to oneself . . ."

Bertie's ears appeared unimpressed, but then his great eyes widened in surprise. "Turn around, Harriet," he hissed.

I turned to see Miss Olivia shrugging a coat on over her dirty shirtwaist. Garish yellow-green and a few sizes too large —it was Byerley's coat.

"Where did you get that coat?" I stammered.

"Do you like it? It was a gift. A very kind gift to remember my father by."

"Olivia," I said, dropping the formality, "you need to be careful of Byerley. He is not the friend he seems to be. The fact that he gave you that coat—"

"But Mr. Langford gave me this coat," she said. "He gave it to me the day after my father died."

"What? But Byerley was wearing that coat on Thursday!"

"He has one too," she said, giggling. "Father had these coats made for all the horsey members of the family. See?" She indicated the embroidery on the breast, two rearing black horses. "He called them the 'Becketts Coats.' He had them made for himself, Mother, Byerley, and Mr. Langford. Father considered Byerley and Mr. Langford to be members of the family, you know." She pouted prettily. "I didn't get one, of course, since I couldn't ride. Mother said I should be happy, not having to wear such a hideous color. She refused to wear hers. She said she'd put it on if she ever wanted to ask Father for a special favor. Father himself only wore his coat on very grand occasions, when important breeding clients came to Becketts. I think Byerley was the only person pleased with the coat, but as you know, he's quite taken with gaudy colors."

"And Mr. Langford?"

"Oh, he didn't really want his—it really is a shocking color —but he started wearing it after he and Father made up from their little spat last year. I think wearing it was some kind of gesture for Father. But after Father died, Mr. Langford thought I would like to have the coat. And so I do. I shall always wear it on the anniversary of Father's death. Mr. Langford is a very thoughtful person, which is why I felt so guilty refusing his marriage proposal. I suppose that's the other reason I sold him Brioso."

"Wait," I said. "You told me you sold Brioso to Byerley."

"No, I said Brioso *left* with Byerley," she said, smiling sunnily. "Mr. Langford went home early after I agreed to sell him Brioso. He said he had to get his stable ready, but I think he was a tiny bit devastated that I refused his proposal. Or he just didn't fancy digging in the avenue!" She giggled. "He said he would come back tomorrow morning to get the stallion. But when I told Byerley about it, he said he wanted to deliver Brioso to Mr. Langford himself. Wasn't that kind of him?"

"So Byerley is riding to Maplehurst right now?" My mind raced. Did Byerley intend collusion or confrontation?

"He's probably already there," she said, wrinkling her fine brow in consideration. "He went to talk to Mother first—he said he had something to discuss with her, and he also agreed to tell her about my decision to sell. I didn't have the courage to tell her myself, especially today, of all days. She didn't want Brioso sold, you know. She wanted him destroyed. But I don't think the conversation went very well."

"No?" If Byerley had shared his suspicions with Lady Chedington—

"We heard raised voices, Viv and I, and then Byerley left. He looked so silly, riding that mule and leading Brioso—he bought the mule for himself, you know. For a lord, he certainly has strange taste in horses."

Bertie's voice boomed through the stable, deep and commanding. "She said today is the anniversary of Sir Algernon's death. What is today's date?" Muscles taut and neck held high, he filled the aisle with a formidable tenseness.

Miss Olivia shrank back, blinking at him in awe. When I asked the question, she replied, "September 12th. It's been one year since Father died."

Bertie and I stared at each other as the significance sank in. "I was a fool not to have realized it sooner," Bertie said. "It wasn't Byerley on the moor that day. We know where he was last year on the 12th of September."

"He was in Wolverhampton, standing in the winner's circle with Praxiteles," I said.

"Praxi—what?" Miss Olivia smiled uncertainly, looking back and forth between me and Bertie. "It really is fascinating—it really looks like you're having a conversation! I shall have to try it myself someday, when I find another horse I like."

37

A GALLOP IN THE DARK

"MISS COBB!"

We turned to see Fletcher hobbling through the rear stable entrance, his face pinched and ashen under his old cap. When he saw the young ladies he hesitated, swaying a little. I hurried forward, Bertie's hooves clopping hollowly as he jogged beside me.

"What is it, Fletcher?"

Light sweat stood out on the man's weathered face. "It's her ladyship, Miss Cobb," he said. "She showed up at my place not twenty minutes ago, bangin' on my door an' ravin' about somethin' Lord Byerley told her. 'Did you know?' she kept sayin'. 'Did you know they were switched?' Took me more'n a few minutes to figure out what she were sayin'. Lord Byerley told her Brioso hasn't been here at all, not since Sir Algernon's death. He said Mr. Langford switched the horses that night, brought back his Dolce instead and kept Brioso. I told her, that can't be, Dolce died last year, but she were certain of it."

I nodded, and Fletcher looked at me in surprise.

"This ain't news to you, then?"

"I—it's something I learned today."

"Oh, how funny!" Miss Olivia said, coming up behind me. "Mr. Langford got the stallions mixed up? I shall have to tease him about that the next time I see him."

From the solemn look on Miss Seyward's face, she at least seemed to grasp the situation.

"An' I should've been the first to know," Fletcher said, moving to slump against the front of a stall. "I knew that stallion had changed, but I thought . . ." He shook his head. "Maybe it is time for me to retire, if I can't even read a horse any better'n that." There was heavy silence for a moment and then he said, "There's somethin' else, Miss Cobb, but . . ." his eyes flickered nervously to the young ladies.

"I think Mr. Fletcher could do with a cup of tea," I said, turning swiftly to Miss Olivia. "And perhaps a spot of your mother's sherry?" The two girls nodded and fled to the Hall.

"She went, you know," Fletcher murmured, voice cracking. "Hopped right up on one of the mares out there in the pasture, bareback with nothin' but a bridle."

"Lady Chedington? Can she even ride bareback? She fell off today when her horse spooked."

"Did she?" Fletcher said, frowning. "That'd be strange, that would. Her ladyship's the best rider in the neighborhood, maybe in the county. She performed, back in the day."

Bertie took a step forward, ears pricked, and I gaped at the man. "Performed? You mean, performed on horseback?"

"Oh, aye. You know, in a travelin' troupe. Equestrian acts an' such. Trick ridin', tumblin' 'bout on horseback, an' all that."

My brain felt fuzzy, as though I had been tumbling about on horseback. "I thought Miss Olivia said her mother was on the stage," I said weakly.

"Well, now, Lady Chedington didn't want anyone to know.

Can you imagine if her fancy friends found out she used to ride like that, an' scantily clad too? She wouldn't be gettin' any more invitations to afternoon tea, that's certain. Sir Algernon, he saw her perform all those years ago, an' he fell in love. An' when they married, they kept her history under wraps, like."

Feeling staggered, I looked stupidly at Bertie. Tight wrinkles had formed around his nostrils, and his eyes glinted dangerously.

Fletcher spoke again, and there was a new urgency in his voice. "We could talk 'bout that all night, but that's not what I came to tell you. She *went*, Miss Cobb. Went to Maplehurst." His faded eyes settled on mine. "Went to get her revenge, she said. I think she'd had a bit too much of that sherry she's so fond of, an' there weren't no reasonin' with her. I told her Lord Byerley can handle it, but she just galloped off. I can ride, but with these old eyes, I can't ride at night. So I thought maybe you could stop her before she does any harm to herself or . . . or anybody."

Bertie arched his neck and sidled forward until I was even with his saddle. "Care to try your mounting trick, old girl?"

As I was not a trick rider, I made good use of the stirrup and hauled myself aboard.

"She went by the road," Fletcher said. "Prob'ly didn't want to chance the woods in the dark. But that path in the woods will get you there quicker if you can handle it."

Bertie wheeled and clattered down the stable aisle, shod hooves sliding on bricks, and we burst out into the darkness and headed for the open meadow gate.

If I had thought the branches were hard to avoid in a leisurely canter at dusk, they were much more treacherous while galloping in the dark. I leaned low over Bertie's surging neck, wishing the moon was high enough to at least paint the edges of things.

"Lady Chedington didn't want us to get to Pelgren with that stirrup cup," I said.

"No," Bertie agreed.

"Oh, don't go monosyllabic on me now! Ten-to-one she didn't even have it in her pocket when we started out."

"I'd give higher odds," he said, around steady, whooshing breaths. "That lady is about as trustworthy as a washy chestnut filly on a windy day."

"Less," I grunted. "She's a trick rider. She pulled your bridle off at a full gallop, just before that gorge—she was trying to kill us."

"Perhaps, but only if she knew about the gorge. If not, her fall in the woods was simply a ruse to disappear the stirrup cup."

A thick branch loomed up out of the darkness, and I ducked to one side, only to be swatted soundly in the face by a clump of foliage. "And why," I said, spitting out the remains of a leaf, "would she be so eager to disappear the stirrup cup unless she killed the Major herself?"

"You heard Miss Olivia," he said. "Lady Chedington wanted Brioso destroyed, and any proof the Major was killed by a human would make that unlikely. We do not know for certain that she murdered the Major. We only know that she didn't want anyone questioning Brioso's guilt."

"At least we know who took a shot at Sir Algernon last year."

Bertie snorted. "Do we? It seems there are plenty of those excruciatingly green coats to go around." His body lurched as he bounded over a log on the path.

I found the center of the saddle again, and said, "Byerley

was in Wolverhampton, which leaves Langford and Lady Chedington. So it must have been Langford. He was angry with Sir Algernon, and he wanted Brioso. We also know from the ledger that Sir Algernon suspected something fishy about Dolce's death. He probably confronted Langford about it on the moor that day."

"And Lady Chedington?"

"But I can't imagine her ladyship aiming a revolver at her husband! She's been devastated by his death. It's the whole reason she's so hung up on revenge against Brioso. Although, she has had it in for that horse ever since he was born."

"What did you say?" Bertie said, and then, "Sit tight." He swerved suddenly to the right as the path divided, narrowly missing a heavy tree trunk at the fork.

When my heart dislodged itself from my throat, I replied, "I said, she's had it in for that horse since he was born." We were on a sharp incline now, moving ever closer to the edge of Exmoor.

"Why 'since he was born'?"

"A fortuneteller told her that her husband would be killed by a black stallion."

"Madame Itovsky? But she only came to the Vale last year."

"No, it was long before Madame Itovsky. Years ago, there was another one. Madame something-or-other. Byerley told me about her. She used neighborhood gossip to fabricate fortunes—very clever, you must admit—and she was eventually arrested for fraud. And it was she that first told Lady Chedington her husband would be killed by a black stallion, years before Brioso's birth."

Bertie grunted, but the thrum of his great strides quickened.

In a moment, the leaves thinned and we broke from the

treeline onto a stretch of smooth turf. Ahead, under the wan light of the rising moon, the tidy fences and black chimneys of Maplehurst stood out in sharp relief against the open moor. A timid glow could be seen in the windows of the distant stable —not the gaslight of Becketts, nor the electric lights Langford so coveted, but dim lantern light.

"Bertie," I said, as we aimed for the bordering fence, "I've decided that, when all of this is done, I won't take any more silly saddlery jobs. No more saddles for séances, no more unnecessary adjustments for privileged young ladies who can't even bump a horse. No more bending the truth just to earn a paycheck, because it leads to things like this! From now on, we're going straight."

"Sounds commendable," Bertie said, his ears fixed on the approaching fence. "Commendable, but not half as fun." He rocked back on his haunches and launched into space, flying over the fence in an effortless arc of air and muscle.

38

A DISHEVELED CAVALIER

WE SLOWED to a soft jog as we approached the stable, Bertie's hooves muffled by the thick carpet of grass at the edge of the graveled drive. Motionless in the moonlight, Byerley's mule stood tied to a post outside the front of the stable, but there was no sign of Lady Chedington or her horse.

"It seems we beat her here," I whispered.

As we neared, the mule turned his long, curious ears toward us and whickered a low welcome, but one fierce glare from Bertie cowed him into silence. I dismounted, leaving the reins over Bertie's neck, and we crept toward the stable doors together. Far grander than that of Becketts, Langford's stable entrance was framed by massive columns and an elaborate overhang, complete with decorative spires.

"Trust a poet to truss up the front of his stable like the Palace of Versailles," I muttered.

"Hush," Bertie said, nodding toward a dim column of light that crept out of the entrance. Someone had left the heavy doors ajar, and there were voices within.

"What did you hope to do with him?" came a voice. Only

Byerley could manage that tone, both contemptuous and insipid. "Keep riding him at night, breed only your own mares, keep the foals for yourself and hope no one noticed? I can't see the profit in that. Or were you planning to forge a new pedigree for him yourself?"

"As I've already said," Langford's voice replied, "I don't have to explain myself to you. You're not a magistrate, and while everyone else in the neighborhood might quake and cower in your presence, I find myself unimpressed. Though perhaps I should forgive you your habit of lording it over everyone. It's one of the afflictions of the title, I suppose."

"But you are impressed," retorted Byerley. "You've been impressed with my wealth, my title, ever since we were children—you've hated me for it."

"You were born into the best of everything," Langford said with a twinge of petulance. "The best horses, the best riding masters, the resources to buy winners. Everything has been handed to you on a silver platter, literally. Yet you go around riding mules and buying rogues. Your decisions beggar belief."

Byerley snorted. "Your grasping after wealth has led you to worse decisions. Faking Dolce's death—what a foolish thing to do! When are you going to let go of your ridiculous obsession with money?"

"Only people that have far too much of it ever say things like that. I had to work—"

"We both had to work," Byerley snapped, "or have you forgotten? My father did his best to forget I existed. Sir Algernon took both of us under his wing, you and me, and he taught us together. He gave us equal chances, and he was kind when others were not. He had one blind spot, and that was his daughter. He never gave Olivia any chance at all. Which is why I take exception to you stealing her horse."

"I am trying to protect Sir Algernon's legacy!" thundered Langford.

"So am I," Byerley said. "And I think you'll find that the law is on my side."

I leaned forward and peered in through the space between the doors. With empty stalls on either side, the aisle was remarkably cluttered. Haphazard piles of lumber and bales of straw cast ragged shadows by lantern light, and the chemical smell of fresh varnish wafted out to us. Despite Malcolm's skepticism, it seemed Langford's stable was indeed undergoing some kind of construction. I could see only two lanterns, one hanging on the wall and the other at the feet of the man facing away from me. Beyond him was Byerley, those unmistakable cheekbones sharp and menacing in the guttering yellow light. Dolce stood obediently at the far end of the aisle, looking more alert than I'd seen him in days. No doubt he was relieved to be somewhere other than his stall.

"But the law is on my side when it comes to trespassers," Langford said, raising something from his side. "I could shoot you now, say you were trying to steal a horse." Lantern light glinted dully on the long, angular object in his hands.

"The poet has a shotgun," I whispered to Bertie.

Byerley's laugh echoed in the stable. "A horse thief shooting a horse thief," he mused. "Sounds appropriate. But when the dust settles and both Brioso and Dolce are discovered in your possession, you won't be able to cover your tracks any longer. Or do you have space in that tack room for two stallions and a body?"

I turned to Bertie, eyebrows raised in a silent question. He hesitated, then nodded succinctly. "I think the boys have shared enough brotherly affection for one night," he said.

Yanking the heavy doors open, I stepped inside with Bertie

at my heels. Byerley's white brows shot upward in surprise, and Langford whirled, leveling the shotgun at us.

"Hello, Mr. Langford," I said, flinching a little at the sight of those twin barrels.

Langford dropped the nose of the gun to the floor. "Miss Cobb!" he gasped. "I thought you were—did you come from Becketts?"

"Yes," I said, wondering why that should matter.

"You came alone?" he said, eyes flitting to the open door.

"Yes." Encouraged by the fact that the gun remained lowered, I continued, "And you may as well put your shotgun away. Everyone knows you stole Brioso, so unless you're going to shoot us all, there's no point in shooting Lord Byerley."

He blinked his long lashes as though dazed. Finally, he stalked over to the side of the aisle and set the weapon on the floor. "It isn't even loaded," he mumbled, then straightened and turned to me. "And I didn't steal Brioso. I was trying to protect him."

"From what?" I said, at the same time Byerley said, "From whom?"

Bertie's hooves clattered sharply as he startled and spun, and I heard a new voice behind me, quavering with fury. "Where is he?!"

Standing in the doorway, her face contorted and her eyes roving wildly, was Lady Chedington. She had donned the crushed hat again, and its misshapen brim curled up on one side, lending her the look of a disheveled cavalier. It would have been comical, had the impression not been further reinforced by the revolver in her hand.

"Where is he?" she demanded again, waving the revolver unsteadily. I glanced at Langford, bewildered. He was clearly visible beside me—she wanted her revenge on Langford, didn't she?—but perhaps she was too far gone with sherry to recognize the man. Then the lady's bleary eyes widened and she said, "Is that him? Back there, lurking in the darkness like the devil he is—is that him?"

I followed her gaze. Byerley was edging cautiously toward us, but Dolce remained shrouded in shadows at the end of the aisle. Lady Chedington lurched forward as though to make her way to the horse, and I found myself considering with odd detachment—what would Watson do? Would he trip her, or try to knock the gun from her hand, or grab her arm and wrestle the thing away from her? But just before she was within grabbing distance, Lady Chedington stopped abruptly, some last vestige of logic nibbling at her brain.

"No, no, no," she said playfully, giving a sly wink, "I know your tricks." It was hard to tell whether she was addressing the horse or one of us. She backed away and wagged the revolver at Langford. "You'll show me another horse, then another, a whole parade of black horses—why are there so many black horses? I thought they were rare?—but I demand to see the *one* that I demand to see!" She tilted toward Langford and said, in a raspy whisper, "Where . . . is . . . . Brioso?"

"He's dead—he died," Langford said, but his voice cracked and he glanced furtively toward the tack room door. He was an exceptionally bad liar, which was surprising in a man who had successfully hidden a horse in his tack room for a whole year.

"She'll calm down once she sees the stallion," muttered Byerley, and then he spoke directly to Lady Chedington. "He's not dead. He's—"

"Don't tell her!" thundered Bertie and Langford together.

Byerley's thin mouth snapped shut, but even in Lady Chedington's befuddled state, she had noticed Langford's glance. "Ah, in there, is he?" she said, weaving her way to the tack room door. Langford leapt forward, but the woman pointed the revolver at him and he backed away. "Ah-ah-ah," she tutted. "You're as bad as Fletcher. Sleeping in the barn, indeed. I could have cleared this up long ago, and with much more privacy, if that doddering old man hadn't been patrolling my stable like a palace guard. I wanted it to look like an accident, you know. Poison, or a broken leg. But it's much better this way." She reached for the handle of the tack room door. "After all, the true demon wasn't even in my stable!"

She jerked the door toward her a few inches and craned her neck to peer through the opening. There was only darkness and silence within, and a bit of straw spilled out onto the floor. She frowned and started to widen the gap, but then came the muffled thud of startled hooves and the loud whoosh of a snort. Lady Chedington rocked back and turned slowly to us, smiling triumphantly.

"And there he is," she said. "Soft straw and a cozy room. That beast has been living in luxury while Algernon lies six feet under! It was supposed to be the other way around, you know." Her haunted eyes stared off into nothingness. "Madame Tournier warned me. She told me, all those years ago, that Algernon would be killed by a black stallion. But no one believed me! Not you—nor you—nor you," she wagged the revolver at each of us in turn, apparently forgetting that she'd only met me six months ago. "Nor Algernon himself! When the demon was born, I asked my husband to put him down, and he refused! Over the years, I tried to make him see —I even put on that hideous coat and begged him!—but he was in the thrall of the black beast and he wouldn't listen to reason."

"Lady Chedington," Byerley said, his face very white, "Madame Tournier was a fraud, and Brioso is just a horse. He can't reason, he can't—"

"Quiet!" she burst out, and then she gave a pout that reminded me of her daughter. "You're not a true friend—none of you are. You encouraged Olivia to ride Brioso, and he would've killed her too, make no mistake! It seems I have no true friends left. Even Arthur turned on me. Such a shame, that."

"Arthur?" Langford said, running his tongue nervously over his lips. "Who is Arthur?" It seemed the poet was only trying to stall her, as his eyes never left the narrow crack of the tack room door.

"A friend I thought I could trust," she said. "Arthur was with me all those years ago, when I made my living riding the silly creatures. Oh yes," she said with a mirthless laugh, "I was a performer. The greatest equestrian act in England, that is what the papers said. Arthur was my valet in those days, but he was so much more. He took care of me, tied up loose ends, got rid of the men that hung around my tent after shows. He lived to help me. And all these years later, when I sent word to him in my hour of need, he came to Becketts."

"The Major," I said.

"The Major," she echoed sourly. "*That* was unfortunate. Arthur's flair for the dramatic led him to take an assumed name, the silly man." She ran her sturdy fingers along the edge of the door, toying with it, and invisible hooves circled restlessly behind the opening. "He was supposed to help me save Olivia from the stallion. He was supposed to convince her that she would never be able to ride. But then Miss Cobb stuck her nose in and puffed him up with her praises!" She glared at me, shifting the revolver in my direction.

I scowled. This was really too much. "For the last time, I didn't say—"

"Arthur demanded to be given a permanent position at Becketts!" she exclaimed. "How's that for loyalty? He said life hadn't been easy for him after I left—he was trying to make a living doing poetry readings, the absurd man. He said he wanted a large bed and a comfortable salary for the rest of his life. If not, he said he would tell everyone how I tried to kill Brioso."

She turned suddenly sheepish and giggled like a girl. "Oh, I know! You don't have to look at me that way, you three. I know I shouldn't have told Arthur about that. You're quite right. It was foolish of me, very foolish. But, you see, I had to make him understand how dangerous the stallion is. So I told him about the day that I tried to protect Algernon and failed." She looked sadly down at the revolver in her hand. "My aim was off. I missed. And that black demon carried Algernon away and killed him in retaliation. Just as it was foretold."

39

THE STALLION

IN THE SILENCE THAT FOLLOWED, Bertie said, "She wasn't aiming for Sir Algernon on the moor that day. She was aiming for Brioso."

Byerley looked at the horse in surprise, and at the sound of Bertie's equine voice, the trampling in the tack room grew louder. At the end of the aisle, Dolce sensed the tension in the air and his ears flickered uncertainly.

"Well," Lady Chedington said, drawing herself up and reaching for the door again. "I failed the first time, but I shan't miss this time."

As she turned, Byerley leapt and grabbed for the revolver. Lady Chedington's startled bellow was cut short by the deafening explosion of the gun, and Byerley cried out and fell backward. At the sound of the gun, Dolce panicked. He tore down the aisle toward the only visible exit, plowing between me and Langford. His hooves sent the lantern flying and it smashed against the pile of lumber.

Lady Chedington stood over Byerley, glaring down at him. "Algernon was like a father to you," she said reproachfully.

"You should be helping me destroy his murderer." Byerley only groaned and fell back, a dark stain blooming across his right shoulder. There was a whoosh and crackle across the aisle as the spilled kerosene ignited.

"But it was your own gunshot that caused Sir Algernon's death!" I exclaimed. "Lady Chedington, that day on the moor, the sound of your gun made Brioso bolt. In trying to prevent your husband's death, you caused it!"

"That's just what Arthur said," she mused. "Just like you, he couldn't see how cunning, how devious the stallion is." Smoke was rising now, flames licking up the dry edges of the piled lumber. Langford gazed at the fire in horrified fascination, but Lady Chedington didn't even appear to notice it. Lost in her reverie, she kept the revolver aimed lazily at us. "Arthur was very indiscreet," she said. "Most performers are, you know. So I gave him a little tap on the head—just a little tap!—with that silly cup on the end of the whip, and I stuck his foot through the stirrup and left him to be dragged. He was always so pleased to be of use to me. It was only fitting that his last act should be to help me prove the danger of that demon horse."

"We need to leave," Bertie warned. "From the smell of things, Langford has been rather extravagant with his varnish, and this place is about to go up like the O'Leary's barn. Shall I stampede her?" The air was growing hazy as a straw bale ignited, and from behind the tack room door came a shrill equine squeal and the sound of violent pawing.

"No," I said, my eyes never leaving the barrel of the revolver.

"Now that the chance is before me," Lady Chedington said, "I find I don't care what my neighbors think. Once the deed is done, I shall leave Pelgren Vale and take Olivia to London, where there are certain to be more motorcars than horses. We shall go by motorcar, I think. Yes. That is the way to travel." She reached for the door.

It suddenly burst open, sending her stumbling backward. Brioso filled the doorway, proud and terrible and oily black with sweat. After his long captivity, he was quivering with rage, seething with the pent-up fury of a wild beast unjustly caged. At the sight and smell of the leaping flames, he shied and reared, eyes rolling in panic.

Recovering herself, Lady Chedington raised the revolver.

Brioso screamed like an untamed stallion and plunged violently forward, knocking the woman to the ground. The revolver fell from her hand, and I heard the soft thud of hooves on flesh as Brioso flew over her. He careened past Bertie, out of the stable doors and into the night.

"No!" shouted Langford, running madly after him.

"Wait!" I cried, and then doubled over, coughing in the thickening air. The fire had found the heavy varnish coating the stalls, and rippling sheets of orange flame raced upward toward the wooden ceiling.

Lady Chedington moaned and lay still.

"I can't carry them both," I gasped.

"Get Byerley," Bertie commanded, and I stumbled to the injured man. When I grabbed him roughly under the arms, his eyes fluttered open and he observed me in bewilderment.

"Miss Cobb," he said weakly.

"Yes?"

"You appear to be upside-down."

"Yes. Be quiet." As I dragged Byerley toward the open doors I saw Bertie, framed in shimmering flames, reaching his long teeth toward Lady Chedington's face. In my surprise, I dropped Byerley and he grunted in pain. As I stood frozen,

Bertie locked his teeth on the stiff collar of Lady Chedington's tweed jacket. Backing swiftly, he dragged her down the aisle. I retrieved Byerley and followed them out of the inferno.

When we reached the grass beyond the gravel drive, I flung myself to the ground between Byerley and Lady Chedington, panting hard. Lady Chedington's eyes remained closed, but she was breathing and began to mumble incoherently. Byerley, a sheen of sweat on his brow, twisted his neck to observe his bloody shoulder.

"A pity, that," he managed, through clenched teeth. "This is one of my favorite coats."

"Where are Langford and Brioso?" I said, looking around.

"The stallion is probably halfway to Bristol," Bertie said, shaking himself to get rid of singed bits of straw and ash. "I'd give the poet another hour or so before he comes limping back."

"And Dolce?"

As if on cue, the timid black horse appeared behind Lady Chedington. Curious at the sound of her mumbling, he stretched his muzzle toward her and began playfully nuzzling her face. The lady's eyes flew open. She stared up into his giant nostrils. With an earsplitting shriek, she fainted dead away.

Byerley grunted and said, "I suppose now I owe you and Bertie for saving my life as well as for winning that race. But have no fear, Miss Cobb. As I told you before, I always pay my debts."

"You need to find a less-sinister motto," I rasped, coughing again.

"Bertie?" Byerley said, his voice weak and plaintive. "Before I die, will you tell me how you did it? How you got Praxiteles to win that race?"

Bertie fixed him with an appraising eye. "Yes," he decided. "I'll tell you."

After a long moment of silence, Byerley coughed pitifully and said, "Well?"

"Well, unless lords possess anatomy different to commoners and your heart is somewhere near your collarbone . . . you're not in danger of dying anytime soon," Bertie said, and whuffled a deep, horsey laugh.

We sat on the grass, sooty and singed, watching the flames dance high against the stars as Langford's stable was consumed.

BOOKS AND BENEFACTORS

"Did Tom sneak over last night with a bucket of whitewash?" I said, eyeing our little cottage. From my seated position in the middle of Bertie's pasture, the rough stone walls looked remarkably clean and bright in the late September sun. It was a cottage uniquely suited to our needs. To the observer, it appeared to be quite roomy, but one end of the building was actually an attached stable sharing the sloping thatched roof.

Bertie's warm, broad back shifted behind me as he turned his head to look around my shoulder. "Optical illusion," he declared. "It's the new thatch, old girl. That golden straw makes everything appear brighter." He turned back to the grass at his chin and resumed drowsily nibbling. Even when he was lying down, those velvety lips never stopped searching.

"'fraid I can't tell you that, Miss Cobb," Tom had answered, when I asked him who had paid for the new thatched roof. He had shown up one day with wagons of supplies and a crew of men from the village, all stating they had been hired to replace our roof and all claiming ignorance about the person who had hired them. I had been persistent in my questioning, and Tom had been persistently reticent, and we had ended up with a sturdy new roof and not a peep about the identity of our benefactor. Of course, as Bertie pointed out, we would have to be very simpleminded not to guess who it was.

"Are you going to finish the story?" Bertie said lazily.

I turned my attention back to the leatherbound volume on my knee, *The Sign of the Four* by Sir Arthur Conan Doyle. "This is Watson speaking, in case you forgot—

'I am glad that the treasure is gone. I think we shall be happier without it.'
'No doubt, no doubt,' said Holmes, in his soothing way. 'Still, I am disappointed in my calculations. I certainly did not anticipate that the Agra treasure would prove so intractable. Let us see how the matter will shape itself to-morrow, Watson.' "

I closed the finished book, and Bertie considered for a moment, chewing thoughtfully. "I wonder whether there were any golden bits in that Agra treasure," he said dryly. "You haven't heard anything from Becketts about whether Miss Olivia ever found them?"

"No," I said, climbing to my feet and brushing myself off, "but here's someone who might be able to tell us."

Striding across the pasture in a brilliant coat of coppery orange, Byerley raised a hand in greeting. His other arm was still in a sling, but from his long, purposeful strides, it seemed the bones in his shoulder no longer objected to jostling.

"Ah!" Bertie said. "Our lord has finally come to inspect his vassal's holding." He scrambled to his hooves, shaking off bits of clover and grass.

"I thought Dr. Reed told you that you were not to ride

until that sling comes off," I called to Byerley, noticing the waggish face of his mule peeking around the corner of the cottage.

"Riding doesn't jolt it nearly as much as the gig does," he replied airily. He strode to Bertie and produced a lump of sugar from his pocket, which Bertie accepted with fastidious grace.

"I don't suppose you've noticed anything new about our cottage?" I couldn't keep the accusatory tone out of my voice.

"What?" He swiveled to glance at the building. "No, I can't say I have." He pursed his lips, pale brows furrowed in contemplation. Turning back to me, he said angelically, "A coat of whitewash, perhaps?"

Bertie snorted and narrowed his eyes, but said nothing.

"I've come to ask a little favor of you, Bertie," the lord continued. "I think I shall need your help at Becketts."

"Indeed?" Bertie said. "How is little Miss Olivia grappling with her new circumstances?"

"Oh, it was very hard at first, as you can imagine. There's nothing quite so shocking as finding out that one's mother is a murderer."

"What will happen to Lady Chedington?" I shivered as I remembered the woman's wild babbling when Sergeant Harrison arrived to collect her on the night of the fire.

"It looks as though she may end up in Broadmoor," Byerley said, chewing his lip, "though Dr. Reed hopes she may be moved to Bailbrook in the future, if Olivia can afford it— that's a private asylum in Bath. Actually," he suddenly grinned, "Bertie may have done more for her rehabilitation than any doctor could."

"I?" the horse said, ears rigid in surprise.

"Yes. Apparently, she remembers you dragging her out of

the stable that night. Dr. Reed said it's been quite the conundrum for her. She says she always thought that dragging was one of the methods horses used to *kill* people, but she never imagined that being dragged by a horse could *save* one."

Bertie gave a slow chuckle and said, "And Mr. Langford? Will he be sentenced to prison for his insurance fraud in faking Dolce's death?"

"Well . . ." Byerley said, looking down and fussing with his sling, "I may have pulled a few strings to prevent that—"

"You?" I said, staring at him.

"Yes. After all, we did grow up together."

"And he stole Brioso in an attempt to protect him from Lady Chedington," Bertie put in.

"So he won't be punished at all?" I spluttered.

"Oh, he'll learn his lesson." Byerley smiled grimly. "His stable was well-insured, and the payout he receives for its loss by fire will go directly toward repayment of Dolce's insurance. That, and the sale of his horses, should about cover the fines imposed by the court."

"I can't help but feel a tad sorry for the fellow," Bertie said. "In some ways, he's as silly as his eyelashes, but he does love horses and he'll be left with nothing."

"He may be luckier than he deserves," Byerley said. "Olivia has some idea of hiring him to be the Becketts trainer and stud-groom-in-training—under Fletcher's supervision, of course. She said that will allow Fletcher to stay on at Becketts without being overworked, and Langford will be able to have daily contact with his beloved Brioso—while also earning an honest living."

"A rather good idea, that," Bertie said. "Is it possible Miss Olivia is cleverer than she appears?"

Byerley gave the horse's neck a firm pat. "After meeting

you, Bertie, I've decided that anything is possible. However, I think that idea came from Miss Seyward."

"She's staying on, then?" I said, feeling pleased. "Those young ladies are going to be business partners after all?"

"That's the idea, and that's what I need Bertie's help with. There's still no sign of the golden bits, but I have another idea on how the young ladies can cover expenses until they start to turn a profit. There will be an equestrian gala at Becketts next month . . ."

We looked at him expectantly, but he said, "I promised Olivia that I wouldn't divulge the details to any other human being. Apart from sending invitations, she wants the whole thing to be a surprise. However, as Bertie is not a human being . . ."

"I'll go brew some coffee, shall I?" I said brightly and retreated to our cozy—and dry—cottage.

By the time the two pale creatures came wandering back across the pasture, they were speaking and laughing together in animated tones. I felt a queer hollowness as I watched them through the little mullioned window, and it didn't take much reflection to realize what the feeling was. It was the jealousy of a child seeing her beloved pony being expertly handled by another. Ridiculous. I batted it swiftly away. Bertie was not a horse to be owned, so he was not my horse—you might as well say I was his human. But that was just it. I had thought *I* was his human.

I trudged out the door and delivered an earthenware mug of strong coffee to Byerley, bringing one along for myself. We stood outside with Bertie as the sun fell toward the distant sea and an autumn crispness crept into the air.

"I believe the sight of that new thatch has put me in a

rather expansive mood," Bertie said, sending a sly glance Byerley's way.

"Yes?" Byerley said, with his best butter-wouldn't-melt expression.

"It's also a mood of reminiscence," the big horse said. "I feel the urge to reminisce about a little something that happened in Wolverhampton last year."

The look of dawning hope was oddly touching on Byerley's sardonic face.

"But remember," Bertie continued, "I told you it was neither clever nor replicable. And I'm afraid it was rather uncivilized." His ears flickered uneasily. "I wouldn't have done it if my freedom hadn't been at stake."

"Understood," Byerley said.

"Harriet and I chose your Praxiteles because he was given long odds—he had the physical conformation to make a runner, but he lacked the spirit and confidence to pull off a win."

"Exactly," Byerley agreed. "He had the body to do it, but he was easily intimidated by the other colts and always faded at the finish."

Bertie nodded his great head. "In other words, Praxiteles had the habits we needed, and I was stabled near him. So I started talking to him each night."

"Talking?" Byerley said, looking startled.

"Purely in the equine sense. I delved deep into the equine depths of my brain, taking hold of the instinctual and shunning the intellectual. I glared, pinned my ears, bared my teeth, made the most intimidating sounds I could manage. And then, any time we were on the track together, I escalated the ruse. I never touched him, mind you, but a well-aimed kick or bite, always falling just short—I'm ashamed to admit it, but I made the poor fellow believe that, given the chance, I would turn him into dog meat." Bertie shifted his hooves uncomfortably and swished his tail at a non-existent fly. "Very uncivilized," he said.

"But necessary," I added, taking the reins of the story. "On the day of the race, the 12th of September, I placed my bet—all of it, everything I'd saved from my time in Walsall, I put it all on Praxiteles. Then I just needed to get Bertie to the infield among the crowd at the start of the homestretch. That was easy. By that point, I was a familiar face around the stables, and the groom believed me when I said another track pony was needed."

"When the pack came into the stretch," Bertie said, "Praxiteles was among the front runners, as usual. And then, as was his habit, he started to fall back."

"I remember," Byerley breathed.

Bertie's eyes were brighter now as he warmed to his story. "Just as he passed me, I let out a scream—a savage, primal scream, the barbarous challenge of one wild stallion to another. It was quite similar to the sound Brioso made on the night of the fire. It may have been lost to human ears in the roar of the crowd, but it certainly wasn't lost on Praxiteles."

"And that's when Praxiteles began to run as though his life depended on it," I finished, "because he thought it did. He knew that voice, and he thought the very devil was on his tail."

Byerley began to laugh. "That's it? It had the advantage of simplicity, I suppose. All the same, you were lucky. Very lucky. So many unforeseen things can happen in a race. Praxiteles could have fallen coming out of the gate."

"We were lucky," Bertie said, "and I was taking a larger gamble than Harriet. My display of aggressive behavior—not quite the thing for a track pony, you know—had my owner considering gelding me." His broad, dappled shoulders shivered dramatically. "Luckily, with a portion of our winnings, Harriet made him an offer he couldn't refuse. She obtained my freedom before the crime could be committed."

Byerley looked thoughtful and said, "You may be interested to know that Wolverhampton no longer allows track ponies during races—a rule that was created soon after that race. I don't think that scream was lost to all human ears, and if the Jockey Club stewards hear of it, other tracks may be forced to follow suit."

"And Praxiteles?" Bertie said. "Did I irreparably damaged his nerves, or did the poor chap develop a taste for the winner's circle? I've often wondered. I suppose you could say I've felt a bit guilty."

"I can relieve you of that burden." Byerley smiled. "Since then, Praxiteles has actually seemed to enjoy running. It's as though he's finally realized that he needn't worry about the other horses after all. He just loafs along with a grin on his face, metaphorically speaking. Sometimes he even manages to finish near the front."

"Satisfactory," Bertie said, breathing a heavy sigh of relief.

An odd sound filled the air, a curious, braying neigh. Byerley's mule rolled a questioning eye in our direction, pawing emphatically.

"Ah. My charger awaits," Byerley said. It was meant to be sarcastic, but the affection on his face when he looked at the mule would've given Dr. Reed a run for his money. "I have an appointment this evening with two young ladies regarding a certain equestrian gala."

"Just out of curiosity," I said, walking with him to his mount, "do you prefer the paintings of Waterhouse or Rossetti?"

He looked surprised, then thoughtful. "Neither," he said. "I'm more of a sculpture man, myself."

"The sculptures of Praxiteles?" I suggested. "His Aphrodite?"

"Or his Hermes," he said, grinning wolfishly. "I've never felt a pressing need to choose." He mounted smoothly despite the sling, and I decided that his bright, autumn-colored coat paired rather nicely with the mule's mousy brown one. "We shall expect you both at Becketts in a fortnight," he said, turning the mule and sending him into a smart trot. "Come well-groomed," he called over his shoulder, and I saw a flash of white teeth before he rode away.

I looked at Bertie. "Does he mean you, or me?"

A VERY SOPHISTICATED EVENT

THE DAY of the gala dawned with a crisp October sky and just enough breeze to set the orange leaves whispering. At Bertie's request, I brushed a coat of oil onto his heavy hooves and neatly braided his mane, though he put his hoof down at my suggestion of ribbons.

"No ribbons, I beg you," he said, snorting his derision. "I am not a circus horse, nor am I a carriage horse at a country fair. Today is to be a very sophisticated event." He eyed my outfit in approval. "Although I would never call your usual dark clothing unsophisticated, you look rather nice in a bit of color."

The "bit of color" he was referring to would hardly compete with Byerley's coats, but it was a brave step away from my usual charcoal gray. I had dug the russet-colored herringbone jacket out of the back of my closet—where it had been in exile ever since Bertie referred to it as "dapper." But, I reasoned, in the whimsical air of this gala day, dapperness was exactly what was called for.

"You're quiet this morning," I said to Bertie as we rode across the fields toward Becketts.

"I've been considering the influence of expectations on the human brain," he said.

"And here I was, considering whether they might have those nice little whortleberry tarts at the gala," I teased.

Undeterred, Bertie continued, "Consider. Lady Chedington expected that her husband would be killed by Brioso, and in trying to prevent his death, she caused it. A lovely example of the power of expectations."

"Lovely," I muttered.

"If you prefer something less felonious, Miss Olivia expected that she would never be able to ride, and thus she couldn't—but after you praised her that day, her expectations changed and she found that she could."

I sighed. "You know perfectly well that I didn't . . . Wait. Miss Olivia can ride?"

"Ah—I believe that was one of the things I was not supposed to mention," he said.

We arrived to find the Becketts stable bedecked with autumn-toned flowers, for all the world as though a harvest-themed wedding was in the works. Fletcher approached us, looking vaguely sheepish in one of Sir Algernon's chartreuse coats. When I pointed out the lovely bunch of begonias pinned to his lapel, he snorted.

"Miss Olivia wants everyone festive, like," he grunted. "Grooms included." Treacle Tart trotted past with a large orange chrysanthemum hanging off his collar and a look of indignation on his face. "Cats too," Fletcher added glumly. "Now, if you don't mind, Miss Cobb, I'll take your horse . . ." I handed the reins to the old groom, and Bertie gave me a wink as he was led away.

A crowd had already gathered in the rear stable yard, milling around tables of fruits and cheeses and, to my delight, platters piled high with whortleberry tarts. In the green pasture beyond the yard, a white-fenced arena had been constructed. There was a large booth near the fence with a colorful, fluttering banner that read "Chedington Bits." I smiled. Miss Olivia was going to carry on her father's legacy in one way, at least.

I wove my way through the throng, moving around little clusters of attendees who stood chatting and laughing together with the ease of long acquaintance. Finely-tailored breeches and riding habits abounded. These jovial, capable-looking men and women were certainly the horsiest residents of Pelgren Vale. A few glanced curiously my way, but as I didn't see anyone I'd already been introduced to, I made a beeline for the pastry table. Just as I placed a delicate tart on my plate, I heard a gruff voice behind me.

"Miss Cobb."

I turned to find Sergeant Harrison's red mustache bristling at me like a fox's tail.

"Hello, Sergeant," I said, more brightly than I felt. "I'm surprised to see you here."

He looked startled. "What? Why?"

"It is an *equestrian* gala," I pointed out.

"Oh. Oh yes, quite." He reached up and smoothed his mustache. "A show of support for Miss Olivia. Like many of the people here, I'd say." He looked hard at me. "The people of Pelgren Vale like to help their neighbors, Miss Cobb. That's the kind of place this is."

Since he seemed to require a response, I handed him my plate. "Then allow me to help you to the most delicious whortleberry tart you will ever taste."

He stared at the tart. His mouth remained an unwavering line, but the corners of his eyes crinkled a little. "You've heard, haven't you?" he said gruffly. "That the stirrup cup found in Lady Chedington's bedroom was capable of making those three little lines?"

I nodded and busied myself choosing another tart from the platter.

"Well." He shifted uncomfortably and cleared his throat, and I suspected there was an apology trying to claw its way out.

"Oooh, Miss Cobb!" Miss Olivia fluttered between us like a gilded-green butterfly. She was wearing another of the Becketts coats, and her golden curls were pinned smartly under her stylish black hat. "Oh, Sergeant Harrison, you won't mind if I steal her away?"

The burly man beamed. "Not at all, not at all," he said, and as we moved away, I saw him take out his handkerchief and mop his ruddy brow in relief.

Olivia led me to a place at the middle of the arena fence. "This is the best place to watch," she assured me. "Oh, thank you so much, Miss Cobb, for letting me use your horse! And for . . . well, for everything." Her brilliant eyes turned misty, but she managed a smile and continued, "Do you like my skirt?"

I looked down to see, in fine black wool, an exact replica of my own split-skirt. "I think you have excellent taste," I said.

She giggled delightedly. "Why didn't you tell me, Miss Cobb, that riding astride is so much easier than riding aside? But that's not all I wanted to say. You'll never believe it, but I found the golden bits!"

"What?"

"I did just as you said. I followed your advice, and I found them!"

I blinked at the girl. "But . . . I never gave you any advice about those bits."

"You did, in a way," she said, her eyes large and solemn. "You told me it was useful to talk to horses in the way that one talks to oneself. So I was talking to Dolce about what Madame Itovsky said—I've been learning to ride Dolce because he's so sweet and calm, and Brioso is much too spirited for me—anyway, I was talking to Dolce about it, and it all just became clear! Madame Itovsky said, 'buried among many more of their kind,' and I remembered that there are scads of bits in the tack room. She said, 'branches of oak,' and I thought, all those pegs on the tack room wall are made of some kind of wood, and they could look like branches, in a pinch. And the last thing she said was . . ."

"Buried at the root," I finished for her, "at the root you shall find them."

"And that's where they were!" she said. "Father had hung them at the base of those pegs, buried under all those other bits. I think he wanted to make sure that the person who found them was already interested in his prototypes."

"Miss Olivia," I said, "I think you're a very clever person indeed," and I surprised myself by actually meaning it.

We noticed movement in the arena and looked up to see Byerley, wearing his own bright Becketts coat, leading Bertie across the grassy space.

"If all this goes as planned," the girl whispered, "there won't be any need to sell those family jewels." Giving me a nervous smile, she ducked under the fence and strode across to the big gray horse.

The crowd in the stable yard had dispersed, and people

began to arrange themselves along the fence, murmuring in anticipation. Bertie stood square and proud in the center of the arena, his dappled coat a gleaming mosaic in the morning light. When Byerley boosted Miss Olivia into the saddle, she swung her skirted leg over Bertie's back and settled firmly astride. I was surprised to hear only a few soft murmurs from the crowd—the people of Pelgren Vale were less shocked than I would have imagined at this symptom of the new century. Bertie remained perfectly still as Miss Olivia arranged her skirts and carefully gathered her reins. Retreating a few steps, Byerley turned to face the crowd.

"Welcome, all," he announced. "Like many of you, the late Sir Algernon Chedington had an enduring love of horses. It was that love that led him to spend many years designing and perfecting unique bits for horses. Most of you heard him talk about his bit designs—sometimes at much greater length than you would have liked,"—there was a smattering of laughter from the crowd—"but none of you have ever seen one in action. That is about to change." He gestured to the pair in the center. "As all of you know, Miss Olivia Chedington is hardly an expert in the saddle. Her mount today is merely a retired track pony. But he is wearing one of Sir Algernon's bits, and I invite you to observe the effect it produces." With a flourish of his hand, Byerley stalked back across the arena, ducked under the fence, and came to stand at my side. I looked a question at him, and he gave a tiny shrug and a tight smile—hardly reassuring, as it was the first time I had ever seen his lordly face look nervous.

Bertie moved off, cautiously at first, as though afraid of jostling his rider. Miss Olivia sat very still and straight, and her face remained serene. Sensing her confidence, the big gray horse picked up a trot, arching his dappled neck and delicately testing the brass bit in his mouth. The girl rose to the rhythm of his strides, up and down in balanced harmony. They made their way across the arena at the diagonal, Bertie's strides lengthening impressively and his long body rounding to the work. Watching Miss Olivia carefully, I couldn't see any conscious movement of her hands or legs—Bertie was apparently running the show. I held my breath as the big horse leapt lightly into canter and Miss Olivia swayed dramatically, but then she centered herself and straightened up—like a tall and mighty rampart, one might say.

Soon the pair was dancing in patterns, circles and diagonals and serpentines, every movement a demonstration of the impossible—a heavy, ruthlessly powerful creature turned feathery light in a girl's hand. When the gray horse finally floated to a halt in the center of the arena, the audience was deathly silent.

I met Byerley's light eyes and quickly looked away. He was holding his breath, as I was.

Then, from somewhere down the rail, came the sound of clapping.

"Bravo!" a man shouted, clapping wildly. "Marvelous!" It was Dr. Reed, his thick spectacles tilting dangerously on his nose from the violence of his enthusiasm. At the sound of his voice, as though released from some enchantment, the rest of the audience burst into applause.

Byerley gave me a lofty smile, as though he'd never doubted a thing in his life, and went to join his charges in the arena. Many of the onlookers had abandoned the fence to flood around the "Chedington Bits" booth, examining the various mouthpieces and discussing them with shrewd interest. At the head of the table stood Miss Seyward, in her own vividly green coat, gracefully answering questions and pointing out the features of each bit.

I felt a tug at my sleeve and turned to find Dr. Reed beaming at me from behind his spectacles. "A pleasant day, Miss Cobb, is it not?"

"Much pleasanter than the last time we were here together," I agreed.

"Allow me to introduce one of your neighbors," the doctor said, indicating the small, round man beside him. The man was struggling to keep hold of a rather fractious tortoiseshell kitten. "Miss Cobb—Mr. Hastings. Mr. Hastings lives just down the valley from you, and he has quite a few fine horses that may be in need of your saddlery skills. Now, if you'll excuse me, I need to see about securing one of those bits for my Beauty . . ."

"Glad to meet you, Miss Cobb," the round man said, extending his unoccupied hand.

So, I thought as I shook his hand, this was the Mr. Hastings who had locked himself and his kitten in Mr. Foster's tack room. A "feline fixation," Dr. Reed had called it. The man even resembled a cat, from his pink button nose to the long side whiskers that tufted out to a point on either side of his face.

"I promised one of my kittens to Lady Chedington," he said, "and Dr. Reed says I need to deliver all my kittens as promised, so I brought her for Miss Olivia."

"She looks like a feisty one," I said, wondering at the advisability of allowing a "feline fixation" patient to go around carrying kittens.

"Oh, she'll be a fine mouser," he said proudly. Leaning close, he whispered, "Have no fear, Miss Cobb. I won't be absconding with her to the tack room any time soon." He chuckled, and I felt a little better. I'd had enough of animals in tack rooms, secrets in tack rooms, and treasures in tack rooms.

"I've learned a valuable lesson, Miss Cobb," the tufted man declared. "Being too attached to one's animals causes all sorts of problems. They might find their own happiness in another way, another place. Best let them fly the nest when they're ready, what?"

An odd lump rose in my throat, and I could only nod. I looked over at Bertie. Miss Olivia had left the arena to greet her throng of well-wishers, and Byerley was fondly scratching the big horse's neck.

"Come and see me when this gala business is finished," Mr. Hastings said. "I have about a dozen saddles that could use your attention. And, from what I saw in Mr. Foster's tack room when I locked myself inside, I'd say he's in even greater need of your services." With that startling pronouncement, he carried his kitten away—not in the direction of the tack room, thankfully.

I walked across the empty arena to join Bertie and Byerley, and as I neared, I heard the lord say, "You'll talk to her about what we discussed?" Bertie bowed his great head in assent. With a final pat, Byerley strode away, giving me a nod as he went. He appeared to be very pleased about something, which set my stomach churning.

"Well?" Bertie said when I reached his side. "What did you think of our ride? Miss Olivia is far from polished, but she has mastered the art of sitting still and not getting in the horse's way. Which is, of course, the first step to becoming a rider."

"But it all seems a bit disingenuous," I said. "I know it's for a good cause, but you just pulled the wool over every equestrian in Pelgren Vale. What's going to happen when they buy those bits and find they can't achieve the same results? Your theatrics may have done more harm than good."

"It was hardly theatrical," he said. "Byerley simply instructed me to move in whatever way the bit made me feel. They are remarkably good bits. I wouldn't mind collecting a few for my own personal use. And now," he said, fixing me with his large, liquid eyes, "I have something to discuss with you. Byerley has extended an invitation that is rather too good to pass up—"

"I know," I gulped. "And you're your own horse—you're free to do as you like. It's bound to be a spectacular place, Ashwold Abbey, with a luxurious stable and all those acres of pasture. You'll have the best of everything, and someone civilized to talk to. It's a very good opportunity, I think, and I shall miss you dreadfully, but I'll get by. Oh— does Byerley know about reading mystery novels to you? I can send the next Sir Arthur Conan Doyle—but of course, the library at Ashwold is probably full of—"

"Harriet!" Bertie said, stomping his hoof and glowering down his Roman nose. "I am not *moving* to Ashwold Abbey, nor am I going anywhere without you, old girl. Byerley has invited us, you and me, to come to Ashwold. It seems he needs our help with a little something." He frowned. "Byerley reading mystery stories, indeed. Can you imagine listening to any book in that supercilious tone of his?"

He snorted in surprise as I flung my arms around his neck.

A MESSAGE FROM THE AUTHOR

Thank you for picking up this book! I truly hope you enjoyed reading *Saddled with Murder*. Thank you also to those who took the time to write a review. As an independent author, reviews help immensely as I continue writing Bertie & Harriet's next tale. If you did enjoy this book, please consider recommending it to a friend. After all, it's best to hear things straight from the horse's mouth.

Bertie & Harriet's adventures continue in Book 2: *Murder with All the Trappings*, which takes place at Lord Byerley's ancestral home, Ashwold Abbey. **https://mybook.to/Trappings**

Chomping at the bit for more? Sign up for my newsletter and receive a free *Saddled with Murder* Bonus Scene: Bertie's account of the discovery of the corpse at Becketts. **https://BookHip.com/FGHQAFQ** You'll also be the first to know about upcoming Bertie & Harriet mysteries and get access to exclusive content.

ACKNOWLEDGMENTS

I literally could not have produced this novel without my husband, John. Not only was he incredibly supportive and encouraging through the writing process, he is also responsible for the stunning cover and artwork. His illustration skills brought the characters to life and made this book beautiful.

Adie, editor extraordinaire, provided more than just polishing. She fixed errors, caught plot issues, provided genre-specific advice, made brilliant suggestions, and asked all the questions that needed to be asked. Even while wielding her meticulous red pen, she managed to be a cheerleader.

Lisa, one of the cleverest writers I know, was kind enough to read the entire draft and give me her thoughts. Her suggestions made this novel infinitely more readable.

Vance and Shelley championed this novel from its conception to its conclusion. They read—and re-read—chapters as I sent them, and they never once ran screaming from the room when I brought it up in conversation. I'm so grateful for their encouragement and suggestions, which carried this novel all the way through to its completion.

Ron read early rough-draft chapters—and then asked for more. What writer doesn't love that? His enthusiasm for the story was a great motivator throughout the writing process.

One more person contributed to this novel in ways he might not be aware of, and he deserves a heartfelt thank you: to my Uncle Den, the original horse whisperer, for teaching me how to talk to horses.

ABOUT THE AUTHOR

Philippa Lee Mors teaches English and writes mysteries in the lovely Midwest, where she lives on a small farm with her husband and their menagerie of animals. When she's not teaching or writing, she spends her time drinking entirely too much coffee and trying to decide whether her horses possess the ability to speak.

Sign up for Philippa's newsletter and receive a free *Saddled with Murder* Bonus Scene: https://BookHip.com/FGHQAFQ

Website: https://www.philippamors.com/

Email: philippa@philippamors.com

facebook.com/philippaleemors

amazon.com/author/philippaleemors

bookbub.com/authors/philippa-lee-mors

goodreads.com/philippamors